DATE DUE

SEP 2 9 2001		May-13-02
NOV 1 5 2001		
NOV 2 7 2001	FEB 1 7 2013	
DEC 2 0 2001	AUG 1 8 2015	
DEC 2 6 2001	JAN 1 6 2016	
JAN 2 8 2002	AUG 3 0 2016	
FEB 1 2 2002		
FEB 2 5 2002		
MAR 1 5 2002		
APR 0 2 2002		
APR 2 2 2002		

An Uncommon Enemy

ALSO BY MICHELLE BLACK

Lightning in a Drought Year
Never Come Down

An Uncommon Enemy

MICHELLE BLACK

A TOM DOHERTY ASSOCIATES BOOK
NEW YORK

This is a work of fiction. All the characters and events portrayed in this novel are either fictitious or are used fictitiously.

AN UNCOMMON ENEMY

This book is printed on acid-free paper.

Design by Heidi Eriksen

Map by Ken Ray

A Forge Book
Published by Tom Doherty Associates, LLC
175 Fifth Avenue
New York, NY 10010
www.tor.com

Forge® is a registered trademark of Tom Doherty Associates, LLC.

01-199   Ingram 9-6-01 $26.95/15.31

Library of Congress Cataloging-in-Publication Data

Black, Michelle.
    An uncommon enemy / Michelle Black.—1st ed.
      p. cm.
    "A Tom Doherty Associates book."
    ISBN 0-765-30103-2
    1. Indians of North America—Wars—1868-1869—Fiction. 2. Custer, George Armstrong, 1839-1876—Fiction. 3. Washita River Valley (Tex. and Okla.)—Fiction. 4. Indian captivities—Fiction. 5. Cheyenne Indians—Fiction. 6. Women pioneers—Fiction. 7. Soldiers—Fiction. I. Title.

PS3552L34124 U54 2002
813'.54—dc21

                        2001033976

First Edition: September 2001

Printed in the United States of America

0 9 8 7 6 5 4 3 2 1

This book is dedicated to Maggie Osborne

Acknowledgments

The author wishes to gratefully acknowledge the help and advice of the many experts on this fascinating corner of history, chief among them: Stan Hoig, author of *The Battle of the Washita*, Jeffry D. Wert, author of *Custer: The Controversial Life of George Armstrong Custer,* Anne M. Marvin, Curator of the Kansas State Historical Society, Carldon Broadbent of the Mitchell County Historical Society, and Col. (Ret.) William J. Caffery. A special thank-you to Wayne Leman, author of *Let's Talk Cheyenne, An Introductory Course in the Cheyenne Language*, a book which it was the author's privilege to publish.

She wishes also to thank her editors, Dale L. Walker and Stephanie Lane; her agents, Nat Sobel and Laurie Horowitz; as well as all her early readers, especially Leslie Caldwell, Carol Gates, Paige Marshall, and Lisa Frazell Ruggs.

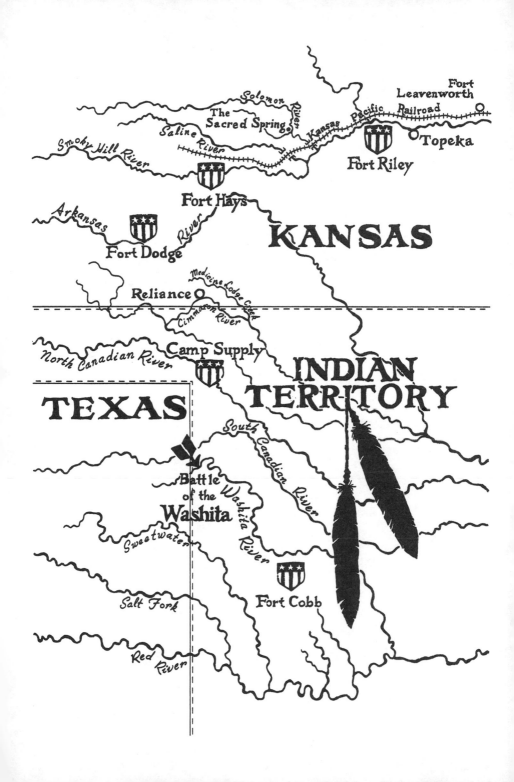

An Uncommon Enemy

One

Custer, I rely on you in everything, and shall
send you on this mission without orders, leaving you to act entirely on your own judgment.

—GENERAL PHILIP SHERIDAN TO LIEUTENANT COLONEL
GEORGE ARMSTRONG CUSTER, FORT HAYS, KANSAS,
SEPTEMBER 30, 1868

We will probably remain out until we can do
the Indians considerable damage. I hope to
find a village in two or three weeks, if I do,
look out for scalps.

—G. A. CUSTER, LETTER TO A FAMILY FRIEND IN MICHIGAN,
FROM CAMP ON THE ARKANSAS, EIGHT MILES BELOW
FORT DODGE, NOVEMBER 8, 1868

NOVEMBER 27, 1868
WASHITA RIVER, INDIAN TERRITORY

In the soft silence between sleep and wakefulness, the
morning began like a hundred others. Seota opened her
eyes thinking she heard a noise. She decided it must be
the faint rustling of little Gray Wolf, her sister Red
Feather Woman's six-month-old baby, another early riser.

The fire in the center of the lodge had died to
glowing embers and now barely advanced against the

morning chill. Seota reluctantly pulled a blanket around her shoulders and crept out to fetch more firewood. She could see her breath in the receding moonlight as she regarded the predawn sky and shook the snow from the twigs and small branches of the little woodpile. A bright star rose on the southern horizon just above the ridge line. It shone there vividly, like a beacon. She paused in the frigid stillness to contemplate its eerie, singular beauty.

The sharp sound of Red Feather's baby demanding attention broke her reverie. She hurried back into the lodge and gently took the baby from its place by its mother so as not to wake her. Poor, frail, little Red Feather Woman was still so weak from the illness that had dogged her throughout the fall.

Seota tossed a few twigs onto the fire with her free hand before she nestled the baby into the crook of her arm and put him to breast as she had done so many times since the stillbirth of her own baby five months before.

Red Feather was grateful to her for volunteering to nurse her tiny son, but in truth, Seota's motives had not been entirely altruistic. Serving as wet nurse to her sister's baby had eased the pain of her own loss. Secretly, she coveted Red Feather's beautiful, perfect, healthy child. Of any prize on earth she could be offered, she longed only for this: a child of her own.

Seota worried about Red Feather Woman. How would her sister ever regain her strength when the entire tribe was starving? The Tsitsistas, the Cheyenne, had spent nearly four years at war. The hardships and privations they suffered grew daily. Buffalo and game were scarce in this new territory. Their shared husband, Hanging Road, said they would be slaughtering and eating the camp dogs and ponies soon. Most of the ponies were too weak to serve a higher function anyway.

Her other sister, Nightwalking Woman, murmured and stretched. She opened her eyes momentarily, exchanged a faint smile with Seota, then turned over on her robe.

The lazy smoke from the small fire now caught the pale morning light as it slowly filtered through the opening in the top of the lodge. Seota luxuriated in this quiet time she spent with little Gray Wolf in her arms.

She heard the far-off sound again. A low rumble, like thunder, yet not quite. She tensed, listened. Surely not trouble. Please, not trouble. Chief Black Kettle had just returned the day before from Fort Cobb on a mission of peace. But he had not returned with any satisfaction. In fact, the man there had warned him that soldiers were already in the field. Controversy had arisen the moment he returned as to what the tribe's next action should be.

Black Kettle had held a council, attended by Hanging Road and all the other important men of the tribe. They smoked on the problem and eventually decided to move their lodges closer to the other villages farther downstream in two days' time. If soldiers were seen sooner than that, they could send out runners to tell them they did not want war.

This decision was met with the loud objections of Medicine Woman Later, Black Kettle's formidable wife. She had good reason to fear white soldiers. Her body carried the scars of nine bullet wounds from the treachery of Sand Creek, four years past.

Upon returning to his home, Hanging Road had informed his concerned wives that he personally doubted the story that soldiers were in their country. Everyone knew the white government seldom made war in the wintertime. He claimed their soldiers were too puny and spoiled to venture out for a winter campaign. "Fairweather warriors," he had called them with sneering contempt and all but Seota had laughed.

"Nightwalking, did you hear that?" Seota asked in a low voice.

Nightwalking sat up sleepily, then also snapped to attention, listening. The sound came from the village dogs, but not the usual break-of-day barking, more like a nervous yipping. She flashed a worried glance at Seota. "Get dressed."

"But I'm not finished—"

"Get dressed!" Nightwalking immediately began pulling on her own dress, leggings, and moccasins. She pinched Red Feather's arm and ordered her to dress, as well.

A single, loud *pop*—like a dry twig being snapped right next to one's ear—broke the calm of the frozen morning.

A warning shot! All three women jumped into frantic action.

"Where is Hanging Road?" Red Feather asked as she took her now-screaming baby back from Seota. Little Gray Wolf kicked and squirmed, searching for the nipple from which he had been so abruptly removed.

"He left last night to see about Lame Dog's child. You know, the one that coughs," said Nightwalking. Hanging Road treated the sick, both the physically and the spiritually ailing; Seota helped him in this calling, though he had not bothered to wake her the night before. Now she wished he had. Being with him, no matter where, seemed preferable to not knowing his fate at such a critical moment.

They they heard the sound they had come to dread most—a distant trumpet—the soldiers of the United States being called to battle.

Red Feather's lips trembled as she looked over at Seota frantically. They could hear the pounding hoofbeats of the approaching horses and men with foreign voices shouting, *"Huzzah, huzzah!"* with a manic fervor.

And above it all, Seota heard strains of music. Band music. A military band. In some far corner of her memory, she knew the tune. An Irish one.

"We must run," Red Feather said, clutching her baby tightly to her chest.

"No, we must wait for Hanging Road to come to us," said Nightwalking.

Seota agreed with Red Feather, but did not wish to contradict the oldest member of the family. She did not know what horror awaited outside the mystical circle of their home, yet any action seemed preferable to cowering in the tepee and waiting for certain doom to arrive on horseback.

Screams and shouts were heard as the cavalry arrived in a thunderous tumult. Gunshots. Shrieking women. Wailing children. Wounded men. Galloping horses. The acrid smell of smoke filled the air from pistols and rifles fired in every direction. A nightmare made flesh in the early light of day.

The three women heard a commotion immediately outside the tepee. Nightwalking thought it was her husband coming to rescue his family and foolishly threw back the entrance flap. A loud blast sounded and she was thrown back into the lodge. Seota and Red Feather stood over her and looked down in paralyzing disbelief. Nightwalking's eyes stared up lifelessly below a neat round hole in her forehead.

The two young women clutched each other in fear, the baby squeezed between them in their embrace.

"We've got to run," Seota urged.

Red Feather shook her head as panic seized her, immobilizing her. She held her baby so tightly, Seota feared she would harm him.

"Come, Red Feather. Follow me!"

"No, no, no. Nightwalking told us to wait for Hanging Road!"

"We *must* run!" Seota didn't want to add this, but she had to. "Hanging Road is probably already dead!"

Seota knelt down over the body of Nightwalking and cautiously peeked out the opening of the tepee. A chaos of flashing gunpowder and running bodies swirled before her eyes as the echoing report of rifle fire pierced the frigid morning air over and over.

She dropped the flap, ran to the opposite side of the lodge, knelt down, and yanked away the tepee liner, careless of the beautiful paintings Hanging Road had so

painstakingly applied last summer. She brushed aside the dried grasses stuffed between the liner and the heavy outer wall and hurriedly attempted to peel it upward.

Snow had fallen to knee depth after two days of freezing rain. The edge of the tepee lay stubbornly frozen to the earth. She pulled with all her might, bracing her elbows against her knees, and finally the leather edge yielded. She peeked out from under it and saw no one in her immediate line of sight. Their lodge sat on the northernmost edge of the village. The cottonwood trees and brush lining the creek lay a mere ten yards away.

"This way, quickly."

Red Feather looked at her with uncertainty, then did as she was told. She crawled out from under the tepee wall, then reached back in for her baby to be handed out.

Something made Seota glance about the lodge one last time before joining her sister. Her eyes fell upon a small beaded bag behind Hanging Road's back rest. His medicine bag. The special one. He hadn't taken it with him last night because he reserved it only for the most sacred occasions. She grabbed the small leather pouch and stuffed it down the front of her dress for safekeeping, then dove out from under the wall of the lodge to join Red Feather.

Flames engulfed the village, fifty lodges and more.

Both women dashed for the frigid, waist-deep water of the river. The little crusts of ice that had formed along the dark red bank of the stream made their descent into the Washita difficult and treacherous. Heedless of the freezing cold, they waded across and sought cover in the brush of the far bank. Once there, they huddled in silence as the battle raged so close and yet somehow removed, like a strange dream in which one merely watches and does not participate. Soldiers of the United States swarmed everywhere, like a plague of hornets.

Baby Gray Wolf still squirmed and cried, not so much from hunger now, but fear. He sensed his mother's agitation. Red Feather covered the child's face with her hand to keep him quiet.

Both women crouched in rigid stillness as they heard the approach of horses. Seota raised her eyes above the prickly branches of the leafless bush that hid her and watched two soldiers on horseback make their way down the creek. They were looking for people hiding, like Red Feather and herself. She ducked under her cover again and glanced over to her sister and the baby. To her horror, she saw Gray Wolf's little face turning dark from lack of oxygen. She gestured frantically to Red Feather, finally caught her eye, and pointed first at the baby in her lap and then at her mouth. Red Feather responded with blank confusion, but then looked down at her child. She instantly removed her hand from the child's face. The baby coughed twice, then howled, immediately alerting the soldiers to their hiding place.

"Over here, Ben!"

The two men urged their horses back across the frigid river.

The women jumped up and ran away from the riverbank, but the two mounted soldiers were quickly at their sides.

"Look, Jim, this one's got her papoose with her." The soldier called Ben reached down in an effortless motion and snatched Red Feather's baby from her.

Red Feather Woman screamed and jumped in the air in a fruitless attempt to pluck the child back from the soldier's grasp.

At Red Feather's scream, Seota turned and looked over her shoulder. She saw a laughing man on horseback dangle the baby by its foot just out of the reach of its hysterical mother.

Seota stopped and watched in horror. The soldier chasing her stopped, as well, either entertained by the spectacle or at least curious what would happen next.

Red Feather Woman shouted, begged, and pleaded helplessly in her Cheyenne tongue, as the man continued his hideous, taunting game. Then she pulled her knife from her belt and tried to drive it into the man's thigh, but he jerked his horse away just in time to avoid the strike.

"You filthy Injun bitch!" The soldier kicked Red Feather in the face and she fell to the ground, momentarily senseless. The soldier's horse reared and snorted, its hooves narrowly missing Red Feather's prostrate body.

She managed to raise her head and look up in time to see the soldier raise her baby high in the air.

"No, don't do it!" screamed Seota. "In the name of Jesus Christ, don't do it!"

But the plea had not left her mouth before the soldier slammed the baby to the ground with such force it bounced once, before crumpling into a lifeless little heap. Red Feather threw herself on top of her child just as the other soldier shot her squarely in the back with his revolver.

"Damn you all to hell!" shouted Seota.

Both men now halted on their mounts and stared at her.

"Did you hear that, Ben?" asked the soldier nearest to her.

"Yep."

They continued to gape. Seota stood frozen, clutching her red woolen blanket tightly around her head and shoulders.

"What should we do?" Jim said, his eyes never straying from Seota.

The soldier called Ben glanced back to the village where the fires sent billowing black smoke into the November sky obscuring the pale winter sun. "Go get that new captain. See him over yonder? That tall drink of water. Randall's his name. Let's make this *his* problem."

The soldier called Jim rode off in the direction of the captain while the murderer of baby Gray Wolf leveled his pistol at Seota. She analyzed her chances for escape. Before she could break and run, the other soldier returned with the captain.

They rode over the snow-covered ground and crossed the creek bed quickly. Captain Randall was a lean, sandy-haired young man. He blotted blood from a wound on his forehead with a handkerchief.

"She spoke to you in English?" he asked as they approached.

"Yes, sir, she surely did."

"What did she say?" The young captain studied Seota. Every time he removed the handkerchief from his forehead, blood trickled over his brow and down the side of his face. One such drip slid into his eye and caused him to squint and blink.

"She said, 'In the name of Jesus Christ,' plain as day."

The captain frowned as he busily wiped the blood out of his eye. "She probably picked up the phrase from a missionary."

"Then she said, 'Damn you all to hell.' What kind of Injun squaw knows how to curse that good?"

Seota stood motionless as the three men gazed down upon her from their horses. Captain Randall dismounted, fastened his reins to a nearby bush, and walked toward her.

"What is your name, woman? Do you speak English?"

Seota said nothing. Her heart pounded fiercely as she clutched the blanket even more tightly about her head, obscuring her face. The tall young man took another stride nearer and she instinctively stepped back.

"I'm not going to hurt you." He held his handkerchief again to his bleeding forehead, but lifted his other hand in a calming gesture.

A dozen soldiers rode near, splashing them all as they passed. Captain Randall called to the leader of the group. "Major Elliott? I think I've found—"

"No time to talk, Randall. We're giving chase to that bunch who got on down the river. I need volunteers!"

The two enlisted men looked to the captain for direction and he nodded for them to join Major Elliott.

The major called back with a jaunty cynicism, "Here goes—for a brevet or a coffin!"

The group of soldiers rode away at full gallop following the stream. The captain returned his attention to Seota.

"If you understand what I'm saying, tell me your name."

Seota heard the screams of the wounded and dying from the village. Her eyes quickly scanned the surrounding hills for sign of rescue. Farther up along the horseshoe bend of the river lay the Arapaho village of Little Raven and the Cheyenne camp of Medicine Arrows, with Kicking Bird's Kiowas below them. In all, nearly six thousand Indians had gone into winter camp on the Washita that year. Groups of warriors from those villages now gathered on the ridges overlooking the river valley, but they were too late. Black Kettle's village was already lost.

The captain reached out and caught Seota's wrist in his bloody, gloved hand and yanked her toward him so hard she nearly lost her footing. The blanket she clutched around her head fell to the ground, revealing the color of her hair.

Randall gasped and with his free hand examined a tangled, dark auburn lock of it. In bewilderment, he whispered, "Who *are* you?"

Tears of misery and dread filled Seota's eyes. Did she even know the answer to that question anymore? Her chin trembled. She looked up into the young man's face with a frantic, hopeless despair. She drew a long, ragged breath and knew that for the second time in four years,

her life would change forever. She placed her hand to her bosom to press the small medicine bag to her heart, hoping it might give her some sort of strength and at last she spoke:

"Eden Elizabeth Clanton Murdoch."

Two

A white woman has come into our camp. I
suppose her to have been captured by Indians
and rendered insane by their barbarous treatment.

—G. A. CUSTER, LETTER TO HIS WIFE, NOVEMBER 1868

"What'd they do to ya?" one of the soldiers had asked
as he leered at Eden Murdoch that first night at a place
the soldiers called Camp Supply.

"I know what *I'd* like to do to ya," offered a lecherous sergeant.

"Not after she's been with the Injuns," said a baby-
faced private. Some of the others mumbled concurrence.

Eden could only close her eyes to the ugly laughter
that followed. At least Captain Randall had been kind.
Well, not really kind so much as formal and polite. He
seemed always to avoid looking at her whenever he
spoke. She could only assume he felt the same disgust
the soldiers voiced, but was too gentlemanly to express
it in her presence.

Eden took Bradley Randall to be new to his job, judging from how often others had to explain things to him.
They had both been summoned to the general's tent the

second night at Camp Supply. The encampment did not impress Eden. Her father was a mapmaker with the Army Corps of Engineers so she had grown up on one military garrison after another and knew the high and low of them. This place, with its simple log stockade and small city of white tents, had a hurried, temporary look to it, constructed in anticipation of this current campaign, Eden surmised.

"Mrs. Murdoch, may I present to you General Custer?" Captain Randall had said as they entered the spacious round Sibley tent. The tent, with its golden lamplight and sturdy camp furniture, smelled of damp canvas and coffee beans. Eden glanced down to see a makeshift floor of empty coffee sacks. Coffee. A warm cup of coffee on a cold morning. The scent reverberated in her memory like an echo.

The general, a man of medium height in his late twenties, rose from his small writing desk and strode toward them. A warm smile parted the blond mustache and scruffy beard of the man's thin face as he extended his hand. "Mrs. Murdoch, I am delighted to make your acquaintance."

Eden slapped the general's hand away, then braced herself, half expecting him to strike her back.

His piercing blue eyes widened with surprise. He surveyed her with a detached curiosity.

Randall interceded. "I believe she is still a bit disoriented, sir."

"No doubt," Custer said dryly. He walked around Eden with an imperious gaze, as though contemplating an exotic animal at a zoological garden. "Madam, rest easy. Your nightmare is over at last."

Over . . . or just beginning? Eden wondered with a sick feeling in her empty stomach.

"How long have you been with the Cheyennes, Mrs. Murdoch?"

She remained silent, feeling so many powerful and confusing emotions, she feared she would burst into tears; she did not wish to break down in front of these men, she did not want to give them the satisfaction of confirming their self-congratulatory attitude toward her dubious rescue.

Their triumphant march back into Camp Supply from the battle ground still rankled her. The humiliating procession had carried all the earmarks of a Caesar marching back into Rome with his valiant troops and wretched captives on full and exultant display.

"When and where were you abducted?"

She guessed he would be perversely entertained by the titillating details of her capture. Men seemed to take a base delight in hearing stories of a woman mistreated, especially mistreated in a sexual way.

"Mrs. Murdoch, I can understand your reluctance. I have personally dealt with numerous individuals in your unfortunate situation. I know you have suffered greatly at the hands of these savages and that recalling such horrors must be painful to you, but it remains important, nonetheless, that you inform us of the details of your captivity. There are persons in our government who should know just what we are dealing with out here.

Your story would doubtless sway opinions . . . *opinions that matter*."

"I don't wish to discuss it," she finally managed to say. She trembled from either the biting cold of the evening, or from nerves and exhaustion. The fact that she had barely eaten for three days did not help the situation, and before she knew it, the canvas room, bathed in its golden lamplight, spun around her and she dropped to the ground. The soft coffee-sack floor had cushioned her fall. Randall and the general knelt over her. Her head rested on one of the men's laps, she did not know which one. She heard them speaking, but could not organize her mind enough to open her eyes. The general called to someone outside the tent for water.

"What have you been able to find out about her?" Custer demanded of his captain. His courtly manners had evaporated with Eden's faint.

"I think she's a widow."

"You *think*?"

"I couldn't get her to talk much about her husband. She became agitated and upset whenever I mentioned him. When I finally asked if he had been killed in the War, she just nodded and refused to say more. Very odd. She was much more forthcoming about her father. He is with the Corps of Engineers, or at least he was before her capture—whenever that was. When she's in the mood to talk, she seems very intelligent. She must have had some education. She used words like 'ironic.' "

"*Ironic?* In what context?" Custer said, amusement in his voice.

"Last night she asked about the air played by the regimental band during the charge."

" 'Garryowen'?"

"Yes. She said it was ironic that the same tune was played at the reception following her wedding."

The general contemplated this for a moment. "I would call that *coincidental* rather than ironic. Wouldn't you?"

Randall continued. "She asked if she could help out at the post hospital and nurse the wounded Cheyenne women and children being treated there. She said she was trained as a nurse and had served in a field hospital during the War. But I declined to allow her anywhere near the hospital."

Eden knew that Captain Randall had believed her claim of medical experience. When he had pulled her back across the Washita, she had bluntly told him to wet his bloody handkerchief in the river and hold it tightly to his head wound. She said the cold cloth would keep down the swelling. She also told him not to worry about the cut, that head wounds always bleed far in excess of their actual severity. He did as she had instructed.

While he wrung out his wet handkerchief, she used the opportunity to make a run for the shore. He tackled her in the middle of the freezing Washita and they grappled until they were both nearly drowned. He dragged her to the bank where they again wrestled in the snowy, red mud.

Twice her size and weight, he quickly pinned her

struggling body under his and pulled her arms over her head. She sensed he was trying to subdue her without hurting her and determined to employ his chivalry against him. She was certain she could have succeeded had not a young lieutenant come upon them.

"*Brad*," the man said, "do you really think this is the time or the place?"

"I'm not raping her, damn it! And don't shoot her, she's a white woman."

Eden used the moment's distraction to force her knee up between Brad Randall's legs and slam him in the crotch with all the force she could manage. He shrieked and rolled off her in agony, while his comrade calmly placed the muzzle of a revolver against the bridge of her nose.

"And you assumed she would try and harm the prisoners?" Custer ventured.

"Quite the opposite. I feared she would try to arrange their escape."

"Oh, come now, Randall."

"I'm entirely in earnest, sir. I don't think this woman can be trusted. Nothing about her can be taken for granted. I think the trauma of her captivity has deranged her. Not to mention unsexed her."

"Unsexed her?"

"Walking over here tonight, sir, I was detained a moment in conversation with the interpreter on another matter. An enlisted man, who apparently didn't realize she was with me, stepped up and made a crude and insulting remark to her. She shouted something at him in the Cheyenne tongue and I noticed our interpreter, Mr. Romero, laughing. I asked him for an explanation and, according to him, she'd said something like 'Get out of my sight, you little weasel, or I'll castrate you with my teeth!' "

"I guess we'd better watch what *we* say to her from now on," Custer said with a grin.

At that moment, Eden's amber-green eyes fluttered open. She saw the two men's slender, bearded faces hovering over hers, but the images still swam before her.

"She's almost pretty," Custer said.

"Hard to tell under so much dirt," Randall whispered. Neither he nor his ward had fully recovered from their bout of mud wrestling on the slippery cold bank of the Washita. Every item of clothing he possessed seemed now to be stained brownish-pink from the mud of the battlefield.

Custer grinned at Brad's remark, then as quickly sobered. He wrinkled his long nose and knit his freckled brow. "Do you suppose she's pregnant?"

"Could be," Brad said as he awkwardly patted her cheek with his cold hand.

"Most of them are when we find them. I have always left standing orders with the ranking officer of any garrison where my wife remains that they are to shoot her rather than allow her to fall into enemy hands."

"Shoot Mrs. Custer?" Randall asked in horrified tones.

"Of course. I would not have a moment's peace on a scout were I not to leave such an order. I can assure

you, my wife heartily concurs. Think about it, Randall.
Would you really care to see that beautiful Amanda of
yours ending up in this sorry state?"

The captain looked down and saw that Eden was
fully awake and listening to their comments.

She sat up and drank a sip of the water they offered
her. The general helped her to her feet and led her to a
small folding camp chair next to his writing desk. How
long had it been since she had sat in a chair? She was
amazed at how novel it felt.

"Did you know that the flour and sugar we found at
the village were supplied to them less than a week ago
by General Hazen at Fort Cobb? We fight them, Hazen
feeds them!" Custer snorted. "I wish someone would
explain this anomaly to me. I am at a complete loss to
understand it!"

Then his manner softened and he merely sighed
with irritation. "If this matter is not handled correctly,
the press will have a field day with it."

In that instant, Eden realized why she had been assigned such a prominent position in the parade into
Camp Supply to meet Custer's commanding officer,
General Philip Sheridan. She was their prize, their justification to the world for their attack on the sleeping
village. They had found a white captive—proof positive
that Black Kettle was not the peace chief he pretended
to be.

Custer looked down at Eden where she sat and
smiled thinly. Eden fought the urge to recoil from that
smile. She felt like a powerless child in the presence of

a stern and autocratic parent, though she and the young general were nearly equals in age.

"That is why it is so important to tell the truth of the story. A truth that can only be told by our Mrs. Murdoch here. This conflict must be brought to a swift and decisive end. We cannot allow godless savages to go on terrorizing our settlements and ravishing our womenfolk." He gently placed his hand on top of Eden's where it lay on his writing desk.

She bristled at his patronizing tone and jerked her hand away.

"Godless savages?" She spoke up archly. "Your own men are taking lustful advantage of the Cheyenne women prisoners right now, as we speak. What, pray, motivates them, sir? The *love* of God?"

Custer exchanged glances with Randall, then chuckled. "Touché, Mrs. Murdoch."

Three

Brad had just enough candle left to proofread his letter to his fiancée, Amanda, one last time before retiring for the night. He would leave with a detail of men for the nearest town tomorrow at daybreak with the woman, Eden Murdoch, in tow.

He had worked on the letter sporadically since leaving Camp Supply. Never getting the opportunity to post it until the regiment returned there, he had just kept adding on passage after passage.

My beloved Amanda,

Forgive me this long space between letters. The events of the past week and beyond precluded my communicating sooner. I pray this note will find you well.

My happiness depends on yours, my dearest. You are the first thought in my mind each morning and the last as I rest my head each night. This necessary separation is painful to me—painful to us both, but this week I have been presented with evidence of the most shocking and graphic nature to cause me to be grateful for our decision to postpone our wedding until after I return to the States.

Our company headed south out of Fort Dodge on a mission to punish the hostile tribes for the reign of terror they have perpetrated on our border residents this fall. The most recent depredation involved a Kansas Pacific track crew, brutally attacked, leaving seven men dead and twice that many wounded. Four days later, a farm family fell victims. A husband, wife, six children, and the wife's brother—all slaughtered, their bodies hideously mutilated. Concern for your delicacy forbids me to share the gruesome details, but one could not come away from such a sight unmoved.

My admiration for General Custer grows daily. So does my gratitude to him for taking me onto his personal staff, as well as into his family circle. As I indicated in my last letter, our trip west together afforded me the opportunity to learn much of my new mission.

As your father intimated, the general definitely enjoys the patronage and confidence of General Sheridan, who abruptly replaced General Sully with General Custer on the current campaign. I believe General Custer still feels ill-used in the matter of his court-martial last year. He claims he was made the scapegoat for the abject failure of the Hancock Expedition to subdue the hostiles.

I learned more of the incident, which I feel you

might appreciate, Amanda. It seems the "personal mission" alluded to in the newspapers for which he marched his troops so unforgivingly was to see his own dear wife!

I cannot condone his actions, especially since they resulted in the loss of two of his men, but as a soon-to-be married man myself, I can at least understand how someone could act so. Still, his command is not without controversy, though I daresay the man thrives on it. For this current campaign, he has outfitted himself in a uniform made entirely of fringed buckskin, and goes everywhere accompanied by a fine pair of Scottish staghounds, called Blucher and Maida, on whom he lavishes the affection one usually reserves for one's children.

Many who were under his command prior to his suspension cast him in the role of petty tyrant. I have not seen evidence of this. Either he has turned over a new leaf, as they say, or he is the target of a certain jealousy. I suspect the latter owing to his extreme youth. He is, after all, but eight-and-twenty and so many of his junior officers are his senior in years by more than a decade.

He can display a temper, though, while in the field. On the morning we were to depart on the current mission, he apparently felt some—namely his younger brother who is my age, Captain Tom Custer—were tarrying too long over their breakfasts. He strode into Captain Custer's tent and kicked the man's breakfast table out from under him, sending food and dishes flying in all directions! He turned on his heel and left the tent without another word while the remainder of our group stood by aghast and speechless.

Poor Tom Custer, who sat there with his fork still in his hand, blithely announced to all those present, "If anyone thinks it's an easy job being the brother of a general, they are sadly mistaken."

Everyone laughed.

Speaking of laughter, your poor intended was the target of one of the Custer brothers' legendary pranks. Some of my more soft-hearted fellow officers had warned me to be on the lookout as every newcomer to the regiment was subjected to some level of horseplay—a kind of baptism to the frontier. I intended to bear this with as much good humor as I could summon, but how was I to know that the rattlesnake—yes, *live* rattlesnake, that I found in my bedroll one night was actually Tom Custer's pet? I pulled out my revolver and shot the odious creature. The good captain sulked and refused to speak to me for three days.

General Custer said a curious thing on the train ride west that I have yet to fully understand. He remarked with an uncharacteristic gravity, "Don't count on coming home the same man who left this week. Once you've spent time on the frontier you will never look at life in the States quite the same again." We'll see about that, I suppose.

Well, I have digressed from my story of the recent encounter with the Cheyennes. We marched south out of Camp Supply on the twenty-third of

November with eleven companies, unable to wait any longer for the Kansas volunteers.

A blizzard commenced the day we left, making it so difficult to see, General Custer had to use a compass to direct our march. The following day, the weather cleared and, by the twenty-fifth, we reached the north bank of the South Canadian River, seventy miles out of Camp Supply.

Our scouts, nearly a dozen friendly Osages plus four seasoned frontiersmen, followed a trail which eventually led to a large band of Cheyennes camped on the south bank of the Washita River in the western part of the Indian Territory. If you will look on the map, Amanda, you will find this place due east of the Antelope Hills.

We neared the Washita late the following evening—certainly the strangest Thanksgiving Day of my life to date—and hung through the night under orders that there be no conversation above a whisper, no fires built, not so much as a match to be struck as we waited in silence—and bone-chilling cold—for daybreak and the order to attack.

When the trumpeters sounded the charge, the band struck up "Garryowen." (Do you remember the tune?) Our men stormed the village from four different vantage points, taking it utterly by surprise. Women and children ran screaming, while their warriors mustered an astonishingly quick defense. Within minutes, we had secured the village and their chief, Black Kettle, was dead.

I found myself slightly injured. Do not fret, it

was but a trifle. An arrow grazed my forehead, slicing the skin above my brow. I did not require the attention of a surgeon and the wound will no doubt heal without a scar. (I am almost sorry for this last. When you and I are an elderly Mr. and Mrs. sitting in our rocking chairs by the fire with half a dozen grandchildren at our feet, and they ask me if it was true I was once an Indian fighter on the great frontier, I could proudly point to the scar as a memento of my heroic youth! Ha!)

The general ordered the entire village be destroyed so as to make utter paupers of those who had escaped the morning's battle. This tedious and unsavory task did not appeal to my sensibilities, but do not make mention of this to your father as I do not wish it to be taken as a criticism of my superiors. Before the afternoon had finished, we became increasingly aware that Black Kettle's village was not alone in this country, but rather the first of many encampments on the Washita. Warriors from these neighboring tribes grouped themselves in threatening numbers on the surrounding ridge lines and minor skirmishes continued throughout the day.

As we were nearly twoscore miles from our pack train, the situation could have proven grave indeed (pun intended!) had not our commander resourcefully executed the most astounding and clever maneuver. He ordered us back on the march in the direction of the enemy camps with band playing and guidons flying at full glory, all the while

knowing we were nearly exhausted of ammunition and supplies. Our enemy, thankfully not aware of this, scurried at once back to their respective villages to take a defensive posture.

At approximately 10 P.M., we countermarched, retracing all our steps of the previous day and night under the cover of darkness. The bold feint achieved its goal. We were not followed. We pushed through the night and went into bivouac about two in the morning. We caught what we could of much-needed sleep, then resumed our march at daylight, mercifully reuniting with our pack train by ten the next morning.

Our losses were few in number. One officer killed—regrettably Captain Hamilton (I think I mentioned in a previous letter he was a grandson of Alexander Hamilton). Two wounded, one seriously—Captain Barnitz—the other, Tom Custer, only slightly. Concern mounts, however, over the fate of Major Elliott and a detail of men he took with him after a group of escaping warriors. I think I may have been the last officer to see them alive before they left the Cheyenne village. We can now only assume the worst.

On the day of the battle, I and numerous others were assigned the task of rounding up the women and children for transport back into Camp Supply as prisoners. I found among their number a white woman, apparently taken captive a number of years ago. Our scouts had not informed us of her presence and now I believe they were not aware of it. The level of her degradation was so complete, we at first mistook her for a Cheyenne.

When I attempted her rescue, she actively fought against me. She seems to align her loyalties more with her former captors than her own kind. I am anxious to learn more of her history, though I fear she has lost her reason. Perhaps by my next correspondence, I will have more light to shed on this strange enigma of a woman.

I must close for now and will write again as soon as I can. You will be able to reach me by telegram in the city of Reliance, Kansas, should an emergency arise, otherwise send my mail via Fort Dodge. They will forward it if necessary. I remain here, either at Reliance or Fort Dodge, until my white captive has found her way back to civilization.

All my love always,

Bradley

Eden Murdoch peeked around the blanket partition that separated her cot from Captain Randall's in his tent. He had moved her in with him after her second escape attempt. He was so engrossed in reading something at his little camp desk that he did not notice her.

She knew this might be the last opportunity she had to visit the Cheyenne women prisoners. He had told her to prepare to leave at first light for the States, heading to some little town whose sole attraction was a telegraph office and, thus, contact to the wider world. Though she longed to be reunited with her father, she

was desperate to learn the fate of Hanging Road.

Eden quietly slipped out and made her way among the countless tents, some illuminated by lamplight, others already dark, their canvas walls vibrating with their occupants' snores.

She knew that the Cheyenne women and children were being housed in two large tepees salvaged from the Washita village. She saw their high peaks glowing in the distance above the Army tents and quickened her step.

"Mrs. Murdoch!"

Eden spun around to face an angry Captain Randall who stood both hatless and coatless in the bitter night's chill. He reached out and clutched her arm.

"Please, Captain, let me visit the women just for a moment. It's terribly important."

Randall frowned and debated the matter. "Well, we're already here. I'll let you go in on one condition. You must hold my hand at all times just like a little child."

Eden grudgingly acceded to this demand and they proceeded, hand in hand, looking like a pair of sweethearts, though Randall's firm grasp was far from lover-like. When they ducked into the first tepee, Eden hoped he would release her hand, there being an ample supply of soldiers standing guard, but he did not.

Several blanket-clad women jumped up as they entered, their dark faces apprehensive and defiant. When the identity of their late-night visitor became apparent in the flickering light of the lodge's central fire ring, several more women approached.

"Well, Seota," snarled a young woman named Making Trails, "I suppose you're happy now."

"Everyone knows that you're the reason the soldiers came down upon us," shouted an older woman called Little Day who shook her wrinkled fist at the young white woman.

"That's not true," Eden cried in Cheyenne. "Please, do any of you know what became of Hanging Road?"

"Why should you care? You're back with your friends now."

"Stop it! Just tell me if you know about Hanging Road."

"Look how he holds her hand," taunted Making Trails.

Eden fought back tears. "Please just tell me. One of you must have seen him that morning."

"Ask your *new* lover, Seota!"

Finally, an elderly widow called Evening Woman emerged from the crowd. Her age gave her a status requiring deference from the younger women. She stepped up close to Eden and the captain and whispered, "They shot him, Seota. I'm sorry, but I saw him fall. He was running for your lodge when they cut him down."

Eden managed to choke out a thank-you before Captain Randall led her back to his tent.

"I don't know what those women were saying, but they sounded angry at you," said Randall.

"They consider me one of you now."

Four

"After having her . . . person subjected to the fearful bestiality of perhaps the whole tribe, it is mock humanity to secure what is left of her for the consideration of five ponies."
—General Philip Sheridan, explaining his decision not to allow General Hazen to attempt the ransom of a captured white woman, November 1868

Hugh Christie had just stepped out of the barber's chair at Rhinehart Meeker's Tonsorial Palace, having received a fine shave, and was about to enter the bathing room when a startling trio burst into the shop with much noise and commotion.

"I want a bath, Sergeant! And you're not going to stop me," shouted a bizarrely dressed and spectacularly dirty young woman to a plump, middle-aged cavalry trooper who had just chased her into the shop. A skinny, grinning young private whose uniform looked three sizes too big for him followed close behind.

The sergeant frowned at the agitated young woman who had just shouted in his face. "Look, Mrs. Murdoch, the captain said we was supposed to take you to that doctor and have you checked over straightaway and that's what me and Joe intend on doin'!"

Joe, the skinny private, now stood by silently gawking. He gave Hugh Christie and Rhinehart Meeker a nod and a small wave of greeting.

Mrs. Murdoch glared at Sergeant Yellen. "First of all, I do not need to see a doctor. I can assure you I am in perfect health. And, secondly, even if I did visit this doctor I would not care to do so until I have bathed."

"Oh, no, you won't, lady," said Meeker, the only barber in the tiny border town of Reliance, Kansas. He said the word "lady" in a tone that implied he was being generous in his use of the term. Whether the creature who stood before him was a lady or not had yet to be determined. She was dressed, head to toe, in Indian garb, though her wavy, tangled mass of dark auburn hair and her green eyes announced her a member of the white race. "This here is an establishment serving gentlemen, not ladies."

"Or squaws," piped up Hugh Christie as a joke. He quickly seated himself in the waiting area to watch the action. The arrival of the Seventh Cavalry in town always caused a stir, but when the cavalry arrived with a rescued white captive in tow, Reliance was ablaze with curiosity. To have unexpectedly landed a front-row seat pleased him immensely.

The young woman was a feisty one. Maybe even pretty under all that dirt and matted hair. Christie wondered what her age might be. Her skin was tanned and weathered by the elements, but her voice sounded young—somewhere in the mid-twenties, he guessed.

The woman twisted her mouth at Christie, while the sergeant and private tittered at the joke. She turned back

to Rhinehart Meeker with a pleading tone replacing the strident one. "But where do *women* bathe?"

The barber shrugged. "In their homes, I reckon. I never been asked that question before."

"It don't make no difference 'cause you ain't gettin' a bath now anyways," said Sergeant Emory Yellen. "The captain told us to take you to that doctor and that's what we're gonna do!"

"Why didn't you take her to an army doctor?" said Hugh Christie.

"All the surgeons are busy with the wounded," Sergeant Yellen said. "We had a big fight down on the Washita. 'Sides, we had to come here on account of this bein' the nearest place with a telegraph line. And she wasn't fittin' in at all at the camp. Raisin' holy hell and makin' everybody's life miserable. Now, come on, lady. We're gonna see that doctor."

"Not until I've bathed, Sergeant Yellen, *please,*" Eden said. "I have been forced to wear this coat of mud every day since that battle, for heaven's sake."

"But the captain said—"

Brad Randall, the captain in question strode into the shop at that precise moment. His height was such that he nearly bumped his forehead on the door frame, ducking at the last instant just as everyone winced in anticipation, but losing his hat in the process. The sergeant and the private knew better than to smile at this, but Christie and Meeker shared an amused glance as the young man retrieved his hat from an awestruck little boy who had scooped it up for him. The captain handed the boy a penny and slapped dust off his hat. He surveyed the small, crowded room with a tired exasperation, having located his misplaced charge by following the throng of curiosity-seekers who now crowded the barbershop's large window for a look at the white captive.

"Sergeant, what is going on?"

"Captain Randall, her ladyship here says she won't see the doctor till she gets a bath."

"Well, let her have the damned bath," Randall said irritably. "Forgive my language, ma'am. I fear life on the frontier is eroding my manners as well as my disposition."

Eden smiled weakly at his remark, grateful that he agreed that she could have her bath. She turned expectantly back to Meeker.

"No," said the barber. With the palms of his hands, he slicked back his heavily pomaded hair, parted down the center with the precision of a draftsman.

"Why not?" Randall demanded.

"As I told this *person*," began Meeker, apparently having decided he would no longer refer to her as a lady, "my establishment caters only to men."

"Well, make an exception," the captain snapped.

Meeker set his jaw. Hugh Christie could tell that his friend was not about to have this young brat of an army officer hand him orders as if he were back in uniform. Meeker had served in the Union Army during the war and though he bragged often about his outfit's heroic exploits, Christie knew he had actually hated every minute of army life.

"Mr. —" Randall glanced at the sign on the wall to gain the name of the barber. "Mr. Meeker, forgive me

for my shortness of temper. Allow me to introduce myself. I am Captain Bradley Randall of the Seventh Cavalry—"

"I guessed that much," Meeker interrupted with a superior tilt of his well-shaved chin.

"The Seventh, as you may *also* know, has just engaged the hostiles in a terrible skirmish down in the Indian Territory and we are all quite weary and, I'm afraid, lacking in civility at the moment. If you could but make an exception to the rules of your establishment for this unfortunate woman, you would, sir, be performing an act of Christian charity."

Sergeant Yellen, standing behind his superior officer, rolled his eyes.

"Sounds fair to me, Rhinehart." Christie broke into the conversation, hoping to calm things down and get his friend to ease off a little. He, like all the citizens of Reliance, looked to the army for protection.

Everyone had been on edge during the last four years as both the Arapaho and the Cheyenne nations had declared war on the United States. Though the summer had been a quiet one, a violent autumn had followed. No one dared to cross the prairie without some sort of escort. At times, a state of siege prevailed.

Still, the look of disgust on Meeker's face conveyed his true feelings. Christie could tell that the barber did not want this filthy woman who had lived among the savages and looked like a savage herself using his fine brass bathtub. He was as protective of that tub as a mother of her only child.

"Much as I'd like to oblige you, Captain," Meeker

said, not sounding very sincere, "the truth is, this gentleman here is waiting for the bath I've just drawn."

The woman and her entourage collectively turned to Hugh Christie with dismay.

"I'm a gentleman?" asked Christie in mock surprise.

Meeker grinned at his friend, then noticed that the filthy woman had helped herself to one of his combs. "Wait a minute," he yelled. "Give me that. You probably got lice."

"I do *not* have lice." She refused to yield the comb and continued to yank it against the tangled mass of her hair.

"She does not have lice," Randall assured the barber.

Meeker picked up a hairbrush and attempted to pull it through Eden's matted auburn hair. He seemed to forget for the moment how distasteful he found her presence in his shop and rose to the professional challenge her hair presented.

"It's hopeless," he declared, after a few tries. "Too bad we can't just cut it."

Eden, apparently inspired by this remark, impulsively grabbed a pair of scissors and whacked off a large handful of hair and dropped it to the ground.

"Now, come on," Meeker cried. "I didn't mean you had to. Gimme them scissors back."

But Eden had already successfully made several more cuts.

"Mourning," remarked Randall as he watched Eden cut her hair. He explained to the other men, "The Cheyenne women we took as prisoners—they all cut their

hair off, too. One of our scouts told me it was a gesture of mourning."

"What's she got to mourn about?" the barber asked.

"Might I take my bath now?" Eden demanded as she continued to hack off lock after lock of her hair.

The captain turned to Hugh Christie. "Sir, if I could persuade you to relinquish—"

"My pleasure, Captain," Christie said with a gallant gesture. "Anything for the grand and glorious Seventh Cavalry."

"Grand and glorious," Eden Murdoch muttered under her breath as she tried to pull a comb through the tattered remnants of her hair which now barely reached her jawline.

The remark caused Emory Yellen's temper to give way. "A body would think you'd have the common decency to be thankful to the men who risked their lives to save your sorry hide!"

"Save my hide?" repeated Eden, her sarcasm dripping. She pointed the comb at the sergeant's plump belly. "Is that what you are calling the carnage I witnessed?"

"Don't start up again, Mrs. Murdoch," Randall warned. He sighed in irritation, obviously not wishing to be pulled into a public debate with the woman. "Sergeant, I am off to the telegraph office to begin the search for this woman's family. Carry out your duties with the least fuss, if you please. I shall meet you later at the doctor's office."

He turned and left. Christie watched Yellen frown

after him. He looked as though he resented taking orders from a man young enough to be his son. Randall appeared to be no more than twenty-four or-five, yet he was only slightly younger than the regiment's commanding officer, George Armstrong Custer. Christie had seen the Boy General once before in early 1867 and was struck by how similar the two young men were. They could have been mistaken for brothers, both lean and handsome and well-spoken, though Captain Randall was considerably taller.

"What's a captain doing on a job like this?" asked Christie of Sergeant Yellen.

"Captain Randall is General Custer's aide-de-camp," explained the sergeant. "He gets to do any damn thing the general thinks needs gettin' done."

"He's Iron Butt's errand boy," the smirking private added.

"Shut up, Joe," Yellen growled.

"So I guess that makes you two the errand boy's errand boys," remarked Hugh.

Yellen leveled a glance like a warning shot at Christie, while Meeker and the young private stifled their smiles.

"I wish to take my bath now," Eden Murdoch said.

While the men became embroiled in a new debate, Christie watched her remove her moccasins which, though caked with mud, showed fine and intricate beadwork. The dress she wore also carried elaborate decoration. The woman seemed remarkably well dressed for a former captive.

"Who's gonna pay for this bath?" demanded Meeker.

"Invoice the army out of Fort Dodge," said the sergeant.

"The last time I billed the army, I got stuck for three officers' haircuts and two shaves and I ain't never been paid yet!"

"Not my problem," said Yellen.

"The water has probably gone cold by now," Eden said, but the men took no notice.

Christie tugged on one side of his long, dark mustache as he watched the woman's exasperation grow at being ignored. He raised his eyebrows when she began unfastening the shoulder lacings on her grimy doeskin dress. He alone noticed this action as the other men continued to argue over the bill.

Eden let the dress drop to the floor in a single motion and stood in the barbershop stark naked from the waist up, clad only in her breechcloth, which hung loosely from her hips, and her leggings, which began just below her knees. The crowd at the window let out a collective gasp and the quarreling men in the shop fell silent in utter astonishment. Hugh Christie grinned.

"I had a feeling this would get your attention," Eden said, hands on hips.

Christie appraised her figure with a practiced eye. The white skin of her body stood out in shocking contrast to the tanned skin of her hands, face, and throat. Her breasts were swollen, with the distended nipples of a nursing mother. A beaded leather pouch hung between her breasts from a cord about her neck. Sinewy muscles defined her slender arms and thighs, indicating her years among the savages had not been idle ones.

And then there were the scars. Most noticeable were bright red stripes of newly healed flesh arranged in parallel tracks across the fronts of both her thighs like a run of railroad ties.

"My bath?"

Rhinehart Meeker, his eyes wide and mouth gaping, could only point mutely to the door at their immediate right.

She moved to the door, but turned back to stare at the heap of clothing on the floor. A strange, unreadable expression crossed her face, then she raised her eyes to her two army keepers. "Prior to seeing this doctor, I will require clean clothing, a blouse and skirt, at least—and don't forget the undergarments. Also, some breakfast would be welcome. Eggs, over easy, bacon or sausage, bread—biscuits would be even better—preferably with jam or honey, and coffee with cream and sugar."

The men continued to stare dumbly.

"You eat all that and you're gonna get fat," warned Christie playfully. He was still the only man in the room not overwhelmed by her sudden nakedness.

She narrowed her eyes at him. "Of what possible interest could my appearance be to you, sir?"

He shrugged amiably. "Just an appreciator of the female form, I guess."

She rolled her eyes and he thought she almost, *almost* smiled before she entered the bathing room and slammed the door behind her. The men continued to stare at the closed door as if they could still see her.

"She's got more curves than a snake," murmured the awestruck private, who looked as if he had never until

this moment seen a naked woman. His Adam's apple bobbed as he swallowed several times.

"She's got the disposition of one, too!" grumbled the sergeant, the spell now broken.

Christie stood up and spoke to the soldiers in mocking imitation of their young captain. "Gentlemen, I believe she's given you your orders."

Emory Yellen shook his head with a frown. He headed for the door of the shop. "Come on, Joe." Over his shoulder, he called, "We'll be back in a while. You won't let her leave, will ya?"

"I'm not her keeper," Meeker said.

"If she slips the leash again, there'll be hell to pay."

"Why's that, Sergeant?" asked Christie. "You act like she's under arrest or something."

"It ain't that. I don't know why the general's givin' her such special treatment, but he's made poor Captain Randall bird-dog her day and night since the morning we found her. The captain got so fed up with her tryin' to run off, he threatened to put her in irons. *That* brought her to heel."

Christie and Meeker looked at each other and could scarcely contain their amusement at the sergeant's ludicrous story that a slip of a girl who couldn't have weighed a hundred pounds soaking wet had placed the United States Cavalry in such an uproar.

"She sounds like a powerful threat to your safety, boys," Christie warned.

The sergeant and the private angrily marched out of the shop.

"Was that or was that not the damnedest thing

you've ever seen?" said the barber, motioning toward the bathing room door.

Hugh shrugged and rose from his seat. "I've seen a lot."

"You're not gonna leave, too, are you? I don't care to be alone with an obvious lunatic."

"She don't look big enough to take you, Rhinehart."

"It ain't funny. Stay here till those troopers come back."

"I got a saloon to run, remember? Leavin' Marco in charge with the army in town wasn't such a good idea." As he reached the door, he called back over his shoulder, "If she gets to beatin' you up too bad, you just shout for help, all right?"

Brad Randall did not go straight to the telegraph office as he had told his men. Rather, he decided to grant himself the luxury of an hour in a quiet place to write some letters. He found a saloon open with no patrons inside and no proprietor on duty, just a curly-haired boy who was sweeping up. The boy inexplicably ducked out the back door of the saloon the moment he saw Brad enter.

He made himself comfortable at a table far from the cold draft of the door and pulled from his haversack his beloved walnut writing box, a gift from his mother. She had carefully stocked it with pens, nibs, ink, and countless sheets of rolled paper with the admonition that he write home as often as possible. She had tended to smother him with care since his older brother had been killed in the War of the Rebellion.

He found that such letter-writing proved a delightful diversion in this desolate place so far from the comforts of home and his anxious pen flew over the pages.

Hugh Christie returned to his saloon and saw the young officer in the corner. He walked over and offered Randall a drink.

"Thank you, but, no," Brad said. "I'm on duty, technically."

"Coffee?"

"Yes, that would be great. I didn't realize this was your establishment."

Christie brought the coffee, poured a cup, then offered his hand by way of introduction. "Hugh Christie."

"Bradley Randall. Pleased to make your acquaintance. I want to thank you again for your assistance during that difficult situation in the barbershop."

"Oh, it got a lot more interesting after you left. You missed the best part."

The smile fell from Brad's handsome face. "Oh, Lord, what did she do now?"

"Ah, nothin' really. Don't worry." Christie made a gesture to ask if he could sit down.

"Of course, of course." Brad rapidly shuffled together his papers, eager for conversation. He hated to admit it, but he was lonely. He was not allowed to fraternize with the enlisted men he had brought with him on this detail and he was reluctant to do so with his own junior officers for fear of losing his fragile authority over them. The Seventh Cavalry's notoriously high desertion rate had been made well known to him prior to his arrival on the frontier. Being a staff officer did not help, either; they seemed universally ill-regarded.

Christie poured a cup of coffee for himself. "That little gal looked like a handful."

Brad made a comic groan of concurrence. "You don't know the half of it, Mr. Christie. I foolishly thought looking after her was going to be an easy assignment—almost a furlough—but she has been nothing but trouble since the day we rescued her. Such a strange woman. So angry at everyone. Calling us *murderers*." He shrugged. "When I questioned her on how to locate her family, it was as though she dreaded the thought of being reunited with them."

"Some of those captives—they spend too long out there, they don't want to be found."

"I can't fathom that. Well, anyway, it should only take a week or two to locate her father." Brad leaned forward. "I could sympathize with her desire to bathe. I haven't shaved or had a proper bath since we left Fort Dodge. I plan to enjoy the comforts of city life every day that I am here."

"Calling Reliance a city might be a stretch, but as one of its fine citizens, I'll accept the compliment."

"Everything smells *new* here."

"Just about everything here *is* new." The saloon-keeper chuckled, then grew more serious. "Was that battle down on the Washita your first?"

The young captain shook his head. "I came to this posting eight weeks ago. We were under attack the very night of our arrival. We had just sat down to our supper." He sighed. "This is nothing like the War. The land is so vast. And the enemy so . . . unpredictable."

"They don't line up nice and neat and stand their ground like Jeb Stuart's boys, now do they?" Hugh said.

"This new type of warfare—to attack the enemy in his home where he sleeps with his wife and children . . . I've never . . . Frankly—just between you and me—I'd rather be back in Washington. I had a nice post in the War Department on the staff of General Markham. Do you know of him?"

"No."

"I'm engaged to marry his daughter. He decided at Easter last year—" Brad cleared his throat and made a theatrically serious face to imitate his future father-in-law. " 'The peacetime army is no place for an ambitious man.' "

"So here you are," Hugh said with a wide grin.

"So here I am. How long have you been out here?"

"Long time. Near fifteen years. Left St. Louis when I was just boy of twenty, twenty-one. Went out to Denver City when they discovered gold. Stayed there a goodly while, then came back here when they were building Fort Dodge and tried to get the sutlership. Didn't get the contract, but I've done all right for myself here in Reliance. 'Course, like everybody else in town, I'm marking time, waiting for the railroad to come. That's when I change careers once again."

"What are you planning?" On the frontier the future seemed to Brad Randall as limitless as the prairie horizon. He often wondered what he might have ended up doing with his life had he not locked himself into a military career when he proposed to Amanda.

"Cattle. Gonna bring longhorn herds up from Texas.

I got it all planned out." He paused and smiled. "Trust me, this country'll grow on you, my friend."

"I don't know. This was not . . . not what I expected." Brad pulled out his watch and glanced at it. His host read this not-so-subtle sign that the conversation was over and rose from the table. They nodded their goodbyes as Christie returned to work behind the bar.

"Good Lord, who did this to you?"

Eden did not answer Dr. Ashcroft's brusque inquiry as she sat on the examining table. She hurriedly closed the blouse the local minister's wife had given to Sergeant Yellen. She did not wish the doctor to stare at her breasts any longer than necessary.

"I suppose I know the answer to that question well enough," he said.

She raised her eyes to the elderly man and studied his jowly face. The story of how she came to have several scars upon her breasts in the shape of human bite marks was not a pretty one and the passage of four years had not softened the memory of it any. She refused to oblige his curiosity.

He took her hands and turned them palms upward, examining the numerous scars on her wrists. He looked her in the face for an explanation, but she said nothing.

He walked around the examining table and lifted the back of her blouse. He glanced at the scars over her back and shoulders, but did not ask about them. He then eased her down on the examining table.

She held her breath. This was the part of the ex-

amination she had been dreading. She shut her eyes as the doctor lifted her skirt.

"Pray tell me if I hurt you in any way," he said. "I apologize for the invasive nature of this examination, but the army always wants a full report on persons in circumstances such as yours. Intimate diseases, you understand."

Well, the army must not be disappointed, she thought bitterly. She winced only once under the pressure of his probing fingers. He was mercifully efficient, soon pulling her skirt back down over her limbs, decency restored. He turned his back to her as he washed his hands in a bowl on a nearby stand.

"You've had a child recently." He dried his hands on a towel, keeping his back to her as she sat up again.

She drew a deep breath. "Yes." Her voice was barely above a whisper.

"And what became of the child?"

She gazed at the faded calico of the skirt curving over her knee. She carefully considered her answer. She did not wish to tell the doctor that the child she gave birth to five months ago had been stillborn. Then she would have to explain why her breasts were still swollen with milk. If she had to talk about either her own baby or Red Feather's little Gray Wolf, she would dissolve into tears again. Each day was a new struggle to contain her grief.

And when would her breasts stop swelling and leaking? A week had passed since she had last nursed. The pain of the first few days had been excruciating, keeping her awake at night, when the tears did not. Warm milk seeped from her nipples at the slightest provocation, leaving her sticky and chilled as she rode along with the Seventh Cavalry in the November cold. The pain throbbed like a constant physical reminder of all that she had lost so suddenly.

"Dead." She hoped the doctor would not attempt to pry more detail from her.

She did not look at the doctor's face. She had been subjected to all levels of curiosity since her "rescue" and was coming to recognize a certain look on people's faces concerning her intimacy with the *enemy*. She tried to harden herself to it, but their attitude filled her with an angry contempt—allowing her the luxury of the shameless display in the barbershop which she had perversely enjoyed.

She let the doctor help her down from the examining table and adjusted the ill-fitting skirt and blouse as best she could. As he turned from her, she caught the edge of that look again.

That staining look.

She had naïvely assumed that upon arriving in Reliance, she could escape the stares and comments of the townspeople by casting aside all visible remnants of her years with the Cheyennes. She now knew that the breach was deeper than a bath and a change of clothing.

And General Custer's remarks to Captain Randall that night in the Sibley tent returned once again. About how he would rather see his wife dead than in Eden Murdoch's "sorry state". Her blood chilled with the contemplation that her own husband would undoubtedly share this view. Four years had passed. Four years of his life, four years of hers. Had Lawrence Murdoch searched for her all that time? Did he think she was dead? Did he *hope* she was dead?

Eden was now more certain than ever that she had chosen the correct path in intimating to Captain Randall her husband had been killed in the War. If she had thought the matter through, she would have given Randall only her maiden name when he had demanded it that dreadful morning on the bank of the Washita.

Five

In all these military movements I fancy I see
another Sand Creek massacre. If these Indians
are to be congregated at Fort Cobb or elsewhere, under promises of protection, and
then pounced upon by the military, it were far
better that they had never been sent for or any-
such promises made them. I . . . would re-
spectfully request that you promptly call the
attention of Lt. Gen. W. T. Sherman to this
subject.
—THOS. MURPHY, SUPERINTENDENT OF INDIAN AFFAIRS TO
THE COMMISSIONER OF INDIAN AFFAIRS,
NOVEMBER 15, 1868, TWELVE DAYS BEFORE THE
WASHITA ATTACK

Eden stood silently in the hall of the minister's house
and listened through the closed parlor doors as both
Captain Randall and the minister, Mr. Elias Lowell, tried
to convince the minister's wife to allow Eden to stay
with them while efforts were made to locate her father.

They had already been turned away from the only
boardinghouse in town that accepted women boarders.
The elderly widow who ran the boardinghouse had
snarled, "They'll be no Injun whores livin' under my
roof. I run a respectable establishment!"

Brad had quickly ushered Eden out of the boardinghouse and apologized for the woman's rudeness. She had trembled at the humiliation of the incident, but she had managed not to cry. She did not wish to let anyone—and they were now followed by a crowd of onlookers wherever they went in the town—see her break down.

Randall had seemed stymied by this lack of success and turned to discuss the matter with his two subordinates.

Eden had drawn her woolen blanket more tightly about her shoulders and surveyed the town of Reliance. Impressive wooden sidewalks down each side of Main Street bespoke a touch of elegance the raw and new little city strove for. The cold air rang with the sound of pounding hammers and grinding saws as buildings and dwellings were under construction in every direction. All manner of wagons and carriages filled the muddy street before her.

An Indian, perhaps a half-breed, man passed them. He wore white men's clothes, but his antecedents were unmistakable. He glanced at Eden with a curiosity that seemed to be of a slightly different character than that of the general run of gawkers.

She spoke to him in Cheyenne, but he did not respond.

Randall and his two men stopped their conversation and turned toward her.

She held out her left forefinger and stroked it with her right forefinger.

The Indian man surveyed her critically, then responded with a different hand sign.

Eden nodded and the man walked on.

"What was all that about?" asked Sergeant Yellen.

"I asked him if he was Cheyenne. But he's Kiowa. Or once was."

"What was the sign you made with your fingers, Mrs. Murdoch?" Randall asked the question with genuine curiosity. He attempted to copy it, slicing his own right forefinger over his left.

"The Cheyenne tribal sign. It means, roughly, 'cut finger.' "

"Cut finger?"

"The Cheyenne often cut off the finger of an enemy. Other tribes started calling them that."

"*After* the enemy is dead?"

"One would hope."

"And scalping—they only do that *after* their victim is dead, right?"

"I think the victim might squirm around too much otherwise, don't you?"

He nodded. Behind him, his two men barely contained their laughter. They, unlike their callow superior, realized Mrs. Murdoch was teasing him.

"It's also the sign for mourning," She sensed that Brad Randall had an honest interest in his "enemy." "The Cheyennes cut off strips of their own flesh in a gesture of grief. And sometimes as an offering, of sorts."

She thought of the gashes she had made on her legs after her baby was born dead the summer before. Typically such sacrificial acts were done only by those mourning a warrior killed in battle, but her grief had been so consuming she had wanted to suffer. Only a blood sacrifice would purge the darkness that overwhelmed her soul. Simply cutting her hair had seemed too superficial a gesture.

They approached a saloon—a saloon with no name, Eden noticed. Out of its double doors came the man with the long, dark hair that she had seen in the barbershop a few hours before.

"Well, she cleaned up real nice now, didn't she, Captain?" the man offered jovially.

"Good afternoon, Mr. Christie. We meet once again."

"Call me Hugh," he said. "Where you all headed now?"

"We are looking for accommodations for Mrs. Murdoch and having no luck, I'm afraid."

As Randall spoke these words, a small, dark-haired woman walked out of the saloon and joined Christie on the sidewalk. She surveyed the group with an arrogant eye as she wrapped one arm around the saloonkeeper's waist. He hung his arm over her shoulder. From her manner and dress, she was clearly a sporting woman, probably employed by the saloon to entertain its customers.

Eden noticed that the man called Hugh Christie did not bother to introduce his companion, further confirming the woman's low status. Eden watched the middle-aged woman, who was attractive despite her slatternly manner, stare boldly at Brad Randall, scrutinizing his potential as a customer, no doubt. Her unsmiling gaze was so brazen, the young officer blushed.

"Why, she could stay there with you, couldn't she, Tessa?" offered Hugh. "You've got plenty of room."

The woman frowned at this suggestion, glancing up at Christie fiercely.

"Um, no, I don't think so," Randall answered, to Eden's relief.

"Beggin' your pardon, sir, but what about askin' that minister?" said Sergeant Yellen. "He was a whole lot of help on the clothes."

The mention of the clothes brought a touch of embarrassment to Eden. She felt ridiculous in the garments they had provided for her. The woman who had last worn them had not only been at least a head taller, but probably seventy or eighty pounds heavier. The sleeves of the blouse hung beyond her knuckles and the hem of the skirt dragged the ground, requiring her to constantly gather it up to keep from tripping as she walked. The waist of the skirt was so large, Eden had been forced to fold it over several times, finally securing it around her slender midriff with a length of twine given to her by the doctor at his office. She hugged her red woolen blanket about her for warmth and occasionally pressed the little medicine bag between her breasts to reassure herself it remained in safe obscurity there.

The mention of the minister brought a snicker from the woman at Hugh Christie's side.

"Now, Tessa, be polite," Christie warned, grinning down at the small woman.

"The minister and I aren't on good terms at the moment," Christie explained. "He's misguided enough to oppose my choice of profession."

"Temperance," Tessa said in a low voice, barely parting her lips.

"Ah, yes, well . . ." Randall made a motion to wind up the conversation. "Perhaps he will help us, though."

"Good luck," offered Christie as the captain and his party continued on their way down the sidewalk. He and Tessa watched them go.

"I know what you're thinkin'," Tessa said, looking up at him with a sly and mirthless smile.

"You're wicked, Tess, just plain evil." He laughed as they returned to the saloon.

Tessa just gave her tousled head a rueful shake.

"I don't know. I just don't know," came the minister's wife's fretful voice through the closed parlor doors.

Eden's stomach twisted, sensing yet another rejection. She sent up a silent prayer, hoping to change the woman's mind. She wondered who might be up there to hear it. She had stopped believing in a merciful God so long ago. And yet, still she prayed. *Please, please let me stay here.*

She could not bear another night at the soldiers' encampment on the outskirts of town. The captain knew how unpleasant she found that and had assured her they would find some sort of accommodations for her in town.

"What will the congregation say, Mr. Lowell?" asked Mrs. Lowell in a hushed voice.

"They will say we are doing our Christian duty, my dear."

"But many have lost loved ones at the hands of the

savages, Mr. Lowell. They will not see it as a kindness to take in one of their number."

"She is as white as we are, ma'am," Captain Randall interjected.

"Why, yes," said the minister. "We should pity this poor woman's circumstance, not hold it against her, Mrs. Lowell."

"It is said that she bore a child—or children—while . . . while . . . What kind of woman would—"

"Who are we to judge, my dear? Remember what our Lord said of the adulteress."

"I'm not casting stones, Mr. Lowell. Truly, I'm not. It's just that—" She broke off.

There was more conversation in the parlor, but Eden could not hear it due to the sudden commotion of three children, ranging in age from seven to twelve, bursting in the front door. Their noisy chatter ceased when they came upon their visitor.

"Who are you?" asked a little boy of about nine. He and his older and younger sisters stared at Eden.

"It's her," whispered his older sister. "The one everybody's been talkin' about."

"The children!" exclaimed Mrs. Lowell from the parlor and she and the two men quickly emerged. When Mary Lowell saw Eden for the first time, she clapped her hand over her mouth, then whispered to her husband in a voice loud enough for all to hear, "She's so young."

Eden met the woman's gaze for an instant, then glanced down. Apparently the minister's wife was astonished to realize that the white captive looked neither like a savage nor a raving lunatic—just a young woman in ill-fitting clothes and unkempt, awkwardly cropped hair.

Mary Lowell was as tall and plump as her husband. The couple, both in their middle thirties, looked so much alike they could have passed for brother and sister. Her golden-brown hair was parted in the center and pulled neatly back into a chignon at the nape of her neck. She leaned near her husband's ear to whisper some remark.

The minister smiled and nodded. He said to the captain, "My wife and I will be most pleased to provide lodgings for this young woman."

Eden looked at Mrs. Lowell and saw deep dimples appear in the woman's kind face.

"Thank you, ma'am," said Eden. She again dropped her gaze to the floor, self-conscious because of all the staring eyes.

"Thank you," repeated Randall, heartily shaking the minister's hand, visibly relieved to have completed this task.

"I'll show you to your room, dear," Mary Lowell said. "Perhaps one of the gentlemen could bring your things."

"I don't have any things," Eden said.

"Mrs. Murdoch," Randall said, "before I depart, might I have a word alone with you?"

She allowed Brad Randall to separate her from the large Lowell family.

He drew a long, uneasy breath and confided in a low voice, "Mrs. Murdoch, might I ask you, for your sake as well as my own, to please behave yourself. My men gave me a full report on that incident in the barbershop after I left."

"I'll bet they did."

"No more of such behavior and no more outbursts. Please. If you cannot control your conduct I shall have no choice but to confine you to a doctor's care."

She frowned. She resented being treated like an errant child, but knew well enough from the miserable way she had treated him and his subordinates in the previous days that his warning was justified.

"These people seem very kind. I will behave as a lady should. I assure you I have not forgotten how."

"Thank you," he whispered, then bid adieu to the Lowell family.

Eden watched him leave. In some vague way she almost envied the "beautiful Amanda" alluded to by General Custer.

Mary Lowell motioned Eden to follow her upstairs. She took her to a small room just off the landing. She told Eden it was used as a sickroom from time to time, but not to worry—it had been thoroughly cleansed since it was last occupied.

Eden sat on the little bed, adequate for a large child, but barely long enough for a grown woman, and marveled at the softness of the mattress. She could not resist the urge to bounce up and down a couple of times.

"I hope you will be comfortable here," Mrs. Lowell said.

"Oh, yes, ma'am."

"Dinner will be at six."

"Yes, ma'am."

"I'll fetch you a bowl and pitcher, if you care to freshen up."

"Thank you, ma'am."

Eden rose and walked to the washstand. There she beheld her mirror image and scrutinized it. She looked so much older! And thinner. She had once been so vain of her looks.

Mary Lowell turned to leave.

"Mrs. Lowell, do you know about the War?"

"Which war, dear?"

"Not the war against the Indians. I mean Mr. Lincoln's war against the Confederacy."

Mary smiled at the question. "I expect just about everyone knows about that, dear."

"Is it over?"

Six

But who were the parties thus attacked and slaughtered by General Custer and his command? It was Black Kettle's band of Cheyennes. Black Kettle, one of the best and truest friends the whites have ever had among the Indians of the plains.

—Thos. Murphy, superintendent of Indian Affairs, report to the commissioner of Indian Affairs, December 4, 1868

Brad reread his fiancée's letter, which had arrived by courier four days after he came to Reliance, then tore it into little pieces and tossed the shreds to the prairie winds. He watched them flutter away like tiny birds and tried to calm his anger. How could Amanda run on for seven pages describing one party or reception after another, knowing full well all the discomfort, hardship, destruction, and death that was his daily burden?

Did she think he would find entertaining her fretful complaint over the lateness of the seamstress with her new party frock?

If it were not for her stupid father, he would not even be *in* this godforsaken country. Amanda would be entering those lavishly decorated homes on *his* arm, not that of her father.

And to think he had actually looked forward to this new assignment. Last summer, the idea of it seemed like a grand adventure—escaping the stifling heat of Washington, seeing the great frontier. General Custer's last-minute reassignment at the end of September and his offer to bring Brad out with him as an aide—at the request of Amanda's father, of course—had seemed too good to be true.

Brad sighed with the thought that Christmas was coming. Endless Washington social events for Amanda loomed on the horizon. Tea with the newly elected president, no doubt; perhaps even dinner. Grant and Amanda's father were good friends, after all. And what would he be doing? Eating army food, fighting chilblains, and risking his scalp every day.

He closed his eyes and tried to imagine what Amanda looked like in the watered-silk gown she had so meticulously described in the letter he had just destroyed. Instead, his brain could not halt the image of Major Joel Elliott's desecrated body and the mutilated bodies of the seventeen men who had fallen with him.

Their remains had been found when the Seventh Cavalry had returned to the Washita battleground to give General Custer's commanding officer, General Phil Sheridan, a tour of the area. Elliott's lost party had apparently been surrounded by Cheyennes on a high knoll and slaughtered to the last man.

Brad had morbidly drifted through the carnage that day, watching Surgeon Lippincott examine the corpses and catalog the wounds.

"*Corporal William Carrick,*" Lippincott dictated to

the orderly at his side making notes. "Bullet in right parietal, both feet cut off, left arm broken, penis severed."

The stench of death had been pervasive, almost intolerable, causing Brad to hold his woolen neck scarf over his nose except when speaking. The surgeon and orderly moved on to the next victim. The naked body was so frozen to the ground, Brad had to help them turn it over.

"Corporal James Williams . . ." Lippincott continued, "This is Williams, isn't it?"

"Yes, sir," answered the orderly.

"Bullet hole in back, both arms cut off. Penis severed. Deep gashes in the back."

"I believe I was the last officer to see Major Elliott alive," Brad offered aimlessly. "He rode off with such a cavalier expression. I remember him shouting, 'Here goes for a brevet or a coffin.' "

"Well, Joel didn't get his brevet, did he?" The doctor looked up briefly at Brad before they all moved on to another corpse. Lippincott began to examine it, then scratched his head. There was not enough face left to identify.

"I'm damned if I know who this one is. Any ideas, gentlemen?" Brad and the orderly exchanged shrugs. "Oh, well, just put down 'unknown' for now. Perhaps we can figure it out by who's unaccounted for. Head, right hand, and penis severed. Three bullet holes and six, seven, eight arrows in the back."

"I would have followed him that morning, if I had not been detained with Mrs. Murdoch," Brad remarked.

"Lucky you," said Lippincott without looking up.

"Did any of the dead have their fingers cut off?"

"Elliott did. The little finger of his left hand. Why do you ask?"

"No reason."

"What do you reckon they're doin' with all them peckers they cut off?" the orderly asked.

Lippincott smiled sardonically. "I think it behooves us not to speculate."

They buried the bodies of all the men, save Elliott, on a small hill overlooking the Washita. Elliott's body was to be shipped on to Arbuckle for a proper burial. A large trench was dug and each corpse was wrapped in a woolen blanket and placed in the pit. Their gruesome and mournful task did not fall on completion until well after midnight.

Icy winds blew down the Washita River valley and caused the torchlight to waver and flash wildly as they toiled at the mass grave. The doleful sound of the prairie winds moaned like the keening of the Cheyenne women singing their death songs.

As Brad fought back the nausea brought on by the reeking odor of rotting flesh he thought of the Osage scouts. On the first night back in camp after the battle, they had fired rifles over the Cheyenne scalps they had taken to drive away the recently departed spirits. Brad had wished, that bitter cold night, that he could as simply drive the ghosts of Elliott's men from his thoughts.

Their fate weighed heavily on the regiment. Many officers criticized their commander for abandoning the field without determining the fate of the detail. Some of the officers were mutinously angry over what seemed to them a heartless decision, though Brad felt the abrupt countermarch that night had been mandated to save the Seventh from a nearly certain doom. The fate of Elliott's long-overdue party appeared all too certain to risk the entire regiment.

Rumors floated not far from Brad's ears that one such disgruntled officer, Major Benteen, was actually circulating a petition critical of General Custer's decision.

Brad Randall's face was as easy to read as a newspaper headline when he entered Hugh Christie's nameless saloon. Hugh Christie and the woman called Tessa exchanged sly smiles as they watched the young captain wander around the nearly empty tavern on a Thursday afternoon pretending to find interesting the odd collection of posters pasted on the walls.

"Bet it took him most of the day to work up the nerve to knock on your door, Tess. Only to find out your sportin' lounge don't open till seven."

"What's his name?" she asked in a whisper.

"Captain Bradley Randall. Comes from back East. Had a fancy office job with the government before he came out here."

She studied the tall, good-looking captain with a chilly smile. The young ones were the best—quickly aroused and quickly satisfied; in other words, easy money.

"Want me to talk to him?" Christie offered.

"I'll handle that."

"I thought you might."

Tessa made her way over to Brad and waited for him to turn and face her.

"May I help you?" she asked with a pleasant smile.

"I . . . um . . . I was just . . ." Brad's voice trailed off uncertainly.

"Were you looking for some company?" she asked in an intentionally neutral voice. She knew better than to address someone shy like Randall in suggestive overtones.

He looked at her apprehensively.

"My place don't open till later," she said. "But . . . if you'd like to spend an hour in my company, I'd be happy to entertain you."

"How much?" Brad asked abruptly. He had no idea what the going rate was for services such as these.

Tessa thought for a moment. She could roughly guess a captain's salary and today was payday. Every good whore knew when the military paid its help. She wanted to get as much as he could pay, yet she did not want to let someone this attractive slip through her fingers on a matter of a dollar or two. It was a rarity for her to actually fancy one of her clients.

"Five dollars."

Five dollars. Brad swallowed hard. "All right."

He turned toward the door of the saloon, but she caught his arm.

"We can go to my room through this back way," she said.

He gratefully allowed himself to be led through the side door near the back of the saloon. As he passed the bar, Hugh Christie gave him a nod and a smile.

*   *   *

Tessa guided him down a hallway. They stopped in front of a door which she opened with a key. Brad glanced nervously up and down the hall, but no one saw him enter her room.

Once inside, he drew a five-dollar coin from his pocket. She took it and disappeared behind an ornate folding screen. Brad surveyed the room. A washstand stood near the small window that faced the alley. A generously sized bed sat waiting in the corner of the room with its walnut carved headboard draped in colorful tapestries.

He heard the swishing sounds of her undressing behind the screen. He unbuttoned his jacket and draped it over the back of a straight chair which sat near the door. He unbuttoned his vest and hung it over the jacket.

Tessa stepped out from behind the screen wearing a long silky robe of Oriental design. She walked over to the bed confidently and sat on its edge, waiting.

He smiled at her, then he self-consciously peeled the suspenders from his shoulders and began to unfasten his trousers with his back to her.

"You've never done this before, have you?" she said.

Brad turned to her. "Of course I have."

She drew a lock of her long, dark hair across her face to coyly hide her smile.

*   *   *

"How'd you get to be a captain so young? You do something real special in the War?" Tessa asked as they lay abed together after the successful completion of their commercial venture.

"No, I'm just good at taking tests."

She turned a quizzical eye on her handsome customer.

He explained. "After the war, they cut back the staff positions considerably and gave all the officers a written test to place them in the regular army. I scored high, I'm told, so they made me a captain."

"I could tell you was real smart."

Brad shrugged modestly. "I thought it an honor to be promoted. I was still only a first lieutenant at the close of the War. Most officers fell in rank once they left the Volunteers. My own commander, in fact."

"Custer? You mean he's not a real general?"

"He's a lieutenant colonel. Major general is his brevet rank."

"How come you still have to call him 'general' then?"

"Courtesy, I guess. It's just the way these matters are done. Sometimes it all seems like a silly game to me. Actually, I thought of studying law or philosophy after the War. Maybe even spend some time in Europe. But . . . well, my fiancée's father was in a position to help me a great deal in a military career. And Amanda expects . . . Amanda, that's my fiancée, she—" His voice faded. Amanda longed to be a general's wife, just like her late mother before her. She had already had plenty of experi-

ence, as she had served as her father's hostess since the age of sixteen.

Tessa read the familiar guilty look on Brad's face. "You don't need to feel bad. Your sweetheart's never gonna find out about this and what she don't know won't hurt her. 'Sides, you've been riskin' your life fightin' Indians. You deserve—"

"Could we change the subject?" He nervously fingered a wide gold ring which hung on a chain against his bare chest. The ring had belonged to his grandmother and he planned to place it on Amanda's finger on their wedding day.

The gold band was the only thing he owned that had belonged to his father and he loved the family story behind it. When the elder Randall was a young man growing up in England, he decided to come to America to seek his fortune. His family objected and were so angry with him, they refused to say goodbye, but as he stood on the dock, waiting to board the ship, his mother came rushing up. She pulled off her wedding ring and gave it to him, saying if ever he needed money, he was to pawn the ring. He swore he would never do such a thing, but after he got to America, he did get into bad straits and was forced to use the ring for collateral on a loan. He worked for years to pay off his debt, but by the time he finally redeemed the ring to return to his mother, he got word that she had died.

Brad wore the ring as a kind of talisman, his love for both Amanda and his family sheltering him somehow. He wished he had taken it off with the rest of his clothes, since his love seemed tarnished now, profaned by what he had just done with this whore. In some strange, superstitious way, though, he could not bring himself to remove it.

Tessa ran her finger delicately over the scab above his eyebrow. "This from the Washita?"

"An arrow did that." He gingerly touched it, as well. "It's nothing. Just a graze. Didn't even require a plaster."

"How's that woman doin'? That captive you rescued."

"Not too well. The people here don't seem to want to have any contact with her. Her presence makes them uncomfortable, I think. And her disposition doesn't help her cause. I never seem to say the right thing to her. No one seems to know the right thing, where she's concerned."

"Did she really have an Indian baby while she was livin' with them Cheyennes?"

Brad felt as if he had already said too much, not that the details of Eden Murdoch's strange history were confidential for any reason other than courtesy and deference to her regrettable circumstance.

"I don't know," he lied. Dr. Ashcroft's report had informed him she definitely had given birth to a child, though he had been relieved to learn she was not currently pregnant. "I'm frustrated that I haven't been able to locate her father yet. I just assumed I would receive answers to the wires I sent almost immediately. I can't imagine why we haven't heard something."

"Must be he's dead."

"Quite possibly. What I can't understand is why no

one knew of her capture. It took place the week before Christmas in 1864."

"Sixty-four! That's four years ago. I never heard tell of a woman being held captive that long. What all did them savages do to her? You can tell me. I'm pretty hard to shock."

He rolled onto his side and reached across Tessa to read a small clock which sat on the shawl-draped table next to the bed. "I'm afraid I must be going."

"Don't rush off." She unexpectedly threw her arms around him and hugged him with a pretense of affection that caught him off guard.

He grinned down at her and tried to kiss her, but she quickly turned her face to avoid his lips. He thought it odd that kissing was not included in the price. Five dollars was a lot of money.

She read the confusion on his face and smiled up at him as she closed her eyes. He let out a startled laugh when he felt her hand guiding him back into her. He groaned with the unexpected delight of it, then stopped suddenly in an economic panic. "Will this cost extra?"

Brad hurriedly adjusted his greatcoat as he reentered the saloon through the back door from Tessa's room. He wiped beads of perspiration from his face.

"You look downright refreshed," Christie observed with a grin.

As Brad passed by his long oaken bar with its gleaming brass foot rail, his ears flushed bright red as always happened when something embarrassed him.

"Your sergeant was lookin' for you."

A shade of panic briefly swept over Brad's lean face, just smoothly shaved by Rhinehart Meeker that morning.

"Don't worry," Christie said. "When he stopped in, I told him you was out back." He yanked his thumb in the direction of the privy in the alleyway. "He left this for you."

He handed a small leather satchel over the bar. Brad pulled out a note and read it with a frown.

"Bad news?" the barkeeper asked.

"Not really. I've just been asked to pull together a last-minute birthday party for General Custer. Next Sunday evening. I hardly feel like celebrating after all that's happened recently."

"Well, you have to make the best of it."

Brad returned Hugh Christie's smile, but thought it odd that he already felt more comfortable in Hugh's and Tessa's company than he did with his own regiment. Where was the esprit de corps that fighting men were supposedly famous for? He'd felt it, to some extent, during the War. But then, everyone had been united in their actions, fighting for a cause they believed in. They had shared a profound sense of purpose.

The frontier army was an altogether different matter. It seemed composed of soldiers-for-hire, men who literally could not find a better job. The enlisted men were a sorry lot, ruffians of every stripe. Large numbers were recent immigrants who could not speak enough English to understand orders. The officers were hardly more impressive. Many were dissolute in their habits, some outright inebriates.

"I've been given explicit instructions to escort Mrs. Murdoch to the party. That should make the night interesting," Brad said, comically looking heavenward in despair. "I'm supposed to invite some guests, some women, especially, so that Mrs. Murdoch won't feel uncomfortable. Do you think the Lowells would come?"

"I think gettin' to meet someone as famous as the Boy General would please just about anybody."

Brad had gotten to know Armstrong Custer so well in the last two months that he had come to forget that the rest of the world considered him a celebrity. Who wouldn't want to meet someone they had read about in the newspapers? "Would you like to come, Hugh? And bring your wife?"

"I'd love to come. So would Tessa."

All the color drained out of Brad's face. "Tessa's your *wife*?"

Christie threw back his head with a grand laugh. "Lord, no, but she'll play the part if I ask her."

Brad laughed now, too, and wiped his brow in mock relief. "Don't scare me like that."

"You're an easy target, son, way too easy."

Seven

We destroyed everything of value to the Indians . . . 875 ponies, horses and mules, 241 sad-
dles, 573 buffalo robes, 390 buffalo skins, 160
untanned robes, 210 axes, 140 hatchets, 35 re-
volvers, 47 rifles, 535 pounds of powder,
1,050 pounds of lead, 4,000 arrows and arrow-
heads, 75 spears, 80 bullet molds, 35 bows
and quivers, 12 shields, 300 pounds of bullets,
775 lariats, 940 buckskin saddlebags, 470 blankets, 93 coats, 700 pounds of tobacco . . . all
their winter supply of buffalo meat, all their
meal, flour, and other provisions, and, in fact,
everything they possessed.
—G. A. CUSTER, REPORT TO GENERAL PHILIP SHERIDAN,
NOVEMBER 28, 1868

"Mrs. Murdoch, dear?" Mary Lowell called softly through
the door of Eden's bedroom.

"Come in," came Eden's choked voice.

Mary Lowell found her houseguest sitting on her un-
made bed, her legs tucked up under her, hugging a pillow.

"Oh, you've been crying again." Mary sat down next
to Eden. "What's wrong, dear?"

Eden smiled through her tears and wiped her wet
face on the edge of the bedsheet. "It's nothing, really."

"A problem shared is a problem halved. That's what I always say."

She knew Mary Lowell would not really want to hear the story behind her tears. No one she had met since returning to white society wanted to hear about her life with the Cheyennes, unless the story contained graphic descriptions of rape and torture.

She could supply those if she wished, but she cried instead about the beauty of a particular summer evening, now six months into memory. She recalled it as vividly as if it were yesterday. The sun had stayed long in the sky, so it must have been near the solstice. The air had cooled somewhat. Where had they been camped? Not the Washita, which she knew as Hooxe'eo'he'e, the Tepee Pole River. That came later. Somewhere farther north than that.

A lazy evening it had been with all of them lolling in the lodge, each pursuing some favorite pastime. Red Feather Woman had just given birth to little Gray Wolf three weeks before. She sat nursing him with the beatific expression common to all new mothers gazing at their firstborn child.

Nightwalking's busy hands sorted porcupine quills into four separate piles according to their length and color. She belonged to the honored and exclusive quilling society, one of its youngest members. It was said that a woman who quilled thirty robes would be granted a long and healthy life. Nightwalking was already at work on her twenty-first.

Hanging Road earnestly decorated the inner wall of the lodge with paintings of Sweet Medicine, the sacred prophet. He said he painted them for his little son and his child on the way, carried by Eden, its birth expected any day. Eden sat next to him holding his little dishes of paint.

The base of the lodge had been rolled up to catch the cool, southern breeze of the summer evening. Eden had felt so uncomfortably warm for so many nights recently with her advanced state of pregnancy that the cool breeze enveloped her like a delicious, hypnotic drug.

"It's important for them to learn these stories," Hanging Road said as he dipped the horsehair paintbrush in the yellow paint pot.

"Then I'd better learn them, too," Eden said. "I want to be a good mother to my little one."

Hanging Road smiled at her. "You'll be a fine mother. No one in this village is more caring than you."

"I'm a good nurse. I don't know if I'll be a good mother." She had never told them of her first child, the son she'd lost three years before. She blamed herself for his death. She still could not think about it without getting a lump in her throat.

"Seota, you're being silly. Besides, you'll have plenty of good help, won't you?" He glanced over at his other wives.

Both looked up and smiled. Then Red Feather Woman teased, "Sorry, I'll be too busy with my own baby."

Nightwalking, Red Feather's older sister and the widow of Hanging Road's older brother said, "I'll be too busy, too. You're on your own, Seota."

They all chuckled at Eden's expense. She could not remember being happier than at that moment. The mutual love in the air felt almost palpable. She finally had a family, a real family, a husband and sisters. Though she could never have guessed she would enter into a polygamous marriage, she had found happiness there.

Odd that she did not feel immoral. Within their village, their living arrangements were commonplace, so no shame was attached to it. She did occasionally feel a pang of jealousy, a longing for Hanging Road to show some preference for her over Red Feather. She had at times even kept track of how often he had lain with Red Feather as compared with her. On the other hand, she knew the sisters often envied the way Hanging Road allowed her to help him heal the sick and injured. That he felt she had been favored by the Great Spirit in some inexplicable way had caused resentment in the early days. Eden had picked up on the recurring friction even when her grasp of the Cheyenne language had been limited.

But all that seemed far in the past. Soon the baby would come after the nine long months of eager waiting. Then her life would at last be complete.

She dated the child's conception to have taken place the previous fall, just before Hanging Road had journeyed with the others to the Medicine Lodge Creek where the treaty had been signed. That treaty—what a joke, what a waste of time.

She planned to give this child the loving home life she had longed for herself, but had been denied by circumstance.

When her mother died, Eden had been sent to boarding school in Pennsylvania because her father traveled too much to properly care for an eight-year-old girl.

"Stop your tears, Edie," her father used to chide her. "Summer will come and I'll get my leave and we'll go traveling, you and me. Think how lucky you are to be getting this fine education."

But she did not want an education if it meant giving up her father ten months of the year. Between the ages of eight and eighteen, she saw her father a total of eighteen months.

She delighted in the knowledge that her baby would grow up with not one, but four parents to love and care for it. She suddenly grabbed Hanging Road's hand, paintbrush and all, and pressed it to the side of her belly where the baby kicked.

He grinned with delight. "A boy, I'm certain of it. With a kick like that."

"No, it's a girl," said Red Feather playfully as she laid little Gray Wolf on a soft blanket before her. "You don't deserve two sons in one summer."

"A boy and a girl would create a nice . . . balance. A boy and a girl would be just fine with me," remarked Hanging Road.

He yawned and stretched his arms languorously above his head. He put away his paints as the twilight grew in the lodge. All the happy family eventually settled onto their respective sleeping robes. He produced a flute and played a delicate, haunting melody as he reclined against his elaborately decorated back rest.

Eden recalled slowly sinking into the most peaceful

sleep that night, lulled into tranquility by her husband's seductive, reedy music that arced and circled over them in the summer night. She thought Hanging Road must have come from some place other than this mundane earth, born of mortal woman. His fascinating way of sliding in and out of ordinary existence intrigued and mystified her. She knew from conversations with the sisters that he had always been different, even as a child. A dreamer, a believer in dreams, he could easily have been chastised as lazy had he not possessed such an astonishing wisdom and a voracious, inquiring intellect.

She had never been happier or more content than at that moment; in fact, she had felt the closeness of the Great Mystery that Hanging Road had spoken of so often, the knowledge of all that was unknowable. It felt so close that night as she lay half-dreaming that she thought she could almost reach out and touch it. But as always, the image, the feeling, skittered off, just out of reach, and slipped away like the shimmering heat waves rising from the endless prairie.

As Eden watched the cold, gray winter rain blur the window of her bedroom in the Lowell house, she reflected on how, of that happy family group last summer, only she now survived.

The last alive. And it was not the first time such could be said of her. She touched the medicine bag that hung between her breasts with its secret contents. Hanging Road had once dared to show them to her, but only after threatening her with death if she ever revealed to anyone that he had allowed her to see the sacred items. Such sights were forbidden to women and he showed her only because he remained convinced of her supernatural powers to heal.

She did not really believe his death threats. She could no more imagine him killing someone than she could imagine him sprouting wings and taking flight. Still, she kept his secret and revealed to no one that she had been privileged to see the shocking contents of his most sacred personal medicine bag, the one handed down to him from his grandfather, the one he planned to give to a child of his own one day. Tears welled up in Eden's eyes once again at the thought that he would never have a child to give this hallowed present to. Why did she keep it? She would probably never have a child either.

"You have an exceedingly kind heart, Mrs. Lowell. I'm afraid I was crying for the silliest of reasons. I'd be embarrassed to admit it."

"It couldn't be silly if it made you cry."

"Oh, but it was. I was thinking about the ponies. They killed them, you see. The army. They killed all the Cheyenne ponies. There must have been a thousand in the herd."

"Indian ponies? That's what's troubling you?"

"I told you it was silly. I just can't stop thinking about it." Easier to pretend to cry about the ponies, instead of Red Feather Woman's baby. Or all the other babies she'd lost, one way or another.

Mary Lowell did not know how to respond to this, so she awkwardly patted Eden's knee. "I have some exciting news, dear. Captain Randall is downstairs."

Eden brightened. "He's heard from my father?"

"No, I'm sorry. It's not that. He came to invite you to a party. It's that General Custer's birthday and they're throwing him a dinner party and he wants you to come."

"No, I don't think so." Eden's glum face returned. She had no love for General Custer. She hated him for his ruthless attack on her sleeping village. On a more personal level, she had not quite recovered from overhearing his stinging remark to Brad Randall about how he would not want his "beautiful Amanda" to end up in the same *sorry state* as Eden Murdoch. And what manner of husband would order his officers to shoot his own wife to prevent her ending up in the same *sorry state* as Eden Murdoch?

The implication of his words was obvious. He—and every one else she encountered—considered someone in her circumstance better off dead. She not only heard the opinion voiced often enough by the soldiers at the camp, but she could feel it in the stares of the townspeople of Reliance. Even their most furtive glances cast shadows.

Mary Lowell bustled off downstairs to deliver Eden's verdict on the party invitation. She left the bedroom door open and Eden could hear their muffled voices in the hall.

"She says no, Captain."

"Did she give a reason?"

"She doesn't like going out. She doesn't seem to tol-

erate too much company. She won't even take her meals with us. Says she can't handle whole conversations yet, or something like that. I don't know. We try not to push."

"She doesn't take meals with you? Surely she does not expect you to carry up all her meals on a tray?"

"Oh, no, she won't have that, either, although I tried. No, sir, she just comes down to the kitchen after each meal and, while Bonnie Sue cleans up, she eats whatever's left. I personally don't think she's up to a party, sir, with all due respect to your general. We finally pried her out of her room long enough for her to attend a prayer meeting on Wednesday night and . . . well, it just didn't work out."

"How so?"

Mary Lowell issued a pensive sigh. "We got her all nicely fixed out in a dress we remade from one of Sarah's. Sarah, that's my oldest girl. And Mrs. Murdoch looked real fine. Of course, we still haven't figured out quite what to do about her hair and all, but anyway, she didn't look bad. Still, some of our congregation did not receive her in as generous a Christian spirit as we had hoped. About half just got right up and left the church the minute they laid eyes on her. And poor Elias was planning to introduce her and all, but after that, he just went on with the meeting and Mrs. Murdoch sat there with Sarah and Josiah. She was too proud to cry, but I know she wanted to."

"I confess I don't fully understand their reaction."

"They all say she's a traitor—kind of like a traitor in

war, but not exactly. A renegade, maybe that's a better word. A person who's turned against her own kind and, well, crossed over, so to speak."

Brad knew this opinion could honestly be held of Eden Murdoch, but wondered how the townspeople of Reliance had become so intensely aware of it. He asked this of Mrs. Lowell.

"Well, in my opinion," she said, "those men of yours have been doing a great deal of talking and they seem to care nothing for poor Mrs. Murdoch's reputation, much less her feelings."

He inwardly groaned. He would have to have a talk with the six men assigned to his detail. He knew only too well their opinion of his charge. They were simple, crude men and there was little hope of them understanding much less accepting someone as complex as Eden Murdoch.

"Still, it is vital that Mrs. Murdoch attend this dinner. If I could convey the invitation myself and make her understand its importance. Oh, and I was hoping you and your husband might attend as well."

"Oh, dear, oh, dear," breathed Mary Lowell with delight. "Mr. Lowell and I . . . meet General Custer? Dine with him? Oh, my."

She hurried back upstairs, breathing deeply with the effort, and poked her flushed face back in Eden's door.

"Mrs. Murdoch, Captain Randall asks that he might have a word with you."

"Please, Mrs. Murdoch?" Randall called from the bottom of the stairs.

Eden rose from her bed and reluctantly shuffled after

Mrs. Lowell. She ran a hand through her awkwardly bobbed hair. Mr. Meeker had insisted on giving her a cropped hairstyle befitting perhaps a twelve-year-old boy, not a woman of twenty-seven. She had to admit it looked better than the rough, funereal hacking she had given herself, but that still wasn't saying much.

Brad Randall stood waiting for them, impatiently spinning his hat by its brim. He made an attractive figure in his greatcoat with its short cape tossed back over his shoulders.

"Captain Randall, please let me take your coat." Mary Lowell hustled over to where he stood.

"Thank you. Mrs. Murdoch, may we speak for a moment?"

Eden entered the parlor and placed herself on the settee, spreading her borrowed skirt about her. She looked up at the handsome officer who stood opposite her in the well-appointed room next to a large brass birdcage. Brad tapped a finger on the cage bars to attract the attention of the canary within.

Eden waited for the captain to initiate the conversation since, he, after all, had requested the meeting. When he did not commence right away, she said, "Why is it, Captain Randall, that I should wish to attend a party in honor of a man I despise?"

"I'm sorry to hear that, Mrs. Murdoch. I can assure you that General Custer holds you in the highest regard." He was extemporizing. He had no idea how his commanding officer felt about this woman. All he knew was that Custer was impatient to get the details of her years among the Cheyennes for a magazine article he wished to write. "He requested your presence specifically."

"Well, he would be the only person I have yet encountered who regards me so," Eden snapped. "To everyone else, I am apparently no more than a repulsive curiosity."

"Mrs. Murdoch, you are among friends here."

She wanted to shout, If I am among friends here, why can you not look at me when you speak to me? "May I ask you one more question?"

"Anything."

"Why did you choose to attack Mo'ohtavetoo's village of all the Indian villages you could have chosen? Were you not aware of his—"

"Excuse me?" He frowned in confusion. "Mo-ta-va—"

"Black Kettle," Eden translated. "Were you not aware of Black Kettle's peace efforts?"

He pulled a small notebook from the breast pocket of his frock coat along with a pencil. "Could you spell that? Black Kettle's name, I mean."

"Um . . . no. I mean the Tsitsistas have no alphabet like ours, I would have to guess at a rendition of the word."

"Tsitsistas?"

"The Cheyennes. They don't call themselves Cheyennes."

"They don't?" He raised his eyebrows at this revelation as though it had never occurred to him.

Eden sighed irritably, wanting to pursue her original line of questioning. "Black Kettle had only returned

from Fort Cobb the day before you attacked. He asked General Hazen for asylum there."

"We didn't know it was Black Kettle's village when we attacked."

"You didn't *know*?"

"Good Lord, no. For half the night, we didn't even know if it was a village at all. We huddled in the cold, listening for signs of life in the distance. We could make out a herd of some sort in the darkness, but couldn't tell if it was your ponies or a herd of buffaloes. The final confirmation came when we heard the sound of an infant's cry."

She gasped and clapped her hand to her mouth. Red Feather's baby? Little Gray Wolf?

"Oh, my dear Mrs. Murdoch, was that *your* child?"

The distraught look on Brad's face caused Eden to feel more kindly toward him. "No, not mine . . . How did you know I had a baby?"

Brad blushed and did not answer.

"Oh, the doctor. Of course." Eden guessed by the captain's embarrassed manner that there must have been some fairly intimate information imparted in the doctor's report.

The matter of Red Feather Woman and her baby still burned in her heart. She longed for justice. She decided at that moment that she would attend this ridiculous celebration and use the opportunity to confront General Custer over the incident with Red Feather Woman. "Tell your commanding officer I will attend his birthday celebration."

He strode forward and extended his hand. "Oh, excellent, excellent. I will look forward to seeing you then."

She shook his hand and tried to appear pleased. "You look nicer without the beard, Captain."

He chuckled self-consciously and ran his hand over his smooth cheek. Only a long, neatly trimmed set of mustaches remained. "I paid a visit to our mutual friend Mr. Meeker this morning."

She smiled at him. "Captain Randall, I want to tell you that I know my conduct toward you has been wanting in civility. What I'm trying to say is that, well, my feelings are not personally directed at you. I hope you understand that."

"Mrs. Murdoch, say no more. I understand, at least, I'm trying to understand. Please know only that I want to help you."

"I appreciate all you are doing to help locate my father."

"I'm happy to be of service."

"I don't expect your friendship—"

"But my dear Mrs. Murdoch, you have it whether you desire it or not. And is not your knee already on a first-name basis with a rather private portion of my anatomy? I mean, I had hoped for Randall heirs, but—"

Eden had to giggle at this unexpectedly risqué comment. She covered her blushing cheeks with her hands. "Surely I did not do you any lasting harm."

Randall's mustaches crinkled with a delighted smile. "No, of course not. I don't know why I'm so fresh today. But at least I've succeeded in making you laugh."

He pulled her to her feet. As they neared the hall

and the eager Mary Lowell, who had been eavesdropping at the etched-glass parlor doors, Eden thought she caught the trace of a woman's perfume on the person of Brad Randall. She did not mistake it for the scent of shaving soap from Mr. Meeker's establishment. The captain smelled faintly of that, too. Cavalry officers were known to smell like leather and saddle soap, rain-soaked wool and sweated horseflesh on occasion, but not lilies of the valley.

Though many years had passed since she herself had used ladies' toilet water, her sense of smell remained exceedingly acute, and the memory of such scents was indelible.

Perhaps he was not the perfect gentleman he pretended to be. Eden sensed in that one whiff that "the beautiful Amanda," wherever she might be, very probably had an unfaithful sweetheart.

Eight

In the excitement of the fight, as well as in self-defense, it so happened that some of the squaws and a few of the children were killed and wounded.

—G. A. Custer, report to Major General Philip Sheridan, November 28, 1868

The moment Eden entered the dining room of the rustic hotel where the birthday dinner was to take place, she decided it might be the oddest collection of party guests ever assembled in one room.

Captain Randall ushered the Lowells and herself into the small, dark chamber, lit by unsavory-smelling oil lamps, as his redoubtable assistants, Sergeant Yellen and the skinny private whom Eden knew only as "Joe," scurried about to place the room in readiness. The man Eden remembered from the saloon, with the wild mass of black hair and cascading mustache, stood in the far corner of the room where he chatted with the small, dark-haired woman whom Eden had sized up as a prostitute when she had met them on the sidewalk that first day in Reliance.

Randall greeted the Lowells and thanked them for coming. Eden had to hide her amusement at this. Mr.

and Mrs. Lowell were so excited by their invitation to dine with the famous Boy General, she wondered if they could contain themselves long enough to wait for the appointed hour to arrive.

The Lowells froze for a moment when they realized they would be dining with Hugh Christie. They staunchly opposed the consumption of alcohol for any but medicinal purposes and viewed those who sold it to be morally and spiritually lacking.

Mary Lowell squeezed her husband's arm. "We must be polite."

Elias Lowell glowered across the dining room, but said nothing. The tension soon broke with the arrival of the guest of honor.

"General," Randall called and advanced to greet his commander.

Armstrong Custer, clad in a suit of fringed buckskin, entered the room with a frown and a long sigh. He had already removed the fur hat and heavy buffalo coat he wore and held them out to be taken by a man Eden deduced to be an orderly of some sort. The orderly quickly took his place with Sergeant Yellen and Joe at the far end of the dining room.

"My dear Mrs. Murdoch," Custer exclaimed in a somewhat forced-sounding tone of conviviality.

Eden ducked her head, but accepted his proffered hand this time. She had grown too fond of the Lowells in the course of her short residence in their home to embarrass them with a public lack of manners. She would not be rude to their idol, regardless of her feelings toward him.

"You are much altered in appearance since last we met. Are you not?" he said.

She gave him a barely perceptible nod. She did not like people commenting on her appearance and, in any event, felt ridiculous in the Lowell daughter's made-over dress with its bright calico flounces and ruffles, especially coupled with her bobbed hair. Instead of a child playing dress-up in her mother's clothes, she felt like an adult masquerading as a child.

Custer did not release her hand immediately, which also annoyed her. Instead, he closed his other hand around it and gently pulled her slightly nearer to him. She thought this terribly familiar; perhaps Captain Randall did, too, in that he stepped up next to her in an almost protective fashion.

"Your cropped hair is most attractive, Mrs. Murdoch," Custer said. "No, don't look away. You look fine, really you do. And anyway, the wonderful thing about shorn hair is, it grows. Mine grows so quickly, I cannot keep up with it. Yours will grow back."

"And perhaps my heart will, too, someday." Eden looked up into Custer's face and fixed his pale eyes in her darker ones.

"Interestingly put, Mrs. Murdoch. I wish you the best in that regard, too."

The odd spell between them was broken by the arrival of three additional men, two cavalry officers and a small gentleman clad in ordinary street clothes.

Brad deftly handled introductions all around. The two officers were Captain Tom Custer, the general's younger brother, and a Captain Thomas Weir. Brad had been instructed to introduce the third man only as Mr. Keim, without making any reference to his profession, but Brad knew he was a newspaper correspondent.

Tom Custer was unable to shake hands in the normal way as his right hand was heavily bandaged and hung from a sling on his chest. He laughed about the injury when Mr. Lowell dutifully inquired after his welfare, complaining only that it reduced him to a mere spectator on the hunt that afternoon.

"You were able to get in some hunting on your way here?" Brad asked genially of his commander.

"But with a noticeable lack of success, I'm afraid. Though the weather was awfully fine today. A pleasure to be out."

Randall thought Custer seemed distracted, not at all in the mood for the party he had instructed him to organize. While the remainder of the group made polite small talk, Custer drew Brad into a corner of the poorly lit room.

"What have you got for me?" he demanded.

"Not a lot, yet, I'm afraid. I hesitate to push her too hard. Her moods are most unpredictable. I'm still uncertain about her mental state. She *has* calmed down a great deal since the last time you saw her."

"Time is now of the essence. Wynkoop has resigned his position over this matter!"

"Wynkoop?" Brad still struggled to keep all the players in this complicated game straight. He hated to appear so uninformed in front of a man he revered, but he still knew so little of the background of this tangled affair.

Custer frowned with impatience at Randall's ignorance. "Ned Wynkoop. He is—or was—the Indian agent
representing the Cheyennes and the Arapahos. He's resigned in protest over our actions at the Washita. Calling
it another Sand Creek! Calling me another Chivington!
It's outrageous. The nerve of the man. He wasn't there.
What does he presume to know? By God, it was the
rifles he gave to the savages that they used to fire upon
us. The surgeon confirmed it, you know. Captain Barnitz
was shot with a *Lancaster* rifle."

Everyone knew the military used only Springfields.

Brad glanced over his shoulder. Everyone in the
room heard Custer's brief outburst and looked vaguely
uncomfortable, except Tom Custer who undoubtedly
took his brother's temper in stride.

"Is Wynkoop making a formal complaint of some
sort?"

Custer shrugged. "We can only assume. Oh, but this
is rich—guess who is defending us?"

"I have no idea."

"Hazen! Can you believe it? Never thought I'd see
the day he'd come to my aid. Oh, well, I think he's just
defending his own actions in the matter. In any case, we
need to pull something together, and quickly, concerning our fair captive there. She now looks quite handsome. That will help the situation all the more."

At this moment, the hotel proprietor and his wife
entered the dining room carrying steaming tureens of
soup. "Here comes our dinner," Randall announced. "I
think it's time we were seated."

He tactfully ferried each member of the group to a

carefully assigned seat at the long wooden table in such a manner that no one in the group, save Custer—who had dictated where he wanted everyone seated—ever suspected that their place had been preselected. Each thought they had arrived there entirely of their own volition. During his one-year engagement to Amanda, a hostess of no small gifts, he had learned the art of hosting a successful evening.

Custer had decreed that, with himself at the head of the table, Mrs. Murdoch would be seated on his right, with Brad next to her—to gently assure her good behavior if necessary. An amiable couple were to be seated to his left to keep the conversation moving. Brad chose Hugh Christie and Tessa for this. He knew Hugh could converse with anyone on just about any topic, while the Lowells seemed somewhat overawed by the presence of one of their war heros. He additionally feared Custer might find the Lowells a bit provincial.

Christie, on the other hand, carried an air of the roguish frontier eccentric about him, with his wild hair and extravagant mustache. Brad knew Custer delighted in such unorthodox characters, given his fondness for the company of his extremely unconventional scouts.

Mr. Keim was to be seated at the far end of the table in such a way as to afford him a good view of Eden Murdoch. Then there were Captains Custer and Weir, both amiable in the extreme, to be placed opposite the Lowells. Brad suspected Tom Custer could keep the jolly Mary Lowell in giggles all evening. Though not as polished, nor as educated as his famous brother, Tom Custer was much more relaxed and easy to get along with.

As the soup was served, Eden spoke up, turning her head from right to left, to address both Custer and Randall. "Did I hear you mention Sand Creek? Might I ask the reason?"

"Are you familiar with Sand Creek, Mrs. Murdoch?"

"I believe you could call me one of the bitter legacies of Sand Creek, General. A legacy shared by all the people living along the Solomon and the Saline and the Republican. Of course, I didn't know it at the time, but the stagecoach on which I rode to meet my father four years ago was attacked in retaliation for Sand Creek. The atrocities committed at that sorry place caused the final break between the advocates of peace in the Cheyenne Nation and the Dog Soldiers."

"How are Dog Soldiers different from other warriors in a tribe?" Brad Randall asked, unable to contain his curiosity.

"The Dog Soldiers are a military society," Eden explained. "One of several. Within a Cheyenne village, the various military societies keep order." She wanted to tell them more. She knew a great deal about the subject. Her mind briefly slipped back to the summer night Hanging Road lovingly painted the story of Sweet Medicine, the prophet, on the inner wall of their lodge. According to legend, Sweet Medicine had brought the four oldest military societies, the Dog Men, the Kit Fox Men, the Elk Soldiers, and the Red Shields. Later came the Crazy Dogs, the Bowstrings, and the Chief Soldiers.

Eden thought the Kit Fox Men had the best songs. When someone decided to organize a war party, the night before they left the members of the society would walk through the village and each would take a turn with his own song. Upon arriving at the lodge of the man who called for the expedition, they would gather and often sing love songs to their sweethearts. Eden wondered how long she would remember these songs before they faded away.

"But now these Dog Soldiers, as you call them, have been actively conducting the raids that the railroad crews and the border residents complain of," remarked Custer with authority. He took a sip of the rich pumpkin soup, mindful to avoid staining his blond mustaches. "Is that not the case, Mrs. Murdoch?"

"I cannot say with any accuracy."

"And yet it happens that it was just such a raiding party our scouts traced directly back to the village of your late, lamented Black Kettle, your so-called Peace Chief."

Eden could not refute this. Black Kettle had lost the support of the younger men, those fed up with a peace that offered nothing, that only subtracted from their existence. And yet she remembered hearing that a war party of Kiowas, allies of the Cheyenne, had just returned, not from an attack on any white citizenry, but rather from a strike against their ongoing enemies, the Utes. She wanted to mention this, but she had no proof, only rumor and a vaguely remembered one at that.

"I remember Sand Creek," remarked Hugh Christie. "I was in Denver City when the Colorado Third came back. They did some pretty nasty things, those boys."

"What do you mean?" Randall asked.

"Things I'd rather not mention in the presence of

the ladies. In fact, things I'd rather not think about while I'm eatin'."

"State militias are not equal to the task of keeping the borders safe," Custer said, with disdain. "I'm afraid your own Kansas Nineteenth has had their problems on this mission."

"What sort of problems, General?" inquired Elias Lowell. "I'm frankly proud of the Volunteers. And of Governor Crawford for his efforts to lead them."

Custer was obviously trying to suppress a smile as he answered Lowell. "I'm sorry to report your Volunteers got themselves lost in that blizzard we experienced the week before Thanksgiving. I'm told they wandered aimlessly over and around the Cimarron between Fort Dodge and Camp Supply for several days before finally arriving at their destination. Unfortunately, we were unable to wait for them. It was reported that they lost over seven hundred of their horses to exhaustion and exposure."

Captains Custer and Weir shared a derisive chuckle over this.

"Just be glad, Mrs. Murdoch, that the regular army, exercising proper military procedure and restraint, were in charge of the attack on Black Kettle's village that morning."

"And exactly what would your definition of restraint be, sir?"

Before Custer could reply, the main course arrived. Fine steaks of buffalo meat, roasted over coals, together with heaping bowls of potatoes, turnips, beets, and corn were laid upon the table. A large loaf of fresh-baked bread steamed as the innkeeper's wife struggled to slice it.

Everyone chuckled as they watched Mary Lowell cut the injured Tom Custer's steak for him.

"Oh, heavens, I do this for my children all the time," she exclaimed. "I could do it in my sleep."

"Every man needs a mother, no matter what his age," rejoined Tom Custer, obviously relishing the momentary limelight.

Brad felt grateful for the distraction of the meal. He could sense the tension brewing between his commanding officer and his charge. He had hoped to charm the recalcitrant Mrs. Murdoch into good behavior and thought he had made progress in that direction. He felt responsible for the success of the evening even though this party had not been his idea and its true purpose far from the celebration of Armstrong Custer's twenty-ninth birthday.

He saw the reporter, Mr. Keim, at the far end of the table making sketches in his lap. How long did he think he could get away with this activity before someone remarked on it? And then who knew what sort of outburst from Mrs. Murdoch might ensue, when she found out her story and her likeness were already scheduled to appear in several Eastern newspapers of wide circulation and a national magazine, as well?

The thought of magazines gave Brad a sudden inspiration on how he might change the subject and defuse the building animosity.

"Mr. Christie," he said across the table. "I recall your

telling me you had a collection of *Harper's Weekly* magazines going back several years."

"I surely do."

Eden glanced across the table to Hugh Christie and eyed him suspiciously. She did not believe for a moment that the woman named Tessa seated next to him was his wife even though she had been introduced as such and was now dressed in a demure black silk without a hint of face paint or gaudy accessory. Eden also noticed Tessa glancing slyly at Captain Randall. Every time she successfully caught the young man's eye, he blushed and smiled, then quickly looked away. Eden concocted in her imagination a love affair between Brad and this slattern, though she thought them an odd couple, indeed. She knew that to call theirs a love match was a great stretch of fancy. Romantic nonsense. Undoubtedly the young officer was just another of this woman's paying customers. A service rendered. A frontier cavalryman's loneliness or lust temporarily assuaged, nothing more. Still, somewhere deep in her battered heart, Eden Murdoch regarded herself as a romantic.

"Mrs. Murdoch might be interested in taking a look at them sometime." Brad turned in his seat toward Eden. "Mrs. Lowell mentioned you longed to catch up on events for the years you were . . . when . . ." His conversational ploy expired before his sentence did.

"Harper's Weekly?" repeated Eden, showing some interest.

"Why, ma'am," Christie said, "it would be my pleasure to share my collection with you. I go back and read 'em myself now and then when I get lost for somethin' to do."

"That would . . . that would be nice," murmured Eden.

The Lowells looked at each other in alarm. Mary Lowell cleared her throat in a manner to advise her husband he needed to speak up.

"I do not believe Mrs. Murdoch would care to visit an establishment such as Mr. Christie's, Captain Randall," offered Mr. Lowell piously.

"What sort of establishment would that be, Mr. Christie?" asked General Custer. He did not bother to look up as he spoke, but rather continued to attack his plate with a furious gusto, eating as if he thought someone would take his dinner away if he did not hurry. His restless energy set everyone around him in a state of anxiety.

"A saloon, General. An establishment offering strong beverages to the strong-hearted and the occasional friendly game of cards or chance."

Custer looked up in interest. "Do you offer faro?"

"I employ a faro dealer every Friday and Saturday night."

Custer smiled broadly and looked relaxed for the first time all evening. He was about to make another remark when his brother snorted with laughter. "Was that a comment on your part, Tom?"

"The old lady's not gonna like this, General," he warned, smiling mischievously at his older brother.

The remainder of the dinner party looked to their

host for an explanation as to the identity of the "old lady."

Custer grinned boyishly. "My brother refers to my wife. She does not approve of playing cards for money. But I suppose we do not have time for such frivolous pursuits anyway. We return to the Indian Territory day after tomorrow and will most likely not return to these parts until early next spring."

These words chilled Eden's blood. The army's campaign against the tribes living south of the Arkansas was only beginning, not ending. She summoned all her courage and, with heart pounding, she fixed her eyes on the so-called Boy General.

"Earlier in the meal, General, you spoke of restraint. You did not answer my question."

Randall tensed as she spoke.

"Have you a specific instance in your mind, Mrs. Murdoch?"

"Do you or do you not sanction the killing of women and children?"

Brad Randall murmured, "Oh, God."

Custer sobered instantly, and stated, "The killing of women and children is strictly forbidden unless they take up arms against us and we have no choice but to defend ourselves."

"And yet I have personal knowledge of the wanton murder of women and children by your soldiers." Eden hoped no one picked up on the quaver in her voice.

"I do not mean to contradict you, madam, but I find that difficult to believe. Do you have evidence of this?"

"The evidence of my own eyes, sir. One woman, my sis—" Eden caught herself just before calling Nightwalking her sister. This type of remark would stir up contempt in her audience and hurt the effect of her story. "My . . . *heveono,* she merely—"

"Excuse me, your what?" the general interrupted.

Heveono was a word to denote a cowife. Why had she so thoughtlessly used it? That term would probably cause even more problems than "sister." They would be appalled by a reference to her polygamous marriage and might ignore the true importance of her question. Her nervousness was ruining her presentation. "Um . . . there is no English word. She was a woman in whose lodge I slept. Anyway, she merely looked out of the tepee and was shot dead."

"It might have been a deliberate act," reasoned Custer. "But it could easily and more likely have been a stray bullet."

Brad had to agree with this assessment. Bullets were flying everywhere in the chaos of destruction that morning. If he were perfectly honest, he would have to admit he did not know whether an arrow or a bullet had creased his forehead. He proudly told everyone an arrow did the deed, but all he really knew was that something whizzed by his head and laid open the skin of his brow with the searing precision of lightning.

"I know of more instances," she continued, gaining momentum. "I saw the soldiers involved and they were not threatened in any way. One tore a nursling babe from its mother's arms and taunted her with it in a . . . in a gross perversion of sport. When she fought to re-

trieve her child, he threw her baby to the ground with enough force to kill it instantly. The other soldier shot her as she cradled her dead child in her arms."

Mary Lowell gasped at this story and covered her lips with her napkin. Even the silent, mysterious Tessa winced in horror. The men fell silent and waited for their host to respond.

"Such behavior would be in total contravention of my explicit orders. Would it not, gentlemen?"

"Yes, sir," Brad quickly answered.

"Absolutely," chimed in Captain Weir. Tom Custer nodded his concurrence.

"If you can identify these two men, I will see to it that they . . . that they are brought before a board of inquiry."

Brad whispered into Eden's ear. "Were these the two men I found you with?"

She nodded.

"Excuse me, sir, but an inquiry will not be necessary."

Custer turned a disdainful smile on his young aide, apparently amused by Brad's audacity and presumption. "And just why would that be, Captain?"

"The two men of whom Mrs. Murdoch speaks . . . they followed Major Elliott."

A distinct pall fell over the military men at the mention of Elliott's name.

"Well," said Custer, as he threw up his hands. "I guess that matter is settled then."

Eden looked to Randall for an explanation.

He leaned in close once again and informed her that

all the men in Major Elliott's detail were found dead. This news gave Eden cold comfort, though any comfort was better than none.

"General Custer," spoke up Elias Lowell, anxious to change the subject. "Is it true you personally accepted General Lee's flag of surrender at Appomattox?"

"Indeed I did, Mr. Lowell. And the flag you mention was no more than a white towel."

"And were you present at the signing of the terms of the surrender?" enthused Mary Lowell.

"Not only was I present, but my superior, General Sheridan, purchased the table on which the surrender was signed and gave it to my dear wife as a gift."

"Did you really have ten horses shot out from under you during the War?" Hugh Christie asked with a skeptical smile.

"Eleven, actually. Not that I wish to tempt fate by counting,"

"This is dangerous," warned a smirking Tom Custer. "You get him started on war stories and we'll be here all night."

"That would suit me right down to the ground," Christie rejoined. He gave voice to the feelings of all in the group from Reliance. They would treasure for a lifetime the memory of hearing the famous Boy General regale them with his daring exploits in the War of the Rebellion.

Christie watched Custer please and charm his listeners with a practiced grace. He wondered how a man of such obvious high esteem for himself and his abilities as a warrior took to the news that his great "victory" at the Washita was now being compared to the Sand Creek Massacre. Such an inference had to be galling in the extreme.

The saloonkeeper had read plenty of newspaper stories about the attack on Black Kettle's village four years earlier. The Cheyennes were camped near Fort Lyon in the southeastern corner of the Colorado Territory. He remembered how the Colorado Third, the Bloodless Third as they were derisively called at the time, under the command of Colonel Chivington, a self-righteous former minister, had marched south from Denver City with the single purpose of slaughtering Indians wherever they could find them. Folks said Chivington felt pressed for time as his hundred-day volunteers' enlistment period was due to expire. So find Indians they did, on the south banks of Sand Creek, only thirtysome miles distant of Fort Lyon where they'd just been promised sanctuary by Ned Wynkoop. Lyon, in those days, was a post more on active lookout for Rebels up from Texas than hostile Indians.

The story went that Black Kettle had flown an American flag from his tepee and a white flag, as well, when he saw the approaching troops. He had been given the flags as a gift so that he might fly them to demonstrate his peaceful and friendly attitude toward the white government. He told his people to gather around the flags for safety.

The Colorado troops opened fire on the unresisting group and, in the bloodbath, scores of women and children were killed, bodies mutilated. White men took Indian scalps. Cheyenne women's private parts cut off and dangled on sticks in the big parade back into Denver City to celebrate their victory. The *Rocky Mountain News* sung their praises.

No wonder the Cheyenne Dog Soldiers went looking for revenge after such a bloody orgy of treachery. And poor Eden Murdoch, to have had the confounded misfortune to have crossed their path. How could she possibly have survived their vengeful fury? Christie thought he would have sooner faced the wrath of the Almighty himself than a Cheyenne warrior with blood in his eyes and the image of his dead wife and children crushing out all else in his mind.

There had been a hearing on the Sand Creek incident, an inquest of some sort afterward in the Colorado Territory. Someone whose testimony had been critical of the attack had been murdered for his efforts. Hugh remembered that part vividly. Rumor had it that Chivington himself had hired the assassin. The killer was captured, but then escaped amid more rumors of conspiracy.

He watched Eden as she diffidently picked over the remains of her dinner. She seemed to take little interest in Custer's war stories, though the rest of the group sat silent and spellbound, especially the oafish minister and his plump, good-humored wife. The two captains looked as though they'd heard it all before. And what was that man on the end, that Keim, what was he up to? Hardly talked all evening and never took his eyes off Eden Murdoch.

The dinner plates were cleared by the innkeeper and his wife, who had been excitedly eavesdropping on

their famous guest. The landlord offered the gentlemen a round of brandy on the house to toast the health of the birthday boy. All accepted this offer, save the temperate Elias Lowell and Custer himself, who drank only water and cider during the evening.

Tessa almost slipped in her role as the decent and dutiful wife when she raised her glass to take some brandy. Hugh nudged her and she quickly backtracked.

The party broke up just after ten with Mr. Keim and Captains Weir and Custer heading out with the enlisted men to see to the horses.

As Tom Custer passed Brad at the door, he whispered with a grin, "Better watch out, Randall. That saloonkeeper's wife has got eyes for you."

Brad met this tease with a doubtful chuckle.

"Well, if you aren't interested," Tom Custer continued in a low but smirking tone, "at least put a good word in on my behalf."

Brad hushed him with an embarrassed grin.

Tom Weir, privy to this little exchange, playfully punched Brad in the shoulder as he passed out the door. The two Toms walked off laughing.

Christie and Tessa delivered their thanks and birthday congratulations to the young general and drifted toward the door. Armstrong Custer lingered at the table and placed a hand on Eden's arm when she rose to leave with the Lowells.

"Mrs. Murdoch, would you be offended if I told you that I am put in mind of Persephone whenever I see you?"

She sat back down with a confused frown. "Excuse me?"

"Persephone was carried off to the Underworld by—"

"I *know* who Persephone was!"

"So then you'll understand me when I ask if you ate the pomegranate seed while there?"

Brad watched with dread as this odd inquisition proceeded, though he too wondered if Eden Murdoch was destined to return to that strange Underworld from which she had so reluctantly reemerged. Did some adoring Hades, wearing war paint and eagle feathers, wait for her there?

The Lowells stood by silently, mystified and confused.

"What do you want of me?" she demanded irritably.

"I can't help wondering why you have been so reluctant to let us help you. I still long to learn more of your story."

"I do not feel under any obligation to share the intimate details of my life with you or anyone else."

Custer narrowed his pale blue eyes at his target as his playful mood vanished and his true objective resurfaced. "My report remains unfinished so long as I am unable to give an accurate account of the circumstances of your captivity with the Cheyennes, Mrs. Murdoch. You owe me that much, I believe."

"I owe you nothing, sir."

Mary Lowell visibly blanched at Eden's brazen rudeness to the general.

"You are living on the generosity of the United States Government at this moment. I think the very least you could do is cooperate."

"I've done all I intend to do."

Custer slapped his hand flat against the table in anger. "Perhaps we should have left you out there, then."

"I wish to heaven you had!"

Brad was so astonished at this remark that he forgot himself and spoke out. "How can you say that? How can you possibly say that?"

Custer shot Brad a fierce look that clearly said *I'm handling this, not you.*

"Look, General, I've given Captain Randall all the information he needs to find my relatives. The basic facts have been revealed. I was traveling west to meet my father for the Christmas holidays four years ago. He was then with the Corps of Engineers—I assume he still is. The coach on which I rode was attacked by a party of Cheyennes two days west of Fort Riley. Everyone was killed, I believe. Everyone . . . except me."

"But tell them about little Samuel," urged Mary Lowell. "They should know about your poor little boy."

Eden turned a furious face to the innocent Mary Lowell. She wished she had never divulged the existence of baby Samuel. Samuel was her secret, her precious memory, her terrible agony.

"You didn't tell me you had a little boy, Mrs. Murdoch," offered a stunned Brad Randall. He felt wholly inept as an investigator.

"I don't wish to talk about it."

"It wasn't your fault, dear," said Mary in a soothing voice. "You couldn't help it."

"What happened?" Custer addressed Mrs. Lowell, rather than Eden. He propped his chin up by his elbow.

"She was on her way out to visit her father and show him his new little baby grandchild when the stage was attacked. She took off running with her baby in her arms and those savages were after her and one of 'em caught her and grabbed her and she dropped her poor little Samuel in the buffalo grass and she could hear him screaming for her as they dragged her away."

Custer pinched his narrow chin thoughtfully.

Eden propped her own elbows on the table and covered her face with her hands. She said to Custer without looking up, "Are you satisfied now?"

Custer rose from the table without speaking and Randall followed him to the door, chagrined that Mrs. Lowell knew so much more about Eden Murdoch than he did. Of course, it only stood to reason that Mrs. Murdoch would have felt more comfortable confiding in another woman on such painful matters. He hoped Custer would understand this and not hold it as a failing on his part.

"General?" Eden called before Custer left the room.

He turned back as he pulled on his great buffalo coat.

She rose from the table to face the man whom she felt had engineered the demise of her Cheyenne family. "As you continue on your mission to subdue these people, you will understand them better it you keep in mind what Milton said of Lucifer."

"Milton who?" whispered Mary Lowell to her husband, only to be abruptly shushed by him.

Custer smiled bitterly at Eden's warning. " 'Better to reign in hell than serve in Heav'n'? We'll see about that."

He held her defiant gaze for more moments than anyone else in the room felt comfortable watching, then turned to leave once again. "But I thank you for the advice, madam."

"There is no word in the Cheyenne language for 'forgiveness,' " she called after him.

Brad hurried out the door of the inn to follow his commander and found him on the wooden sidewalk with his arms folded across his chest, staring up into the starry, cold night sky.

Custer smiled faintly and remarked, "Degraded by savages for nearly four years, yet still able to quote Milton. Curious. When I sit down to write my memoirs, I'll have to save a chapter for her." He turned to join the remainder of his group.

"I'll get more information on her, I promise you," Brad called, as Custer swiftly walked to join the others in his party.

"See that you do." The general did not even bother to face Brad as he spoke, but kept walking, fastening up his buffalo coat as he strode away. "Messenger any information to me by way of Fort Cobb. Oh, and I'm putting you in charge of moving the prisoners from Camp Supply to Fort Dodge within the week."

"Yes, sir." Brad watched the party of men ride off. "Happy birthday, General," he mumbled into the cold night air, but no one heard him.

${\mathcal{N}}$ ine

As to "extermination" it is for the Indians
themselves to determine. We don't want to ex-
terminate or even fight them. At best it is an
inglorious war.
—LIEUTENANT GENERAL W. T. SHERMAN, COMMANDER OF
THE MILITARY DIVISION OF THE DEPARTMENT OF THE
MISSOURI, TO MAJOR GENERAL PHILIP SHERIDAN,
OCTOBER 15, 1868

Eden felt guilty about deceiving such a nice and honorable person as Mary Lowell. Still, Eden longed to read
Hugh Christie's magazine collection and knew Mary's
opinion of that particular gentleman well enough to realize she would have to visit him on the sly.

On a bright, cold morning, Eden slipped out of the
Lowell house with only a word to Bonnie Sue, the
kitchen girl, that she intended to take a walk. The girl
possessed so little wit, Eden was certain the Lowells
employed her only out of their well-known Christian
charity.

Mary was off attending a meeting of her ladies' suf-
frage and temperance society. Mr. Lowell was seeing to
his weekday profession as a shopkeeper. His congregation was far too small to afford a full-time minister, so

he supported his family with a thriving general store. Eden wondered if he might employ her in his store until it grew obvious to her that her presence would drive away business, at least once the curiosity factor had diminished.

She wrapped herself in one of Mary Lowell's woolen shawls and left the house for the first time since the night of the Custer birthday party a week ago. Reliance had begun its life on a trade route, a precursor to the Santa Fe Trail. The town was only four years old, though people had begun to gather at that spot on the Cimarron River for nearly a decade. Now the city grew in every direction, with population pouring in following the end of the war.

Eden drew in a deep breath. The whole town seemed to smell of new-sawn lumber, a scent filled with promise of the future.

The coming of the railroad was the only piece of the puzzle missing and the town anxiously waited for that development. Iron rails meant the arrival of the civilized world.

Mary Lowell told Eden that she and her husband had first moved to Kansas in the late 1850s with the noble ambition to help establish Kansas as a free state prior to its entry into the Union.

"Oh my, those were wild days," Mary Lowell had remarked of her years in Leavenworth, Kansas. "Those border ruffians, such lawlessness. I was as afraid of them as I am of the dreadful savages. Oh, I'm sorry. I shouldn't have said—"

"No, please, it's all right. I know you worry about

the Indians and I'm not going to tell you that you have nothing to fear."

"No, I guess you, of all people, know the truth of it."

"Yes." So much easier to agree than to elaborate. No one wanted complex answers to any question.

The Lowells had left Leavenworth three years earlier to settle in Reliance. Mary remained oddly silent on exactly why they had moved.

Eden faced a wintry blast of cold air as she attempted to locate Hugh Christie's saloon. She tried to remember its location from that first day in Reliance, but misjudged the distance. She recalled that the sign out front of the establishment said only Saloon, no name or fancier designation. She concluded this man, Hugh Christie, lacked a great deal in the way of imagination.

She paused at the window of Mr. Lowell's Mercantile. She did not wish him to see her, but the jolly display in the window caught her eye. Christmas decorations—ornaments, ribbons, and garlands of all sorts—bedecked the window. The Lowells had not yet decorated their home for the holidays, so Eden had almost forgotten the proximity of the occasion. For nearly four years, she had not even heard the word "Christmas."

If only her father could reach her by that date. How she longed to see him again, to throw her arms around him and hug him tightly and feel his full beard scratch against her cheek.

She could feel safe and loved again if only she could see him. She recalled climbing into his lap as a child; how he would read her stories or tell her of his travels.

Her mother would cluck her tongue and say he spoiled her, his only child, and he would laugh in response to this gentle criticism. Thinking about him made Eden imagine that her life had a chance of returning to normal. He would have to forgive her disobedience in marrying Lawrence Murdoch without his blessing. She would admit, for the hundredth time, that he had been right to oppose the match. She remembered with chagrin the frantic telegram he had sent her, just before her wedding, begging her to wait, to postpone the marriage at least until the end of the war. She had angrily thrown his telegram away and blithely proceeded to run off with her handsome soldier bridegroom, whom she had known for all of five weeks.

Her father couldn't stay angry forever, could he? That wouldn't be like him at all. But how would he react to her life among the Cheyennes? Would he consider her tainted, ruined, despicable, as did the citizens of Reliance? Would he expect her to pretend her life with Hanging Road and the sisters had been dreadful instead of joyous, as everyone seemed to demand?

Eden heard two women pass behind her on the wooden sidewalk and whisper, "Is that her? Is she the one?"

She clutched Mary's shawl more tightly around her head and shoulders and marched down the street. She arrived at Hugh Christie's drinking establishment in a moment's time, but the doors were locked. She peeked in the front window and dimly saw a figure occupied in some task behind the bar.

She rapped on the window with her bare knuckles

as she owned no gloves. She caught the attention of the figure and soon she heard the sound of the door being unbolted.

"Why, it's Mrs. Murdoch. I'll be bound." A smile stretched across Hugh Christie's broad, angular face.

"I've come about your magazines. I mean, if you wouldn't mind my taking a look at some of them."

"Wouldn't mind at all. Come in, come in. Get out of the cold."

He ushered her inside with a gallant gesture.

"I keep them all under my bar," he said. He led her through the long, narrow room between numerous mismatched tables and chairs. Sawdust powdered the floor and spittoons sprouted in strategic locations. A large gilt mirror reflected their walk down the center of the room. Eden could not remember ever having been in a drinking establishment before.

She had never so much as tasted alcohol, though she had administered plenty of whiskey to wounded soldiers during the war for a variety of medicinal purposes prescribed by the surgeons. They treated whiskey as something of a cure-all to deaden pain when laudanum or morphine were unavailable, to induce sleep in an overanxious patient, or to warm up a chilled one.

For all other purposes, however, Eden's views on liquor did not vary much from those of the Lowells. She had too many unpleasant memories from her brief marriage to Lawrence Murdoch to view the consumption of alcoholic beverages as a harmless pleasure. She could still feel the sting of the back of his hand when he would hound her with his endless, groundless accusations of adultery every time he got drunk. Then came his pathetic pleadings for forgiveness.

But the mere whiff of whiskey brought back still another memory, more revolting than any of her unpleasant confrontations with Lawrence. There was the night of a drunken half-Kiowa trader. How he reeked of it. An overpowering, sickening stench. Little shreds of that night came back to her when she least expected it, causing her to tremble uncontrollably. She drew a hurried breath to cleanse her mind.

Eden thought Mr. Christie seemed somewhat nervous. This was certainly at odds with her first impression of him—that of a wiseacre with a smart remark for every occasion.

They walked around the large, carved oak bar. Its marble top hid shelving that carried row after row of glasses, from large beer mugs to tiny whiskey shot glasses. The bottom shelf held stacks of *Harper's Weekly* magazines.

"I'm sorry these aren't in any order," Christie apologized as he pulled out two armloads and carried them to a table that sat close to the bar. Eden likewise gathered up a large stack and followed him.

She seated herself and hungrily dove into the last four years of the rest of the world as presented by the self-proclaimed "Journal of Civilization." He offered her coffee, which she graciously accepted, then he left her to her reading. A young man with dark, curly hair came and went throughout the morning. Hugh Christie called him Marco, but did not bother to introduce the boy. He carried in crates of whiskey and other strong drink from

a delivery wagon outside. He and Hugh both labored to carry in several kegs of beer and get them set up for dispensing.

She passed the morning in silence, only once pausing to exclaim in shock: "President Lincoln was assassinated!"

Hugh Christie grinned at his guest. " 'Fraid so."

Eden had blushed at her ignorance. She was reading the news events of years ago, she had to remind herself.

At noon, Hugh told her he needed to open his establishment. "You can take some copies home with you, if you like," he offered, knowing she would not care to remain in the saloon once it stood open to receive its customers.

"Thank you, but I'd better not. The Lowells, you see, don't even know I'm here and—"

"Say no more. I know the rest. But you're welcome to come back as often as you like, you know. I sleep kinda late, most mornings, but I'd get up early if I knew you was coming."

She gathered up all the magazines and carried them back behind the bar. "Would it be possible, I mean, would you mind at all, if perhaps I stayed back here—in your office, out of sight—and continued to read? I'm just enjoying it so much I can't stop."

"The back room?"

"Yes, sir. Would you mind? I won't get in your way, I promise."

Hugh smiled and scratched his chin. "Go ahead, if that's what you want."

Eden nodded her thanks and gathered up her magazines. She found a desk and chair in Hugh's disorganized back office. Both were piled high with old newspapers, bills of lading, discarded mail, and other sundry items. She carefully set the pile of clutter covering the seat of the wooden chair on the floor. She hoped Mr. Christie wouldn't mind her rearranging his things. She was down on her hands and knees clearing a space for her feet when she heard him enter the back room. She looked up, startled, to see him grinning down at her.

"Is something wrong, Mr. Christie?"

"Not at all, Mrs. Murdoch. Seein' you down there like that just reminded me of Tessa, that's all."

"Tessa?"

"My neighbor." He jerked his head toward the brothel next door. "The woman I brought to the party. She's not really my wife. Brad and I just thought it might sound better, you know?"

Eden's smile faded when she realized she was somehow being compared to a prostitute.

"First time I ever saw her," Hugh continued, "She was down there on the floor where you are now, hidin'."

"Hiding?"

"From her husband. Or whoever the fella was she was travelin' west with. She decided to part company with the gent and he wasn't quite convinced, so she took off and hid in here until he gave up and left town. Guess that was about three years ago just after I opened this place."

"You offered her shelter?"

"She didn't have nowhere else to go." He chuckled at the memory. "Been takin' in strays since I was a kid. Can't seem to break myself of the habit."

Ten

I have always done my best to keep my young
men quiet, but some will not listen, and since
the fighting began I have not been able to
keep them all at home. But we all want
peace.

—Black Kettle to General Hazen, Fort Cobb,
November 20, 1868, one week before the
Battle of the Washita

My beloved Amanda,
I have just returned to Reliance, Kansas, after an
eventful week's absence—

Brad set down his pen in frustration and rubbed his
face with his hands. His eyelids seemed to contain a
thousand fine grains of sand. He felt washed out from a
miserable night of fitful, tormented sleep.

The cook at the little Reliance restaurant brought
out a serving of steaming peach cobbler, the last course
of his large lunch. The aroma distracted him from his
present misery of guilt and self-loathing.

He felt like such a worthless hypocrite, addressing
Amanda as his "beloved" when he had sinned against
their love three times since leaving home and was fight-

ing the urge to do so again even as he tried to write this letter.

His shameful guilt haunted him day and night. Even in his sleep, he could not avoid it. Only last night, his dreams began lasciviously, and not in Amanda's beautiful, lithe arms, but in those of the whore, Tessa.

Soon, however, the character of the dream shifted ominously. Gone were the sexual images. Now he saw Eden Murdoch make the tribal sign for the Cheyenne people. She looked at him unsmilingly as she sawed her right index finger over her left, over and over again, until blood appeared on her fingers.

In the dream, Brad looked down at his hands and beheld his own fingers dripping with bright red blood. Then he lay naked in the frozen grass with the men of Major Joel Elliott's detail. All of them lying there, but he was not dead. Why was he with them if he was still alive?

A grotesquely painted Cheyenne warrior appeared above him. He knelt down over Brad's body. A single eagle feather adorned his straight black hair. Red paint obscured his face. A necklace decorated with three severed human fingers was suspended around his neck. Brad observed the necklace with acute clarity. The skin of the severed fingers had dried an odd yellow color so that Brad could not decide if they came from white men or red. The fingers had shrunk back from their fingernails, rendering the horny surface of the nails large and bulging in comparison to the taut flesh that surrounded them. The fingers hung upon a beaded necklace of sky blue and white alternating bands.

The warrior did not look crazed with blood lust. Rather, he appeared composed and methodical, like someone about to perform a ritual, not a killing. The warrior drew a long, elaborately decorated knife from his belt. He softly sang a strange, ragged song as he ran the flat metal blade slowly in circles over Brad's chest, then down his white belly as though drawing a picture. Brad could feel the cold, faintly scratchy sensation the metal made against his flesh as it lightly moved over him. Lower and lower the blade drifted. Brad's hysteria grew. He strained to move, but could not.

I'm not dead... I'm not dead! he screamed, but no sound came out.

The warrior reached for Brad's penis . . . to sever it for a grisly trophy of war.

No . . . no . . . no . . . NO! Brad sat up on his camp bed, gasping for breath. In the total darkness, several seconds passed before he came to realize he was still in his tent. Bathed in his own sweat, he shivered uncontrollably and wondered if he had actually cried out or just imagined it as part of his nightmare. He ran his hands over his face several times and tried to shake off the horrifying spell of the dream.

Brad took a large bite of peach cobbler and tried to think of something to write to Amanda. He had much to report on since his last letter to her, but his thoughts inevitably returned only to the fact of his inconstancy. He thought about his last night with Tessa, after that miserable birthday party for the general.

She had talked him into walking her home. His judgment was impaired by all the brandy he had consumed at the party, at least that was the excuse he made to himself. He had drunk just enough to feel light and silly and utterly invincible. Not to mention profoundly randy, once they had neared Tessa's house and Hugh's nameless saloon. Both of their establishments were closed on a Sunday night in an odd gesture of reverence to a Sabbath neither celebrated.

Hugh had bid them good-night and tossed Brad that age-old smile that one man gives to another when one is going home with a woman and the other is retreating to an empty bed.

"Tessa, if I had not found you, I would surely have drowned," Brad had said with heartfelt, if improvident, sincerity as he held her in his arms.

"Drowned? Kansas ain't known for its water."

He chuckled softly. "That's not exactly what I meant." He tried to decide if he had enough energy to muster a full-blown explanation of the concept of metaphor.

"You like comin' here 'cause when you're with me, you don't have to think about nothin' else."

She knew the concept of metaphor after all.

"Your little captive better watch herself around that reverend," Tessa had warned him with unexpected gravity.

"What do you mean? The Lowells are an awfully nice couple, it seems to me."

"Can't say anything against the missus, 'cept she looks down her nose at everybody that don't wanna

take an oath to swear off liquor. It's him, the minister, that the girl's gotta look sharp after. 'Course, I don't know. If she's been layin' with Indians, I expect she ain't too choosy about who gets up her skirt."

"I believe you're wrong about Mrs. Murdoch. But on what do you base your suspicions of the good Mr. Lowell?" Brad rolled over on his side and, in the dim candlelight, found a smirking half-smile on Tessa's face.

"Oh, no!" He grinned. "You can't be serious. You mean you know him . . . *professionally?*"

"Not me, myself, but some of the girls who work here."

Brad flipped back over and clapped his hands together in scandalized delight. "This is too rich! And I thought I was bad."

"How's he worse than you?" she teased, tickling him.

"*I* don't pretend to be perfect. I'm a professional soldier, not a man of God. No one would mistake me for a saint."

"That General Custer of yours. He seems kinda saintly to me."

"He's a man of temperate habits, but I would not call him a saint. I would call him . . . a celebrity."

"What about Sheridan? What's he like?"

"Small, no taller than you. They don't call him 'Little Phil' for nothing. Custer served under Sheridan in the Great War as well. Whenever I am called in to speak with him, I can barely keep a straight face because I am always reminded of an illustration I once saw in *Harper's Weekly*. It was during the war, after Sheridan drove back Jubal Early's troops in the Shenandoah Valley, I think. Anyway, the picture—and I assume it was based on an actual occurrence—showed Armstrong Custer picking General Sheridan up in the air and dancing him around the campfire to celebrate their great victory. I just can't get that picture out of my mind."

There were a great many pictures he wished he could rid his memory of lately. He finished off his peach cobbler and debated whether to talk to Mrs. Murdoch about Tessa's concerns over Mr. Lowell. On the other hand, who would board her if the Lowells were not available? He knew she did not want to sleep in a tent in his small encampment, nor did he wish to resume his duty of referee between her acid tongue and his belligerent men.

He decided to say nothing. Tessa did not like the Lowells. Perhaps she was just spreading malicious gossip. And besides, was not Mrs. Murdoch quite adept at defending herself? He remembered her knee in his groin only too painfully well. Any woman capable of threatening to castrate a man with her teeth could surely fend off the advances of a lecherous minister.

He picked up his pen, dipped it in his little bottle of ink, and tried to start his letter to Amanda once again.

My beloved Amanda,
I have just returned to Reliance, Kansas, after an eventful week's absence in which I was charged with the responsibility of moving prisoners up

from Camp Supply to the more established and better equipped Fort Dodge. The weather held up well for the journey. Transporting fifty women and children proved less of a travail than I had anticipated. I expect the nomadic existence of the Plains tribes prepared them well for our journey.

Three of their number left with General Custer and the rest of our regiment to head farther south into the Indian Territory. They took the women to aid in negotiation with the hostile tribes, though I do not know why any faith should be placed on their loyalty. One claimed to be the sister of the slain chief, Black Kettle. Early on, she seemed to appoint herself spokeswoman for the group and even endeavored, on the day of the Washita battle, to marry General Custer to a young woman among their number. (I wonder what Libbie Custer would say to that!) The general politely declined the honor, once his interpreter informed him of its nature.

The daughter of the slain Cheyenne chieftain, Little Rock, was also chosen to accompany them. Her name is Monaseeta. Many a rude remark is being hoisted at the general's expense over his choice, given that the girl he picked is easily the prettiest of the captive women. Many question his motives in a manner his wife would find most offensive. I think their randy jests fail the mark in that the young squaw in question is obviously on the verge of giving birth to a baby. I suppose this fact was not apparent to casual observers, given

the heavy robes in which the women bundle themselves against the prairie winter. (Do you mind my
speaking so frankly? I consider you as delicate as
any of the female sex, and if anything I write makes
you uncomfortable, please inform me, my darling.)

I continue on my "White Captive" duty. Her
name is Eden Murdoch and I am under pressure
from both General Custer and General Sheridan to
learn more about her. Before I left Camp Supply
with my prisoners in tow, General Sheridan called
me to his tent. He furiously slapped a letter down
on his camp desk and told me he "Will not stand
for it, will not stand for it!"

"Will not stand for what, sir?" I dutifully inquired, all the while wondering what had excited
"Little Phil's" choler in such a way.

"This, this outrage!" he shouted, handing me
the letter, which turned out to be a copy of a letter
of resignation from the Indian agent, Edward Wynkoop.

I scanned the missive as quickly as possible.

"I have just been informed by an associate of
mine in New York that the *Times* plans to print this
in its entirety no later than the twentieth of this
month," continued General Sheridan. "That is why
I have called you in here. I am fortunately being
allowed to deliver a response and a firm response
is what they'll get."

"Sir, if I might ask for a clarification on this letter of Colonel Wynkoop's? It says here that his orders were to proceed to Fort Cobb to bring in all

the tribes of his jurisdiction to the reservation."

"Correct," snapped my feisty little commander. (Amanda, I keep thinking of that time you told me how uncomfortable it made you to dance with Sheridan since his face seemed in too close a proximity to your bosom! That should teach you, my very tall darling, not to display such cleavage—except when dancing with me, of course! Please know I am laughing as I write this last.)

"If our dear Colonel Wynkoop had been doing his job, this whole matter might not have gotten started in the first place," Sheridan continued to fume.

"But sir, if Colonel Wynkoop was under orders to proceed to Fort Cobb to peaceably bring in the tribes, why was General Custer likewise under orders to attack those selfsame tribes? Were we not working at cross-purposes?" I knew I skated a thin line between honest inquiry and insubordination here, but I just had to ask this question.

With a loud sigh of exasperation, my commander rose from his desk and angrily strode about the tent. He threw his hands in the air. "Of course, of course we are working at cross-purposes. Look at what Hazen's up to. Custer informs me he found coffee, sugar, and flour in Black Kettle's village. They came from Hazen!"

I kept my tongue after this extraordinary outburst, but I could sympathize with the general's frustration even if I could not fully understand the situation.

He finally sat back down again, shuffled his papers, and appeared to regain his composure. "All this will right itself, once Grant takes office. I'm certain of that. The Congress will vote soon on transference of the Indian problem from the Department of the Interior to the Department of War, where it rightfully belongs. Then we will have a clear policy to follow."

At this point, he bid me draw up a chair before him and sit. "Until then, it's all quite mad," he continued. "To the defenseless people on the frontier, getting scalped and ravished, we're soulless monsters if we do not protect them and maintain an adequate peace, yet whenever we attempt to do just that, we are the same soulless monsters to the peace advocates in the East who burn us in effigy for our 'barbarous' acts against the 'noble Red Man.' "

I had to concur in his frustration. We are in truly an untenable situation, Amanda. Do not believe the condemnations of our actions you may soon be reading in the papers. If those same advocates of peace could but come west and stay a simple month on the frontier and experience the fear and anxiety endured by the residents of Kansas—if they could have viewed the viciously mutilated remains of Major Elliott, a man I had come to know and respect a great deal in the few short weeks of our acquaintance—they might find their views considerably modified.

And yet, that is not the whole answer, either. The native tribes are caught in this awful web, as well. If I am to take the word of Mrs. Eden Murdoch, not all of these people are truly savage. The more I learn of Mrs. Murdoch's strange sojourn among them, the more I find I have yet to know. Though she undoubtedly suffered more at their hands than any living person I have yet come to witness, she cannot and does not condemn or hate these people. I was at an utter loss to understand this, though the information I have since gained may shed further light on the issue.

And our government has behaved in a most confusing and contradictory manner. They bully the tribes into signing treaties in which the tribes give up their claims to vast areas of territory in exchange for promised goods and annuities. Then Congress, in their divine neglect, never bothers to ratify said treaties and the goods and commodities promised are never forthcoming as the needed funding has never been authorized. I am told the terrible depredations committed last autumn by the tribes we now seek to "punish" were inspired by their frustration at not being awarded the goods we had promised them.

I'm sorry, I digress from my meeting with General Sheridan. Following his diatribe on the chicanery of politics, he brought home the reason I was summoned to his presence. "In drafting this response to Wynkoop's resignation, I must have as much information as possible on Black Kettle and why it was necessary to eliminate him from the scene."

This order left me at a momentary disadvantage for reply. We had no knowledge that it was Black Kettle's village in those predawn hours before the advance. It struck me as vaguely dishonest to now justify our actions in retrospect. When I hesitated in my response, I incurred the wrath of my little commander whose temper seemed as short that morning as General Custer's was on any given day in the field.

Brad set down his pen and thought about his uncomfortable meeting with Sheridan.

"The woman," Sheridan had snapped. "Custer said he put her entirely in your charge, man."

"Yes, sir. Mrs. Murdoch. A sad case."

"Details. I need details. Custer said she was quite attractive to look at, but thoroughly out of her mind."

"That might be overstating it, sir."

"Are you contradicting your own immediate superior, Captain?"

"No, sir. Might I simply suggest that I have had longer exposure to Mrs. Murdoch and, though she remains difficult and uncooperative at times, she seems to have full possession of her faculties."

"Well, Custer told me she took off her clothing in a public place in Reliance, a barbershop or something."

"Yes, sir."

"Doesn't sound like the actions of a rational person

to me. Does it to you, Captain? Custer also told me that he discovered this tidbit of information, not from you, but rather from camp gossip."

Brad squirmed at this implied rebuke. Did Custer not only think him inept, but duplicitous, as well? He would have to do something to get back in the man's good graces.

He hurriedly blurted out all that he knew of Eden Murdoch's capture, how the stagecoach was attacked by Cheyennes in retaliation for the atrocities of Sand Creek, how she ran and tried to escape but dropped her baby in the process. How she had heard the baby screaming as they carried her away to a night of unimaginable horror at their camp.

"Little Phil" eagerly jotted notes as Brad spoke. He nodded with satisfaction over the part about the lost baby. "Raped? Was she raped?"

"She hasn't said so, but one assumes—"

"Yes, one does assume, doesn't one?" snapped Sheridan irritably. "Custer said the doctor's report indicated she had given birth to a baby or babies during her time with the Cheyennes. If one takes for granted the basics of human biology, I think one can fairly assume they enjoyed carnal knowledge of her person—absent another immaculate conception. Would you not agree, Randall?"

Brad did not see the point of his commander's sarcasm, but managed a tight remark of concurrence.

"And the husband, where is he? Alive or dead?"

"Killed in the war, I believe."

Sheridan grunted with dissatisfaction at this and

mumbled, "Damn. If we could but include the outrage of the wronged husband. Much more powerful effect. What about scars? I'm told the doctor's report included an extensive list of scars."

Brad still found the contents of the doctor's report on Eden Murdoch revolting. One remark in particular stuck in his brain like a gnawing thorn: *"Significant scarring about the vaginal area, not all of which can be attributed to childbirth, even a complicated delivery."*

"Yes, sir. Lots of scars, though I am told some wounds on her limbs may have been self-inflicted. I have not personally viewed them. I was not present during the barbershop incident. But some are in rather intimate locations. Scars in the shape of human teeth—bite marks—on her breasts, so we must assume—"

"Torture!" crowed Sheridan with satisfaction. He scribbled furiously on his pad of paper as he growled, *"Fiends."*

Brad sighed and resumed his letter:

After concluding my less than enjoyable interview with General Sheridan, Amanda, I embarked on my mission to deliver the Cheyenne women and children to Fort Dodge, a distance of about one hundred miles from Camp Supply.

The morning of the journey began in a quiet and orderly fashion. We had more than enough horses to accommodate the group in that General

Custer had had the foresight to allow each of the captive women to pick a mount for herself and her children from the Indian herd prior to their destruction. Some were still healing from wounds of the battle, but almost all were able to ride with no difficulty.

I and my detail of six men headed out just after breakfast with our charges. As we rode north on a reasonably fair day, we chanced to encounter a white man and his Indian wife. I had previously seen this man, a trader of some sort supplying the army with canned goods and tobacco, at Camp Supply. His name was Brighton.

He rode to my side and asked if his wife might join our party. He needed to travel elsewhere and wanted his wife safely transported to Fort Dodge. I told him this was fine with me, though I was not in a position to guarantee Mrs. Brighton's safety, given the limited size of our escort. He cheerfully accepted these terms and introduced his wife, a Cheyenne woman, though she was not in intimate acquaintance with any of our party.

The trader bid us and his wife adieu and was soon off. Before Mrs. Brighton had drifted too far from my position, a sudden inspiration seized me. If she spoke English, and this was far from certain in that her husband had communicated with her in the Cheyenne tongue, she could serve as an interpreter betwixt myself and my party of prisoners. I slowed my mount to draw alongside the woman and asked her if she spoke English.

"Some," was her reply.

"Could you ask a few of these women nearby what they know of Mrs. Murdoch?"

Mrs. Brighton called over to the two women riding closest to us. They were elderly squaws with dark, deeply creased faces. Unburdened by children, the pair were seeming to enjoy the bright morning with its bracing air.

Both looked puzzled by my question when it was addressed to them by Mrs. Brighton. At first this answer astonished me. The village had not been so large that the existence of a white woman among their number would have escaped their notice. Then I realized my error in thinking. They might not have known her by her English name, so I asked Mrs. Brighton to convey this new slant to the question.

The women's reaction changed markedly when the object of my inquiry was made more plain. Their wizened faces now bore noticeable agitation.

"They don't want to talk about her," was my interpreter's reply.

"Why not?"

"Afraid. Them very, very afraid."

"Please convey that no consequence will attach to their remarks. No retaliation is in store for them." The woman stared at me dumbly so I simplified my remarks as best I could. "Tell them I will not be angry with them, no matter what they tell me. I will not punish them in any way."

Mrs. Brighton and the two elderly squaws con-

versed a good long time over this. Then Mrs. Brighton rode as close to me as possible and stated, "Them not afraid of you. Them afraid of her."

I almost laughed out loud. There must have been a miscommunication of some sort. "Why would they be afraid of Mrs. Murdoch?"

"She called Seota. She have big medicine. She don't like somebody, she make them die. She make lots and lots—nearly whole tribe—die."

I stared at my interpreter. Her report was so ludicrous, I had to conclude I was the butt of an elaborate practical joke on the part of these old women. They no doubt thought they could tell me anything and I would be gullible enough to believe them. Rather than become angry, I chose to play along, just out of curiosity. We had a long and tedious ride ahead of us, remember, and I needed a good diversion to pass the time.

"Why did she make all these people die?" I queried.

Another long conversation ensued among the women. Then Mrs. Brighton returned to my side. "A man, a Kiowa, hurt her real bad and she made everybody take sick and die."

"If she had the power to kill an entire tribe, why did she not simply escape and return to her own people?"

This elicited an even longer conversation between the women. Mrs. Brighton then asked me rather timidly, "You sure she not gonna find out about this?"

"I promise you, Mrs. Murdoch is far from here and unable to work any black magic from such a distance."

Mrs. Brighton regarded me suspiciously. I do not think she understood my reference to witchcraft and I am certain she did not think me powerful enough to control a force of nature with the reputation of Mrs. Murdoch.

"She make everybody sick and they die and die. But she take care of them and fetch them water and food and not run away. No one understand this. Just one in the village does. E'kotsemeo, a medicine man, only one not afraid of her. He tell chiefs that she the favorite of the Great Spirit. Don't know why. Some want to kill her, but others afraid to. This E'kotsemeo take her into his lodge and marry her when some come to kill her. Then people get well again."

"I confess, I'm completely confused by your story, madam."

She shrugged. "Them not gonna talk no more. Them maybe said too much already. They don't want no trouble."

So my quest for knowledge resulted in a greater quandary than I was in before concerning Mrs. Murdoch. Why were the women so afraid of her? How was it that she came to hold power over them? She was their captive, their slave, for all intents and purposes, to use and abuse as they chose, if I am to believe the other stories concerning the treatment of captives by tribes such as these.

I tried a different tack. I questioned them on the subject of captives generally. Once again, they showed reluctance to speak, still apparently fearing some reprisal on the part of the government of the United States.

Mrs. Brighton, however, felt free to speak on her own as to such matters. She informed me that the taking of war captives was a time honored practice among all the tribes, that it had gone on for as long as anyone could remember.

Stealing an enemy's wife and children served a number of practical purposes over and above the obvious grief and forbearance caused to the victim's family. A captive was a valuable commodity who could be bartered, sold, or gambled away at his or her owner's whim. The captive could be made to work at all sorts of menial and difficult activities as well as perform tasks considered taboo by the tribe for one reason or another. And, as you no doubt have heard before, a captured woman of any age above childhood was used in the most indecent manner by the warriors of the tribe. I don't think I need to elaborate on this aspect, though you might keep it in mind when considering a too-harsh judgment as to some of my Mrs. Murdoch's eccentricities.

Though we take a reproachful view of the barbarous treatment meted out by these savages to their unfortunate captives, is there a great difference between their attitude and that of a slaveholder in the Rebel states before the War?

I will write more as soon as I talk to Mrs. Murdoch. I must confess I do not know what to make of the charges against her lodged by the Cheyenne women.

I still have not received any responses to my search for her father, who is apparently the only family the poor woman has left. Christmas is only a week away. I was previously certain I would have accomplished my task by that time and be on my way to rejoin the regiment. They are now on their way to Fort Cobb. If you look on the map I left with you, you will see Fort Cobb farther south on the Washita than the site of our engagement with Black Kettle.

Try not to have too much fun without your intended present(!!), although if I pass the holiday in the agreeable, if raw and rough, little town of Reliance, it will still be more jolly than spending it in the field with my regiment. I have made several new friends here.

All my love now and always,
Bradley

He decided to order another slice of peach cobbler. He didn't believe in drinking his problems away. Maybe he could distract himself from his worldly cares through gluttony. He had joked about his news of Mrs. Murdoch, but in reality, he had no idea what shade to place on this newfound information.

He folded his letter to Amanda and sealed it to post. He finished off his second serving of cobbler, then left

the restaurant to walk to the post office and telegraph station.

He realized that the walk would take him directly past Hugh Christie's nameless saloon and Tessa's house. He ought to stop in and say hello to Hugh and at least wish him the tidings of the season. Of course, Tessa might be there. Tessa often seemed to linger about Hugh's saloon in the afternoon. What would he do if he saw her?

As he strode down the wooden sidewalk of Reliance, the rough-hewn boards creaked in the chill of the overcast December day. His thoughts wandered back to the last night he had spent with Tessa. Oh, the glorious things they had done together. The slightest memory was enough to excite him. He picked up his step down the sidewalk and hummed an old favorite Christmas carol.

Eleven

No better time could possibly be chosen than
the present for destroying or humbling those
bands that have so outrageously violated their
treaties and begun a desolating war without
one particle of provocation.
—Lieutenant General W. T. Sherman, report to J. M.
Schofield, secretary of war, September 17, 1868

"He's back," Tessa announced with satisfaction as she
entered Hugh Christie's saloon from the side door.

"Who's back?" Hugh asked from a table near the
front of the establishment. He wiped up a beer spill
from a recent customer, though the bar had welcomed
few patrons since it opened two hours before.

Eden had just opened the door of the back room to
collect another armload of magazines, but froze so as
not to attract Tessa's attention. She was certain the
woman had not seen her and stood silently out of view
of the open door.

"You know who!" Tessa teased. "Mabel just saw him
at the café, eating his dinner."

"You knew he'd be back. Don't Loverboy tell you all
his secrets?"

Eden wondered who "loverboy" might be. She

couldn't help but eavesdrop . . . and enjoyed it.

"You just make sure and come get me if he shows up here, all right?"

Eden peeked into the main room and saw Tessa head back toward the side door to leave again when someone entered the saloon. The moment Tessa saw the identity of the bar's latest patron, her expression came closer to smiling than any Eden had previously seen on the dour-faced woman. And the boy called Marco, who had been quietly sweeping up, ran for the back room when he saw who entered. He nearly knocked Eden down in his hurry to exit the building.

"*Scusi, signora,*" he whispered as he flew out the back door and into the alleyway behind the saloon.

A cold shock hit Eden when she recognized the voice of Brad Randall proclaim season's greetings to Christie and Tessa. She debated whether to make her presence known while she overheard the three people chat amiably for a moment, exchanging the news of the week gone by. She was glad she had remained in hiding when she realized the reason for Captain Randall's visit. She watched through the opening as Tessa almost dragged the young officer by the elbow through the side door and the pair vanished.

Eden entered the back of the saloon and beheld Hugh's smiling face. She could tell he knew she had just witnessed the little interlude. His infectious grin eased her embarrassment. Everything she had guessed about Brad Randall and Tessa had turned out to be true.

She could feel the heat rise in her cheeks, but she could not help returning his smile of amusement.

"Guess our young captain came back to town feelin' kinda amorous," Hugh observed with a twinkle in his dark brown eyes.

"He's engaged to be married," came Eden's scandalized whisper.

Hugh raised his eyebrows. "Then he's bein' a real bad boy."

She covered her mouth with her hand, but couldn't help laughing. "Her father is a very important man in the War Department and he gave a ball to celebrate Captain Randall's engagement to his daughter and the president of the United States attended!"

Christie grinned at this information. "I reckon old Johnson was lookin' for any friend he could find in the War Department just about then." The observation flew over Eden's head. She had not reached in her reading the story of President Johnson's recent impeachment trial, brought about by a vengeful Republican Congress seeking to punish him for firing the secretary of war.

"Sergeant Yellen is quite an old gossip. He gave me an earful one night when we were briefly on speaking terms. He claims that Captain Randall's fiancée is considered the most beautiful woman in Washington City."

"Do tell."

Eden blushed again. "I'm sorry. I'm gossiping worse than Sergeant Yellen, aren't I?"

"If there's one thing a bartender's used to, it's plenty of gossip. Bet I hear more confessions than a priest. Do you need anything? 'Cause I could get you something to eat or drink."

"I'm fine. Really."

"Not even a glass of water?"

She smiled warmly at the man's persistence. "Thank you, no."

"Suit yourself." He returned to work and Eden returned to her reading, filling her eager brain with every detail she could absorb from the printed pages before her. So much had happened in four years. She ran across the name of General Custer several times in articles about the war. She vaguely remembered hearing of his exploits before her capture, but now the stories came back to her recollection more vividly.

He no longer sported the long, golden curls so often mentioned in the articles about him. He had to be the only Federal officer whose appearance was as commented upon as his deeds of valor. And his deeds were impressive. No wonder the Lowells were so in awe of him.

Randall emerged through the side door an hour later and this time he saw Eden squarely as she knelt behind the bar and replaced many of the magazine issues she had completed.

"Mrs. Murdoch," sputtered the obviously startled young captain. "I . . . I didn't expect to find you here."

The poor man looked so ill at ease, Eden had to pity him. The edges of his ears turned such a bright shade of scarlet, she thought they might burst into flame at any moment.

"I was just leaving, actually." She struggled to pull herself into an upright stance. "I was following your suggestion, you see."

"Yes, yes." He strode over, leaned down, and offered her his hand, while Hugh propped his chin on his elbows at the other side of the bar to watch the action.

"I was just on my way to visit you, Mrs. Murdoch," Brad said as he pulled her to her feet.

"Sounds like you get the chance to walk this fine young lady home, Brad."

Eden did not care for the familiar way Hugh Christie spoke to her, but politely thanked him for the loan of his reading collection. Any man who liked to read could not be all bad. She had often thought that, if Hanging Road had been born in the white world, he would have read voraciously. She had never encountered a man who hungered after knowledge with such intensity.

A tiny pain stabbed her heart with the memory once again that Hanging Road was now dead. She had to remind herself of this fact and break the habit of three and a half years of thinking of him as a partner in her life. Hanging Road, Red Feather Woman, Nightwalking, little Gray Wolf—dead, all dead. She would never see their faces again, never hear their laughter, never listen to the hypnotic music of Hanging Road's flute round their fire in the evening, either entertaining them or lulling them gently to sleep.

Now Hanging Road would never make good on his promise to take her to the Sacred Spring whose legendary maiden was her namesake. How many long hours had he spent telling of his pilgrimages there. The way he described it, the place sounded as supernatural as he claimed it to be. Yet she was of a stubbornly realistic frame of mind. She required proof of everything. Hanging Road used to tease her about this characteristic, this flaw, so common to the white race.

His stories about the mystical healing powers of the Sacred Spring made it seem as lost in time as the Cheyenne maiden whose spirit resided in its waters and imparted its wondrous healing qualities. Hanging Road called the maiden Seota. But had she been a Cheyenne maiden or a Pawnee, or perhaps a Kansa, a Lakota, a Comanche? All the plains dwellers shared the myth and each had their own manner of telling it. All gave the maiden a different name. All came to make sacrifices there, to bathe in the sacred waters, or to drink them. Intertribal hostilities were suspended when they came to the Sacred Spring.

But did it even exist outside Hanging Road's imagination? Eden sometimes wondered. He spoke of it so concretely, described it so precisely, it must be real. Somewhere up along the fork of the Solomon, that was all she knew for sure about its location. A huge limestone dome rose out of the earth, eight times the height of a man and five times in breadth. At its center lay a mystical circle of bubbling cold water like a giant eye staring at the heavens.

Eden checked herself. She must stop thinking about Hanging Road and the sisters and her old life, just as she once told herself to stop thinking of her life as it existed before she met them.

Upon leaving the saloon, Brad Randall courteously offered her his arm as they traversed the wooden sidewalk. This bit of gallantry surprised Eden. Perhaps he

did not feel so superior to her now that she knew of his recent indiscretion.

"Captain Randall, I'd be obliged if you did not mention to the Lowells where you found me this afternoon. They don't approve of Mr. Christie and would take offense at my having gone to his establishment."

"I would hope that I might ask a similar bit of discretion from you, Mrs. Murdoch. I was, of course, just visiting a friend."

"Who just happens to be a prostitute." She tried to keep from smiling.

Brad pulled his broad-brimmed hat off and raked his fingers through his hair.

"Captain, I apologize if I am not quite the innocent you hoped I was. I spent three years working in and around army encampments during the war. I know how those type of women earn their living. I'm not trying to embarrass you. I just don't fancy artifice, especially if it serves no purpose."

"I . . . I'm not proud of my actions. I have no explanation, no excuse."

"I am not in a position to pass judgment on others, I assure you."

"Our situations are in no way similar. A right-thinking person would never hold less of an opinion of you for your ordeal, Mrs. Murdoch. You had no choice."

Eden smiled strangely and turned to look up at her tall, lean escort. She studied his firm jaw and broad, clear brow that hooded his gray eyes. She noted that the wound on his forehead had faded to a dark pink crease now.

Her mind fell back to an evening nearly a year and a half into memory when she had made a decision to willingly break her marriage vows to Lawrence Murdoch. She tried to justify her decision on the grounds that she would never see him again, that he might have been killed in the war, but the truth remained that she was still married by the laws of God and man and she wanted to break those laws.

She and Hanging Road had gone off together on a mission to find a particular plant he thought would yield spectacular healing results. The plant had been described to him by a medicine man in another village. They traveled for two days following a river's course south, stopping to examine the undergrowth along its banks every mile or two.

She knew why he had brought her along on the little expedition. He did not require her assistance or her company, though he enjoyed both. Rather, he did not like leaving her alone in the village. He did not admit it, but she could tell he still worried about her safety. A faction in the Cheyenne band still harbored a lingering fear and suspicion of her.

Whatever the reason, she relished her journey with him. She liked having him all to herself, even though he seldom gave her or anyone his undivided attention. The natural world and the spiritual world encompassing it fascinated him too completely.

The days were still hot along the trail at that time of year, but the evenings had begun to grow delightfully cooler. On the second night out, she and Hanging Road had laid their sleeping robes side by side and watched

the moon rise and make its journey across the sky.

"Are we near the Sacred Spring?" she had asked.

"No, we're far from that. The spring lies near the fork of the Solomon, probably a seven- or eight-day ride from here."

She bided her time as she worked up the courage to ask what she really wanted to ask. But how does a woman ask her husband of two years that she wants him to finally consummate their marriage? So much time had passed, the whole subject had become awkward to broach.

"Are we really married? Do you consider me your wife?"

He nodded as he chewed on the stem of a sweet blade of grass.

"And yet you don't treat me as your wife . . . in some regards." She turned her face to study his reaction by the flickering light of the campfire.

He tossed her a curious frown, as though suppressing a smile.

"Have you ever thought that we might have a child together someday?" she blurted out.

He chuckled, taking her true meaning. "Of course I have."

She sat up and looked down upon him in surprise. "You have?"

"I wouldn't be a normal man if I didn't, would I?"

She did not have an answer for this. She had long since assumed he found her ugly or repulsive. She had accepted the fact that theirs was a marriage of convenience, that he did not bear her the same affection he obviously felt for Red Feather. And Nightwalking, that was another matter entirely. She knew he thought of her as an older sister, not a wife. He had married her to honor his slain brother and both parties accepted the relationship as such.

But Eden wanted a child desperately.

"I've always worried that it wouldn't be safe for you to bear a child, Seota. After what that Kiowa did to you. I don't know. It could be dangerous. Didn't those soldier doctors you worked for teach you anything about that?"

"No, they didn't, as a matter of fact. There was a war on. They only treated soldiers."

Soldiers and—one hot July day—a pregnant woman. Baby Samuel had decided to arrive abruptly while she had been at work. For hours, she had tried to work through the labor pains. Finally, they grew so powerful, she could not remain standing or even speak as they came upon her. When Surgeon Brinkley observed this, he knew instantly what Eden sought to keep secret.

An empty bed was found for her and Brinkley delivered the baby amid the sounds of bursting shells less than half a mile distant. A throng of nearly three dozen wounded soldiers watched in awe as a new life came into the world amid so much death and destruction. Many wept and all applauded when the surgeon shouted, "It's a boy!"

"I'm not afraid to take the risk, Ameo. Truly, I'm not. I feel completely healthy and normal."

He smiled up at her ruefully, then reached out his arms to pull her close. "If you're sure."

"I'm sure. I've never been more sure. I want a child. I want a dozen!"

"I can't feed a dozen," he said with a grin. "You know how much I hate to hunt."

"You don't really know anything about me, Captain Randall. You know nothing of my life for the last four years."

Brad cocked his head to one side. "I know a good deal more about you than you think, Mrs. Murdoch. Or should I say . . . Seota."

She gasped. She had never heard a white man utter that name before. "Who have you been talking to? Who told you that was my name?"

"I spoke with some elderly women on the trip from Camp Supply to Fort Dodge."

"How are they getting on?" She was intent on changing the subject. "Your prisoners, I mean."

"Fine all around, I think. Even the wounded ones were able to make the trip. Only two required transport in an ambulance. All the rest could sit a horse."

"Good," Eden murmured. As they walked toward the Lowell home, several passersby noticed them, some rudely pointing, others merely staring.

A boy, tall and lanky but still in knee pants, waited for them to pass, then shouted, "Injun whore!"

Brad halted and turned to launch a furious retort.

"No, no," Eden begged. "Let's just walk on. He's only a child. Please." Eden was much more offended by the grown women who made a point of crossing the street to avoid her.

"All right," Brad sighed angrily. He grasped her arm more tightly and hurried them quickly along the sidewalk. "I would like to continue with our first topic, Mrs. Murdoch. I wonder why the old women I spoke to last week were afraid to talk about you. They were afraid of some kind of retribution, and not from the government, from you . . . Seota."

"That's silly," she said with an awkward smile. "You cannot seriously believe I could harm anyone."

"According to my informants, you are capable of killing scores of enemies, at a whim."

"You don't believe that." They reached the yard of the Lowell house and paused before mounting the porch steps.

"I don't know what to believe anymore," he said with such a miserable and wayward exasperation, Eden did not know if he referred to her or to some larger question. He looked down at her with a penetrating intensity. "They told me someone hurt you, hurt you very badly, and you took revenge on the entire tribe by making them ill."

"That's absurd."

"You said you were a trained nurse. I could not wholly dismiss the proposition."

She sighed with annoyance. "They are possibly referring to a smallpox epidemic. I don't think I could be held accountable for that, do you?"

"Someone hurt you, they said. A Kiowa? What did he do?"

Brad watched a terrible shadow cross Eden Murdoch's delicate features. Her chin trembled slightly. "What did they say? What did they tell you?"

"Just that he physically abused you in some terrible way."

"Nothing more?"

He shook his head, feeling he had crossed some line he had not fully intended to cross.

Mary Lowell burst from the front door to the porch at just that moment. "Mrs. Murdoch, you've had us ever so worried. Where have you been, dear? Bonnie Sue said you left this morning to take a walk, and now it's almost gone to supper."

"She was with me, Mrs. Lowell." Brad glanced down to see Eden's fierce expression melt into a grateful half-smile. "I am just returned from business at Fort Dodge and Mrs. Murdoch has graciously agreed to teach me some words and phrases in Cheyenne."

"Well, that's a relief. I was worried sick. I just didn't know what to think."

"I'm sorry, Mrs. Lowell," Eden said. "Truly, I didn't mean to cause you alarm."

"Now Captain Randall, you must stay to supper. You will, won't you?"

"What a kind offer. I'd enjoy that very much."

As they followed Mrs. Lowell into the house, Eden whispered, "Words and phrases in Cheyenne?"

"Would you?"

"Are you serious?"

"Very much so."

"To what end? Do you wish to greet them and po-

litely inquire after the state of their health before you
kill them?"

"I don't appreciate your sarcasm, Mrs. Murdoch. For
your information, I would like to learn these skills in
anticipation of *peaceful* negotiations. Surely you cannot
criticize that."

She did not give an immediate answer, but busied
herself hanging up Mary's shawl and taking Brad's hat
and coat.

The Lowell children descended upon the entryway
once they heard the sounds of a visitor. They quickly
spirited Brad off to the parlor, while Eden wandered toward the kitchen to see if she could make herself useful.

Twelve

That night, for the first time, Eden joined the Lowell
family for dinner. She felt responsible for Captain Randall's dinner invitation, almost as though he were her
guest and she felt obligated to attend.

Mary seated her opposite Brad at the center of the
table, between the youngest daughter, Annie, and the
boy, Josiah. The twelve-year-old girl, Sarah, sat next to
Brad and Eden could tell by the dazzled expression on
the young girl's face that she had already developed a
crush on their tall guest in his dashing cavalry uniform.

Mr. Lowell asked the family to bow their heads for
grace. Eden stared off into space with a vacant expression. Mr. Lowell glanced up at her suspiciously several
times during the short prayer of thanks for the Lord's
bounty.

"Mrs. Murdoch, did my prayer of thanks offend you in some way?" inquired Elias Lowell. He carved the duck as he spoke.

"Offend me? No, not at all."

Mary tactfully changed the subject, wishing to shift the focus to her guest. "Captain Randall, what is your opinion of the newly elected president?"

"I hope he will perform the duties of the office well," offered Brad. He did not know whether to mention that Amanda's father was a close friend of Grant's. He feared it would sound like bragging. He really wondered what kind of president the general would make. He had never thought of him as a politician. "You know, I believe there was not a single man in all of Fort Dodge last month that even remembered Election Day when it occurred."

"You were no doubt busy preparing for your big campaign against the hostiles," remarked Lowell. "Far too preoccupied to concern yourselves with *political* campaigns."

"Well put, Mr. Lowell," said his adoring wife.

"And entirely correct," said Brad. "I came out west with General Custer and he had only a few weeks to drill his troops and prepare them for battle. In any case, the concerns back in the States seem so far away when one is outside them."

This innocent observation upset Mary Lowell. "When are people going to start to recognize that Kansas is indeed a state? Everywhere I go, I continually hear people talking about how they are *outside the States* or

that they are *returning* to the States when they prepare to leave here."

"Oh, Mrs. Lowell, calm yourself," said her husband. "Such a trivial matter."

The well-mannered Lowell children giggled at this and Brad glanced across the table to Eden, comically raising his eyebrows in an expression of *I'd better watch what I say more carefully.*

"I can't help it. That's how I feel," said Mary Lowell.

Eden had to admire the gentle way Mary stood up to her husband occasionally.

"What are you getting for Christmas, Captain Randall?" asked little Annie Lowell.

Brad swallowed his mouthful of mashed potatoes and smiled at the blond seven-year-old. "I may not get anything. The mail shipments are not as prompt as one would hope."

"What do you want to get?" the little girl persisted.

"Hush, child," scolded her father. "We need not pester our guest with such personal questions."

"That's all right," Brad said. "What do I want? Warmer weather, more socks, and . . . to get married soon." He carefully avoided looking at Eden when he said this, but turned to face her directly when he concluded with, "Most of all, peace on these plains."

"Here, here," said Elias Lowell. "Certainly a fitting toast to the season." He raised his glass of cider. "To peace."

Everyone raised their glasses and drank the toast.

As they resumed their meal, Mrs. Lowell said to the

captain, "The ladies of the church wanted me to ask if you and your men might like to attend the small social gathering we are planning on Christmas Eve. We feel sorry for all you brave men so far from your loved ones on the holiday and all."

"Why, Mrs. Lowell, your offer is a delightful one. I'm sure I speak for all the men of my detail in heartily accepting your generous invitation."

Mary beamed and the Lowell children squirmed with delight at the prospect of the cavalry troopers attending the church Christmas party. Eden realized just how much the Lowells and probably the townspeople of Reliance held the cavalry in awe and respect.

After the meal, Brad told the Lowells he needed a word alone with Mrs. Murdoch. They allowed him the use of their parlor and made themselves and the children busy in the kitchen where they set about to decorate holiday cookies and cakes for the coming party.

"Cheyenne lessons?" Eden inquired.

"Yes." Brad placed himself in a chair opposite her settee.

She sighed. "I have mixed feelings about cooperating with you in the slightest. Why would I wish to do anything to make it easier for the government to make war on the Cheyennes?"

"We may not be making war any longer."

Eden frowned skeptically.

"I've heard rumors that Grant wants peace. We may

well spend the winter negotiating rather than fighting."

"*General* Grant? A peace advocate?"

"*President-elect* Grant. And yes, that's exactly what I've heard. My fiancée's father travels somewhat close to Grant's inner circle. He serves in the War Department. Congress votes this month on whether to transfer authority over the Indians to the War Department or leave it in the Department of the Interior."

Brad hesitated to say more. He knew that information about Eden was already being prepared for dissemination to the newspapers. He had himself sent a report by courier to Custer, who had now proceeded to Fort Cobb.

The New York Times had printed Colonel Edward Wynkoop's angry letter declaring his resignation as Indian agent for the Cheyennes and Arapahos. The paper ran a rebuttal by General Sheridan the next day, vilifying Black Kettle as a dangerous troublemaker and claiming his band had led recent raids along the Arkansas, as well as having held a white woman captive for four years. The paper, in an editorial the following day, sided with Sheridan and congratulated Custer on his great victory.

Brad knew Custer himself had been contacted to write a magazine article on the battle. He also knew Custer's writing skills to be far more persuasive and eloquent than Little Phil's and what use he might make of Mrs. Murdoch's story could be easily imagined. Poor Eden Murdoch. She would soon be a national celebrity, with or without her permission.

"If you wished to spend more time reading at Mr.

Christie's, I could certainly offer an excuse to the Lowells for your absences." He added this in a low voice, should the Lowells be eavesdropping.

"I would appreciate that," Eden murmured. Her expression softened.

"I already know a few words of Cheyenne," he boasted with an eager smile.

Eden looked attentive and appeared impressed.

Brad pulled out of his jacket a note pad. "The Cheyenne women, the prisoners I guided to Fort Dodge, they called me 'Ve-ho-oxha-esta' . . . I think."

Eden smiled broadly. "They called you 'Tall Whiteman'."

He looked faintly disappointed at this prosaic appellation. "Did I pronounce it correctly?"

"Close."

"What does Seota mean?"

Eden shrugged. "Ghost Woman. Dead Woman—something like that. E'kotsemeo, that is, Hanging Road, gave me the name because I reminded him of a woman in a legend who dove into a spring—a sacred spring—to save her wounded lover and was never seen again. Her spirit still resides in the water and gives it healing powers."

"Hanging Road?"

"Yes," she said cautiously. "He was . . . a medicine man." So strange to speak of him in the past tense.

"Hanging Road, that's a pretty frightening name, itself."

"Oh, no, not at all." Eden shook her head with a sudden smile. "It refers to that bright band of stars

across the sky that you can see on clear nights. That's the Hanging Road. The dead travel that road to reach Seyan."

He looked up from scribbling notes on his little pad. "Heaven?"

"Not exactly. It was simply the place of the dead. Everyone went there, I think. They did not believe in a hell."

Brad nodded thoughtfully, then made more notes. "Tell me more about the smallpox epidemic."

"There is really nothing more to tell."

Brad studied her. He could tell she was debating whether to reveal more. If only he could gain her confidence, convince her to confide in him. Her glimpses into this foreign world held him enthralled. He no longer sought to gather information for his commanding officers. He had already supplied them with what they wished. Now he wanted to learn for his own education.

"If everyone in the village fell ill, you must have had the opportunity to escape," he prompted.

"Yes . . . that's true." Her eyes wandered to some vague location, far away from the small, well-furnished parlor. "But how could I? I was a nurse. Treating the sick. That's all I've ever done. That's all I know how to do. So much suffering, so much misery and death. I almost left one afternoon. I'd gone to fetch water, alone, no one watching me. No one would ever have seen my departure. I could have stolen a horse, undetected. I had planned to do so often enough. But when I reached the river I saw a young child, a little boy of no more than two years. He was crying and pulling at the hand of his mother who lay in a delirium on the ground. He looked to me for help. He couldn't understand that his mother had fallen ill, that she was near the point of death. I could not turn my back on such suffering."

Eden narrowed her amber-green eyes as she looked back into the past. "I can still remember how hot it was that afternoon. How the flies had swarmed over the woman's pox-covered flesh. I managed to pick her up in my arms and carry her back to the village. Her little child tagged along, tugging at my skirts. I did not know the woman personally, but only a month before two women, two sisters, all but strangers to me, had shown me a similar kindness, for no other reason than that I was a fellow human being."

As one in a trance, Eden rose and crossed the room to where Brad sat in the small, velvet-upholstered side chair with its carved walnut arms. He sat up apprehensively as she approached. She delicately placed two fingers on the flesh of his throat, just at the spot of his carotid artery. He looked up into her face and beheld the strange, eerie calm of her slight smile. Where ordinarily he might feel arousal at such an intimate touch by a woman to his throat, his reaction was a disquieting fear, like the cold sweat of his awakening from the horrifying nightmare of the warrior with the necklace of human fingers. His breath came quickly. He grasped the carved arms of the chair more tightly. What was she up to? Why did she touch him in this odd way?

"It all comes down to this," she whispered.

"To what?" he asked in a hoarse voice, still feeling

the pressure of her fingertips on his artery as it pounded fiercely against them.

"The rhythm of a pulse. It's the same in all. Man or woman. Red or white or black or yellow. It all comes down to this." She dropped her hand and returned to the settee, fanning out her skirts gently as she sat down.

Brad felt bathed in relief when she left his side. She made him uncomfortable. So ridiculous and yet he had to admit it. Her eerie calm bothered him the most. Her anger had been easy to deal with by comparison. She sat on that gaudy sofa looking like a Renaissance Madonna. Was she a demon . . . or a saint? An angel of mercy or an angel of death? What had those savages done to her in those four years?

A gentle knock at the parlor doors broke the spell.

"You must take some holiday treats with you, Captain Randall," said Mary Lowell as she peeked into the parlor. "I'm sorry, did I disturb you?"

"Not at all." He rose from his chair with a broad smile. He was plainly relieved to see her enter the room.

The remainder of the Lowell family followed. Their festive mood brought life and spirit into the little parlor. Lively chatter replaced the exotic aura left by Eden's remarks. Brad laughed and talked with the family on a variety of Christmas-related topics and barely noticed Eden's departure from the room until the etched-glass parlor doors rattled as they closed.

Everyone looked up, startled.

"Perhaps I should be leaving," said Brad.

Mary rose and ushered the children off to bed.

"Don't rush off," insisted Elias Lowell. "We enjoy your company so much."

"I fear I've done or said something to upset Mrs. Murdoch."

"If we worried ourselves every time Mrs. Murdoch abruptly leaves a room or starts to cry or does something bizarre and completely without reason, we would have no peace at all, Captain."

"Has she been behaving strangely?" Brad worried that there might have been a recurrence of her outrageously immodest behavior in the barbershop.

Lowell stretched his long legs out before him on the settee and removed his spectacles. He pulled a handkerchief from his vest pocket and cleaned them with it. "Three nights ago, the weather grew unexpectedly stormy. Too warm to snow, it thundered and pelted us with a cold, hard rain that later turned to ice. Our daughter Sarah woke us up at an unconscionable hour to tell us that Mrs. Murdoch was standing in the yard, amid the thunder and the lightning, soaked to the skin. My daughter had called to her repeatedly and the woman acted as though she did not hear. I was forced to don a rain slicker and go out into the storm to drag her indoors. We feared she'd catch her death, but she seems to have survived the incident."

"Did she give a reason for her behavior?"

The minister shook his head. "She was sobbing and talking in that blasted, infernal savage tongue, saying something over and over. I finally slapped her face. With my wife's permission, of course. I can assure you, I do not normally go around slapping women in the face, but

I did not know how else to bring her to her senses. I wanted to summon Dr. Ashcroft, but Mrs. Lowell wouldn't let me. She feared the doctor would recommend that she be put in an asylum. She's convinced that all Mrs. Murdoch needs is to be reunited with her father. I, however, have my doubts."

"I shall call on her tomorrow," Brad said. "I will keep an eye on her so that you and your wife are not so troubled."

Thirteen

Undoubtedly this war would have been prevented had Congress made an appropriation
for the purpose of continuing the supply of
subsistence to these Indians [required by
treaty], thus following the dictates of humanity and justice. The expenditure of a few
thousands would have saved millions to the
country.

—EDWARD WYNKOOP, CHEYENNE AND ARAPAHO INDIAN
AGENT, REPORT TO THE COMMISSIONER OF
INDIAN AFFAIRS

Brad called for Eden at the Lowells' house promptly at
nine the next morning, as he had promised. He re-
hearsed a happy, smiling countenance to chase away the
pall left by the dream that had awakened him before
dawn. The same dream as always. The warrior wearing
a necklace of human fingers bent over him and threatened his frozen, death-stilled body with a large cere-
monial knife.

"Why, Mrs. Murdoch, you look stunning," he exclaimed as she showed off the black silk taffeta dress
Mary Lowell had made for her as an early Christmas gift.
White braid accented the bodice and sleeves, with
white lace adorning the high collar and cuffs. The full

skirt wafted in an airy circle about her as she twirled to display the garment for Captain Randall's appreciation.

A beaming Mary Lowell asked Eden to go upstairs and retrieve a dark shawl from the clothes press in the Lowell bedroom. "That shawl will set the dress off just perfect, dear, and you'll need something for your shoulders. The morning's turned out nice and warm for December, but there's still a chill in the air."

The moment Eden disappeared up the stairs, Mrs. Lowell leaned close to Brad Randall to speak in confidential tones.

"I learned a new bit of information on our dear Mrs. Murdoch, Captain. You seem to care about her and I thought you might want to know."

"Indeed I do, ma'am."

"Well, the other day the three of us—that would be me and Mrs. Murdoch and my girl Sarah—were out in the yard hanging the wash to dry. Well, I got called to the kitchen by Bonnie Sue—one of her usual disasters in the making—and when I came back, Mrs. Murdoch was giving Sarah quite a talking-to.

"You see, Sarah was all pouty and carrying on because Mr. Lowell and I have decided to send her to school in St. Louis next year and she doesn't want to leave home and all. She's been fretting about it and giving us all grief—"

"And Mrs. Murdoch?" Brad prompted to keep Mary Lowell's story on track.

"When I came back I could hear the two of them talking and they didn't know I was there because of all the sheets on the line. Well, anyway, Mrs. Murdoch tells

Sarah she must never disobey her parents because they know what's best for her even when she don't. And Sarah gives some flighty response like young girls sometimes do and Mrs. Murdoch says, 'I learned that lesson the hard way, Sarah. Trust me. I married against my father's wishes and I lived to rue the day in more ways than you can count.' "

Mrs. Lowell concluded her account with a triumphant smile just as Eden returned to join them.

Brad paid more solicitous compliments to the two ladies while he mulled over the new information. The possibility that there had been trouble in the Murdoch marriage had previously occurred to him. Eden had exhibited a great reluctance to speak of her late husband. Her vagueness seemed tinged with something other than traditional grief. Now he cast her odd reticence into a deeper range of speculation.

Eden left the house on the captain's arm with an almost joyful feeling, the first day she had felt truly happy in many weeks. They talked about the Christmas season and how Brad would bring his men to attend the Christmas Eve party at the Lowells' church.

"My men are all quite excited about it," he said as they rounded the corner to Main Street and stepped up onto the wooden sidewalk. "I think they hope they'll get to meet young ladies there."

"Tell them not to get too excited," she warned with a smile. "I've seen some of these church ladies. First of all, they are few in number. Second, most are married.

And third, well, beauty is in the eye of the beholder, but . . ."

Brad threw back his head in a laugh. "You must recall that my men aren't much to look at, either."

They neared Hugh Christie's nameless saloon and quickened their pace, ignoring the occasional gawking passerby.

"Do you think you might spend some time teaching me the Cheyenne language, Mrs. Murdoch?"

"You're still serious about that?"

"Absolutely."

"Do you swear you would use such knowledge for only a peaceful purpose?"

"Upon my life." He placed his right hand over his heart and looked sincere and guileless. He could feel the press of his grandmother's wedding ring against his bare flesh where it hung tethered on its chain as always.

On those occasions when he had lain abed with Tessa wearing nothing but the ring, he had entertained guilty imaginings of the ring suddenly turning white-hot and searing the flesh beneath it in punishment for his carnal transgressions.

He envisioned himself left with an ugly red scar as a vivid reminder of his sin. He thought about a book he had read once of a convicted adulteress in Puritan times who was forced to wear the letter *A* embroidered on her bodice to mark her shame for all to see. He felt an ugly red scar on his chest was the very least punishment he was entitled to for consorting with whores.

He knocked at the closed door of Christie's bar.

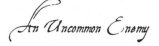

They waited. He knocked again. A commotion was heard from within and the tousled head of the proprietor appeared in the door, once it finally opened.

"Oh, Lord, you caught me sleeping late," Hugh said as he ushered them into the saloon without further ceremony.

"I'm sorry, Hugh. We didn't mean to rouse you from your bed."

"It's not a problem. I just forgot you all were coming. Had a late night."

Eden tucked a smile away at Hugh Christie's disheveled appearance. His long, curly dark hair flew in all directions, even more wildly than usual. He hiked up his suspenders and pulled on a vest coat over them as he stuffed his long shirttail into his trousers.

"I know my way," Eden said and proceeded to the back of the bar to retrieve an armload of magazines. She returned and seated herself at a table with good light streaming in from the front window. She positioned herself so that the shutter of the window blocked a view of her from any passersby on the street.

"I'll just step back here and get some coffee going," said Hugh.

"Let me take care of that," offered Brad. "Mrs. Murdoch has graciously consented to allow me to spend the day with her."

Christie pulled down a tin coffeepot from a shelf and directed Brad to the back of the saloon for access to the pump. He then returned to his lodgings upstairs saying he wanted to "get presentable."

Eden plunged into her reading, but soon found herself interrupted by Brad, who set before them steaming cups of coffee.

"I have some news to share, Mrs. Murdoch. I wanted to wait until we were comfortable and alone here."

"What have you heard?"

"I have managed to answer a question that has been troubling me from the start. I could never understand why there seemed to be no information on your capture. The army always takes these matters very seriously and I couldn't figure out why no one seemed to know of it. I think now I have an explanation though it seems to be a very strange story. I have verified this information with a man in charge of post records at Fort Riley. When your coach was overdue at its next stop, a search party was sent out. They found the coach just where you indicated—two days west of Fort Riley on the usual route.

"The bodies in the coach were burned past recognition, so they were unable to make a positive identification, but all persons traveling on the stagecoach that day were accounted for when compared to the passenger manifest supplied by the stage line. Thus no search party was ever sent to look for you."

He watched as Eden digested his hurried words. He wondered how all the passengers listed by the Overland Express Company could have been found. Eden Murdoch seemed more like a ghost woman than ever.

"No one came looking," Eden murmured vacantly. "No one came looking."

*   *   *

The coach had been overloaded that day so close to Christmas, with everyone trying to reach their destination before the holiday. Even the many reports coming out about the growing Indian peril did not dissuade them. Eden would have braved any danger for this promised and longed-for reunion with her father.

She recalled the coach's occupants with indelible clarity, though she never learned their names. There was a soldier on leave from the fighting in the East traveling home to reach his parents' farm on the western border.

Two businessmen were returning to Denver City after an unsuccessful trip to St. Louis to raise capital for a gold mining venture.

A woman of about fifty and her fourteen-year-old grandson were returning to her son's home, near Denver City. The pair had traveled east to bury the mother of the boy with her family in Michigan. The woman gave a long explanation of why the boy's father did not accompany them to bury his wife in the East, but Eden had briefly dozed off before the story ended.

Two young men rode cheaply outside the coach. They braved the prairie December, bound for the California coast. The two businessmen gossiped about the young men riding outside. They must be deserters from the army, they surmised. Why else would two able-bodied young men not be in uniform?

The young soldier agreed. He allowed as how every person able to do so should serve the war effort in whatever way they could.

"I served the war effort." Eden spoke up with pride.

The two businessmen chuckled in disbelief.

"Bet you was a nurse," said the young soldier.

"Yes, I was." Those had been happy, busy days, filled with such a sense of purpose. She had worked right through her pregnancy with little Samuel, garnering the stern disapproval of the woman who owned the boardinghouse in which she lived.

Of course, even she had to admit that working while obviously pregnant flew in the face of all that was sacred, holy, and enshrined about motherhood and social propriety. But there was a war on and ordinary rules no longer applied. That was what she told herself to justify her actions, not the least of which was the outright disobedience to her husband Lawrence's command that she stop working after their marriage.

"Why must I stop?" she had cried on the day before he left to return to his regiment after their brief honeymoon.

"I will not have my wife in such an environment."

"But that's how I met you."

"You are Mrs. Lawrence Murdoch now and you will comport yourself in a manner above reproach. Your . . . unconventional behavior was the talk of that hospital ward. As a single girl you may have flaunted your charms in any manner you chose, but—"

"Lawrence, I never flaunted myself at all. I dress as plainly as a spinster schoolmarm. All I need is a wimple and I could pass for one of the Catholic sisters."

He had sighed with exasperation. "That aside, I do not wish to have my wife seeing—"

"Sights unfit for virgin eyes? Lawrence, I'm not a

virgin anymore and, believe me when I tell you, I've seen sights unfit for *anyone's* eyes!"

His reply to this impudent assertion, intended by Eden as a humorous remark, was a hard cuff across the face which knocked her to the floor. After that, she dropped the subject of the nursing work. Lawrence spent the last night of his honeymoon out with two friends in a tavern. The next morning, after a silent breakfast, he gave her a brief kiss on the forehead and left to catch the train that would return him to service in Virginia. Eden waited only until he left her sight before she donned her plain gray nursing apron and departed for the hospital as though nothing had happened.

Surgeon Brinkley was delighted to see her. He congratulated her once again on her nuptials, then asked, somewhat hesitantly, about the bruise on her cheek. Before she could think of a reply, a train of ambulances arrived with newly wounded.

She saw her husband only twice during the long, lonely nine months of her pregnancy. It was on the second visit that he discovered her disobedience to his wishes. Eden guessed that the disapproving landlady had to have been the one to tell him where she was when he showed up in Washington a day earlier than he had originally planned.

At least he had behaved like a gentleman in the hospital, quietly telling her it was time to leave. The moment they reached the street, he started in. "How dare you parade around this town and work in that horrid place, looking like you do?"

"They needed me, Lawrence. The hospital is desperately shorthanded. I dug a bullet out of a man's arm with a penknife yesterday. There was no surgeon free to do it."

"Shut your impudent mouth. When we get home, I'm going to teach you a lesson you will never forget!"

She said nothing more as they walked back to the boarding house. She knew her pregnant appearance was a shock to him. She was nearly through the seventh month, a great change from the last time he had been home. Then she had only been four months along and barely showing at all.

Lawrence was right, she would never forget what happened when they reached home. Even the miserable old shrew of a landlady had gotten frightened enough to summon the authorities. When the military police arrived, they did not do much, they simply told Lawrence he would have to leave the premises or they would place him under arrest.

Eden hated to remember that terrible day. She closed her mind to the memory as she rode on the Overland Express coach. The stage line had its own military escort, a detail of six soldiers whose long and tiresome days were occasionally punctuated by brief moments of mortal danger.

When the coach unexpectedly lurched to a stop in the middle of the vacant prairie, the fourteen-year-old boy climbed halfway out the window to see what was the matter. Everyone leaned forward anxiously. Eden clutched her sleeping baby to her chest.

"Help us, help us," cried a woman's voice, barely

audible over the sighing prairie winds. The driver got down from his seat and walked round to inform the passengers of the situation.

"We saw the smoke in the distance," he explained. "The troopers went off to investigate over yonder there."

The passengers all strained for a look outside. The two businessmen climbed out, followed by the young boy. The older woman stayed behind with Eden, who wished she could step out herself, if for no other reason than to stretch her cramped legs, but she did not want to wake baby Samuel. Poor little Samuel, who had never even met his soldier-father and, if Eden had her way, never would.

Out the small window, she could see a dwelling in the distance, smoke pouring from its roof, far more than a normal stove or fireplace would produce. She could see someone half walking, half running toward them who was soon met by two of the troopers on horseback.

Within minutes the cavalrymen returned with a woman and her toddler. The young woman's face and dress were covered with black soot from fighting the fire at her homestead. The little child, who appeared to be a boy, though it was hard to tell, was likewise blackened from the soot.

The woman trembled as she spoke in short bursts to the troopers. "You've got to find him, you've got to find him!"

"Your husband, ma'am?" asked the lieutenant.

"He's gone, he's gone and they burned everything and they didn't find us and you've got to go looking for him and what if he comes home and we're not there? He'll not know what's become of us!"

"Calm down, ma'am. We'll find your husband."

"All is lost, all is lost," she fretted, insensible to those around her.

"Bring her and the kid on inside," said the driver. "We'll take her to Fort Larned."

"You may not want to stop at Larned," said the lieutenant. "We heard there was cholera there. We were planning to ride on ahead and see about it before you all reached there, but now we'll be off to chase these Indians. When we'll be back, I can't say exactly."

Eden recoiled at the mention of the word "cholera." She had watched the dreadful disease kill more soldiers than bullets or shells once an outbreak got started in a camp or a hospital.

The driver frowned and looked around as if the prairie horizon could give him some kind of answer. "Well, I don't know what to say. But we'll take her someplace."

"Grandma, can I ride outside?" asked the young boy. "The lady and her kid can have my seat."

"Oh, I guess so," his grandmother called, not looking too happy at the prospect.

"Good boy," said the lieutenant with a smile. He tried to encourage the young woman and her child to enter the coach, but she resisted.

"I have to stay. He might come back. I need to be here if he comes back."

"Ma'am, we're going off looking for your husband and for the Indians what done this to your house. We'll

find 'em. Don't you worry. Get on in that carriage and get yourself and your child to safety. That's the best way you can help your husband."

The woman continued her deranged fretfulness.

"Come and sit with me," Eden called to the woman in a calm and cordial voice, as if they were attending a Sunday social in a park. "I have a baby, too. We shall talk and keep each other company."

The woman turned with a look of confusion, then nodded faintly. Eden smiled and held out her hand. She knew from experience in the hospitals that speaking to an irrational person in a soft and ordinary manner often reached them in ways shouting and reasoning did not.

The lieutenant and the stage driver helped the woman and her child up into the coach while the other men remained outside and discussed the situation in tense, low voices.

Soon the coach set out once more, but lacking its military escort. Eden never saw the soldiers again.

"My father—he was told I had perished?" Eden asked Brad.

"I suppose so." He sat back and watched her for several seconds. "I'm sorry."

"It's not your fault."

"Think how happy he will be when he learns the truth."

She sat silently with an odd, unreadable expression on her face.

"If you don't feel like undertaking the lessons today, I can certainly understand. I don't mean to pressure you. It's just that my time here is so short."

Eden sighed. "Tell me what you want to say and I'll translate. Where do you wish to begin?"

"With 'hello'?"

Eden paused thoughtfully and looked puzzled. "I know you'll think it strange, but I don't know a Cheyenne word for 'hello.' "

Brad frowned in dismay, perplexed that his would-be teacher did not seem to know the simplest word in any given language.

"I'm sorry, but I really can't think of any such word. How about 'good day'?"

"Even better."

"Pahaveeseeva."

"Pah-va-shev," Brad carefully repeated, sounding out the syllables several times as he noted it in his book.

"*Ve'ho* is their word for 'white man.' "

"Vay-ho?"

"You're missing the little sound in the middle of the word," Eden corrected. "Say 'uh-oh.' "

"Uh-oh?"

"Did you hear that little sound you made in your throat?" When Brad grinned and nodded, she continued. "You'll have to learn to make that sound all the time if you're going to learn to speak the language of the Tsitsistas."

"*Ve'ho,*" Brad tried again, using the new pronunciation. "Does *ve* mean 'white' and *ho* mean 'man' or the other way around?"

"No, *ve'ho* actually means 'spider.' "

"How curious," Brad remarked, jotting another note to himself. He studied Eden's thin face and wished he could see inside her head. He longed to have an explanation for her strange behavior the night of the storm Elias Lowell had described.

"Mr. Christie told me there was a terrific thunderstorm the other evening, before I returned to Reliance. Odd weather for this time of year, don't you think?"

Eden looked up from her magazine and smiled. "The Winter Man usually fights the Thunder in the spring and fall, doesn't he?"

"The Winter Man?"

"It's a Cheyenne story."

"Please tell it. I'd like to hear."

She tilted her head at him with a searching look. "Really?" When he nodded emphatically, she proceeded. "When Heammawihio—the Creator—made the first man and the first woman, he put them in separate hemispheres, the Woman in the north and the Man in the south. The woman was given control of the Winter Man who represents the storm, the cold, the sickness. Death, too, I think. The Man in the south controls the Thunder. The Thunder gave the people fire to defend themselves against the cold, but twice a year the Thunder and the Winter Man do battle for control of the earth and each spring, Thunder drives the Winter Man far north and warm weather returns."

"And every fall, the opposite?"

"Precisely." Eden smiled warmly at Brad. "I could tell you a hundred stories."

"I wish you would. Where did you learn them?"

"The man I lived with, Hanging Road. I think he knew every story that could ever be imagined. He used to tell them every night. I can't tell them as well as he could. He would often paint the stories on the walls of our lodge. He was a wonderful artist. My favorite stories were always the ones about Sweet Medicine." In her mind, she always pictured Sweet Medicine to look like Hanging Road. She never told anyone this as she was afraid they might think it blasphemous, like remarking that someone looked like Jesus Christ.

"And who is Sweet Medicine? Their god?"

"No . . . he's more like a prophet, I think. Someone who came to the Cheyennes and taught them things. He brought the Sacred Arrows. The Sacred Arrows are very important, you must understand. I believe Hanging Road always secretly longed to be the Keeper of the Arrows. I think he wasn't chosen because he was . . . a little bit flighty at times, a little on the unreliable side. He was a deeply spiritual man, but sometimes he had trouble keeping track of the real world. He could forget to eat, forget to come home. Then he would just show up as though nothing whatsoever had happened.

"His childhood name was Whirlwind because he used to chase the dust devils that swirled around the prairie. Have you seen them? If you haven't yet, you will. They're like little miniature tornadoes. Anyway, I can just picture him as a little boy running off trying to catch a whirlwind." Eden could have gone on to tell Brad more about tornadoes and whirlwinds, but she didn't want to embarrass him.

The Cheyennes considered tornadoes to be potent phallic symbols, appearing in the spring when the earth came verdantly back to life. She, herself, had never fully adjusted to the free manner in which her Cheyenne family spoke of sexual matters. Even the sisters would join Hanging Road in making elaborate, bawdy jokes.

Hanging Road would often be the one to start it, making some teasingly boastful remark about how his appetites were so great not even three wives could satisfy him. Red Feather would take her cue and opine that she had not seen any evidence of this recently and Nightwalking would pretend to complain that she had not seen any evidence of this *at all*. Soon the playful insults would ricochet around the lodge with good-humored, risqué abandon while Eden—who had never spoken out loud of the marital act to anyone on earth including her husband, Lawrence Murdoch—sat blushing as red as a prairie sunset at the ribaldry of the proceedings.

Eden decided she had better change the subject.

"Ameo—that is, Hanging Road, but I called him Ameo—had a long, jagged scar along the edge of his chin that looked like a bolt of lightning." Eden dreamily traced the line of Hanging Road's scar on her own chin.

"From battle?"

"Oh, no. He would never have willingly engaged in fighting of any sort. He might defend himself or his loved ones, but that was all. No, he got the scar as a youth. He went out on a vision quest and had fasted I don't know how many days. Four, I suppose. Four is the sacred number. The last thing he remembered was standing on a rocky precipice and reaching for the sun. He thought he could touch it, but then he fainted dead away. He cracked his chin open when his face hit the rocks. He used to joke about it. He thought he was accident-prone. What? Why do you look at me so?"

Brad shook his head to dismiss her question, but he wanted to say, Whenever you reminisce about your Cheyenne family, you get the most luminous look in your eyes. How different from the face you wear at the mention of the late Lawrence Murdoch.

Eden continued, "I used to envy how Hanging Road viewed the world. Everything was alive to him. Everything had meaning. He believed in so many things that I could not comprehend. He used to believe the rain was a blessing, that if you stood out in it and let it pour over you, all your bad thoughts, your worries and cares, would be washed away." She turned a sad, rueful smile on Brad. "It doesn't work."

He paused before asking the question he could not remove from his mind. "You speak with such affection for this man whom you came to think of as your husband, but . . ." His voice trailed off. "Forgive me for asking this, but I still find it almost impossible to imagine how you could so completely forgive those people after what they did to you."

"The men who abducted me . . . treated me very badly, but Hanging Road never did. Would you blame one person for the actions of another?"

"Well, no, but—"

Eden cynically finished his line of thought: "But they're all Indians, right?"

"You think I'm narrow-minded, I suppose."

"You must understand how Ameo allowed me to help him heal the sick and injured."

"As you did during the War."

"Yes, but with a difference. When I was at Ameo's side, no one called me a *whore*."

He flinched at Eden's unexpected use of such a vulgar word, but he knew what she was talking about. The nursing profession was held in questionable regard. Many thought the women were little more than prostitutes looking to ply their trade closer to the field of battle than was allowed of civilians. Brad could guess the type of comments Eden must have had to deal with in the medical wards and makeshift field hospitals.

"No, quite a different situation prevailed in Black Kettle's band. Though I was never universally accepted or trusted, many came to value my skills and were grateful for them. Ameo thought me gifted, special, capable nearly of—please don't laugh at me—of performing miracles."

Brad held Eden's strange, otherworldly gaze so completely he was ready to believe she was capable of miracles.

"Ameo—I mean Hanging Road. Please excuse me, I keep forgetting to translate. He honored me in a way no man ever has. You can't imagine what it's like to be a woman so you cannot possibly know what it's like to experience that for the first time. Honor."

Brad had no response.

"I know how men like you think of women. They come in two varieties, either pure and golden and stand-

207

ing on a pedestal—fragile flowers made of porcelain so delicate a strong wind would shatter them—or . . . or . . . residents of the gutter, like your little friend Tessa. Men like you have no comprehension that there might exist some middle ground between those two extremes, but I can assure you that I am neither a porcelain rose nor a whore, despite the fact that name has been applied to me with liberal abandon lately."

"I think you are too quick to judge me, madam. I do not recall ever expressing an opinion on the female sex in your presence and I'd be obliged if you did not make assumptions on matters of which you are ignorant."

Eden stiffened. She had not seen the captain's ire raised before, but she had obviously overstepped the boundaries of their acquaintance.

"I apologize," she said. "Perhaps I did oversimply."

With a gentle wave of his hand, they both relaxed again.

"Tell me more about Hanging Road," he said.

"He was a good man. An interesting man. I miss him."

"You loved him very much, didn't you?"

The smile faded from her lips. "I respected him. That's something even deeper than love, I think. Love can often come about unbidden and unearned." She straightened herself and seemed to visibly shut doors. "The word for arrows is *maahotse*."

Their brief moment of candor was over and the formal language lessons were to begin, and so they spent the morning thus engaged. Brad would request words and phrases and Eden would pronounce them several

times so that he could write them down in his notebook in a phonetic style he could remember.

She watched him as he wrote. He gripped his pencil just above its point and rapidly filled the pages with small, careful printing.

At noon, Hugh Christie, who had hovered on the sidelines throughout the morning, broke in on their discussion and offered to bring them both lunch from the café.

"I'll go with you," Brad proposed and the two men departed.

Eden was only alone a few minutes when the slatternly Tessa arrived through the side door of the saloon.

"Did they leave?" she demanded.

"They went to fetch some dinner."

Tessa blithely sat down uninvited in the chair Brad had vacated. Eden shuffled her magazines together.

"Ain't that Brad somethin'?" Tessa said.

"I guess so." Eden shifted uncomfortably in her chair.

"I think he's just about the handsomest thing I ever laid eyes on."

"He's very good-looking," Eden agreed in a prim tone.

"That gal he's engaged to sounds like a real bitch."

Eden did not care for the crudeness of this observation. "I wouldn't have call to know about that."

"He's told me all about her," Tessa boasted, apparently oblivious to the discomfort she was causing her audience. "She's after him all the time to get promotions. Her father's a big shot in Washington and she won't be happy until Brad's a big shot, too. And he's afraid once they're married she's gonna spend him ragged. She's got real expensive tastes."

And he spends his money on prostitutes, thought Eden sourly. It seemed to her at that moment neither future member of the Randall household had much sense.

"She's real tall. He says he's six-three and he just outstands her by four inches in his stocking feet."

"That's a tall woman," Eden said.

"And she's older than him. By four years!"

"Well, I guess it's obvious he likes older women."

"And you know what else he told me?" Tessa continued, not catching Eden's little joke about Tessa's own ten-year age difference with Brad. "She ain't even a virgin!"

"I really don't feel the need to know—"

"Oh, it's a good story. Trust me."

Eden sighed.

"She was engaged to marry somebody else before she met him. Somebody during the war. And she had a dream, a premonition, he was gonna get killed. Do you believe in dreams? I do. Anyway, the night before he left to go back to the front"—Tessa paused and took a deep breath to heighten the melodrama—"she *gave* herself to him. Two weeks later, sure enough, she got word he'd been killed in battle. Probably doin' something real heroic. Ain't that the most romantic thing you ever heard? She confessed all this to Brad the night he proposed. So he could back out if he wanted to. I guess that means she's got some sense of decency. 'Cause he

probably wouldn't of guessed if she hadn't let on. You know most men don't know any better."

Eden frowned skeptically. "Captain Randall actually told you all this about his personal life?"

"That and lots more. He's a real talker, once he gets goin'. I don't think he's got anybody else to talk to but me."

Eden caved in to her own curiosity. "Was he disappointed she wasn't a virgin?"

"No, he was not," Tessa announced with an odd pride. "I asked him that, too. He told me he didn't think the less of her one whit. Imagine hearin' a man say that. He said what she did for love was brave and selfless. Those were the exact words he used—brave and selfless."

Brave and selfless, Eden mentally repeated, impressed.

"I think one thing worries him, though. He never come right out and said this, but I think he worries that she's still in love with that fiancé what got killed. He said something like, 'How can a living man compete with a ghost?' "

"He has a point, I suppose."

"But how could any woman in her right mind not be ass-over-teacups in love with a man as handsome and smart and perfect as Captain Randall?"

Eden once again flinched at the woman's vulgar way of expressing herself. "I wouldn't call a man perfect if he betrays the woman he has promised to marry." She left the words "with you," unspoken.

Tessa bristled at this. "He was just evenin' the score, now wasn't he?"

It took a few moments for the meaning of this re-mark to sink in. When it did, Eden was both astonished and appalled. "You mean to say that you were the first woman he ever—" Decency shut Eden's mouth before she could wallow further in this degrading conversation.

The sly, superior smile on Tessa's face and the ar-rogant tilt of her chin answered the question.

Eden wrinkled her nose in disgust, mortified to be discussing such personal matters. She looked out the window to hide her embarrassment and noticed that Brad and Hugh Christie now crossed the street carrying trays of food. They entered with a loud clatter.

"Hey, Tess, if we'd known you were here, we'd have brought more food," said Christie as he set his tray down on the table.

"I'm not very hungry. I'll share mine," Eden offered.

Tessa glanced at her, then rose quickly from her seat. "I gotta be goin'. Thanks just the same."

Eden could tell by the look on the woman's face that Tessa considered Eden's food to be tainted somehow. Even prostitutes treat me like a leper, she thought. It doesn't get lower than that.

Fourteen

Had each member of Congress seen what I
have, of the injustice practiced toward these
Indians, they would imagine that there was
not sufficient money in the United States trea-
sury to appropriate for their benefit.
—EDWARD WYNKOOP, CHEYENNE AND ARAPAHO INDIAN
AGENT, REPORT TO THE COMMISSIONER OF INDIAN
AFFAIRS, OCTOBER 7, 1868

Brad and Eden's mutually agreeable routine proceeded
in the same fashion each day until Christmas Eve. Every
morning he would call for Eden at the Lowell house and
escort her to Hugh Christie's nameless saloon for a day
of language practice and reading. Eden was astonished
at how quickly the young officer could grasp and remember information. His mind seemed to possess nearly
total recall of every Cheyenne word or phrase, everything that was said to him. He even picked up on subtle
shifts in verb form that Eden did not know she was
using. Soon they were carrying on very simple practice
conversations in Cheyenne.

When she remarked upon his impressive memory
skills, he was pleased but said, "I've always been this
way. It's almost a nuisance. I can remember every date

in history my schoolmasters ever mentioned, names of schoolyard playmates I haven't seen in fifteen years, passages of the Bible, the solutions to math problems I did when I was twelve. It's ridiculous, really."

"I must say I think you're amazing, nonetheless."

Brad favored her with a delighted smile.

"Captain, have you received any news from your regiment? Where they are and what they are doing?"

"The last I heard, they have proceeded south to Fort Cobb. General Custer has taken three of the Cheyenne women with him for help in finding and communicating with the tribes."

"Which ones?"

"The sister of Black Kettle and a friend of hers, plus the daughter of Little Rock."

A curious smile crossed Eden's lips. "Why were they in particular chosen?"

"Because they were, well, royalty of sorts, I suppose. The general boasted of their antecedents."

She was forced to chuckle.

"What amuses you, Mrs. Murdoch?"

She tried to hide her merriment behind her hand. "Are you not aware that the position of chief is an elective one?"

"Elective?" Brad looked stunned, but delighted by the prospect. "You mean they have a democratic form of government like our own?"

"I guess you could say that. If your father served as chief that would make a strong qualification for you becoming one in his place, but it is by no means assured. It takes a certain temperament to be a good chief. Not just anyone can fill the bill. And once elected, the chiefs exercise power by consensus, not fiat." She paused to allow him time to catch up with her on his note-taking. "There are ten bands within a tribe. Each band elects four chiefs and then the tribe as a whole has four chiefs of larger significance. All together, they make up the Council of Forty-four."

"Like our Congress," he murmured as he anxiously made notes to himself. He glanced up with an almost malicious joy. "I can't wait to share this information with my commanding officer."

"The tribes are perplexed by the army's insistence on always speaking with one chief as if he had the power to act or speak for the whole tribe."

"He doesn't?"

"No, that's why it was so unfair of you to attack Black Kettle's village. I'll acknowledge that some of the men might have made those raids you described, but why punish the many for the acts of a few? It wasn't a concerted effort. It wasn't a *political* act."

"What you're saying is that though a murderer or a thief may reside, say, in the city of Topeka, the army doesn't plot military actions against the entire town." Brad stared intently at the center of the table as he contemplated this new point of view.

"The Council of Forty-four doesn't convene all that often," Eden continued. "I only knew of one such meeting during the years I lived there."

"Were you with Black Kettle's village the entire time?"

"No, not at first. A raiding party of Dog Soldiers kidnapped me. A man the whites called 'Roman Nose' was their leader."

"I know that name. He was killed at Beecher's Island a few months ago. I spoke with some of the men in that fight." He paused and wondered if he dared to broach an intimate topic. He had felt their friendship and intimacy grow during their week of lessons. "Recalling that time must be painful to you, Mrs. Murdoch. It must have been . . . I suppose you are not comfortable speaking of—"

"I don't think it was quite what you imagine. I'm sure we have heard the same frontier horror stories— that a captured woman is subjected to the lust of every single warrior in the tribe. No, I was spared that particular outrage."

"Thank God for that."

"Instead, I became the exclusive property of the man who captured me. Of course, he felt obliged to use me in any manner he saw fit. You might as well know that after the first time, I no longer put up a fight. If you did not resist, you risked less injury." She hardened her jaw and narrowed her amber-green eyes at Brad. "I suppose you think me cowardly, even degenerate for that."

"I would not sit in judgment upon you for the world, Mrs. Murdoch. Not for the world."

Eden softened, grateful for Brad's compassion. "Yes, it was a dark time. Probably worse than I actually remember. You see, I was so crazed with grief over the loss of my son that I didn't really care what happened to me. I was almost insensible to what went on around

me and so close to total despair there came a day when I tried quite seriously to end it all."

"I'm happy you didn't."

"No, a man talked me out of it. Not a Cheyenne, but a Negro man who traded goods with them. He was once a slave but ran away from his master as a young man and found a life of freedom outside the States. He came upon me whittling away at my wrists with an unsharpened arrow. Not a very effective means of suicide."

She pulled at her left cuff to show Brad the scars. Brad's cheek twitched when he viewed her damaged wrist.

"The man told me to stop my work long enough to listen to a story. I ignored him at first, but soon I realized why he told it. It seems that when his mother was a young girl in Africa, slavers kidnapped her and carried her away in bondage to America. There she was sold into slavery in a strange country, made all the more frightening by the fact that she did not speak their language nor understand their customs and way of life. She endured incredible hardship, privation, torment, but she lived to tell her son one special thing. She always said to him, 'Only the weak let their troubles defeat them. The strong feed on their own misfortune and grow stronger still.' "

"That's an unusual manner of looking at the world. But it must have helped you."

"A few months later, I was traded to an old man in Black Kettle's band called Spotted Calf. Actually, I think he won me in some sort of gambling game. He did not need me to play the wife, in the sense you imagine. Rather, he needed someone to look after his own ailing wife and carry out her chores. She was partially paralyzed. I managed well in that role and I rather grew to like the old man . . . were it not for the night—"

Brad looked up from his notes expectantly, but found Eden's expression had changed radically. The far-off, trancelike look she always wore when reminiscing about her Cheyenne days had vanished.

After several moments of silence, she asked brightly, "Are you looking forward to the party tonight?"

"Oh, yes, ma'am." Brad quickly tried to cover his disappointment that she had changed the subject. "Especially looking forward to the holiday treats. If I were back home in Vermont in my mother's kitchen, I'd be smelling the aroma of her cinnamon apple bread right now." Brad closed his eyes with a dreamy smile. "Cinnamon apple bread fresh, hot from the oven with cold cream poured on top. Life does not afford finer moments than that."

"Finer than what?" asked Tessa, who had sidled up behind him and placed her hands on his shoulders.

"Mrs. Murdoch and I were talking about memorable Christmas treats."

Tessa brazenly massaged her lover's shoulders, without a care for his reputation. Eden could tell he was embarrassed by this public display of affection. He said nothing, but the edges of his ears turned bright crimson.

He stilled Tessa's hands and asked if he might have a word with her. He rose and walked her over to the back of the room, beyond Eden's earshot. Eden watched

them converse out of the corner of her eye. Brad appeared to be admonishing Tessa, but then Tessa stood on tiptoe and whispered something in his ear that caused him to giggle like a schoolboy. The pair disappeared out the side door to Tessa's room.

Eden shook her head and resumed her reading, more than a little disappointed in Captain Randall. He seemed to suffer such a weakness of the flesh, she wondered how he had stayed a virgin until he came to Reliance.

Hugh Christie breezed in the front door with an armload of mail and sat down at Eden's table.

"Did the captain go off and leave you all alone, Mrs. Murdoch?"

"I believe he had an assignation with your neighbor next door," she remarked dryly.

Hugh heaved a comic sigh. "Oh, these young boys; they do need their love and comfort."

"Is that what you call it?" She studied Christie with a quizzical eye. She liked his unflagging good humor, the way he joked about everything. At first, she had found his manner too free and easy, but now she was more used to it. She was even beginning to grow accustomed to his eccentric appearance, the long, wildly unkempt black hair, the rakish long mustache, the dark, dancing eyes.

"I've seen his type come through here before. That's a boy that's missin' his mama as much as his sweetheart."

"Oh, Mr. Christie." Eden giggled and blushed at this assessment of Brad Randall. His view of Brad's motives had never occurred to her, but it made the young officer's surprisingly intimate confidences to Tessa more understandable.

"I'm kinda worried about Tess," Christie said. "I've never seen her in such a state about a customer before. If customer he be. I wonder if she's even chargin' him, and with Tessa, that's gotta be a first. She's gettin' way too attached to him for her own good."

Hugh's concern for his neighbor or employee or lover or whatever the woman was to him impressed Eden. "Captain Randall will certainly be leaving soon. Most likely by the first of the year, I should imagine. I believe I've already detained him many days longer than he or his superiors originally intended."

"Yep. He'll be gone and she'll be cryin'. That's the way of the world, ain't it?"

An impudent impulse caused Eden to ask, "And have you left someone crying, Mr. Christie?"

He raised an eyebrow with a roguish smile. "Quite the opposite, Mrs. Murdoch. I was on the receiving end of love's cruelty once." He placed his right hand on his chest. "Got this heart broke so bad, it cured me of ever wanting to take the risk again."

"Well, I'm sorry to hear that for your sake," she returned in a teasing tone, not able to discern if this was yet another joke. "And for the sake of all the women in the world, of course." She resumed her reading and Hugh sorted through his week's worth of mail. She paused to ask about something that had puzzled her many times.

"May I ask a personal question, Mr. Christie?"

"The more personal the better, Mrs. Murdoch." He

arched one dark eyebrow with a mischievous grin.

"Why doesn't your saloon have a name? Don't places like this have names like the Lucky Lady or the Silver Dollar?"

He sighed. "It could use a name, I'll grant you that. I've just been waiting for the right name to find me, I guess."

Eden nodded thoughtfully, satisfied by this explanation. She began her reading, only to interrupt herself again.

"One other thing, Mr. Christie, why is it that the young boy called Marco always seems to run and hide whenever Captain Randall appears?"

Hugh smiled. "Poor Marco. He deserted from the army last year and is scared to death they'll find him and haul him back in irons. The army didn't suit him like he thought it would. Bad pay, bad food, and Marco—bein' from Italy and all—didn't hardly speak enough English to understand commands so he was always gettin' punished for something. I felt sorry for him and took him in. I been takin' in strays since—"

"You were a kid! You do make a habit of it, Mr. Christie." Eden smiled, impressed with the man's kindness to the boy. They both returned to their reading.

Hugh suddenly looked up from a newspaper. "Why, Mrs. Murdoch, you're famous."

"What?"

"Look here." He passed the newspaper over to her and pointed to a line. There was her name: *Mrs. Eden Murdoch.*

Eden's mouth dropped open in shock. She read the

article in stunned disbelief. She followed the story to an inside page and there found an etching of her likeness, cropped hair and all. The article's author was General Phillip Sheridan and in it he sought to defend General Custer's actions at the Washita. He was apparently writing the piece in response to criticisms lodged by one Edward Wynkoop.

Wynkoop, Wynkoop—that odd name was so familiar. The Cheyennes' Indian agent, that was it. Black Kettle had considered the man a friend, one of the few friends the Cheyennes had in the United States Government.

Now it came back to her. The resignation of this Agent Wynkoop had incensed General Custer that night of his birthday celebration. Wynkoop had compared the general to Colonel Chivington, calling the Washita engagement "another Sand Creek" and Custer had been furious.

Sheridan attempted to vilify Black Kettle and justify his killing, listing among his evil deeds the kidnapping of a beautiful young white woman, a wife and mother whose husband and father were both actively engaged in the defense of the Union. The article went into a lengthy description of her capture, the heartrending loss of her infant, and how she had been spirited away into the most bestial form of slavery and kept thus degraded for nearly four years. That she had survived such ill use and abasement was listed as a wonder of human endurance. Sheridan exhorted every citizen of the United States to extend their thanks and gratitude to the valor

of the men who risked their lives to save this unfortunate woman from further horrors.

Eden's blood boiled up inside her. "How dare they? How dare they?" she whispered over and over, the further she read.

She stood up, furious and ready to spit fire. "Where is he? Where can I find him?"

"Brad? Oh, don't you think we better wait? I mean, you know. He's off with Tessa and I think we both know what they're up to."

"Tell me this instant!"

With a sigh, he rose and led her to the hallway leading to Tessa's room. He stayed in the entrance to the hall, wanting to view the action, but only from a safe distance.

As Eden reached the door she could hear through it a rhythmic creaking of bedsprings. She swallowed hard and almost lost her nerve. Then the anger generated by the awful article filled her again and she rapped loudly on the door. The creaking noises instantly ceased.

"Go away and come back later," came Tessa's annoyed voice from within.

"I need to speak with Captain Randall this minute!"

"Mrs. Murdoch?" It was Brad Randall's voice.

"Come back later, damn it. We're busy," shouted Tessa.

"I don't care how busy you are. I need to speak with Captain Randall right now."

"Just a minute, Mrs. Murdoch," came Randall's voice.

Eden heard the low sounds of the pair of lovers quarreling, but in a couple of minutes, Brad emerged in his bare feet and trousers, hurriedly buttoning his shirt. Eden could see underwear and socks in a heap next to the bed. Tessa had apparently retreated behind the privacy of a large screen. Brad looked flushed with embarrassment. His golden-brown hair stuck to his forehead in sweaty clumps. Eden watched him drop a ring on a chain of some sort down inside his shirt.

"What do you need, Mrs. Murdoch?"

"I need an explanation!" She slapped the newspaper against his chest.

He took the paper and scanned its headlines. Quickly, his hooded gray eyes fastened onto the offending article. He sighed and ran his hand through his hair as he read.

"Mrs. Murdoch, if you will permit me to finish dressing, I shall escort you home and speak to you directly on this matter."

"Yes, if you please!"

Once they were safely ensconced in the Lowell parlor, Eden started in: "This article is absurd. It seeks to paint me as a damsel in distress, longing for the Seventh Cavalry to swoop down from the heavens and rescue me at all costs!"

Brad shifted uncomfortably in his chair. "There are those who see the situation in exactly those terms, Mrs. Murdoch."

"Let's speak plainly here, Captain. Those terms are the ones in which the army *hopes* the people will view

the situation. Don't pretend they don't know the truth of the matter—and have deliberately distorted it for their own ends."

"You must understand that there are many persons, from the highest ranks on down—and, yes, I am speaking of General Sheridan himself here—who cannot imagine and certainly cannot comprehend your position on this matter. They have presented your case to the world at large in the only terms they understand."

"They have presented *lies*, sir. Don't say you disagree with me on that."

"I will admit, for the sake of argument, that I know your opinion of the matter and that you considered yourself abducted, rather than rescued by our forces. You have made that plain enough on many occasions, but I confess that I still do not really understand how you can feel that way. Many would simply describe you as insane. I know that's not true, but I still do not appreciate how and why you came to love your captors—the very people responsible for the death of your infant son. The people who exacted on you a revenge—however righteous—in which you were made to suffer outrageous cruelty for acts of which you were personally innocent. You once said I really knew nothing of you. Well, you are right. Despite the month we have spent in each other's company, you remain a frustrating enigma to me."

Eden sat quietly through this long speech, turning a handkerchief over and over in her lap as she tried to regain her composure.

"I trusted you, Brad." This marked the first time she

had ever addressed him with such familiarity.

"I know that."

"Did they order you to spy on me?"

"I wouldn't call it spying. When you would not give General Custer the information he desired that first night in his tent, he instructed me to keep close to you, to gain your trust if possible, and to learn all I could about you. He was under a lot of pressure from his own superiors, and still is. The incident at the Washita has garnered many critics, as you can tell from that article."

Eden changed the topic back to the personal once again. "Why do you want to know about me? Why is that so important to you? You have already provided your superiors with all the lurid details they required to make a compelling defense of their actions."

Brad rose from his chair and walked behind it to the parlor window, where he looked out past the curtain at the street.

"I just . . . do. I cannot explain it in any manner. You haunt me, Mrs. Murdoch, or Seota, or Ghost Woman or whatever your name happens to be on a given day. You stalk my dreams, you haunt my waking hours. And please don't think I mean that in a romantic sense. I'm not trying to make love to you."

"Yes, we all know you satisfy those needs elsewhere."

"Don't mock me," he implored, with a note of misery in his normally strong voice. "In shaming me, you cannot make me feel worse than I do already." With a sigh, Brad dropped the curtain and walked around the perimeter of the room. "I don't know what's happened

to me. I'm not the same man I was. I don't seem to know the difference between right and wrong anymore. I have lost whatever guiding moral principles I once relied on . . . or maybe they have never been put to the test before this."

"I know what you mean," Eden said quietly. His problems replaced, for the moment, her anger over the political controversy.

He strode to the sofa on which she sat and placed himself at her feet. As he looked up at her from his seat on the floor, she could not wholly exempt herself from the pain and confusion distorting his face.

"Do you, really, Mrs. Murdoch?"

She nodded. "We all sometimes find ourselves in situations for which we have nothing to prepare us." She placed her hand gently to his cheek and he held it there. She regarded him for several seconds, then angrily snatched her hand away. "Don't try to divert me from the subject we are here to discuss! Don't make your moony, boyish eyes at me and think I will melt. That may work with ignorant prostitutes and even your foolish Amanda back home, but it will not make matters right with me!"

He immediately stood up. "Do not speak of Amanda. Now or ever."

"I'm sorry. You're right. Let us leave personal matters out of this entirely."

"Agreed." He retreated to the edge of the room again. This time he faced her, though, leaning his long body against the frame of the parlor doors and crossing his arms over his chest.

"The newspaper Mr. Christie gave me was from St. Louis. Do you think anyone outside that city would have read the story?"

Brad smiled mirthlessly. "That article was a reprint from *The New York Times,* Mrs. Murdoch. I've no doubt it has been widely circulated and probably has been read by thousands."

"Thousands?"

"You may as well know there are more articles to come. General Custer has been contracted to write a magazine article specifically about you and will no doubt do so as soon as the current campaign is completed."

Eden slowly shook her head as she tried to cope with all he had just said. "So there is controversy, as I understand it? Voices are being raised against the actions by the army this winter?"

Brad nodded. "Colonel Wynkoop's protestations have been registered loudly and strongly and not just in the newspapers. In the halls of government, as well. I understand from dispatches that he was scheduled to speak to a congressional investigating body yesterday."

"Can you at least understand why I'm so upset?"

"I'm sure it is unpleasant to read in a newspaper about such personal experiences being made public. The damage to your privacy and delicacy, to your reputation."

Eden was nearly compelled to laugh. "My delicacy? My reputation? Good God, do you really think that is what concerns me? The United States Army, by its own ignorance or blunder or arrogance, managed to kill the

only Cheyenne chief interested in making peace and *I* am now being used as their fabricated justification for this travesty. Don't you think I'm a little more than angry about that? The fact that the fiend you call your commander is being lauded for his actions—"

"General Custer is not a fiend," Brad interrupted. "He is not the monster you imagine. I know what you witnessed that day at the Washita seemed heartless, but I have personally seen the man cry over the death of puppies."

"The death of puppies?" Eden made a face of disgust and confusion.

"Yes, it's perfectly true. We were in the field. His favorite hunting dog gave birth to a litter of pups in the night. When he found her in the morning, the pups had all frozen to death. I saw him carry the bitch into his tent with tears streaming unashamedly down his face." On the other hand, Brad had heard stories told of Custer ordering men's heads to be shaved in a humiliating fashion for merely failing to salute him.

"He *killed* my family, Brad. *The army killed my family.* And you expect me to quietly allow them to use *me* as their excuse."

Brad turned on Eden with a sudden anger he was not used to displaying in front of anyone and particularly not a woman. "You call them your family? Those people? Those savages who were responsible for the death of your son? Who harmed you in ways I can't imagine? Or maybe I can. I've read the medical report on you, Mrs. Murdoch, and the inventory of the damage to your person is shocking, indeed!"

"You don't know what you're talking about."

"Then why don't you enlighten me? I've asked you often enough. Tell me your side of the story. I want to know, truly."

"So that I can provide the army with more ammunition to use against my friends?"

"No! I want to . . . to . . . understand. I want to make some sense of all this."

"You would never understand. No one does. No one wants to hear my story. It does not satisfy their expectations."

"Don't be so sure. I am not the enemy." He paused to regard her hostile face, all pinched and peaked in its agitation. He added in a whisper, "Not anymore, at least."

"Could I ask you a question about this article by General Sheridan?"

Brad nodded.

"He states that the scalps of two expressmen—expressmen, what are they?—were found at our village. Is this true?"

Brad sighed uneasily. He had questions of his own relating to this particular aspect of Sheridan's account. "The men he refers to were couriers on their way to Fort Dodge with the mail. They were killed and scalped just before the Washita fight. He says that the mail they carried was also found in the village." Brad sighed with a tormented look drawing out his handsome young features. "To be perfectly honest, I do not know where or how he got this information. General Custer had every bit of goods in the village carefully catalogued before they were destroyed and I know that these articles were not on that inventory. General Sherman himself did not view the scene until the following week. As everything was burned, he could not have personally viewed anything but charred ruins."

"So you believe he is lying."

"You must understand that it would be treasonous for me to make such a statement. I can only say that I do not know the whole of it. And neither do you, if I might suggest it."

Eden sat quietly, but was far from quiet of mind. "It's nearly dark, Captain, and you have a Christmas party to attend. Good night and goodbye. I have nothing more to say to you."

"Will you be at the party tonight?"

"No, I will be too busy to attend. I have some letters of my own to write."

Brad approached her with an apprehensive look. "You can't mean that."

"I think the secretary of war as well as the commissioner of Indian affairs—and let's not forget the reading public of the United States of America—needs to hear the story of the Battle of the Washita from one who saw it from a slightly different perspective. Namely, from the *other* end of the cavalry's rifles. We'll see if General Sheridan's argument that Black Kettle needed to be eliminated holds up when it becomes generally known that General Custer and company did not have the slightest idea whose village they attacked and whose people they slaughtered on the day after Thanksgiving."

Brad's expression grew more agitated with every

word she spoke. "I told you that in confidence. I beg you, don't repeat it."

"Ah, Thanksgiving. That wonderful holiday when we all celebrate the Pilgrims and the Indians feasting together in peace and harmony. And did not the story go that the Pilgrims would have perished that first harsh New England winter but for the intervention of the neighboring tribes who taught the foolish Europeans how to survive in the wilderness?"

"Mrs. Murdoch, do you know what will happen if you write such letters? The army will do everything in its power to discredit you. They will label you a madwoman and *they* will be believed. Most who've encountered you would say that already. I know it's not true, but nobody else does."

"I'll take that chance. It's time for you to leave, sir. And Merry Christmas."

She rose and nearly pushed him through the glass parlor doors and on toward the front door, shoving his coat and hat into his arms on the way.

She slammed the door behind him and collapsed back against it. She panted as though out of breath from running. She had one more reason to dread the release of those articles about her, one that she could not share with Brad Randall or anyone else. A personal reason far removed from the lofty world of politics or justice.

Lawrence Murdoch might read those articles.

Fifteen

> Agent Wynkoop publishes in our morning pa-
> pers his letter of resignation as agent for the
> Cheyennes, assigning as a reason that this at-
> tack of General Custer was like that on Sand
> Creek made by Chivington, some years ago.
> General Sheridan's report was emphatic that
> General Custer had recovered [a] . . . captive
> white woman—a simple fact, conclusive to
> my mind that General Custer did strike a hos-
> tile camp.
> —LIEUTENANT GENERAL W. T. SHERMAN, LETTER TO THE
> ADJUTANT GENERAL, DECEMBER 12, 1868

Randall and his men attended the Christmas party at the
Lowells' church that night, but he found it hard to ex-
hibit the festive enthusiasm the event required. His ac-
rimonious afternoon with Eden Murdoch scratched at
him like a hair shirt.

He tried to chalk it up to simple homesickness. He
missed his family and he missed Amanda. He had never
gone a Christmas without seeing his mother and younger
sister, even during the war years.

He noticed immediately upon arriving that Eden had
stayed home, no doubt carrying out her threat to write
retaliatory letters. And what would be the outcome of
such missives? Would she mention him as the source of
the information on the attack?

Even if she did not, his superiors would undoubtedly guess the source. Could he be court-martialed for this? He had not, after all, given any intelligence to the enemy. At least he had not thought of Eden Murdoch in that light when he had so foolishly blurted out the information that day in the Lowells' parlor. In fact, he had naïvely assumed they had a *common enemy*. How wrong he had been.

He sat on the periphery of the party, sipping some punch as floor space was cleared and a fiddler tuned his instrument for the coming dance. Brad saw tall, stout Mary Lowell make her way toward him. He rose to greet her.

"I have a favor to ask, Captain Randall."

"Anything, ma'am, anything at all."

"Would you mind taking one dance with my girl Sarah? I know she's too young to be at a dance like this, but she begged and begged because you were going to be here."

"I'd be delighted, Mrs. Lowell. But you must also save a dance for me, if I can secure your husband's consent."

She giggled with delight. "Oh, you silly boy." She started to leave, then turned back. "Please don't let on that I asked you to ask her."

"Never." He placed his hand over his heart with mock gallantry.

She paused. "Mrs. Murdoch wouldn't come tonight, Captain. She wouldn't tell us the reason, but she was upstairs in her room all upset about something from the moment you left our house this afternoon. We could

hear her pacing around even more than usual."

"Yes, I know she was upset. There were some news-paper articles about her that she found . . . unflattering. It can't be helped though, I'm afraid. I'm sorry you and your family have to deal with all this, Mrs. Lowell."

"Don't say another word. You know we're happy to help out. Now you go have some fun and lose that long face, Captain."

Brad ended up dancing with twelve-year-old Sarah Lowell four times, to the girl's obvious delight. The dif-ference in their heights required considerable dexterity and course correction, but they managed somehow. Sarah's girlfriends whispered and giggled on the side-lines as they watched.

Brad grew bored with the party after a couple of hours and wandered outside the overwarm church so-cial room to take the brisk December air. He eventually found himself walking toward the Lowell house.

He strolled past and saw a light on in the upper window, a room he presumed belonged to Eden. She was probably writing her damning letters just as she promised. He sat down on the middle step of the Lowell porch and wondered if she might come out. Did he hope she would come out? He was not sure. She was so angry with him. He could not decide whether to feel guilty or not, but he knew he did not enjoy her being angry with him. It bothered him more than he cared to admit.

Sitting so long gave him a chill so he rose and started walking again to warm himself. He returned to Main Street and saw two of his men leaving the nameless saloon of Hugh Christie with whiskey bottles in their hands. The temperance atmosphere of the Lowells' church party had apparently not satisfied their idea of a proper celebration.

He smiled to himself. He had not specifically authorized his men to get drunk on the holiday, but rather had made general remarks to indicate that their services would not be needed at any time on Christmas Day unless an emergency arose. At that point, Sergeant Yellen had offered in a loud, theatrical whisper, "He means we can sleep it off all day, boys!" to the chuckles of all those present.

Brad idly wondered what Tessa was doing on this Christmas Eve. Several times he had thought to call on her, longed to call on her, but had ultimately refrained. Though he did not consider himself a religious man, the holiday seemed too sacred to spend in the bed of a whore.

He wistfully looked up into the prairie night sky, so clear and cold. There he beheld the Hanging Road arching across the inky dome with a dazzling clarity. He admired its majestic beauty for several seconds before realizing he had referred to it in his thoughts as the "hanging road." Eden Murdoch's influence reached deeper into his consciousness than he had guessed. He chuckled quietly. Sometimes he half convinced himself she really was a witch and she had taken possession of his mind, even his soul.

He returned to the church hall and quietly trolled the ruins of the buffet table as the holiday party wound down.

*   *   *

Eden found herself in the unlikely company of Rhinehart Meeker as she knocked upon Hugh Christie's door on the morning after Christmas Day.

"Hello, Mr. Meeker," she said when she saw him heading for the same door as she on that cloudy, brisk December morning.

"Good day, miss," was his curt reply. He did not remove his hat, or even tip it in her direction.

She thought he eyed her with suspicion. "Mr. Christie is expecting me."

"Not surprising," snorted the barber.

Eden frowned. She did not understand the man's comment, but before she could pursue the matter, Hugh answered the door.

"Greetings of the season!" he called to both his guests.

"I wish you the same, Mr. Christie. I'll leave you two gentlemen alone and get straight to my work."

She retrieved her magazines, but not before carefully sorting them. She now sought only recent ones that might carry information about the Indian Wars or divulge more names of persons she might contact on her letter-writing initiative.

Christie and Meeker sat on the far side of the room, speaking earnestly about some matter. She could tell by their serious expressions and hushed tones that this was not a social call.

She worried about what Meeker had meant in his odd comment at the door. Was her presence assumed to be illicit in some way? Decent women did not frequent saloons. She knew this well enough, but shrugged off the implications. She no longer cared what people thought of her reputation. Not that she had ever cared much. During the war, many thought it scandalous that she performed her nursing work, her husband chief among them. After all, in the hospitals she was exposed not only to the shocking sight of hideous wounds, but to—horror of horrors—*naked men.*

She had been denied a nursing position more than once because she was deemed too young and pretty. Her motives were placed under suspicion. Her unmarried status was such a handicap, she had to invent an imaginary husband in order to get her first job and called herself *Mrs.* Clanton, rather than Miss. And even that was as an unpaid helper, volunteering only to fetch water, read to the men, write letters for them if they were unable.

She was eventually "promoted" to a level similar to an orderly, which meant she could now empty slops and scour blood and vomit off the hospital floors—still without pay. She subsisted on the allowance her father sent her. She did not complain. She felt that for the first time in her life she was accomplishing something important. Not that the job was utterly without compensation. She possessed as much vanity as any young woman, nineteen years old and freshly graduated from the Female Academy. She demurely soaked up the compliments of wounded men whose lives she made more comfortable. They called her their "Angel of Mercy" and a "Heavenly Vision."

"If I must look upon my last sight on earth, Mrs. Clanton, I pray God it be your lovely face," said one ailing private, recovering from the amputation of both his legs in the fall of 1861.

The woman in charge of the volunteer program overheard the remark and promptly fired Eden for flirting with the patients.

She simply moved again, this time to Washington City, itself, where eleven hospitals were in operation. The first ten turned her away—too young, too pretty. Only plain-looking married women over the age of thirty met the strict requirements decreed by Mrs. Dorothea Dix, "Dragon Lady Dix," who autocratically ruled the army nursing program.

At the final hospital, Eden had wandered about the convalescent ward looking for a surgeon named Brinkley. Before she found him she came upon a soldier choking. She immediately tugged at his collar to loosen it. She then sat him up, turned him sideways, and beat upon his back until the wad of chewing tobacco dislodged itself from his throat and flew out to land— plop!—on her boot. When the man recovered sufficient breath to speak, she fended off his attempted thanks with a stern lecture on the evils of tobacco use.

The sound of a single round of applause caused Eden to look behind her to behold the Surgeon Brinkley she had been seeking.

"Well done!" the doctor congratulated her. "I shall recommend you for a raise, young lady."

"I'm not employed here, sir, but have come hoping for employment."

"Consider it done, madam. Would that I could have but ten of your mettle on my staff."

How clearly Eden recalled the hot, humid summer of '63, the summer she met Lawrence Murdoch. The relentless success of Lee's Rebel forces had turned the whole of Washington City into a field hospital for the Army of the Potomac. Daily the hospital ships docked at the wharves on Sixth and Seventh streets to unload their endless columns of stretchers to be borne away in the waiting ambulances. One day, Lawrence Murdoch arrived on such a ship, fresh from fighting in McClellan's forces, which had just been repelled from Richmond.

Though dirty and disheveled from the fighting, Murdoch was easily the handsomest man Eden had ever seen. She took a personal interest in his care and, from that moment on, catered to his every need.

"Mrs. Clanton," he had managed to say through the pain of a shattered kneecap, "you are the kindest woman on this godforsaken earth."

"It's actually *Miss* Clanton, but don't tell anyone," she had whispered to him.

Hugh walked over to Eden's table after Rhinehart Meeker left.

"Where's your military escort today, Mrs. Murdoch?"

"If you mean Captain Randall, I don't know his whereabouts nor do I care."

"Those are harsh words for our good captain. Are you two still on the outs because of that article I showed you?"

"More than that. He betrayed my trust. I find it hard to think of him as a friend now."

"Sorry to hear that, ma'am. You know, I been thinkin' of something I been wantin' to say to you ever since you started comin' here."

She waited expectantly, not having even a vague idea where he was leading. She watched him shift uncomfortably in his seat and slick down his long mustaches.

"If it turns out that your family can't be found, I just want you to know that . . . well, you could find a place here, if need be—"

Eden's mouth dropped open in horror. "You cannot be serious, sir."

He pushed back his chair and raised his hands in a defensive posture. "I don't think you understand—"

"I understand perfectly! How dare you pretend friendship to me when all the while you were planning to reduce me to the level of your disreputable neighbors. Just because I have suffered misfortune, I am not so without hope that I would degrade myself so willingly." She stood up, but Hugh blocked her exit.

"Hold on, now. First, you got it all wrong. That's not what I was suggestin'. Second, don't talk that way about Tessa. She's a friend of mine and I don't let anybody bad-mouth my friends without a fight. You don't know her or anything about her, so you don't have the right to sit in judgment."

"Just let me out of here before you claim that prostitution is one of the sacraments!"

She ran for the door, only to hear him call after her,

"Your virtue's in a lot more peril at the Lowell house and that's a fact!"

The nerve of the man. Insulting the Lowells as well as her. The unmitigated gall! Had she still been standing near him, she would have soundly slapped his face. Since she had already reached the door, she could only turn and shake her fist at him.

On the last day of 1868, Brad Randall stood on the porch of the Lowell house. Both Eden and Mrs. Lowell reached the door simultaneously and opened it. When Eden saw him, she angrily tried to close the door in his face, but he prevented her with a swift movement of his arm.

"I have news of your father," he said.

"Oh, glory be," exclaimed Mary Lowell with delight. She clapped her hands together over her ample bosom with a smile of thanksgiving to the Almighty on her lips.

But Brad Randall was not smiling and Eden knew what that meant.

The cold, white winter sunlight shining through the uncurtained front window of the Lowell parlor did not flatter Eden as she stared straight ahead and stoically received the captain's news. Her twenty-seven-year-old face wore care lines more befitting a woman twice her age. Dark circles from a sleepless night further marred what was left of her once-vibrant beauty.

"Your father, Captain Samuel Clanton, perished in a

flash flood at Fort Lyon in April of last year."

"There was no letter?"

"No, just a tersely worded military communication. Perhaps more information will be forthcoming in the near future." He hoped his lie was not showing. He did not want to share the full contents of the letter with Eden for fear the sad news would overwhelm her. The post commander's aide had described Captain Clanton's last years in service as unhappy ones. It was said of him that he never recovered from the death of his only daughter and that he had taken to drink. He skated on the thin edge of court-martial for his inability to carry out his duties near the end when the flood extinguished his life.

"It took Captain Landers a good deal of time to piece together the information as all the men who had served with your father were away from the fort with Major Carr. He, as you may know, is also participating in the current campaign, along with Major Evans from New Mexico.

"He found what he could from post records, but then, by a stroke of luck, spoke with a laundress who had worked at the fort since the time you were captured. She said the news of the attack on your stagecoach was the talk of the garrison, owing to the high esteem in which your father was held by his fellow officers.

"He became frantic when your coach failed to arrive at its appointed time. His post commander authorized a search party in which your father participated. They traced the route of the stage line and found it two days hence, near the border at about the same time the search party from Fort Riley reached it."

With a weary sigh, Brad seated himself next to Eden on the settee. She still did not turn to look at him.

After a moment of silence, she said, "Well, I guess your job is done here, Captain."

"I'm sorry the news wasn't what we had hoped. There must be some other relation you have. Your late husband's family, perhaps?" He watched Eden stare at nothing for as long as he could stand it, then finally added, "I hope you'll not think me too forward if I suggest that it's all right to cry. And I have a perfectly good shoulder to lend."

She turned to him with the saddest smile he had ever seen on a woman's face. "It's not all right to cry."

He thought these to be strange words, especially coming from a woman. But then, what about this woman was not a bit strange? He held his offer of a shoulder open by gently placing his arm around her. She did not resist and placed her cheek against his collar. He could feel her soft breath against his throat.

He took her hand in his. A small hand, still a little rough from the heavy labors of her Cheyenne days. She tucked her legs up under her and practically sat in his lap. She appeared comfortable and she did not cry.

Several minutes of this odd embrace passed. Brad's arm started to cramp. He wondered how he would explain this indiscreet familiarity to Mary or Elias Lowell, should they happen into their parlor at such a moment. This did not look good. Highly irregular, in fact. They

might be insulted to find such impropriety going on in their home.

Many more minutes passed. He thought she might actually have fallen asleep on his shoulder. He heard the regular sighing of her breath and saw the soft rise and fall of her small bosom, encased in its firm black silk. Brad moved his shoulder slightly to try and cure its cramp. He hoped this would cause her to sit up, wake up, something. No luck, she only accommodated his change of position.

Worries for their reputations battled with vague feelings of lust as Brad resigned himself to this awkward embrace and pulled her closer. For a moment, he allowed himself to pretend he was Eden's lover. Erotic images of Eden floated through his mind, dark imaginings in which she gazed at him with the same eerie, mystical smile she had worn the night she had made his flesh crawl with her unnatural composure.

What's come over me? he berated himself. Why am I thinking these thoughts? I'm a scoundrel. I'm—

Brad's battle of self-reproach ended when little Josiah Lowell came to his rescue. The sturdy lad burst through the parlor doors, unaware the room was occupied.

"Captain Randall," the boy greeted him with delight. He snapped to attention and saluted Brad.

Brad grinned and awkwardly returned the boy's salute with his left hand, his right still trapped around the now awakening form of Eden Murdoch.

"Josiah, could you fetch your mother, please? I need to speak with her."

"Yes, sir!" The boy saluted once again and left on his mission.

Eden ran her hands over her face. She looked away and arched her back slightly.

Brad noticed her cropped auburn hair had turned up in an unruly way from her nap upon his shoulder. His collar now felt moist from perspiration caused by the pressure of her cheek against it. He could not help blushing at the inappropriateness of the situation.

Mary Lowell entered the parlor with an invitation to dinner for the captain. Eden quickly excused herself, giving Brad the opportunity to relay to Mrs. Lowell all the unfortunate news about the late Captain Clanton.

Eden retreated to the privacy of her little bedroom, still too dazed to cry or even think straight. She sat on the quilt-covered bed and pulled out from under her pillow the letters she had been working on. Through much trial and error, she had constructed, she felt, the best presentation of her thoughts.

Organizing them in a coherent fashion had proved a difficult task. She was not eloquent by nature and she had not exercised her writing skills in so many years. If only someone as polished and well presented as Brad Randall could write the letters, Eden was sure they would be given much more notice and weight. That was out of the question, of course, since he had begged her not to write the letters in the first place. Would her remarks jeopardize his career?

She felt vaguely uneasy at getting him in trouble

since he had shared the information with her so guile-
lessly. She mulled these thoughts over for many minutes
until a singular fact clutched her from the inside out.

Everyone I have ever loved is now dead.

Sixteen

A beautiful girl, just ripening into woman-
hood, was exposed to a fate infinitely more
dreadful than death itself. One could only
wonder how a young girl, nurtured in civilization and possessed of the natural refinement
and delicacy of thought which she exhibited,
could have survived such degrading treatment.
—G. A. CUSTER, *MY LIFE ON THE PLAINS*

Eden lay on her small bed in the early darkness of the
winter evening. She did not know how long she had
lain there, but she heard the sounds of dinner being
prepared on the floor below.

A soft knock caused her to rise and stretch.

"Mrs. Murdoch?" came Elias Lowell's voice through
the door.

Eden thought this odd. Mr. Lowell never came to her
room. "Yes, sir?"

"Might I speak with you, Mrs. Murdoch?"

She advanced to the door and opened it halfway.

He drew a deep breath and looked down his spectacles at her. "The good captain has informed Mrs. Lowell and me of your sad news, Mrs. Murdoch. I just wish
to offer my most heartfelt condolences."

"Thank you, Mr. Lowell."

"We have invited the captain to stay for supper. Is it at all possible that you would feel up to joining us? The captain is awfully worried about you and wishes to be assured of your welfare."

"Yes, I'll join you for dinner. I'll just freshen up a bit." She started to back away from the door, only to have Mr. Lowell follow her into the bedroom.

"My dear Mrs. Murdoch, please know that you may continue to reside under our humble roof for as long as need be."

"Thank you, sir,"

"If you should find the need for a private session of prayer—"

"That will not be necessary."

"Oh, but it is, my dear. I have counseled many in situations as unfortunate as yours and all have thanked me for it." He placed his arm around Eden in a manner she found too intimate.

"Tonight will be the night. Tonight I shall bring you back into the light of our dear Savior's holy realm, that you may rejoice in His mercy and accept His Will."

Eden felt his hot, sweaty hand now massage her shoulder in a most unseemly way. When she tried to wriggle free, he clenched her more tightly.

He continued to speak, but now his voice took on a husky quality, almost a whisper, but without the gentleness of a whisper. "We shall pray together. We shall experience the glory together. To bring a sinner to salvation is the experience of a lifetime."

"Mr. Lowell, I can assure you that such ministrations will *not* be necessary." She firmly removed his hand from her shoulder, deciding she could no longer remain polite.

He was about to respond when his eldest daughter, Sarah, reached the top of the stairs to announce that supper was on the table.

Eden entered the dining room on the arm of Mr. Lowell. Everyone in the room, save the Lowell children, wore the same concerned expression, the same sad smile, common to all those in the presence of one they presume to be grief-stricken beyond repair.

Eden did not know how to react to this. Was she expected to put up a brave front and feign cheerfulness? Was she expected to act numb? Was she to give in to despair and start sobbing?

Strange how all she felt was tired, so profoundly tired. Even the irritating and odd encounter with Mr. Lowell did not faze her. She just wished she could sleep for days on end. Had she actually fallen asleep in Brad Randall's arms? How completely absurd. He must think her an idiot. She was too embarrassed to even mention the matter. She hoped he was too gentlemanly to bring it up himself.

She smiled and nodded to everyone present.

Lowell asked them all to bow their heads for the blessing and, as usual, Eden did not participate. The minister glanced up several times during the short prayer and observed her blunt lack of faith.

"Mrs. Murdoch, I would be remiss in my duties if I

did not suggest that you should look to the Lord in your time of sorrow. Now more than ever do you need His love and guidance."

"Mr. Lowell," his wifc interjected, "perhaps now is not the time to inquire after Mrs. Murdoch's spiritual well-being."

"Quite the contrary, Mrs. Lowell. I believe that now is the perfect time. There is never a better time than the present to discover God's love. To give up our selfish worldly desires and abandon ourselves to His divine will."

Eden's eyes met those of Brad Randall, seated directly across from her as he had been the last time he had dined with the Lowells. His face carried an uneasy look. He tried to smile when her gaze caught his, but she could tell he did not know how to act toward her.

Eden ignored Mr. Lowell's remarks as she had done on previous such occasions. Tonight, however, he did not seem to wish a graceful retreat from his lack of success in converting her back into the fold of Christianity.

"If you'll forgive me the ill manners of disagreeing with my host, sir, I must say I agree with Mrs. Lowell," Brad said. "I think we should allow Mrs. Murdoch some quiet time to come to terms with the tragic news I have unfortunately brought her."

Eden sent Brad a slight but grateful smile across the table, then noticed a strange twist to Mr. Lowell's plump lips. She sensed he did not care to be contradicted or perhaps he did not like another man taking his wife's side against him.

"Captain, you may or may not be a godly man, but

you are not a man of God. My duty in life is to bring sinners to Jesus Christ and I will not rest until I have executed that goal to the best of my abilities. Especially when one such sinner resides under my very own roof."

Eden glanced up at this unexpectedly harsh remark. She saw the captain's back straighten, as well.

"I'm hungry," announced young Josiah.

"Yes, well, pass the peas, dear," said Mary, uneasily eyeing her husband.

"Have Bonnie Sue feed the children in the kitchen," Mr. Lowell ordered.

Mrs. Lowell rose without further comment and ushered the children out of the dining room with their dinner plates in their hands. Twelve-year-old Sarah cast a look of longing over her shoulder to be leaving the dashing presence of Brad Randall, whose wide brow furrowed over his hooded gray eyes. Eden shared his uneasiness. What was Lowell up to with this insistence on converting her tonight?

Mary returned to the table and began to pass the plates of food. "Captain, will you be rejoining your regiment soon?"

"Alas, yes, ma'am. My men and I will be leaving your fine city on the second day of the New Year."

"So soon," murmured his hostess.

"We will be proceeding to Fort Cobb in the Indian Territory. I must say I will miss Reliance and all the friends I have made here during my short stay."

"I'm certain our young captain can find houses of ill repute in virtually any city where an army ventures," the Reverend Mr. Lowell opined.

Brad dropped his knife and fork onto his plate with a clatter, obviously outraged by the remark.

"Husband, whatever possessed you to say such a thing?"

Lowell sliced his pork as casually as if he had just made a comment on the weather. "I do not believe I have said anything untrue. Have I, Captain? I mean, it is common knowledge in this town that you have spent inordinate amounts of time in the company of a known prostitute."

The edges of Brad's ears turned four shades of scarlet as he pushed his chair back from the table to glare at his plump host.

"I don't understand why you wish to insult me, sir."

"I merely wish to force you to confront the error of your ways, Captain. That is why I sent the children away."

"I don't think 'my ways'—whether they be the right ones or not—are any of your concern."

Eden's appetite, what little she had, vanished with this unprovoked confrontation. As angry as she had been with Brad over the newspaper articles, she now wished to rise to his defense. "Mr. Lowell, please spare Captain Randall this pious inquisition. He has been kind to me and I will not let—"

"Ah, yes, one sinner will always come to the aid of another." Lowell kept on eating his supper.

Eden stood up and threw her napkin on the table. "I am not a sinner and I will not allow anyone to call me that. You and especially your wife have shown me much generosity, but that does not give you the right to abuse me in this manner."

"My dear, I have no wish to abuse you. I pray nightly for your salvation. Do you think I have not noticed how you do not share in our nightly grace? How you refuse to attend church with us on the Lord's day? God has told me I must bring you back to the flock. He sent you to us for a purpose. Mere chance did not set you upon our doorstep, madam. God's hand is abundantly evident in this matter. The heathens have turned your heart from God, but no soul is beyond reclamation, beyond God's love."

"God's love?" Eden laughed bitterly. "Forgive me, but God's love—if it exists at all—is a cruel joke. I have seen no evidence of God's love in all the years of my adulthood."

"Mrs. Murdoch," Brad intervened, "would you like to take a walk? Some night air might—"

"How can you doubt the love of our Lord in all His bounty to us? He sent us his only Son—"

"I had a son once," cried Eden. "Where is he now? I had a husband and a father. Where are they now? During the War of the Rebellion I watched men die in agony by the score, fighting for causes they understood little, if at all. I had a family among the *Tsitsistas,* a man and two women and a little baby, another precious son. Not born of my body, but just as precious to me. Where are they now?"

"You lived in sin with those people. Those animals. You must repent your errors and rejoice that you are back among—"

"Those *animals,* as you call them, gave me the only unconditional love I have ever known. They took me in

255

after the most terrible night of my life. They saved me. They returned me to the land of the living when I was long past hope."

Lowell's only response to this assertion was to pause in his meal and set down his fork to sneer at Eden.

"Do you doubt me, sir?" asked Eden, the contempt in her voice sour enough to curdle milk. "Would you like to hear the story of the darkest night of my life? I, who am the veteran of so many dark nights, I can tell you a story you'll wish you'd never heard."

"Mrs. Murdoch, please," Brad interrupted, his agitation growing. "Let us take a break in this evening. You need to rest, to calm yourself. Please sit down, at least."

"Standing suits my mood."

"Elias, I do not wish to go on like this," Mary broke in, even more upset than the captain. "Mrs. Murdoch, Captain Randall is right. You need to rest."

"Hush yourself, Mrs. Lowell." The reverand adjusted his spectacles and narrowed his round, heavy-lidded eyes at Eden. "Let her speak."

Eden actually had few memories from that terrible night. Perhaps her mind simply closed out that which was too terrible to contemplate. The only reliable information she could draw on had been the stories shared with her by the sisters.

"Are we going to have to listen to that all night?" Night-walking had demanded of no one in particular, though

the only other occupants of the lodge were Hanging Road, engrossed in a project of sorting recently gathered herbs and barks, and Red Feather Woman, who sat tediously mending the worn-out lacings of an old legging.

She referred to the screaming coming from the lodge closest to their own.

Hanging Road looked up from his work with a sour face. "There's not much we can do about it. If Spotted Calf wants to sell that woman to the Kiowa trader for whiskey, that's his business, not ours."

"Spotted Calf is an old fool," remarked Nightwalking with contempt. "Trading that woman away for a night of drunkenness when he won't be able to get on without her. Who will look after his wife now? Who will look after him?"

"I heard him tell One Eye that she was awfully bossy and wanted to run everything her way," Red Feather said.

"But that's exactly what the old man needs," Nightwalking insisted.

Another terrible scream broke through the humid night air. Nightwalking stood up and paced about. "What is he *doing* to her?"

"Is that really so hard to imagine?" Hanging Road said, without looking up.

"There's more to it than *that*," snapped Nightwalking, not one to meekly defer to her much younger husband's opinions. "I didn't like the look of that man from the start. I didn't even like the smell of him."

Hanging Road grinned at this. "From now on, all visitors to this camp will have to pass Nightwalking's smell test."

Little Red Feather Woman giggled at her husband's joke until another frightful outburst of screaming began anew. She turned a worried face to the direction of the next lodge.

"She's going to have a baby, you know," Nightwalking said.

"Is she?" asked Red Feather Woman. "How can you tell? She's so skinny."

"She told me. I took her with me to gather roots last week. She put her hand on her belly and said '*mesh-ke-votse,*' plain as daylight."

"She was probably just trying to get out of doing work. White women are so lazy," Red Feather Woman said with authority.

"And you've known so many white women, Red Feather," chuckled Hanging Road, enjoying the banter between the sisters.

"Well, that's what everyone says. Nightwalking, did she really talk to you?"

"I wouldn't call it a conversation, but she knows quite a few words."

"A lot of good that will do her." Hanging Road carefully placed each herb in its designated bag. "Spotted Calf told me the other day he was going to trade her south come winter. Of course, that was before this half-Kiowa creature showed up bearing his questionable gifts."

"The cloth he brought was nice," Nightwalking admitted. "And the needles. How our mothers ever got along without steel needles, I will never know."

"Bone needles are fine if they are properly made," said Hanging Road.

Nightwalking still fretfully paced about the lodge. Another moan of unimaginable torment came through the lodge walls. "I can't stand that!"

"Calm yourself, wife. I don't like the look of the man, either, and I don't like whatever is going on over there, but there is nothing we can do about it."

More screaming echoed through the hot night. Nightwalking took a deep, angry breath. "I'm going to take action if you won't!"

She headed for the opening of the lodge. Red Feather Woman glanced anxiously in Hanging Road's direction, then back to her defiant older sister.

With a groan, Hanging Road scrambled to his feet to follow his angry wife out the door. Red Feather Woman hurriedly brought up the rear as the three marched the short distance to the offending lodge.

They had not yet reached it when out of the opening spilled its occupants in a wild tangle of blood and fury, rolling and kicking across the dusty ground. They struggled in the dirt, the woman looking like a child in size compared to the large man with whom she grappled.

Hanging Road and the sisters rushed upon the pair, thinking the Kiowa trader meant to kill the girl, only to find that the young woman, though blood-splattered and nearly naked—the woman whose screams had rent the summer night—was the one who held the knife.

Before they could stop her, she lunged with a maniacal frenzy and buried the knife in the trader's shoulder. Hanging Road threw his arm around the woman's waist from behind and grabbed her wrist. He squeezed it hard enough to cause her to drop the weapon.

The trader grabbed the fallen blade from the dirt. He raised it against his victim-turned-attacker, but Hanging Road intervened, deftly shoving the battered, bleeding woman into the arms of his wives and decisively blocking the trader's path.

"Get out of my way! I want to finish her off," shouted the trader in a broken form of the Tsitsistas tongue.

"You've done enough tonight, you drunken fool. Pack up your things and get out!"

This taunt enraged the staggering trader. Every heavy breath he took caused his large body to waver. The stench of whiskey surrounded him like an invisible fog. He grasped his bleeding shoulder with one hand and turned on Hanging Road in a threatening manner, knife in hand, but Hanging Road refused to yield.

Dozens of people now emerged from their lodges and gathered to watch the spectacle.

Nightwalking folded the skinny white woman into her arms, heedless of the sticky blood and dirt covering her from head to toe. She watched in a horrified trance as her husband faced mortal danger. She had not intended this result. She had not meant to place anyone at risk but her own stubborn self.

Tension hung in the humid night air, closing up every space, rendering the vast open prairie a tight and claustrophobic vacuum as the violent drama played out second by agonizing second.

Armed with only a bold arrogance and an absolute disdain, the young medicine man stood his ground. He placed his hands on his hips as though he were a father standing down an errant child. He did not even bother to raise his voice as he spoke. "Leave here, you pathetic excuse for a man. Go make your filthy mischief somewhere else."

The trader's drunken eyes widened, not able to comprehend his opponent's insane bravery in the face of his upraised knife. He took a step closer, his bloody knife blade only the width of a man's hand from Hanging Road's throat.

The younger man made not the slightest motion, either to protect himself or to fend off the Kiowa trader's advance. Rather he looked upon him, his gaze never wavering. He jutted out his scarred chin and waited.

Whether Hanging Road employed some kind of potent medicine to back the man down or whether the trader simply feared he would, he dropped the knife with a frightened look.

"Just get out," Hanging Road shouted.

The trader bolted and ran off like a scared dog in the direction of the pony herd.

Everyone watching sighed collectively in relief. Hanging Road's valor astounded his audience almost as much as it had stunned his enemy.

"It's over, it's over," Hanging Road announced to the group with a wave of his hand. "Time for sleep."

He and the sisters carried the unplanned guest into their lodge. Nightwalking busily wrapped the girl in an old blanket in an effort to stop her shivering. As she worked to make the suffering young woman more comfortable she caught in a sidelong glance the sight of her husband breathing deeply in relief. Beads of perspiration covered his forehead and upper lip as he tried to catch his breath. His moment of spectacular bravery had exhausted him.

"What was I thinking?" Hanging Road murmured, apparently addressing himself. "He could have killed me."

"But he didn't," said his senior wife. They smiled sweetly to each other.

She could not help but shake her head. So like his brother, her first husband. Though Hanging Road had never chosen the warrior's path, he was every bit as brave as the older brother he had grown up idolizing.

Nightwalking tried to clean the girl, who had slipped into unconsciousness. As she wiped the blood and soot from the girl's bosom, she grimaced to note human teeth marks covering her small breasts. Some were merely bruised impressions, while others cut through the flesh. In running her hand over the girl's belly, with its hard round swelling of early pregnancy, she felt the muscles contract. The girl's thighs were covered with blood.

"She's going to have this child tonight. She's in labor, I can feel it."

"After her ordeal, I'm not surprised," remarked Hanging Road.

"You're not afraid of a woman's blood, husband?" asked Red Feather delicately.

"Only warriors are afraid of a woman's blood."

That any man exposed to the potent medicine of a

woman during the time of menses would likely suffer death in battle was a fact universally acknowledged. That Hanging Road felt himself exempt from this hallowed taboo perplexed his wives, but they knew better than to challenge him on the issue.

Nightwalking clearly felt a medicine man ought to behave in a more solemn fashion, but he was still so young and had so much yet to learn. She examined the girl more closely, then suddenly cried out in disgust and horror.

"What is it?" asked Red Feather and Hanging Road in unison.

"He must have used a knife on her," Nightwalking said, her face twisted with the thought of it.

Hanging Road and Red Feather both joined Nightwalking. Red Feather turned away quickly after taking a peek between the girl's thighs, but Hanging Road scrutinized the wounds in detail, unflinching as always in his curiosity.

"I think I know exactly what happened," he announced. "The wretch was so drunk he couldn't perform the act in the usual way, so he substituted his knife."

"That's so disgusting," groaned Nightwalking. "If that man were here right now, I'd kill him with my bare hands."

"She'll need something for the pain when she comes around," her husband said. "If she comes around, that is." He reached for one of the pouches he had been working on earlier in the evening.

Red Feather Woman jumped up to go fetch more

water for Hanging Road to use in brewing a tea for the pain medication. She took a long time to return. When she did, she explained that everyone wanted her to stop and talk. Those who had missed the appalling event all wanted to hear the story retold.

Before daybreak, Eden Murdoch delivered a five-month fetus, the product of her time spent in the Dog Soldier camp after her capture. Twice during her labor her pulse grew so weak they were certain she had died.

"Seota'a," Hanging Road had whispered each time he thought she had slipped away. Dead woman. Ghost.

But back she came for another dose of life, again and again, surprising them all with her tenacity.

When Eden finished her story of the Kiowa trader, embellishing any details she could not remember, she observed with perverse satisfaction that her words had produced the desired result: her audience had been shocked into silence.

Mary Lowell sniffled quietly. She had begged Eden to stop on several occasions.

Elias Lowell sat with his elbows still on the table, only now he covered his face with his hands.

Brad sat back in the uncomfortable dining chair with his long legs stretched out under the table. His hands were laced together across his chest as he stared down at the tablecloth. Only occasionally did he dare to raise his eyes to meet Eden's during her story. Eden guessed he may have been better prepared for it than the others. She knew he had read the doctor's report on her. He no

doubt had imagined how some of the injuries had come about.

"It's late. I must be going," the captain announced in a quiet voice after clearing his throat. Before him lay the remains of the dinner, cold and untouched. Congealed lard now floated in great, unappetizing chunks on top of the gravy. He rose from his chair without his customary speech of thanks to the Lowells for inviting him to dinner.

Eden walked him to the door. "Captain, I never said anything to the Lowells about you. I hope you know that."

"About me and Tessa?" Brad smiled bashfully. "I know it wasn't from you. I think I know exactly where he got that information." As he pulled on his greatcoat, he shook his head. "It doesn't really matter."

He paused on the doorstep. "I don't feel right about leaving you here. I don't like what's happened tonight. I know all I can offer is a cold tent surrounded by a bunch of men you can't stand but—"

"I'll be fine. I don't know if I will be welcome here after tonight, but I'll be forced to make another arrangement soon anyway."

"I'll call on you in the morning. I have some ideas I want to discuss with you."

She held out her hand. When he took it, he impulsively pulled it to his lips and kissed it.

Seventeen

"Honey, wake up, for heaven's sake." Tessa vigorously shook Brad's shoulder. "You're havin' a nightmare."

Brad sat up and rubbed his face with his hands. "I can't believe I fell asleep," he groaned. "What time is it? I've got to get back to camp."

He jumped out of bed and began to pull on his clothes as if the devil were chasing him.

"What in the name of God were you dreamin' about? You was moanin' and thrashin' fit to beat all."

"I don't remember," he lied. He did not want to admit that he had dreamed the awful dream again about the warrior with the necklace of severed human fingers. He thought it unmanly to admit to being frightened about anything. He wondered if such a weakness made him a coward. He had never thought himself a coward. He had never flinched in battle or failed to carry out an order. But why did he continue to have these nightmares in which he lay naked and impotent on the frozen prairie ground, at the mercy of that frightening man with

267

his horrific necklace? The images were always the same, the cut finger, the blood on his hands, and lying helpless among the men of Major Elliott's lost detail.

It was all Eden Murdoch's fault. He had the dream whenever he had been around her. She had planted the nasty thought of cutting off an enemy's finger on that first day in Reliance. And then to hear her gruesome story of the sexual torture to which she had been subjected. How could she even remain sane after such horrors?

When fully dressed, he returned to Tessa's bed and knelt next to it. "Tess, I've only got three dollars. Can you carry me until payday?" He comically raised his eyebrows in an attempt to look as pathetic as possible.

"*Now* you tell me," she teased with a playful giggle. She stuck out her bottom lip in a pretend pout, then hooked her little finger around the chain he wore on his neck and drew out the gold band. "You oughta give me this."

"Sorry, it's spoken for."

"Saving it for your bride, I suppose." She slid the ring on her finger.

He leaned over her to give a kiss of thanks. As always, she quickly dodged his lips. "Tessa, I'll be leaving soon. I've just got to ask—why can't I kiss you?"

She narrowed her eyes at him. "Save your kisses—and your stupid ring—for your bride."

He headed out into the blustery, cold night, the last night of 1868. He checked his watch: three twenty-five. The new year of 1869 had begun without him. A couple of sweaty hours of lovemaking in Tessa's arms had left

him exhausted. The little bottle of brandy she had brought to toast in the New Year had finished him off and he slept through the stroke of midnight without giving it a thought.

Hugh Christie's nameless saloon was dark. The revelers drinking in the New Year had all gone home now. Brad vaguely remembered hearing guns being fired into the night. They must have been saluting the start of 1869.

A dry, icy snow swirled in the prairie wind and danced in patterns across the empty street. The arc of light from a lonely street torch on the corner caught the glittering snow as it formed a tiny whirlwind down the center of the hard-frozen dirt road. He tried to imagine a little Indian boy chasing after the spinning shape, trying to catch it, as Eden Murdoch had claimed of her Cheyenne husband.

The frigid air stung his nostrils with every breath. The ride back to his camp on the outskirts of town would be a miserable one, made worse by the thought of how uncomfortably cold his cot would be after leaving Tessa's warm, soft bed behind, not to mention her warm, soft body. After the loathsome dinner at the Lowells' house and the reverend's insulting remarks, he had headed straight for Tessa's, just for spite.

He mounted his horse and drew his coat collar as close to his face as he could manage. A squall of arctic winds thrashed him over and over as he rode down Main Street. He squinted against the blasts and pulled his hat down low. The shifting clouds made the full moon play a game of peekaboo, bathing the sleeping town in gray moonlight one minute and shadowy black-ness the next.

If his horse had not jerked at a rolling tumbleweed that had skittered into their path, he might never have noticed her. She sat curled up like a cat in the slim shel-ter of Rhinehart Meeker's barbershop door. And if he had not seen the edge of a petticoat peeking from be-neath the dark skirt, he would not have known the form was female and might have ridden on by.

"Ma'am? Are you all right?" he called. The cold was severe enough to be dangerous.

The form did not move. He reluctantly dismounted and tethered his horse at the rail. He leaned over the huddled form and discovered it was wrapped in a woolen army blanket. He gently shook the woman's shoulder. She did not respond.

What a night for this to happen. He was not in the mood to play the good Samaritan. The skin of his face had begun to ache with the cold and his eyes stung and watered copiously. He grabbed the woman by the shoul-ders to sit her up.

"Mrs. Murdoch! What are you doing out here?"

Her face looked deathly white in the gray moonlight. She opened her eyes, but said nothing. Brad gathered her up in his arms and decided he would have to carry her—where? Tessa's? That would not be a good idea. He chose to wake up Hugh Christie instead.

Eden seemed light in his arms at first, but after he had covered the span of the block he looked forward to finding a place to put her down. He shifted her in his arms and considered bracing her over his shoulder, but

that seemed too rude a thing to do. He reached Christie's saloon and walked round to the alley. He shouted for Hugh until a light could finally be seen in the upstairs window.

"She's got frostbite on her earlobes," Hugh remarked after he and Brad had placed Eden in bed under many blankets.

Hugh tried to spoon-feed her some lukewarm coffee.

This caused Eden to rouse herself enough to start shivering uncontrollably. She looked about her, uncomprehending.

"Mrs. Murdoch, what were you doing outside at such an hour?" Brad asked.

"Looking for you," she managed to say, through chattering teeth. "I walked all the way to your camp, only to have them tell me you had stayed the night in town."

"That's three miles each way!"

"And according to the thermometer outside my window," Hugh added, "it's twelve below zero."

"They were all drunk," Eden continued. "But the young private—Joe—he gave me this blanket. I left the Lowells' without a wrap. Your men said rude things to me and they made a lot of crude remarks at your expense, too, I'm afraid."

"You went out in this weather without a coat or cover of any sort?"

"Had to get away." Eden shivered, tears welled up in her eyes. "He . . . Mr. Lowell tried to—"

"That psalm-singing bastard!" Hugh growled. "I warned you about him. Didn't I warn you about him?" Hugh angrily left her bedside to retrieve some bricks he had warming on the woodstove in the corner of his room. He wrapped them in towels and carried them back to the large brass bed. Eden gratefully placed her blanket-swaddled feet upon them.

"You oughta arrest the son of a bitch, Brad."

"I don't have any civil authority. Mrs. Murdoch, did Mr. Lowell attack you?" He clenched his jaw in anger.

"I think he would have. But I defended myself with a paperweight from his desk in his study. I did not knock him unconscious, but his forehead was bleeding when I ran out. Mrs. Lowell left not long after you did, Captain. She went to tend one of her friends who was having a baby. Mr. Lowell called me down to his study. He said he wanted to apologize for upsetting me. I should have known it was improper to see him alone without Mrs. Lowell on the premises, but he sounded so sincere. I really needed a place to stay and I was afraid they would turn me out after all I told you at dinner. I don't know what possessed me to tell you that story. I must be insane."

"What story?" asked Hugh.

"Don't tell him," Eden begged. "Don't tell anyone. Please Brad."

Brad sat down on the bed next to Eden and put his arms around her. "There, there. Don't say that. I'm glad you told me."

"What story?" Hugh said again, obviously feeling left

out. He stood at the end of his bed, frowning at its occupants.

Eden could feel Brad make some gesture to Hugh, but could not see because he was pressing her face against his chest. Hugh announced he would heat some more coffee. When they were alone, Brad released her and faced her with an awkward grin. "I don't think our host approves of my familiarity toward you. I suppose it did look improper. I'm sorry, it just felt so natural. Forgive me, won't you? I don't want you to think that—"

"Oh, Brad, just shut up." But Eden smiled at him to show she did not really mean it in a cruel way. Her shivering had abated somewhat. "I don't wish to stay here. Mr. Christie made a most insulting proposal to me just after Christmas."

"I can hardly believe that. Hugh seems like a splendid fellow to me."

Eden sniffled miserably and wiped her nose. "He suggested that I stay in this place and work as a prostitute like all those other women who work for him."

"Those women don't work for Hugh. They work for Tessa. Hugh is Tessa's landlord and Tessa's best friend, I should guess. Nothing more."

"Oh. Perhaps I owe Mr. Christie an apology," Eden murmured.

Brad reached for his frock coat where it lay in a heap on the floor with his heavy greatcoat, gloves, and hat.

"Must you leave?" Eden asked, suddenly miserable.

"I need to get back to camp."

"Please stay. Just tonight. I'll never ask another thing of you, if you'll stay here with me tonight." She reached out weakly and he returned to her side in an instant. She hung around his neck and wept. "Stay, please stay."

Brad held her tenderly. "Do you mean me to stay with you . . . here? In Hugh's bed?"

"Please? I'm so cold, I don't think I'll ever be warm again."

"You poor thing. Of course I'll stay. Just let me pull off these boots first." He tugged off his tall riding boots and climbed under Hugh's quilts to fold Eden's small, chilled body to his as tightly as he could. She rested her head on his chest and he idly combed his fingers through her cropped auburn hair. He pressed one of her hands against the warm skin of his face and held it there.

"Comfortable?" he asked.

"Yes, thank you."

Despite the chastity of their fully clothed embrace, Brad knew this conduct was throughly improper. Consorting with prostitutes was bad enough, but sharing a bed with a woman he considered to be of his own class—however innocently—would be considered scandalous by the entire rest of the civilized world.

And he was woefully negligent of his professional duties in not returning to his camp all night. If he weren't in charge, he would be obliged to declare himself absent without leave. Fortunately, his men seemed to be having too good a time in Reliance to complain of his neglect.

He pulled Eden closer still, relishing the intimacy. He hoped she didn't notice how aroused he was getting

by their pleasing nearness. The last thing he wanted was for her to think that he would try to ill-use her like every other man she seemed to come in contact with.

Instead, he hoped she felt safe in his arms, safe from the howling of the wild world. He fell asleep wishing he could hold her like this for the rest of his life.

As the winter sky grew bright and midday approached, Eden woke up alone in the brass bed. She heard the sound of loud voices nearing the bedroom. Brad, Tessa, and Hugh all entered the room in a rush.

"Hugh, don't do it," Brad said.

Hugh marched into the room and opened up a clothes press. "He's already spreading rumors around town. Rhinehart Meeker came and told me first thing. Says he's gonna press charges. The bastard—I'm gonna teach him a lesson he'll never forget."

"What's going on?" Eden asked in confusion.

"I'm gettin' dressed and goin' callin'," Christie announced as he laid out a vest and jacket and clean shirt on the brass foot rail of the bed.

Tessa slouched in wearing an Oriental-style silk dressing gown and a long shawl. She seated herself on the edge of the bed and surveyed Eden cynically. "The Right Reverend Mr. Lowell's goin' around town sayin' you went crazy and tried to kill him."

Eden gasped at this new outrage.

"Hugh, let me handle this," Brad insisted. "I can get Lowell to recant."

"I'll make him 'recant' all right. He'll be preachin'

out of a whole nother part of his anatomy when I get through with him."

Eden leaned forward. "Don't place yourself in danger on my account, Mr. Christie. I'm flattered, but please don't."

Hugh stood and debated the situation. "Damn it all. I can't let him get away with this. I can't."

Brad turned to Hugh and announced in a low voice that he intended to be out of Eden's earshot, "At least let's wait until dark."

A broad smile spread across Hugh's face. He slapped Brad on the shoulder. "That's my boy."

The two men departed, conversing in whispers.

"I'll go make you some coffee or tea if you want it," offered Tessa with her usual sour face.

"I really just want to sleep, but thank you anyway." Before she could say more, she broke into a coughing spell that shook her entire body. A tight, dry cough. She had often heard that cough in the hospital wards where she had worked as a nurse.

They're coming for me. They're coming to take me. They're coming to kill me. It's not my fault, it's not my fault. Angel of Mercy, Angel of Death.

Eden woke from her feverish dream wondering if the past was about to repeat itself. Her dreams had taken her back to the horrible days of the smallpox epidemic.

More deaths every day. The village grew weaker and anxiety slowly gave way to panic that everyone might perish. Though Eden worked day and night to make the

ill more comfortable, following Hanging Road from lodge to lodge, the fact that she alone did not succumb became more and more apparent.

She wanted to tell them how she had been vaccinated as a child, that she was immune to the deadly plague that raged among them, but she lacked the language skills.

Some began to fear her presence. "Why does she survive? Why is she alive and strong when all about her perish?" They advised Hanging Road that they did not want her near them.

"But she's helping me," he would say. "She knows about treating the sick. I need an extra pair of hands. She's come to me for a purpose. She doesn't fear the ill or the dying. She doesn't flinch when there is unpleasant work to be done. I call her 'Seota' because she makes me think of the maiden of the Sacred Spring. She's gifted with the power to heal. If there is a purpose in any of this, then let it be that she was sent to me to help me heal the sick. I know this. I feel it and I will not let anyone speak otherwise."

Slowly, Hanging Road convinced more and more in the village of Eden's powers to heal. As she bathed the feverish faces and applied his ointments to the oozing and crusting pockmarks of the suffering, more grew comfortable accepting her aid and comfort.

But a faction still smoldered with resentment. A counsel was held in secret. Hanging Road was not invited—a highly irregular move. Yet those who feared and distrusted the *ve'ho'a momoo*, the white captive, Seota, thought she might have deluded him, spiritually seduced him with her evil. His opinion could perhaps no longer be trusted.

Was she a *hestanova,* a life-taker? The faction marched on Hanging Road's lodge and demanded she be brought out.

"A life-taker?" Hanging Road was shocked that they, his friends, would suggest such a thing. He grabbed Seota's arm and pulled her to her feet, for she had been cowering in fear behind his legs. "She is my wife!"

"You're a man of many talents, Brad Randall," Hugh said as they walked back to the saloon in the cold darkness. "Where'd you learn to throw a punch like that?"

"I was once a professional boxer," Brad said.

"Well, I'll be damned. And I had you pegged as a college boy."

"How do you think I earned my tuition? I didn't have any family money to rely on. My prizefighting career was cut short when the school officials found out how I was spending my Saturday nights." He paused to rinse the blood off his hands in the frigid water of a horse trough. He had to break a thin crust of ice first. "But I'm pleased to report I won a fair share of the fights I was in before they made me stop. I was always the tallest in my weight class."

They returned to Eden's bedside the following morning. "You've got nothing to fear from Elias Lowell," Hugh said.

"What happened, Mr. Christie?"

"We had a nice and neighborly chat with the reverend. Told him how his congregation was gonna be disappointed in him when the whole town finds out just how often he visits my friend Tessa's place."

Eden's amber-green eyes widened at this revelation.

"Turns out he got into some trouble with private prayer sessions back in Leavenworth."

"Private prayer sessions? That's exactly what he said to me! The moment he got me alone in his study he said he wanted us to pray together. When I declined, he got forceful. That's when I grabbed the paperweight and whacked him with it."

Eden broke into another fearful coughing spell.

"Mrs. Murdoch, I'm concerned that you're becoming very ill," Brad said.

"I'm sure I'll be fine. I just don't know what I'll do next with no money and no place to live."

"Well, it's true you can't go back to the Lowells'."

"I'll miss my friendship with Mary."

"I'm afraid she has denounced you even more forcefully than her errant husband," Brad said. "She is completely deluded as to her husband's true character and cannot believe a word spoken against him. She is howling for you to be locked up louder than anyone."

Eden shook her head in dismay, unable to believe Mary's defection. And yet she knew how Mary worshiped her husband. She undoubtedly believed every word he said to her. "You're certain they won't press charges against me?"

"Not anymore," answered Hugh with confidence.

MICHELLE BLACK

"What did you do to him?" Eden demanded. "Did you resort to physical violence?"

"He'll be fine," the feisty barkeeper insisted with a wicked grin. "Eventually." He turned to leave. "Now if you'll excuse me, I got a saloon that needs tending."

"Oh, dear," Eden sighed.

Once Hugh was out the door, Brad approached the bed. "I feel wretched to have to leave you like this."

"I shall miss you, Captain Randall."

"Please call me Brad, now. And get well soon. Hugh told me he wants you to stay here for as long as you wish. I feel his intentions are honorable, Eden. Truly, I do. I think you'll be safe here. Though I admit it is highly irregular to venture the proposition that a lady's virtue would be safer if she stayed in a saloon than in a minister's house."

Eden chuckled at Brad's joke, but conceded, "I may not have a choice."

"I shall bid you farewell now. My men and I march by noon if we are to make Camp Supply by nightfall. May I write to you from the field? To tell you of our progress?"

"I would enjoy that very much." He was nearly out the door when she called him back one last time. "Brad, I know you've promised your future to someone else. Rest assured that I fully accept that the other night didn't change anything."

He glanced at her from under his hooded gray eyes with a look of complete confusion. What was she talking about? They had spent a night in the same bed, but nothing more inappropriate had transpired between

them. Brad was certain of that. True, he had experienced a vivid dream in which they had shared a spectacular passion, moaning and writhing, transcending anything he had ever felt with Tessa. He remembered every erotic detail with a shattering clarity which set it apart from other such dreams in an odd way. Dreams were usually remembered in fragments and the sights and sounds, emotions and sensations, came back to him the following morning in jagged disarray like a sunrise reflected in shards of glass.

But his dream of Eden held a blurry, hypnotic authenticity that seemed outside his ususal repertoire of erotic imaginings. Still, it was just a dream. He tried to shake it off even as the memory of it aroused him all over again. Nothing had actually happened with Eden . . . or had it?

He smiled uncertainly.

"I must leave you now, but . . . you will never leave my thoughts." He turned and was gone.

A quarter of an hour later Tessa appeared.

"Where is he?" she demanded. She flounced in wearing a gaudy yellow dress of a style befitting a young girl rather than a mature woman.

"Captain Randall? He left. He breaks camp today and will march before noon, he said."

Tessa did not trouble to hide her crestfallen look. She wandered over to the small window of the bedroom which faced the alley. She stared down intently, though there was nothing to look at but a muddy pathway, some trash piles, and a privy. "He didn't even say goodbye."

Eighteen

The whole force of his nature was concentrated in the one idea of how best to act for the good of his race; he knew the power of the white man . . . his utmost endeavors were used to preserve peace and friendship between his race and their oppressors.

—Testimony of Edward Wynkoop, describing Black Kettle to the U.S. Indian Commission, Washington, D.C., December 23, 1868

In Camp on Medicine Bluff Creek
February 8, 1869

My dear Mrs. Murdoch:

I had strong reason to think of you the other night. Someone wrote a letter to a newspaper that was harshly critical of the Washita Battle and my commander's decisions in regard to same.

The general received a copy of the offending article in the mail delivery as soon as we arrived back at our base camp here on Medicine Bluff Creek. As we and several others dined together in the officers' mess tent, we spoke little and all read our much-loved letters from home. Several officers took turns sharing amusing passages aloud.

Food itself seemed a luxury as the month of January passed in a state of one privation after another. As we traveled to the Red River and back our supplies became terribly short. We went two full weeks without wagons, tents, or shelter of any sort. Both officers and men dined on parched corn—that which we reserve to feed the horses—and horseflesh itself. As our steeds dropped one by one from exhaustion and starvation, they found deliverance at the hands of the rear guard and joined the stew pot and roasting spit each night.

The general paid little heed to the rest of us at the table as he read one missive over and over again. I noticed his unusual silence and saw that he read a newspaper article rather than a letter. His coloring flushed darker red than usual and he tapped his boot against the table leg in an increasingly annoying fashion as his obvious agitation grew.

He abruptly stood up and announced, "Tell the trumpeter to sound 'Officers Call.' "

He left without ceremony, taking the newspaper with him, but leaving the rest of his personal mail untouched. I gathered up his letters to take to him, knowing his distraction must have caused him this oversight. Among the pile, I saw two unopened letters from Mrs. Custer and realized the gravity of the situation must be extreme for him to forsake letters from his wife. He has advised me on several occasions that her letters are among his dearest possessions and he would as soon part with

them as he would part with his own life.

We congregated as ordered within a few minutes. All stood apprehensively as our commander emerged from his tent with the offending newspaper in one hand and his riding crop in the other. He paced back and forth before us like a caged tiger waiting for an opportunity to spring, all the while slapping his rawhide quirt against his boot top as he began his remarks.

"A certain newspaper article, published in the *St. Louis Democrat,* has been forwarded to me by an interested party. In this article someone who could only have had personal knowledge of the Washita Battle—and by that, I mean someone in this group here assembled—has chosen to offer opinions on the said engagement in a manner not only critical, but slanderous to myself and to the actions of the whole regiment."

At this pronouncement, I felt certain my worst fears had been realized, Mrs. Murdoch. I knew at that moment the article must have published the information you desired to share concerning that unfortunate occurrence on the day after Thanksgiving.

"Some cowardly person—one of my very own officers with whom I must trust my life and on whom I must depend through the thick and thin of this dangerous mission into enemy territory—this person has seen fit to anonymously hold my decisions and our actions up to public ridicule before the whole world," the general said.

I wished at that moment to have the earth beneath my feet yawn wide and swallow me, such unbearable humiliation did I feel. Honor would not permit me to hide behind the shield of anonymity and play the innocent. I tried to decide how best to admit my guilt. And at the same time I wondered how it was that your comments, Mrs. Murdoch, would have been published anonymously. Your celebrated status as the "rescued" captive (how well I know you despise that label) would have to have embellished the power of the story immensely.

"When the miserable coward steps forward to reveal himself," continued General Custer, "he will feel my wrath with this horsewhip!" He slapped the quirt against his boot with a resounding crack, causing me and everyone present to jerk in surprise, so heavy did the tension squeeze the air.

I swallowed even harder. So I was to receive physical as well as any other type of punishment the general had in his mind to mete out. Images of my fiancée and her father flashed through my mind—their imagined disappointment in me stung me worse than any degradation I could suffer before my fellow officers, even though that in itself was considerable. I glanced about at the faces near me, innocent men who stood by and wondered at the identity of the culprit and what would happen next.

I decided to wait no longer, to get it over with, and take my punishment in as manly a fashion as I could manage. I drew a deep breath for courage,

and just as I opened my mouth to speak, another officer brusquely elbowed me aside and stepped to the fore.

"Might I take a look at the article to which you refer, General?" asked Major Benteen.

The general narrowed his eyes at this officer and offered him the page of newsprint. My mouth dropped open in surprise that another might have written the offensive tract but you. Yet in a few seconds Major Benteen handed back the paper to his commanding officer and, very noticeably placing his right hand on his revolver casing, said in a clear and stout voice, "General Custer, while I cannot father all of the blame you have asserted, still, I guess I am the man you are after, and I am ready for the whipping promised."

A shocked murmur rolled through the group and everyone then collectively held their breath in wonderment of what would transpire next. Did Benteen actually mean to threaten the general with his hand placed so on his sidearm? He looked absolutely calm and determined in his resolve. In the face of such determination, would the general carry out his announced intention to horsewhip the guilty party?

The general himself proved to be the most stunned of all. His already flushed complexion turned crimson in the utmost. He parted his lips several times to reply, yet no sound issued forth. Had he made his threat idly, assuming no one would dare to come forward and be thus publicly humiliated? If he were bluffing, it was clear to all present that Major Benteen was not.

"Colonel Benteen . . . I . . . I . . . shall see you again, sir!" at last spoke our commander in stammering tones to Major Benteen, (whose brevet rank is that of colonel). Custer then dismissed us all and we quickly dispersed.

Not until I left sight of the general's tent did I grant myself the luxury of realizing I was "off the hook"—at least for the present. Though the evening was well below freezing, I now found myself drenched in perspiration.

If you will permit me, I must ask—what was the result of your letters, Mrs. Murdoch? Were they published and, if so, in what venue or forum? You must take your humble captain out of suspense on this matter.

Your devoted friend and ever your servant,
Bradley J. Randall

P.S. Did you see in the papers that Congress has voted to leave the Bureau of Indian Affairs in the Department of the Interior rather than transferring it to the War Department? This is hopeful news to all those longing for a peaceful resolution of the present scene. Do you not agree? My superiors are not at all pleased by this development, so I mutely keep my own counsel on this subject when it arises in conversation. I stand by my prediction that the new president may turn out to be a man of peace after all.

"Whatcha readin'?" Hugh Christie asked as he breezed in with Eden's dinner on a tray.

"A letter from Brad—I mean, Captain Randall. Would you like to read it?"

The saloonkeeper seemed uneasy. "Only if it's not too personal."

"Personal?" Eden smiled. "It's just filled with gossip from the officers' mess. What did you imagine—a love letter?"

Hugh shrugged. To his mind, Brad Randall owed Eden some love letters, given the fact he had spent the early morning hours of New Year's Day in her bed. The young rascal, jumping into bed with every woman who would have him. And Brad playing cool as ice about it the next day, like nothing had happened. Of course, to the boy's credit, he put an astonishing enthusiasm into the beating he gave the minister. Hugh was still flabbergasted at Brad's prowess with his fists. Who would have guessed it?

He had debated the matter of Brad and Eden at some length with Tessa. Her conclusion was that Eden, for all her airs and arrogance, was a common slut and Brad—being a healthy and virile young man—had behaved neither better nor worse than could be expected, given the provocation.

Hugh set aside Eden's dinner tray and placed a hand on her forehead. "The fever's back. I better call that doctor again."

"Oh, please, no. I can't stand that man. I don't like the hateful way he looks at me."

He did not argue with her, but fetched Dr. Ashcroft just the same. The doctor examined her for the fourth time in the five weeks she had spent in Hugh's bedroom-turned-infirmary, as he liked to call it.

"The infection has returned to her lungs," Ashcroft announced in hushed tones to Christie. "I thought we were rid of it, but we are not. I'm afraid there is not much we can do now but make her comfortable and hope for the best. She's more in God's hands now than ours."

Between the reading of Brad's letter and the exit of Dr. Ashcroft, Eden's temperature had reached a danger-ous level. She was no longer entirely sure of her sur-roundings. "Ameo, help me, help me, I'm drowning."

"Whoever Ameo is, he's not here," Hugh said as he sat down next to Eden on his bed. He had not slept in his own room since the viciously cold night she had been brought to it by Brad. He had taken up residence in his own stockroom just behind the bar on an army cot Brad had dropped off prior to leaving Reliance.

"Ameo, my husband." Ameo was her pet name for Hanging Road. "But where is he? And my baby, Sam-uel . . . where is he? Where is he?"

He awkwardly patted Eden's arm. She needed a fresh nightgown. He would have to ask Tessa to come over in the morning and help Eden change. He did not like the noisy sound of her breathing. Her small chest rattled and scratched with every breath she drew. Her coughing shook the whole brass bed, setting up a resounding clatter.

"Your little fella's gone. Remember? You lost him a long time ago."

Tears welled in her eyes. "I didn't mean to drop him. I tripped. Running through the tall grass. Running so hard. My stays too tight. Couldn't breathe, just like now, couldn't breathe. My boot caught on something, twisted my ankle, I fell, knocked the wind out of me. He was gone, just gone, lost in the tall grass. I could hear him crying, but I couldn't find him. Couldn't stand up, my ankle wouldn't take my weight, then *he* came, he grabbed me, carried me off. I screamed and fought, but I never could get loose."

"It's all right," he said in a soothing tone. "It's over now. All that happened years ago."

"He's alive. I know it! He lives still. Someone found him and cared for him. He waits for me."

"Hush, now. You know better than that. He's gone. You gotta let him go."

With a sudden manic intensity, Eden sat up and grabbed Hugh by the lapels of his vest. Her watery eyes shone wild with fever. "If I had another baby, I would take such good care of it. I would protect it with my life. Nothing bad would ever happen, nothing, nothing, not ever. I wouldn't let anything bad happen. I wouldn't!"

He gently forced her to lie back down. "Of course you wouldn't. Now calm down. You need to rest."

Eden began to sob. "I just want a second chance. Doesn't everyone deserve a second chance?"

"In a perfect world, we'd get as many chances as

we needed, honey. But it ain't a perfect world."

She continued to whimper until a knock at the door caused Hugh to rise from the bed.

Rhinehart Meeker poked his head in. "Hugh, you gotta come on down and tend bar. Marco's just not keeping up with the traffic and some of the fellas are gettin' rowdy and out of hand."

"Don't leave me, Hugh. I'm afraid to be alone."

"Now, honey, nothin's gonna hurt you up here. I wouldn't let nobody hurt you."

"Ameo wouldn't, either. He wouldn't let them hurt me. They came for me, but he stood firm. He said, 'Take your hands off my wife!' And they were so surprised, they didn't know which way to look. And I was stunned, too, because he never said anything to me or the sisters about it. He called me his wife, and ever after, I was his wife—at least in name. He did it to save me. I knew he didn't love me, but he wanted to save me. He knew it was the right thing to do. He was such a good man." Eden started wailing even louder than before.

"What in hell is she babblin' about?" said Meeker.

"She's in a fever."

"Well, I kinda guessed that much."

"When she gets these fevers, she starts talkin' about those Indians she lived with." He wet a cloth in the basin he kept next to the bed and sponged off Eden's fevered brow.

"You comin' down or not?"

He started to rise for the second time, only to have Eden frantically grab his shirtsleeve. "I'm afraid I'll fall asleep and never wake up!"

Hugh shuddered out a worried sigh. "Rhinehart, tell Marco he's on his own tonight. I can't leave her. Ashcroft's already been and gone. He's given up tryin'. I got an awful feelin' this might be the end."

Meeker frowned and closed the door.

"I'm stayin'. Stop your frettin' now." He sponged her face and arms and decided if she lived through the night, he would buy her a brand-new nightgown. The one he had on loan from Tessa was entirely too whorish-looking. Not that Eden had been well enough to care about fashion in the last month.

Reluctantly, he untied the ribbons at her throat and bodice and opened the front of the sweaty, stained night dress. He felt vaguely uncomfortable exposing her in this way, as though he were somehow taking advantage of her illness. He was not taking liberties, but still he felt the sting of her accusation after Christmas that his friendship to her was just a pretense to exploit her somehow.

He sponged her feverish flesh, but worried he had overdone his task when she began to shiver. He mopped off her wet skin with a corner of the bedsheet and retied the ribbons of her nightgown. Without thinking, he gave her a quick kiss on the forehead.

Sick as she was, she managed to smile at him. "Still taking in strays, aren't you, Hugh?"

He grinned. She seemed lucid enough to realize who he was for a change. In her many deliriums of the recent weeks, she had mistaken him for her father, her husband Lawrence Murdoch, the Cheyenne fellow called Ameo, a doctor named Brinkley for whom she had apparently worked during the war, and, of course, Brad Randall. In short, she cast him in the role of all the men in her life, except himself.

"Tell me once more why you've never found a name for your saloon."

"I'm waitin' for the right name to find *me*."

"Oh, yes, that's right."

"You need to rest," he admonished in a whisper.

Nineteen

Little Rock's daughter was an exceedingly
comely squaw, possessing a bright, cheery face,
a countenance beaming with intelligence . . .
and a rich complexion, her well-shaped head
was crowned with a luxuriant growth of the
most beautiful silken tresses, rivaling in color
the blackness of the raven.
—G. A. CUSTER, *MY LIFE ON THE PLAINS*

In Camp on the Red River, Texas
March 14, 1869

Dear Amanda,

Did you attend the inauguration of President Grant
as you and your father planned on the fourth? You
must spare me no details. I hope the weather was
better than here. Snow, more snow, blustery wind
that stings the face, unrelenting cold. How tired
you must be of hearing me complain.

Winter wears on but slowly and my thoughts
fly to you. How can March be so forbidding? Would
you like to know what has happened since my last
letter to you? A mutiny! Yes, indeed. Our Kansas
comrades, the Nineteenth Volunteers, decided to

protest the bad food and lack of compensation with a near insurrection, which fortunately proved to be bloodless.

Congress, in their unfathomable wisdom, neglected to appropriate monies to pay the good volunteers. The governor of Kansas, who resigned his office to lead the troops, has now resigned his commission in order to head for Washington to intercede on their behalf. Give him my regards, should he call—Ha, ha!

General Sheridan returned to Camp Supply and the Seventh has been ordered to report to Fort Hays by the end of the month. On the second of March, we left Medicine Bluff Creek with eleven companies of the seventh and ten of the Kansas nineteenth. We headed west, rounding just south of the Wichita Mountains.

General Custer divided the troops in half at this point, about eight hundred men in each group. He sent one contingent back to the vicinity of the Washita battleground where Major Inman was to meet them with additional supplies.

The poor men of the Kansas Nineteenth have it ever the worse than we in the Regular Army, I must admit. To add to their other miseries, the general decided to place them all afoot. He ordered their horses be given to the men of the Seventh. They try bravely to keep up with us, but their blistered feet see it otherwise.

We found few sightings of Indians, for all our two months in the saddle. We did strike one trail

and located a small encampment, but the barking of my esteemed commander's beloved hunting dogs alerted our quarry and by the time we reached the village, its occupants had long since departed for safety.

On March 9, we crossed the Red River into the state of Texas. We bivouacked on the Salt Fork. Our supplies grew scarcer with each passing day. For warmth, we burned all the blankets save one per man and all the extra clothing. We are required to wait until after dark to start our fires as the general fears the smoke could be seen in daylight by our enemy.

Without your letters to distract me, my days are long and dreary. In the last mail delivery, I had a letter from the woman I have spoken of so frequently, Mrs. Eden Murdoch.

I have less than happy news to report on that score. Her attempt to call attention to certain aspects of the Washita Battle which she does not feel were correctly represented by those official reports made to the press by my superiors has met with considerable conflict.

Her efforts were printed in several newspapers of renown by persons sympathetic to the cause of the Peace Advocates. Yes, her remarks were critical of our actions there, but I cannot controvert them, Amanda. I would if I could. She makes several good points and speaks the truth on every count she lodges. Fortunately, she did not quote yours truly as the source of some of her invectives, but I am afraid it is true. Various bits of her information did come from me. I do not wish my feelings to become generally known on this matter as it could be construed as insubordination, but I have grown to have many doubts about our actions of late. (Do not share these misgivings with your father.)

Regardless of the merits of the case she makes, her remarks were drowned out by a swift retaliation on the part of the military, most particularly General Sheridan, I would warrant, though from the information present in the articles Mrs. Murdoch forwarded to me, my own commander, General Custer, had a hand in the depiction of Mrs. Murdoch as being of unsound mind.

On one count, she has only herself to blame. She behaved in an outrageous manner on her first day in Reliance, causing no end of public comment and speculation as to her sanity. The second incident cited against her, however, is totally specious in nature.

They use against her a story that she made an unprovoked attack on the minister, Mr. Elias Lowell, with murderous intent. Nothing could be further from the truth. The man tried to force his attentions on her one night while his wife was away from the house attending to a friend's child-bed.

The ever-resourceful Mrs. Murdoch handily defended her honor with the aid of a paperweight and ran from the house. She unfortunately picked a very severe night to wander abroad without the

protection of a coat and caught a terrible chill
which later manifested itself as pneumonia.

She recovered with the ministrations and aid of
my good friend Hugh Christie and, judging from
the kind words she had to say about him, I gather
that a strong friendship has blossomed between
them. I only wish you would put to rest your
groundless accusations as to some type of romantic
involvement between Mrs. Murdoch and myself.
Yes, I admire her and, yes, care about her future
and welfare, but you do a disservice to us all to
even hint that I had any affections for her other
than that of a sincere friend.

Brad paused, guilt-ridden because his feelings for
Eden Murdoch were so transparent they even shone
through his chatty, trivia-filled letters to Amanda. She
had done everything but come out and accuse him of
being Eden's lover. He decided to steer the course of his
letter away from Eden and Reliance.

But speaking, as we are now, of romance . . . one
of the more questionable tasks to which my new
Indian language skills have been placed is that of
go-between—and, yes, I mean that in a romantic
sense. It seems my commanding officer, yes, none
other than George Armstrong Custer, lieutenant
colonel, brevet major general commanding, finds
himself smitten with one of our Cheyenne captives.

She is the daughter of the slain chief Little

Rock, killed in battle at the Washita. She seems to return my commander's attentions, though I cannot imagine why a woman would find attractive a man who was responsible for the death of her father.

Last evening, before supper, I was summoned to the general's tent to act as an interpreter of sorts. My skills in translation are far below that of our scout, Romero, but I believe in these matters, Custer trusts my discretion to a higher degree.

The girl and her new baby, born at Fort Cobb in January, had already arrived and she and the general were making conversation in signs. I was invited to sit and we formed a circle, cross-legged, on the floor of his tent. I spoke such as I could to the girl, conversing on matters of no greater import than the weather and the relative states of our health. General Custer and I dutifully admired the baby which the proud young mother displayed for our inspection. The general went on at length to me of the girl's phenomenal abilities at discerning a trail.

Whether he longed to impress upon me that his interest in the girl was professional and not personal, I can offer no opinion, but as soon as the baby grew peevish and fretful, he turned to me and asked as casually as can be imagined, "Randall, go take the baby for a walk."

"A walk?" I repeated, nonplussed. Did one walk a baby as one walks a dog? Custer's tone implied such.

"I really don't know anything about babies, sir," I said.

"Oh, there's nothing to it. Now be a good sport."

Nothing to it? And why would he have any knowledge on the subject? He and Mrs. Custer, though having just marked the fifth anniversary of their marriage, have had no children.

For better or worse, Custer took the squirming bundle from the young girl's arms and unceremoniously shoved it into mine. I rose uncertainly and carried my little charge out of the tent whereupon I was immediately attacked by General Custer's pack of hunting dogs. (Did I mention he has added a pelican to his menagerie?)

I kicked and cursed at the miserable curs, hoping the brevet major general commanding did not hear me. As I have stated on previous occasions, he treats the animals better than children and certainly better than his own men.

It took me a moment to figure out how to hold the little boy, whose name I had not even been told, but I got the hang of it eventually. He soon stopped his fussing noises and I walked over to the top of a ridge so the pair of us could watch the sun set. I found a seat on a rocky promontory and placed the baby in my lap with his little head braced against my knees so that we might look each other in the face.

I feared he might be cold so I adjusted his blankets. He was quite a handsome little fellow with his dark eyes and shock of pitch-black hair, and a surprising amount for such a small infant, I would imagine. I marveled at his perfectly formed little hands with their tiny fingernails. He employed them to grasp my index fingers and hold them tight.

I clucked my tongue and made silly faces and soon he favored me with a large smile, his little pink, toothless gums on full display. I felt well rewarded for my nursery efforts. Babies do not seem quite so mysterious and terrifying after all. I decided at that moment I would quite enjoy fatherhood, should heaven choose to bless our union.

"You are certainly a fine-looking little man," I told him. "Of course, you'll probably try to kill me someday. Are you after my scalp, is that it? Well, you'll have to wait a few years. Right now I have a considerable height advantage on you."

I went on in this foolish vein for a time and enjoyed it a great deal. As the sun disappeared on the prairie horizon in all its crimson and purple glory, a noticeable chill crept over the land and the little lad lost his good disposition.

Soon he cried his displeasure and I thought he might be hungry and wanting his supper. That was a situation I had no means to satisfy. I decided I must return him to his mother, whether my commander liked it or not.

I quickly retraced my steps to the general's tent, his striker smirking at me as I passed by. I listened at the door and heard no sounds from within. Thinking the tent unoccupied, I entered through the open flap, only to behold a strange sight, indeed.

No, there was no scene out of French farce, no passionate figures thrashing about in tangled dishabille. Rather something oddly more difficult to categorize and explain. General Custer sat on the edge of his couch with the girl in his lap. She was laughing and fingering the bushy beard he had spent the winter growing, while he, likewise delighted, seemed engaged in the task of wrapping a thick lock of the girl's long black hair around his throat.

The pair looked both startled and dismayed by my intrusion and jerked apart.

"Pardon me," I said and quickly backed my way out.

The infant now screamed in anger or hunger or confusion, so the reason for my abrupt and unannounced reappearance became obvious without further explanation.

Its mother dashed out, grabbed her crying baby from my arms, and quickly disappeared into the city of tents before us.

My commander soon joined me outside the tent and looked distinctly ill at ease.

"Randall, about what you saw in there . . ."

"I didn't see anything, sir. I don't know what you mean." I turned to him with a level and frank gaze that said I knew exactly what he meant.

A broad smile of relief broke over his face. He

gave me a hearty slap on the back. "Good man," he said, and returned to his tent as though nothing had happened.

And what had happened? I have no idea, really. Certainly there exists a faction among his officers who insist in no uncertain terms that the girl is Custer's mistress. But these selfsame officers are also the ones who criticize their commander at every turn, second-guess his every decision, and are never inclined to grant him the benefit of the doubt. In truth, I believe they possess even less personal knowledge of the matter than I do.

That Custer does nothing whatsoever to staunch the gossip about the girl is without question given the amount of time he spends in her company, yet it seems to me, from observing them together, that he presents the demeanor, not so much that of a paramour, but rather that of a curious little boy playing with a rare and exotic new toy.

On whether the foregoing would give his wife any comfort on the matter, I, again, offer no opinion. I must sign off for now.

Love,

Bradley

P.S. Tomorrow we head for the Sweetwater, a tributary of the Red River. I will write again as soon as we reach Camp Supply. From there we will march north to Hays, but hopefully pass through the town of Reliance on the way. And yes, I will probably again see Mrs. Murdoch.

And as to that comment in my last letter which gave you such offense, please know that I did not mean it as a reproach but merely as a suggestion. You must admit that you spend extraordinary amounts of time planning a wedding for which we cannot yet even set a date. Amanda, you are a woman of exceptional gifts and with the luxury of time at your disposal. All I meant by my remarks was that you might consider putting your time and talents to some more worthwhile pursuit than visiting ten dressmakers to find the perfect lace trim for your wedding gown and every silversmith in Virginia and Maryland in quest of the perfect napkin rings for your wedding reception.

Brad hurriedly crossed out this slip and wrote:

our wedding reception. Churches, schools, hospitals, orphan asylums—all seek constantly for help.

And please do not ask me again to surrender up my small savings for this wedding event. The marriage itself is what is important, not the ceremony that creates it. I will not underwrite every extravagance your father declines. I am not trying to be cruel or harsh, but you know I am saving that money to buy our first house and I consider the matter of our living indefinitely with your father to be a dead issue.

He paused to consider this last remark. He had nearly a thousand dollars saved. A thousand dollars was a lot of money, enough to buy someone a new start in life. Particularly in the West. In a land so vast, one could start fresh. In a land so vast, one could simply *vanish*.

Vanish. The word tantalized him like an exotic woman. And with the vanishing fantasy always came the apparition of Eden Murdoch. The Ghost Woman. She would come with him. They would make a new start together. He would take her away from the narrow-minded prejudice of small towns like Reliance that would doom her to a marginal existence.

His rational mind tried to pull him back to reality. He was engaged to be married. And not just engaged to marry anyone, but rather the daughter of his former employer, his mentor, a powerful man who had virtually handpicked him to be his son-in-law and heir. If he broke his engagement to Amanda, he would undoubtedly be subject to a lawsuit for breach of promise. The scandal would shame and hurt his mother.

And what of Amanda? He had promised to share his life with her. How could he abandon her like that? Of course, he had already sinned against their love with not one, but two women. At least he thought it was two. He still struggled to clear his mind, or perhaps his conscience, of what had transpired that night with Eden in Hugh Christie's bed. Why did everything involving Eden Murdoch seem obscured by mystery?

If he and Eden had shared the passion he seemed to remember, honor would demand that he marry her. Amanda would have to accept this. She would surely not remain alone for long. She was beautiful and moved in the highest circles of society.

He knew his reasoning was all too convenient. But the simple fact remained: he had fallen in love with Eden Murdoch and he could not deny it. He could not honorably marry Amanda while feeling as he did for Eden, even if he never confided these thoughts to anyone. But if he returned to Reliance and found Eden again, he would confess his feelings. He knew that much for certain now.

His conflicted revery was abruptly interrupted when the trumpet call came "to horse." He had not expected so early a call, but soon learned the reason. The scouts had struck a new trail. A pony herd stood in sight. A large herd. That could only mean one thing—a large village. After two and a half months of fruitless wandering, the starving army, its supplies nearly depleted, had at last come upon the object of their search.

He took his place at Custer's side as they spoke with the scouts. They reported the village was that of a chief called Medicine Arrows and numbered nearly two hundred lodges. Rumored to be with them were two young white women, captured in the raids along the Solomon River the previous autumn. The Indian herdsmen had seen the advance of the troops and had already set the herd in motion. Custer gave the order to close up the column and announced to Randall that the two of them were going to ride out to meet with the chief.

Brad took a deep breath. A thrill of excitement and terror shot through him at this prospect. He now almost regretted boasting of his language skills, so poor were they in merit to the task of diplomacy. Facilitating small talk between a man and his mistress was one thing. Negotiating an agreement with the lives of hundreds hanging in the balance was another matter entirely.

As they rode forward, a party of three dozen or so warriors also advanced from the Indian camp. The warriors, of all ages and states of ornamentation, halted at the halfway point and awaited Brad and Custer to come forward to meet them.

The leader announced himself to be Medicine Arrows, as expected. He directed all his comments to Brad, ignoring Custer entirely. It took Brad a moment to realize they assumed him to be the soldier chief as he alone wore the blue uniform of the United States of America. His commander was attired in his usual frontiersman buckskins.

Brad surmised his first order of business was to clarify their difference in rank and ask for a parley. He stumbled through his introductions, too nervous to consult his voluminous notes taken during his quick course in the Cheyenne tongue with Eden Murdoch. Somehow, the message was conveyed and accepted and they were directed toward the camp.

The pony herd had been driven through the village and the place was in a complete uproar. Nearly everyone was now mounted on horseback. Men called threatening remarks. Women chased down their children to cart them off to safety. Though a cold, sharp prairie wind blew off the Sweetwater, he felt uncomfortably warm. His wool uniform stifled him as they made their way through the camp. Everywhere he gazed, angry faces glared at them, shouted at them, and taunted them.

"Well, look who's here," Custer remarked as they continued their mounted promenade through the village. Brad directed his attention to where the general motioned with his head. In the crowd he picked out the elderly face of Black Kettle's sister.

"How did *she* get here?"

"We sent her to a village to negotiate and she never came back. That was in December when you were still detained in Kansas. Look how she laughs at us now." With a grin, Custer saluted the smirking old woman. She clapped her hands in malicious delight and shook a brazen finger at them.

Brad, himself, was too nervous to enjoy this byplay. How could Custer be so utterly calm? He looked as if he were having the time of his life.

Their entourage halted before a large tepee in the center of the village. The lodge measured at least twenty-five feet in diameter and was decorated with splendid artwork. All dismounted and filed into the dwelling. Brad recalled Eden's instructions to enter to the right and proceed in a circle, as etiquette dictated.

The village crier walked through the camp announcing the counsel and in a short time some fifteen chiefs assembled in Medicine Arrows's lodge.

Medicine Arrows was a handsome, gray-haired man in his middle years. The other chiefs present seemed much alike in dignity and age. Nearly all had seated themselves when a much younger man, no older than Brad, burst in upon them, apparently uninvited. Several of the chiefs spoke in terse whispers that Brad could not hear, but he surmised by the expressions and gestures that the young man was insistent on being allowed to stay. The older men eventually acquiesced, whether because the young man had convinced them of his right to be present or because they simply did not wish to introduce any more tension and conflict to an already strained meeting.

The young man made a vivid impression. His long hair hung loose upon his shoulders, decorated by a single eagle feather. His broad face and piercing dark eyes carried the boldest challenge. His clothing consisted of simple buckskin, well worn and lacking in adornment. They did not seem to fit him properly, as though they had been hastily borrowed from another.

When all were comfortably seated, a long clay pipe was produced and lit with great ceremony. An elderly gent that Brad understood to be a medicine man offered the pipe to the four cardinal directions, just as Eden predicted he would. After a long prayer, the pipe was presented to Custer, for Brad had been able to convey, in his broken speech, that Custer was the leader and he the subordinate, not the other way around.

He watched with interest while their hosts required his commander to smoke for a lengthy time. He knew Custer never touched tobacco in any form and thought he was beginning to look a little queasy. The pipe was relit with more ceremony and passed to Brad, also a nonsmoker. He tried with all his might not to cough as the potent smoke filled his lungs.

The pipe made its way slowly around the group, and when it at last reached the end of the circle, it was taken by the young man who had forced his way into the

counsel. After he drew a single puff on the nearly smoked-out pipe, he rose unexpectedly, leaned over, and dumped the ashes of the pipe on Custer's boots.

Custer was startled by this unexpected event, but not half so upset as the chiefs who grumbled and criticized the younger man. The young warrior answered them back in arrogant terms and was promptly asked to leave the circle. He did this without resistance, but threw Armstrong Custer the most angry and threatening look. Brad was reminded of Shakespeare's line "if looks could kill." His commander would surely be ready for the grave were that true.

It wasn't until the young man rose to leave that Brad saw it—the scar on his chin. In a jagged, diagonal line across the man's dark jaw he saw a white scar, looking for all the world like a bolt of lightning.

Medicine Arrows made the opening remarks, only a portion of which Brad understood.

"What did he say?" Custer demanded.

"He said something along the lines of how he is honored that one of the *ve'ho* soldiers has taken the time to learn the Tsitsistas language."

"Well, aren't you the man of the hour," Custer smirked. Brad nearly blushed with pride, but his commander quickly ordered, "Now demand the release of the white captives."

He had expected negotiations on this topic and quickly consulted his notes. He spoke in halting tones, but gained confidence when the chiefs appeared to understand his remarks.

Medicine Arrows responded in a rapid-fire manner

which left Brad utterly confused. He asked for a repetition and was granted one with patience and tolerance. He then turned to Custer. "If I understand correctly from what he said, they claim not to have the power to release a captive. Captives are like slaves. They are considered property and must be purchased from their owners. This would fit with what Mrs. Murdoch advised me on the subject."

"Ridiculous," Custer spat out. "We will not pay ransom. Tell him that. Sheridan says, no more ransom. It just encourages them to take more captives."

Brad conveyed this thought as best he could and the negotiations stalled. To leave the lodge on some semblance of good terms, he inquired of the chief where a good camping place might be for the soldiers.

Medicine Arrows offered to take them to such a site personally and the counsel adjourned without further incident.

As general and captain remounted their horses, Custer leaned close with a grin and whispered, "What in heaven's name were we smoking in there? It wasn't tobacco, I know that much."

"I think it's called kinnikinnick. Mrs. Murdoch described it to me as consisting of the inner bark of the red willow mixed with some dried sage."

"I thought I would get violently ill at any moment. That would have made quite an impression, wouldn't it?"

Brad did not understand how his commander could be so nonchalant given the possibility that they could be slaughtered at any moment. One accidental discharge from the rifle of the Kansas volunteers—who were barely restrainable once they had heard that the missing Kansas girls might be at the village—would start a blood-bath.

Camp was made on the banks of the Sweetwater, at the location given by Medicine Arrows, about three quarters of a mile from the Cheyenne village. As the evening wore on, a delegation of warriors, together with the head chiefs, arrived at the army encampment and made an unusual offer: they wished to entertain the soldiers with music and a display of horsemanship.

A large bonfire was built in front of field headquarters and Brad sat with Custer and the other staff officers as a dazzling show began. Over fifty warriors gathered while a dozen young men, both they and their horses brightly adorned, began the show.

All the soldiers clapped and shouted approval as the horsemen rode in splendid fashion in tightly concentric circles around the inner group of chiefs and officers. As they rode they played music on reedy-sounding flutes. Brad noticed the young man with the scar on his chin was present and never strayed far from the group sitting closest to Custer and his officers. From his display of hostility at the lodge of his chief, Brad had to wonder if the young man was an assassin.

A scout arrived to interrupt the general with a message. Brad overheard the scout tell him that the show was a mere distraction. All evening, the Cheyenne village had been engaged in breaking camp.

When the horse show concluded, Custer took action. He asked Brad to tell the assembled chiefs he was to make an important announcement. He stood with great ceremony and made a show of unbuckling his sidearm and dropping it to the ground.

"Tell them I do not wish any bloodshed."

Brad dutifully complied. The chiefs listened with looks of apprehension.

Custer continued. "Now tell them that they are all my prisoners."

Brad was so stunned by this development, he found himself at a momentary loss for words.

"Tell them!" Custer bellowed.

"But sir . . . they trusted us in coming here. They could have taken *us* hostage earlier today but they did not."

Custer's blue eyes flashed. "Are you questioning an order of mine, Captain?"

"No, sir." He turned to the assembled group of chiefs, but before he could say the words he heard the young man with the scar on his chin shout to his comrades, in his native tongue, "They mean to capture us!"

So the young man knew the general's words before they were translated. Brad should have guessed this the moment he had an inkling as to the man's identity.

The chiefs scrambled for their arms and fought for their freedom, as Custer and all the officers called on the men to hold their fire. In a matter of minutes, all the Cheyennes had vacated the army camp, save four of their number around whom the officers had physically closed ranks. The young man with the scar who had alerted them turned out to be one of those captured.

An Uncommon Enemy

*   *   *

An hour after darkness, Brad heard Cheyenne voices calling out to the camp. "They want to know if the hostages
are still alive," he told his commander.

"Bring Little Rock's daughter to me," Custer ordered.
"I'm going to use her as an intermediary."

The young girl was summoned and informed of her
mission. She looked anxiously to the general and communicated her worries to Brad.

"She's afraid our own sentries might shoot her by
mistake, sir."

Custer folded the girl into his arms and pressed her
head to his breast. He smoothed her hair with a gentle
hand. "Don't worry now. You know I wouldn't let anything happen to you." He turned to the captain and the
other officers present. "I'm going to escort her at least
as far as our last picket."

The pair left holding hands. Major Benteen rolled his
eyes the moment his commander's back was turned.

Brad decided to pay a call on the captive Cheyennes.
He could contain his curiosity no longer and strode into
the tent where the men were being detained. He approached the young warrior through a phalanx of
guards. Something in the young man's fierce expression
put Brad on notice.

"Netonesevehe?" What is your name? Brad asked.

The young man jutted his scarred chin contemptu-
ously and refused to answer.

"I know you speak some English. You translated
what my commander said at the bonfire this evening."

Without warning, the young man spat and a glob of saliva landed squarely on Brad's chest. Several guards rushed up and one raised the butt of his rifle to strike the young warrior for his impudence, but Brad stopped him with a wave of his hand.

As he calmly wiped off the front of his uniform with his handkerchief, the warrior arrogantly turned his back on him.

Before he left, Brad made one last remark. *"Seota . . . Nahene 'ena."* I know Seota.

The young man whirled around with a startled expression. He dropped his threatening pose for half a second and Brad knew his remark had hit its target.

Twenty

This shameless disregard for justice has been the most foolhardy course we could have pursued.

—Excerpt from a letter
by the Reverend H. B. Whipple, of Minnesota,
read to the U.S. Indian Commission to protest
the army's actions at the Washita

"You got a letter here, missy," Hugh called upstairs to Eden. "Come all the way from Washington City."

Eden rushed down the stairs of the saloon and met him in the middle of the room. She eagerly tore open the seal. "It's from Mr. Wynkoop, the Cheyenne Indian agent who resigned, remember?"

Her anxious eyes quickly scanned the four-page letter. Her lips parted in astonishment and her breath quickened with each paragraph. She sat down at the nearest table to finish reading. Hugh, seeing her excitement, sat down as well and waited to hear whatever news had so captivated her. He studied her animated face, marveling at the delicacy of her small chin and the creaminess of her cheeks and brow, grown fair from a winter spent indoors.

"So what's up?" he asked.

She drew a deep breath and her amber-green eyes shone with excitement. "It seems he wants to meet me. He refuses to believe all the stories about me in the press. He said my earlier letters to him sounded far too sensible to have been written by a madwoman." Eden paused to chuckle. "He didn't come right out and use the word 'madwoman.' In fact, he went to somewhat humorous lengths to delicately avoid the term. I suppose he feared affronting my sensibilities. Little does he know what sort of insults I have grown accustomed to!"

Hugh snorted angrily in agreement with this statement. "The army sure ain't been too shy about callin' you names."

"He wants me to come to Washington and appear before his former superiors in the Bureau of Indian Affairs. And possibly some members of Congress and some religious organizations sympathetic to the Peace Cause."

"That's great, honey." Hugh's congratulations carried a detectable lack of enthusiasm, but Eden was too lost in her excitement to notice right away.

"Can you imagine *me* speaking to members of Congress? This is so wonderful! Someone is willing to hear me out, *finally*. I wonder how much the city of Washington has changed since I saw it last? Oh, those were exciting days, during the war."

Then the look of joy fell from her face.

"What's wrong?"

"I don't have funds for such a trip."

He shrugged. "You may not, but I do."

"I can't ask you for that. I wouldn't dream of it.

You've already been far too generous with me. I don't know how I'll ever repay you."

"I never did nothin' I didn't want to do." He sat back in his chair and folded his arms across his chest. "I never ventured too far east of the Mississippi. I might be improved by the experience. We could take the trip together."

Eden frowned at this. "I appreciate your offer. It's terribly kind, but I'm not sure it would look appropriate for me to travel with a gentleman to whom I was not married. I mean, not that I have much in the way of reputation left to lose, but still—"

Hugh laughed out loud in a gravelly howl. "Lord, I wish we'd done half the things this town's been accusing us of."

"I suppose we can't blame them for gossiping. Human nature being what it is, they can't help but assume that an unmarried man and woman living under the same roof . . ."

Hugh's expression grew solemn. "What if you was to make the trip with a man that you *was* married to?"

"You're suggesting we travel together and pretend to be man and wife?"

"No, I was sorta suggestin' the real thing. Oh, never mind. It was a foolish idea. I don't know what I was thinkin' of."

Eden hung her head. "Your offer is a sweet one, Hugh, but I have to decline. I can't really talk about it, but I can't marry you . . . or anyone."

Hugh nodded, accepting the news. He raised his

shaggy head with a bitter smile. He felt he knew the reason for Eden's refusal. After she left the room, he muttered, "That damned Brad Randall. Every woman I know is crazy about him."

Twenty-one

I have been successful in my campaign against
the Cheyennes. I outmarched them, outwitted
them at their own game, proved to them that
they were in my power, and could . . . have
annihilated the entire village [but did not].
Now my most bitter enemies cannot say that I
am either blood-thirsty or possessed of an un-
worthy ambition.

 —G. A. CUSTER, LETTER TO HIS WIFE, MARCH 24, 1869,
   FROM CAMP ON THE WASHITA BATTLEGROUND,
    BEFORE RETURNING TO KANSAS

When the Seventh Cavalry and the Kansas Nineteenth
approached Reliance, the whole town—the first city
they encountered upon crossing the Kansas border—
turned out to greet them. They were to camp there for
one night to allow the weary soldiers the luxury of a
taste of civilization as a reward for all the privations they
had suffered through the winter campaign.

An impromptu street dance was arranged to take
place in the evening. Buffet tables were set up for the
exhausted men, loaded with home cooking from the
kitchens of local housewives.

Brad Randall headed straight to Hugh Christie's
nameless saloon and found Eden Murdoch standing on

the wooden sidewalk before it, watching the troops march in with everyone else. He had decided on a course of action and the mere sight of her told him he had made the right choice. He was going to tell her his feelings for her and weather her reaction, good or bad.

He had gone so far as to write a letter to Amanda asking her to release him from his obligations to her. He had tried to be as kind as possible, though he knew of no way to soften news of that sort. Whether she and her father chose to bring a lawsuit for breach of promise, he no longer cared. Though he had not yet mailed the missive, just the writing of it had lifted from his mind a terrible burden.

There was, of course, the matter of his potential rival. The honorable thing to do would be to tell Eden that the Cheyenne they held in custody might possibly be Hanging Road. But a man in love is a selfish man and while decency would not allow him to keep the man's existence a secret, he was determined to know her state of mind before any complications arose. The matter was settled in his mind.

He pulled off his hat as he bounded toward her, eager as a puppy. "My dear Mrs. Murdoch," he called with a broad smile.

She looked startled and dismayed at his cheery greeting. She opened her mouth to speak but before any words issued, a handsome man of about thirty years of age, with jet-black hair and startling green eyes cut between them with an angry look.

"What business do you have with my wife, sir?"

Brad's lips parted in complete confusion. He looked to Eden for an explanation.

She drew an uneasy breath and said in a low voice, "Captain Randall, allow me to present my husband, Lawrence Murdoch."

"Well, bless my soul," breathed a thoroughly amazed Brad Randall. He recovered his manners and quickly extended his hand. "I . . . uh . . . I am honored to make your acquaintance, sir."

Murdoch eyed Brad suspiciously and reluctantly took his hand, but said to his wife, "Eden, who is this man and how does he know you?"

"Captain Randall was my escort, Lawrence. He was the one charged with locating my relatives."

"Well, he wasn't very good at it, apparently, since he failed to locate me."

Brad felt uncomfortable being an unwilling witness to this domestic scene. "Sir, if I could but have a word with your wife for one moment."

Murdoch shrugged and did not move from his wife's side.

"Alone, sir, if I may."

"I don't think it appropriate for you to say something to a man's wife that you cannot speak in the presence of her husband, Captain."

Brad could not argue with this viewpoint. No married man would wish his wife to speak to a gentleman not of his acquaintance without his permission and his presence. He thought quickly. "I assure you it is not of a personal nature, sir, but rather a matter of military intelligence. Your wife was once a prisoner of war—"

"You don't need to remind me of that!" Murdoch snapped.

"No, sir, but I need to ask your wife a question which I am not privileged to share with nonmilitary personnel." He was extemporizing and hoped the nonsense coming out of his mouth was at least confusing enough to bluff a private word with Eden.

She allowed him to take her elbow and guide her a few feet away from the anxious and intense gaze of her husband.

"Why did you tell me he was dead?" Brad whispered.

Eden sighed. "Please don't ask. Just trust that he and I were both better off with him thinking me in my grave. Unfortunately, Lawrence read those stupid articles about me in the newspapers. He contacted the army and they sent him to the Lowells."

"I don't know quite what to say." Brad's hand now twisted the unsent letter to Amanda in his pocket. With a profoundly sinking feeling, he knew now he would not post it after all.

"What is it, Brad?"

Before he could answer, a group of young boys set off a round of firecrackers, causing everyone in the vicinity to jump in surprise. He stifled his disappointment and introduced his second piece of news. "I need to speak with you on a serious matter. It's about a Cheyenne prisoner we took in Texas. I . . . need you to translate. My language skills are not strong enough and our interpreter is unavailable."

Eden cast a worried glance over her shoulder in the

direction of her husband. He glowered at the pair of them from the door of Hugh's saloon. "I'm happy to help you, but Lawrence won't like this. Perhaps we can say—oh, I don't know. Just, please, do not mention the amount of time you and I spent together in December. He does not tolerate any man paying attention to me, no matter how innocent it may be."

Brad nodded, but wondered at her use of the word "innocent." Was their night together innocent or not? Damn the woman. Had he imagined it after all? Had he spent the entire winter fretting over something that never happened? But no imagining, no dream could have been that real.

"Lawrence," Eden called in a falsely cheerful voice, "Captain Randall needs me to translate while he interrogates a prisoner. I must go with him to the soldiers' encampment outside of town."

Murdoch rushed to his wife's side. He walked with a slight limp. "You'll do no such thing. You know I do not wish you to have any further contact with those savages."

"I can guarantee Mrs. Murdoch's safety, sir."

"That's not the point," said Murdoch. "The sooner my wife forgets those terrible years, the sooner she will regain her sanity."

"Lawrence," Eden began in patently oversweet tones. "Would you like to meet General George Armstrong Custer? You know, the war hero? Captain Randall is aide-de-camp to the general. You could introduce him, couldn't you, Captain?"

Murdoch's mouth fell open in surprise. "I served in

the Army of the Potomac. I was in Sheridan's infantry. But I knew of General Custer. Everyone knew about him. He was the youngest man ever to be made a general—and you are his aide?"

"Indeed, I am, sir. It would give me great pleasure to introduce you to the general." He could hardly keep from grinning at the awestruck look on Murdoch's face. He had barely met the man and already loathed him. But then, he had come to loathe anyone who held Armstrong Custer in higher esteem than he actually deserved. The unexpected doors celebrity would open amazed him.

"Well, look who's back." It was Hugh Christie's raspy, familiar voice. He strode out of the saloon and shook Brad's hand. "You're gonna come on in and have a drink on the house, boy. I don't care if you're on duty or not!"

"I'll be happy to as soon as Mrs. Murdoch and I complete some business at the camp. That is, if her husband will permit me the pleasure of her company."

"Larry, don't you got something you should be doin' right now?" the saloonkeeper pointedly remarked. "We're gonna be plum full up with the soldier boys in town and you know that means Marco's no help."

Murdoch sighed irritably and retreated into the saloon with its proprietor.

"Your husband is working for Hugh?" Brad asked in surprise.

"Hugh's idea of a practical joke. And I do mean 'practical,' " Eden said. "When Lawrence showed up to claim me, Hugh mysteriously arranged for him to lose

all his traveling money in a poker game on his very first night in town. The boy named Marco and Rhinehart Meeker were in on the swindle, though neither of them will own up to it. We've been stranded here in Reliance for two weeks and, of course, Hugh made a gallant gesture of offering Lawrence a job to help him out."

"Hugh is resourceful, I'll give him that." Brad had to chuckle.

"Let's go now." Eden took Brad's arm. "I'll borrow one of Hugh's horses from the livery. We have much to talk about. There's something I need to tell you. Something important we have to discuss."

They began their ride to the encampment in an uneasy silence, but soon Brad felt compelled to ask, "Mrs. Murdoch, might I inquire why your husband made that remark about your regaining your sanity?"

Eden flashed a cynical frown. "Insanity is a grounds for divorce, Captain."

"Divorce? He means to divorce you?"

"I'm fairly certain he wants to marry again. I think he's engaged, in fact. He made a stray remark . . . I don't hold that against him. He had no evidence to believe I still lived."

"No, I guess not. But to accomplish this by having you declared insane? That's barbaric."

"I was perfectly willing to free him from his marriage to me. I was able to give him the necessary grounds for a legal divorce."

Brad looked at her questioningly.

"Adultery, of course. I was willing to go before a judge and admit that I had betrayed my husband with—don't look so frightened, Brad—I was going to say with Hanging Road."

He could feel the heat rising in his face. His ears were no doubt as scarlet as his thoughts. This had to be an admission on her part of their intimacy in the predawn hours of New Year's Day. If only he could come right out and ask her, but there was no earthly way a man can ask a woman, Did I have you or just imagine it?

"If you were willing to do such a thing—and I think it amazingly brave and generous of you, by the way—what was his objection?"

Eden heaved a sigh so sharp in its bitterness it could have sliced fresh bread. "His male vanity would not permit him to publicly suffer the humiliation of a faithless wife."

"So his response is to lock you away in an asylum?" Brad nearly snarled the words, wishing he could practice his boxing talents on Lawrence Murdoch's handsome face. He knew plenty of men like Murdoch. Male pride could be the most vicious progenitor of evil actions. "The scoundrel! Has he no decency?"

Eden knew the reunion with her husband was doomed the very day it occurred. She had just returned to the saloon after purchasing some new stockings and a hat from Reliance's only dress shop in preparation for her

big trip to Washington City. Hugh dashed forward with an alarmed look on his face.

"Honey, I want you to be calm."

"What's wrong, Hugh?"

"He's over at the barbershop. Rhinehart came and told me that he stopped in asking questions, so Rhinehart asked him to sit a spell and he came right over to warn me in advance."

"What in the world are you talking about, Hugh? You're scaring me."

"Your husband, Lawrence Murdoch. A guy sayin' he's one and the same is sittin' in Rhinehart Meeker's barbershop right this minute."

"Oh, God." Eden clapped her hand over her mouth in shock. She sat down in the nearest chair. She put her head down on the table and began to sob into her folded arms.

Hugh moved close to her. "Aren't you happy he's alive?"

She looked up at Hugh with a miserable, tearstained face that answered his question far better than words. She blew her nose, smoothed her hair, and rose to allow Hugh to escort her to the barbershop to be reunited with Lawrence Murdoch.

She thought her heart would stop when she saw him. He looked much the same and yet not the same. Still handsome, the handsomest man she had ever seen, he wore a simple brown business suit. She had never seen him in civilian clothes. If ever a nightmare came wrapped in a pretty package, it was Lawrence Murdoch.

He rose when he saw her, but did not smile or run to her. He offered her his hand and she took it. He awkwardly patted her shoulder.

His first words to her were, "Eden, you're so thin."

She cast her eyes to the floor. "I was seven months gone with child the last time you saw me."

Rhinehart and Hugh chuckled over this remark. Lawrence frowned at the two men with unconcealed contempt and they instantly sobered.

"It's odd that you didn't try to contact me, Eden."

"We thought you was dead," Rhinehart blurted out. Hugh promptly elbowed him to be quiet.

"I did not know where you were living after the war."

A short, angry sigh was Lawrence Murdoch's only response.

Hugh Christie then jumped into action. "I want you two to come on over to my place and we'll all toast this happy reunion."

Eden and the barber both looked stunned by Hugh's unexpected hospitality, but Murdoch seemed innocently flattered. "I appreciate your offer, sir, but just who might you be?"

"A friend to you both," announced Hugh. He threw his arms around the shoulders of Eden and her husband and marched them over to his saloon.

Hugh succeeded in convincing Lawrence that he was renting Eden the "spare" room above his establishment, so her husband moved his traveling case up there. Hugh insisted on taking them both to dinner at the café and then persuaded Murdoch to join him and his friends

in a private game of poker, with drinks on the house all evening.

Eden retired to her room and waited for her husband to return, dreading the moment they would finally be alone together. He stumbled in after two in the morning, much the worse for drink.

He clumsily tried to undress, but had trouble even managing his vest buttons. When Eden attempted to help him, he involuntarily flinched as he pushed her hands away.

"Don't touch me," he whispered.

He did not employ a harsh tone when he said these words. Not an angry pitch, not a threat. More like a recoiling from something unpleasant or unclean.

"So I have reached a pretty pass," Eden concluded. "Hugh has been a dear. He's been trying desperately to help me. He's contacted his brother's attorney in St. Louis, but I don't know if he can come to my aid soon enough. Lawrence has already collected letters from Dr. Ashcroft and Elias Lowell swearing that I am not of sound mind and a danger to myself and others. He needs only one more letter to initiate proceedings."

Brad felt helpless. The regiment would break camp tomorrow and head for Fort Hays. Not enough time to even begin to help her out of this fix. He decided to deliver his one piece of good news.

"I think the time has come to reveal the true reason I am bringing you here, Eden. We took some Cheyenne prisoners down on the Sweetwater in Texas. I think, I mean I have reason to believe that one of them is . . . the man you called 'Hanging Road.' "

Eden gasped and halted her horse's lazy stride.

"He has refused to speak with me at all, but he has a jagged scar on his chin and he noticeably reacted when I mentioned your name. And I know he speaks some English."

"It can't be, it can't be." Eden shook her head in amazed disbelief.

"We took him prisoner along with three others to bargain for the release of two white girls being held in the Cheyenne camp. These were girls who *wanted* to be rescued," he added, to tease her gently. "General Custer promised to hang the men when negotiations broke down. He went so far as to tie nooses around their necks and yank the ropes over a tree limb. The two young women were released unharmed, thankfully, and we avoided an engagement. This last was something amazing given the mood of our Kansas volunteers who were howling to spill Indian blood."

Eden shivered at this remark. An advancing thunderstorm issued a threatening rumble in the southwestern sky. They both set their horses into motion again, and quickened into a trot.

"Yes, I know what you're thinking—another Sand Creek. That was exactly what General Custer sought to avoid. Believe me when I tell you, he has not emerged unscathed from all the furor over the Washita engagement. He has, I believe, gone out of his way to keep the peace this winter."

"The legislature of Kansas passed a resolution last month praising General Custer and his men to the heavens for their valor at the Washita," Eden stated through a clenched jaw.

Brad smiled grimly. "I know. But I also know that President Grant is turning into a peace advocate—just as I predicted, I might add."

"True, you were right about that." She gazed at the multitude of white canvas tents in the distance with distaste. "But why are you still holding these prisoners if the Cheyennes gave up the captives without a fight?"

Eden glanced over to see Brad frown and look ill at ease.

"General Custer refused to keep his end of the bargain, but please do not repeat that. I'll have to deny I said it. The general claimed the release of the captives was only part of the contract. The Cheyennes are to come in to Camp Supply and surrender themselves to reservation life. Only then will he release these men, plus the women and children we took prisoner at the Washita."

"You don't agree with his actions?"

"I feel they were somewhat duplicitous. I believe the tribes are as deserving of honorable treatment as any enemies of our government. I do not imagine General Custer would have behaved in such a manner to the opposing forces during the War of the Rebellion. When a gentleman gives his word . . . well, at the end of the day, what does a man have if his word is no good?"

They reached the enormous army encampment at

last and halted to tether their horses at the pickets. Brad took Eden's arm and led her over the muddy ground into the center of the camp toward the prison tent.

"I have come to speak with one of the prisoners," Brad said to the sentry posted at the opening of the tent. "This woman is the interpreter."

The sentry stood aside and allowed Eden and Brad to enter. The tent was sparsely but adequately furnished with camp beds and a couple of tables. The three elderly chiefs looked on with curiosity as Eden and her tall escort walked over to where Hanging Road lounged on his cot.

"Ameo?" she called out in a voice barely audible.

He sat up in astonishment.

"I'm sorry, but I must remain here," Brad said. "We have to preserve the pretense that you two are strangers."

"How is it that you survived, Seota?" Hanging Road whispered in Cheyenne.

Eden smiled sadly. "The *ve'ho* soldiers would not kill one of their own."

"But they happily slaughtered the rest of our family."

The bitterness in his voice was obvious even to Brad who could only follow bits and pieces of their conversation.

"I tried to save them, Ameo." Tears filled her eyes.

"I'm the one who should have saved them," he said with sorrow and self-reproach. "I was wounded—shot in the shoulder and the thigh. One Eye found me on the

river bank and threw me over his horse when he saw that I was still breathing. I don't remember anything from that terrible day."

The air in the tent was filled with stifling spring humidity. Brad shifted uncomfortably where he stood before them as Eden sat down next to her Cheyenne husband.

"Are you going to help me, Seota?"

"Help you how?"

"Escape, of course. They're going to hang me at the Fort called Hays."

"They won't hang you. They'll release you as soon as the Tsitsistas come in to Camp Supply."

Brad strained to understand their conversation, but their Cheyenne words were spoken too quickly and quietly for him to follow.

"They've already tried to hang me once. Look at this." Hanging Road opened his buckskin shirt at the neck to reveal the healing remnants of the rope burns he had received when Custer had bluffed his hanging at the Sweetwater. "What makes you think that they will honor their promises? They've broken them again and again. I won't live like this. I will escape on my own, if you won't help me. I will not rest until I have avenged the deaths of my wives and son."

"You're talking like a warrior."

"I *am* a warrior. I am now, at least. I spend every hour of every day imagining the joy of taking *ve'ho* scalps."

"Stop talking like that! If you try to escape, they will kill you."

"I've got to try. I have a plan, once I'm free. I'm going to join Tall Bull and his band."

"Dog Soldiers?"

"They will not submit like weak cowards and live in slavery. They are following the right path. I'll escape and join them. I was a fool to believe the promises of Black Kettle. Look where his peace efforts got him dealing with these snakes. Please, Seota, you've got to help me. With the help of someone on the outside, escape would be simple. The *ve'ho* soldier seems to be your friend. Maybe he will help us."

"No, that's impossible. I couldn't ask him. If his superiors found out, they would hang *him.*"

"Seota, we could be together again. Remember what we once shared?"

"Me? Living in a Dog Soldier band? I could never do that. The soldier bands were responsible for the death of *my* son, remember?"

"We were meant to be together. You know the sacred bonds we shared. The secrets."

Brad watched as Hanging Road took Eden's hand in his and squeezed it. She looked away from him with a tormented expression on her face. He now questioned his decision to bring her here, feeling profound moral confusion. Why did nothing make sense anymore? Life on the frontier was touted as being so much "simpler" than life in civilization and yet neither venue seemed to hold easy answers.

"Remember how I trusted you?" Hanging Road said to Eden in a soothing, seductive tone.

"Stop it, stop it." Eden's voice choked with tears.

"It's more complicated than that. So much has happened since I saw you last."

"Come away with me. Leave these fools behind. Life in the soldier bands will be all right. I won't let anyone speak against you. We could be happy again."

In a frantic gesture, Eden covered her ears. "This is all so confusing." She sobbed openly.

"Mrs. Murdoch, do you want to leave?" Brad interrupted. He offered Eden his hand.

"Stay away!" Hanging Road growled at Brad in English.

The three elderly chiefs in the prison tent looked on with interest. They seemed to be eavesdropping to the extent they could.

A sentry peeked in the tent to see what was causing the loud words. Brad waved him back.

Eden looked up. "Captain, would it be possible for me to have one minute alone with him? I need to say something to him that's very private." She glanced in the direction of the three elderly Cheyennes to indicate she wanted privacy from them as well as him.

Brad felt an exquisite pang of jealousy at the thought of Eden and Hanging Road alone together, but found it hard to deny her heartfelt plea.

"I'll tell the sentry—I don't know—that they need exercise or something."

He motioned to the three men to get up and he led them outside, asking the soldier guarding the tent to walk them around the center of the camp.

The moment Eden was alone with Hanging Road she turned to him urgently.

"I have something for you, Ameo," she whispered. "The only thing I managed to salvage of our life before that terrible morning at the Washita. I had no reason to believe you survived and yet something told me I must keep it for you." She pulled a beaded leather pouch from its place of hidden safety in her bosom and handed it to him.

His lips parted in awe as he beheld it. "My grandfather's medicine bundle." He frowned at her momentarily. "Did you show this to anyone?"

"You know I didn't. You know I wouldn't."

He opened the small pouch and withdrew its contents: a blue and white beaded necklace from which dangled three severed human fingers. His dark eyes widened with veneration and astonishment. He clutched the necklace to his breast for several moments before carefully slipping it over his head.

"It's as though my grandfather were alive again. I can never thank you enough, Seota." He enclosed her in an affectionate hug.

Brad's curiosity got the better of his noble intentions and he surreptitiously peeked through the tent flaps as they stirred with the winds of the approaching storm.

He could not see much at first. Hanging Road's back was to him and blocked his view of Eden. He watched as Hanging Road slipped a necklace of some sort over his head, then he and Eden gently embraced. Brad's pulse pounded in his temples to see Eden show such affection to this savage man. Odd that he had not ex-

perienced this level of jealousy when Eden was in the presence of her legal husband, Lawrence Murdoch.

But this emotion was no match for the shock that awaited him when Hanging Road turned and seated himself on the cot. Brad had full view of the gift Eden had given him, a blue and white beaded necklace decorated with *three severed human fingers*!

A cold sweat broke over Brad's wide forehead. He tried to control his breathing as his mind raced to comprehend how he could possibly have seen this very same necklace in his nightmares. He did not believe in the supernatural. He did not embrace the occult. He had often thought himself a hair's breadth from being an atheist, especially since the war. Nothing in his rational mind could sort out the impossible coincidence of this day.

"I must go now," Eden said. She glanced around the tent, and when she was certain no prying eyes could see them, she quickly leaned over and kissed Hanging Road on the cheek. He closed his arms around her and held her tightly.

"You'll help me?" he asked as she rose from the cot.

"I don't know." She drew a worried breath. "I don't know."

"He was asking you to help him escape, wasn't he?" Brad remarked as they rode back to Reliance. They hurried along to beat the thunderstorm that now rumbled closely on their heels.

"Don't be silly. He was simply saying he *wished* he could escape. I told him that would be impossible."

Brad threw Eden a doubtful smile to chide her for her dissembling. He tried to act as natural as possible so she would not guess the turmoil seething inside him since the moment he saw her Cheyenne husband's grisly necklace. He would have given anything to ask her about it, but could not admit to her that he had spied upon them after promising her privacy. The necklace had been removed and stowed away from view by the time he returned the captive chiefs to the tent.

"He seems much altered from the last time I saw him," Eden fretted.

"In appearance?"

"No, in spirit. Saying he spends his days longing to take white scalps. He was never like that."

"He's still grieving, don't you think? I can't imagine what it would be like to suffer such a loss as his. I know that when my older brother was killed in the first months of the war, I couldn't wait to enlist. I was only sixteen at the time and had never aimed a rifle at anything larger than a pheasant, but I couldn't wait to fight Johnny Reb."

"Maybe you're right."

"It's too bad you could not appear before the Congressional Committee. When you wrote me and told me that Wynkoop had invited you, I was so gratified. If they could meet you and see that you are not—"

"The raving lunatic the army paints me to be?" Eden

shook her head bitterly. "Everything I have tried to accomplish has come to nothing, I'm afraid, just as you once predicted."

"I'm sorry. Believe me when I tell you, I wish I had been wrong about that. I think constantly of how things might be different. I long to be some kind of . . . agent for change, but I don't know how."

Their conversation waned and they fell into an uneasy silence, each absorbed in their own thoughts.

Then with a slightly mischievous grin, Eden decided to introduce a topic that might leaven their mood. "Are you going to say hello to Tessa while you're here?"

He frowned. His interest in Tessa had chilled considerably over the long winter as his feelings for Eden grew. The last subject he wanted to discuss was what he now regarded as a sordid interlude in his life.

"I don't think so. Why do you ask?"

"She just misses you, that's all."

I'll bet she does, Brad thought sourly. He had learned from an overheard conversation among his men that she had been charging him over twice the going rate. "I feel quite awkward about all that now. I wouldn't blame you if you held it against me."

"I've gotten to know her a bit in the last few months. The poor woman, I once judged her far too harshly. She's had such a trying life, I feel like a terrible hypocrite now."

"I never really knew anything about her past."

"She had a brutal husband once who knocked so many of her teeth out that she never dares to smile. She's terribly self-conscious about it. She told me she never kisses anyone either for fear they'll notice. But I guess you would already know that, wouldn't you?"

Brad was so stunned by this announcement he did not know what to say.

They reached the livery and dismounted. Eden smiled up at him and said, "I can't thank you enough for this day."

He nodded, but as she turned to lead her mount into the stable, Brad called after her, "Just as we were leaving here, you said you had something to tell me. Something important that we needed to discuss."

She looked back with an awkward smile. She hesitated, then said, "It's nothing. It doesn't matter now."

She haltered her horse, then unbridled and unsaddled him. She needed time alone to digest all that had so suddenly transpired so she picked up a curry comb and began to groom the animal, a task she always found soothing.

She glanced over the tall horse's back to see that Brad had not yet left the livery yard, but stood at the door of the stable watching her. The rain had begun, yet he made no move to shelter himself; he did not even bother to replace his hat.

"What is it, Brad?" The strange, tormented look on his face disturbed her.

He strode to her side and stood mere inches from her. A loud clap of thunder shook the building and the skies opened up with the full force of the storm.

Eden looked up into his lean, distraught face, wondering what could be the matter, but afraid to ask. He stood so close the scent of his rain-soaked wool uniform mingled with the odor of the hay. His long, wet hair stuck to his forehead and neck and sent drips running down his face, yet he made no move to brush them away.

"Eden . . ."

Before he could finish his sentence, two men hurriedly led their horses into the stable to escape the downpour. They laughed and talked loudly as they slapped the rain from their hats.

Brad turned and quickly left the barn, walking out into the storm without another word to her.

Eden wrapped her arms around the neck of Hugh's horse and quietly sobbed into its coarse mane.

Twenty-two

I now hold the captive Cheyenne chiefs as hostages for the good behavior of their tribe. This, I consider, is the end of the Indian War.
—G. A. Custer, *My Life on the Plains*

Two weeks later, Eden rode toward the encampment of the Seventh Cavalry, three miles south of Fort Hays. The April morning bloomed sunny and blustery, a usual spring day on the prairie.

She yawned in spite of her anxiety. She had ridden a day and part of a night, pausing only to catch a few hours sleep when the cloudy night had made it too dark to travel farther.

She could not leave without bidding Hugh Christie goodbye and had awakened him at four the previous morning.

"Let me get this straight," he had said groggily, as he sat on the edge of his cot in his nightshirt. "You're gonna risk gettin' killed on some slim chance you can save that Indian fella?"

Eden nodded as she knelt at his feet. "I came to say goodbye, Hugh, not ask for your blessing."

"You just can't do this, honey," he sighed. "It's suicide."

"I have to do it. I must. Hanging Road saved my life once, he and the sisters. What kind of person would I be if I turned my back on him now? How could I live with myself?"

"You're the least of his problems, honey. You never asked to be in that fix in the first place. I mean, I hear you, I understand what you're tellin' me, but . . . you're a woman. Nobody expects a woman—"

She threw her head into his lap and sobbed. "I've got to do something. Especially after all that's been written about me that's been used against the Cheyennes."

"But livin' with that Indian fella ain't gonna be no picnic," he reasoned. "You'll always be on the run. You won't have no peace or safety at all. There's still a war on, remember?"

"I know. I'm not really happy about the path Hanging Road has chosen." She hung her head in silent misery, then looked back up at him, more miserable still. "But can you really imagine a happy future for me as Mrs. Lawrence Murdoch?"

He ran his hands through her now shoulder-length auburn hair, with a loving detachment. Finally, he shook his head sadly. "No, I don't. How you plan to get there?"

"I'm going to steal a horse."

"Take mine. The bay mare, not the gelding. She handles better. And take this, too." He reached for his money pouch, the one he took to the bank each morning with the previous night's receipts.

"Forty-two dollars! I couldn't possibly—"

"You can and you will. Better see this before you go."

He crossed the room and pulled a large roll of paper from his cluttered desk. He unrolled it before her with a bashful grin. "You said I needed to name this place and I told you I was waitin' for the right name to find me. Well, this is it."

On the paper was a sketch of an elaborate sign bearing the name, The Garden of Eden.

"Oh, Hugh." A tear nearly choked her. "Dear Hugh. Thank God for people who take in strays. Thank God for you!"

She was nearly out the door before he called her back one last time. "What shall I tell old Larry? You know he's gonna wonder."

Eden narrowed her amber-green eyes in bitter contempt. "Tell him the truth. Tell him Eden Murdoch died four years ago."

Eden rode through the center of the city of tents near Fort Hays and passed a large mess tent, then an outdoor laundry, steamy with boiling kettles, and finally an enormous livery stable where a blacksmith's forge clanged loud with the sound of hammers on iron.

She caught sight of Brad Randall, to her dismay. She hoped he wouldn't see her, but a woman riding through a cavalry regiment of seven hundred men was hard to miss.

He waved at her, so she turned her horse in his direction. He held a bundle of clothing in his arms and appeared to have been walking toward the laundry she had just seen.

"What brings you to Hays?" he called when she neared him. "As if I didn't know."

"I have no idea what you mean, Captain. I just came to pay you a call."

Brad twisted his lips and shook his head.

"Don't scold, Brad. I just have to try."

"You have no hope of helping him escape, you know. He's being kept in the stockade at the fort. You'd need a small army to break him out of there."

"I want to talk with General Custer. I want to try to convince him to release Hanging Road voluntarily."

"His office is in the headquarters building at the fort. I'll take you there, but I warn you, you're wasting your time."

She followed him to the stables, where he saddled his own horse and they swiftly covered the three miles from the camp to the fort.

With a deep breath for courage, Eden removed the long, heavy canvas cattle duster that Hugh had given her along with his horse. She smoothed her hair, then placed her hand on the brass doorknob and turned it slowly to enter Custer's office.

"What now?" he barked without looking up. He sat behind a large, plain walnut desk and scribbled furiously on a sheaf of papers. The scratching sounds of his flying pen were magnified in the stillness of the barren office. The room lacked ornamentation, save for a United States flag and a blue and red cavalry guidon draped on the wall behind the man's desk together with a portrait of

the newly sworn-in President Grant. At the general's elbow sat a small daguerreotype of a pretty, dark-haired woman in a wedding gown who could only be Elizabeth Custer.

Eden tried to calm herself, but found her nerves in shreds at the mere contemplation of this interview. She knew that Custer despised her. That fact was implicit in their few dealings. He cloaked these sentiments in exaggerated courtesy and attention to propriety, but she sensed his true feelings lay only slightly below the surface of such courtly behavior. She knew he thought her difficult, duplicitous, ungrateful, and possibly deranged. Simply put, he considered her his enemy. And yet she had always sensed something else there, as well, in the way he looked at her and held her hand longer than was politely necessary and leaned a shade too close when speaking to her. His actions could be categorized as flirtatious, yet the aura of disgust was unmistakable.

She stood silently and waited for him to acknowledge her. She could tell from his frantic attention to his project she had chosen a poor moment to confront him.

He did not realize the identity of his inopportune visitor until he paused to dip his pen in the inkwell. From a sharp look of complete irritation, his visage altered remarkably.

"Why, if it isn't Persephone of the Plains, come to my humble office." He set down his pen and rose to beckon her nearer. He extended his hand across his desk and shook hers in a curt and formal fashion. At his gesture of invitation, she seated herself in a small wooden chair before his desk. "I hope you'll forgive me my abruptness, madam. What brings you to Fort Hays?"

"I've come to request a favor, sir," she said plainly, trying to make it sound as though she were a friend come to ask a simple and humble courtesy, of no real importance. She tried to smile, as well, but could not seem to force her lips to incline as she directed them.

"A favor," he repeated, his voice richly savoring its own sarcasm. "Excuse me for sounding so petty, but I seem to recall once asking you for cooperation and you could not oblige me in the slightest—and have, in fact, since worked actively against my cause. I read those letters you wrote. I found them insulting and unfair. Do you not think it as ironic as I do, that *you* now request a favor from *me*?"

His blue eyes danced with such malicious glee, she squirmed in her seat. To quiet her nerves, she straightened her black skirts, noting mud stains along their hem in several places.

"This isn't easy for me, General."

Custer sighed, already weary of his own game. "What is it you want, Mrs. Murdoch? I'm very busy."

"I merely ask for the release of a man, a Cheyenne you hold hostage here. The youngest one, the one with the scar on his chin. His name is Hanging Road and he's not a chief. If you think that, you were misinformed. He is a simple medicine man, of no *political* importance. I promise you that."

"The answer is no. What you ask is impossible. Now, if you don't mind." He picked up his pen and resumed his scribbling.

"Please, sir, this is important." She impulsively

grabbed his wrist to stop the motion of his pen.

He seemed startled by this, but lay down his pen and motioned for her to resume her seat.

"Out of curiosity, why do you ask this?"

"He is a friend of mine." She folded her hands in her lap and looked down at them. "And he is not a warrior, but a healer, a holy man. Please reconsider. You don't need him. You have the other three. They *are* chiefs, important men." She was lying about this. The three other men he held were only minor in stature, but he obviously did not know this. "They will accomplish your purpose. Please, General, you have so much power—you can afford to be generous."

He sat back in his chair and folded his arms across his chest. "I think our Persephone *did* swallow the pomegranate seed."

"Please, sir. Just answer me."

"Was he your lover?" His blue eyes narrowed with an unsavory amusement.

Eden felt her anger rising, but set her jaw to keep her temper at bay. She could not allow her personal feelings, even her personal dignity, get in the way of her objective. She made a careful, even reply. "I do not believe that is any of your business."

"You're right," he agreed with a cheerful nonchalance. "Now if you'll excuse me." For the second time, he resumed his work.

"At least let us discuss this," she begged.

He looked up from his paperwork, his face a mask of irritation. "There is nothing to discuss. I must finish writing this dispatch at once. I've kept the courier waiting already too long. Please find your own way out."

"Yes, he was my lover," she exclaimed, hoping to recapture his attention.

"I knew you were a whore when I met you," he snarled with contempt.

The depth of his insult shocked her. "Fine words coming from the Chivington of the Washita! By what measure do you sit in judgment of my actions?"

"No decent woman would have wished to survive what you did. There are those of us who would not trade our honor for any price, including mere survival."

"Perhaps those of us who *create* life hold it dearer than the price you place on your honor. But why should you understand this? You make your living destroying life which must, of necessity, cheapen it considerably."

"Do you really think so? You find it that easy to live without your own honor?"

"I can live without the approval of others and without your peculiar definition of 'honor'. I believe I am stronger for my misfortunes—and I have suffered more misfortune than you are capable of imagining. The fire of the forge strengthens the steel, it does not destroy it."

"Strong as forged steel, are you?" His faint smile threatened irony.

"The Kansas-Pacific Railroad could do no worse, sir." Eden raised her chin in defiant challenge.

He threw back his head to laugh at her unexpected humor.

She ignored him and continued. "Only the weak allow their troubles to defeat them. The strong feed on their own misfortune and grow stronger still!"

He leaned his elbows against his desk and thoughtfully tapped the blunt edge of his pen against the glass
desktop. "You make an interesting point. I don't think I
fully agree, but that is of no consequence. I take back
my words. They were said in anger."

"I don't care about insults. After all I've been
through, common words are the least of my worries.
Just please reconsider my request. Please release the
man called Hanging Road. You've killed the rest of his
family. Isn't that enough?"

He studied her critically. "I'm sorry, Mrs. Murdoch,
but what you ask is impossible. Frankly, I think you have
an amazing audacity to even request this of me."

She impulsively planted her hands on the cold glass
of his desktop and thrust her face in his so close she
could not focus on both his blue eyes at once. "I implore
you, sir. I'll do anything to change your mind. *Anything.*"

He raised his fair eyebrows at this. His thin mouth
curved into a near-smile, twisting his bushy blond mustaches in the process. "Surely not *anything.*"

"What the hell's takin' him so long?" The courier fumed
his annoyance to Sergeant Yellen as the two men lounged
against the hitching post in the road opposite the limestone fort headquarters. "That train leaves at 10:05 sharp
and I gotta be on it. He knows that."

"Better go see," suggested Yellen. "It's gettin' nigh
on to two." Emory Yellen had seen the rescued white

captive, Eden Murdoch, enter the building ten minutes earlier. He wondered what she was up to, but he did not like the woman well enough to ask her himself.

The courier adjusted the strap of his leather satchel on his shoulder and marched over to the headquarters building only to return a few minutes later, even more perplexed.

"I went to his office and knocked and he didn't answer, so I tried the door and it was locked!"

"Well, that can mean only one thing," said Sergeant Yellen with a perfectly straight face. The courier waited for some sage pronouncement. "He's obviously got better things to do than see you make that train on time."

The courier groaned and took a freshly rolled cigarette from Yellen. The two men shared a quiet smoke.

After the passage of another twenty minutes, Eden Murdoch emerged from the headquarters building and walked quickly in the direction of the stockade. The two men watched her rush past them. Her canvas cattle duster and her black skirts flew in billows behind her as she hurried down the muddy path. She clutched a folded piece of paper to her bodice.

"See, I told you he had better things to do," offered Yellen with a smirk.

With a sad shake of his head, the courier groaned, "Generals have all the fun."

"Eden, what took you so long?" Brad asked when she rushed up.

"I've got it!" She held out the document for Brad's

inspection and struggled to catch her breath. "He agreed to release him."

"I can't believe this." He took the document from Eden's hand. A raw April wind swept across the prairie and caused them both to brace against it. "How on earth did you persuade him?"

They untied their horses and began to lead them in the direction of the stockade. Eden walked briskly ahead. "I appealed to his reason and sense of fairness."

Brad frowned at this flippant remark and caught her by the elbow. "How did you *actually* persuade him?"

"I used whatever means I found necessary." She averted her face.

"Eden, you've been crying."

"No, I haven't," she lied.

"What did he do to you?" Brad demanded, growing more agitated by the minute.

Her jaw dropped open when she realized what he imagined. "Oh, good Lord, you mean you think he . . . no, not *that*! Brad . . . surely you don't think—"

Brad placed his hands on his hips. "I don't know what to think!"

"Rest your mind, for heaven's sake."

"Tell me what happened right now!" Brad's voice shook with emotion.

She looked up into his face. He seemed, as always, so tall and elegant, the perfect gentleman who took such pains to hide what few flaws were his. She realized that this blustery prairie morning was probably the last time she would ever see him and the acknowledgment of this fact broke her heart.

"It's not what you think! He made me do something terrible, but I can assure you we kept all our clothes on."

Brad frowned and waited, still unconvinced.

With a look of intense bitterness, she said, "Ask *him*. He'll be most happy to tell you, I'll warrant."

She took his hand in hers and fixed her eyes on his. "A day of reckoning will come if there is any justice in the world. I won't rest until he has paid the debt of the Washita. I swear it on my life. I swear it on the souls of my dead children."

The quiet ferocity in Eden's words left Brad aghast. She had never seemed more like a stranger to him, an otherworldly creature capable of anything. She turned and began to lead her horse away again.

"Eden, I've got to tell you something. This is a terrible moment, but it's now or never, I guess."

Eden paused and patted her horse's neck, still reluctant to face Brad. "Tell me what?"

"I love you."

She turned to him, speechless and startled.

"I think I've loved you since that night at Camp Supply when you threatened to castrate that corporal with your teeth. Do you remember?" He smiled helplessly at the absurdity of it.

Her astonishment turned quickly to anguish. They stood in between their two horses and Eden was grateful the animals shielded them from the view of passersby. "Don't say you love me, Brad. Not now. Not when it's too late."

"Eden, I could give you a life of comfort and security."

"And I could give you a life of shame!"

"Why do you say that?"

"I'm not a stranger to Washington society. You cannot jilt the daughter of a powerful man and escape the consequences. And do you really imagine that I could relish such a life? Of course, there was a time when I would have enjoyed sipping tea in fashionable drawing rooms, but those days are long past for me."

"We could live out here. I could learn to love the frontier. I might just surprise you."

"*I* belong out here, Brad. Not you. Not with all your special gifts. You could someday be a powerful man. Someone with influence. Someone who could change the world."

"You flatter me," he remarked with a note of bitterness.

"I love you. And I know you. You said you wanted to be an instrument for change. You could be."

"You just said you loved me and yet you're telling me to go home and marry Amanda."

Her voice turned hard. "You made a promise to Amanda, Brad. 'When a gentleman gives his word . . . well, at the end of the day, what does a man have if his word is no good?' "

"Rather cruel to mock me with my own platitudes, don't you think? There's still the nagging problem that it's you I love."

"Don't say that! It just makes it all hurt so much

more." Tears washed her eyes, making it difficult to speak. "If we stayed together, you could change my life, but if you go home to Washington, you could change the lives of thousands. I don't want to be the reason that doesn't happen."

She dropped her horse's reins in the dirt and threw her arms around him. Brad held her close and pressed his cheek against the top of her head.

"Don't forget the Washita, Brad," she whispered into the breast of his frock coat. "If you *truly* love me, you won't forget."

They reluctantly parted and continued to lead their horses in dejected silence to the stockade. The prison structure was composed of perpendicular logs about fifteen feet in height, driven deeply into the ground. A sentry walk ran the length of the top of the wall.

As they approached the large, reinforced stockade door, Brad unfolded the release document. He halted in his tracks without warning.

"He hasn't signed this!"

"What?"

"He's written out a release from custody all right, but he did not sign it. This paper is worthless."

"Perhaps he forgot. I'll take it back to him," Eden said in a panic. She tried to snatch the paper, but Brad refused to yield it.

"He did not forget anything! His every action is carefully calculated, I can assure you." Color rose in Brad's cheeks and his ears turned bright scarlet to match his temper. "He is playing games with you, Eden. He plays with everyone around him. People—human beings—

are just another form of sport to him. Did I ever tell you what he said to me when he took me on my first buffalo hunt? He said, 'You're going to love this, Randall. Hunting buffalo is as exciting as hunting Indians!' I thought it a curious remark at the time. I've since learned how sincerely he meant it."

Eden hung on Brad's angry words, unable to decide what to do next.

He squashed the release document in his fist. "This is one game he is not going to win!"

He strode off in the direction of the stockade door with twice the speed as before and Eden hurried to keep up.

"What are you going to do? Wait!" she said, half-running.

"Just follow my lead," he snapped without turning to look at her.

"I don't want you to get into trouble, Brad!"

When he reached the door, the guard, a bored-looking infantry private, snapped to an ungraceful stance of attention. "Sir?"

"I am Captain Randall, an aide to General Custer. The general has ordered me to take one of the prisoners to headquarters for interrogation."

"Yes, sir." The guard stood aside and opened the heavy log door. Brad entered the smoky, crowded expanse of interior space, while motioning for Eden to wait at the door.

Eden anxiously peeked in. The sight she beheld pained her heart. The stockade held a series of tents to house the prisoners. A rank odor assaulted her nostrils.

Such crowded, fetid living conditions inevitably bred disease. She knew this awful fact from her war years. She did not know the mechanism of contagion, but she knew its result.

She saw Hanging Road rise from where he sat among a circle of children. It looked as though he had been amusing them with rope tricks. He scrutinized Brad's rapid approach with apprehension. The little children scattered.

When the young officer attempted to take hold of his arm, he angrily jerked away, fists clenched.

"Seota—she's come to help you." Brad motioned for him to look in Eden's direction.

When Hanging Road saw her, he nodded and allowed the captain to lead him toward the door with feigned meekness. They passed quietly through the milling throng of women and children.

They had nearly reached the door and freedom when an old Cheyenne woman shouted, "They're taking him to hang!"

She hoisted up the hem of her doeskin dress and pulled a knife from a secret sheath tied to her knee.

Brad turned, startled, having understood what the old woman had said in Cheyenne. Before he could say a word in response, the woman flew at him and plunged her knife deep into his chest.

The frightened infantryman who guarded the door fired a warning shot into the air above the heads of the prisoners as Brad staggered backward. He grasped his chest with a look of utter astonishment on his handsome face as bright-red blood gushed from between his fin-

gers. He stared at his bloody hands in disbelief.

Bloody hands. Just like in his dream. He pressed them against his chest once again to try and stem the hot, crimson flood. *My life's blood*, he thought sadly. *My life's blood.*

He fell back against the log wall of the stockade and slid down it to the ground. Seated there, he watched the chaotic scene unfold before him. All the players moved with such a graceful, balletlike quality, just like a theatrical, though the lighting seemed poor for broad daylight. Frantic mothers ran to protect their children as more infantrymen arrived on the scene and shots rang out above the screams and shouts. All the smoke from the rifles and cookfires made the action difficult to see and his vision began to deteriorate with his increasing blood loss.

The three captive chiefs stormed the door of the stockade, only to be met with a volley of rifle fire. All three fell.

Through the dense smoke and running bodies, Eden dashed in. She pulled the canvas duster over Hanging Road's shoulders, while he tucked his black hair up under the large-brimmed hat she had brought. They hurried for the door, bending low to avoid the blistering ping and pop of bullets.

The pair had almost reached their goal when Eden turned back, a look of profound sadness shadowing her slender face. She rushed to Brad's side, her long, black skirts billowing around her as she neared him.

Angel of Mercy, Angel of Death.

"Oh, Brad, I never meant for this to happen. Please

forgive me." She knelt down and threw her arms around him, cradling his face into the soft curve of her neck.

He tried to respond, but breathing was so difficult, speaking seemed impossible.

Then he felt her place two fingers against the carotid artery of his throat. *The rhythm of a pulse. It's the same in all.* She lowered her face next to his.

"Your pulse, Brad. It's strong. You're going to live. I know it!"

He tried to accept her hopeful news. He knew she was just being kind.

"You must go," he found words to whisper. "Take my horse."

"Thank you." She rose to leave.

"Wait! Before you go, I want to give you something, Eden." He ran his hand over his bloody chest and then his throat, searching for his grandmother's wedding ring.

"What is it, Brad? Can I help?"

"A ring. I wore a ring on a chain. I can't find it."

"I remember the ring, but I don't see it." Her eyes quickly searched the dirt floor where he sat as well the spot where he was first attacked.

Brad groaned in dismay. "I wanted to give it to you . . . so you wouldn't forget me."

To his surprise, the most startling and radiant smile broke over her face. "Don't worry, my love. There's no chance of that."

She kissed him and he savored the sensation of her warm lips on his. The chaos and noise vanished momentarily. Then she rose to leave. A sudden breeze

tossed and stirred her black skirts about her, creating the illusion in Brad's faltering mind that she was flying on the breeze itself.

I'm losing her forever, he thought with a spirit in greater pain than his throbbing, lacerated body.

He tried to call her back for just one more moment, but he could no longer muster the breath to speak. He could now only helplessly watch her leave him.

Farther and farther away, her willowy form receded. Was she still there? He couldn't decide. He looked up into the morning sun and wondered how many hours would elapse before he would see again the silent, glittering brilliance of the Hanging Road arcing above him.

I'll tread that road, he thought sadly, but without fear. If Eden had left him with anything, it was her eerie sense of calm.

Twenty-three

The efforts of the Peace Commission, composed of civilians and officers of the army, appointed by the President to investigate the
causes of the war and to arrange for peace,
have been attended with success to a great degree, and lasting beneficial results will no
doubt follow a faithful and prompt fulfillment
of their promises to the Indians, and of the
treaty stipulations entered into with them.
—REPORT OF THE COMMISSIONER OF INDIAN AFFAIRS,
NOVEMBER 23, 1868, FOUR DAYS BEFORE THE WASHITA

For three days, Brad floated in the dark and chilly arms
of Morpheus. Only occasionally did the powerful drugs
wear off enough to remind him of an awful pain in his
chest that pierced him every time he drew a breath,
though he could not quite remember why.

Sometimes the fog in his brain lifted enough to allow
him to notice an orderly prop his head up and ladle
some lukewarm gruel into his mouth. He felt mild annoyance when the vile soup ran from the corners of his
lips, down his cheeks, and into his ears, but he could
not quite formulate the words to complain.

On the fourth day, he could look at the ceiling of
the infirmary and realize he had possibly survived the

knife attack, which he now vaguely remembered.

He persuaded an orderly to prop his head up slightly so that he might gaze upon something other than the tall ceiling. Once tilted, he surveyed his fellow patients. A group of four enlisted men were quarantined in one corner of the room with the measles. He tried to remember whether he had ever had the measles as a child. He could remember his sister suffering through a bout when she was just a toddler. He must have been seven or eight at the time and did not catch it then, so perhaps he had already had the disease. If only he could ask his mother. His mother . . . had she been informed of his injury? He hoped not.

He saw one other convalescent in his ward, a man under heavy, armed guard. This was Fat Bear, one of the prisoners from the Sweetwater, who appeared to be recuperating from a head wound. But where were his two comrades? Brad recalled seeing all three chiefs fall together in the barrage of rifle fire from the infantry. The others must have perished. He longed to know the fate of Eden and Hanging Road, but did not dare to ask.

The plump surgeon, Dr. Veddars, with florid cheeks and enormous side-whiskers, passed by and saw Brad's vaguely alert countenance.

"Well, look who has returned to the land of the living." He spoke in a jolly tone. "I'll have to convey this news to your commander. He has requested a report on your progress every day."

Brad smiled weakly in an attempt to be polite.

"Do you know where you are?"

"Hays?" Brad croaked.

"Good, good. And your name?"

"Randall."

"Good boy. Can you tell me what year it might be?"

Brad had to think for a minute. "Eighteen . . . sixty-nine?"

"Excellent. I think your progress is remarkable. Do you have any idea how lucky you are to be alive, my boy? It's nothing short of a miracle. Can't explain it. Part of the fun of practicing medicine, I'll be bound."

He sat down on the edge of Brad's cot, causing the metal springs to complain loudly.

"I have something to show you, Captain." The surgeon dug in his pockets, first his waistcoat, then his trousers, then his apron pockets. "Ah, here it is. I saved this for you. I knew you would want it as a souvenir."

Brad squinted and tried to make out just what tiny object the surgeon held and tossed up and down in his hand.

"I could easily have sewn this right back into your chest, I'll warrant, but by some miracle, I caught a gleaming glimpse of it before we closed you up. I thought it was a crucifix or religious medal like the Catholic boys wear. I must tell you, I called for that old padre to give you the last rites when I first saw that. Yessir, your situation was just that serious, young man. But I dug on in and retrieved this little gem—a charm that saved your life. I believe it diverted the angle of the blade of that old squaw's knife a hairsbreadth and it missed your heart. We all marveled at the luck of it while you were on the table."

Brad grew slightly queasy at the thought of lying on

an operating table with a gaping wound in his chest hanging open to the world. He wished the surgeon would just shut up.

"And no one told me I was operating on a celebrity. If I had known you were engaged to marry the daughter of General Markham, I might have been quite nervous," the surgeon chuckled.

Brad found the surgeon's remarks more annoying than amusing. He instead longed to know what object had been removed from his chest wound.

Dr. Veddars held up the item that had proved his salvation. "Looks like a ring of some sort."

Brad raised a weak arm and took the mutilated piece of gold from the surgeon's hand, but said nothing. He continued to finger the twisted gold band long after the surgeon departed.

He opened his nightshirt and peeled down the dressings as best he could. The gauze was wrapped round and round his chest and the dressing had adhered itself to the wound. He winced and felt slightly faint as he pulled the gauze and padding away to reveal a large, ugly incision. Dozens of black sutures clustered like a colony of ants on the swollen mound of his darkly bruised flesh. If he managed to recover, he would be left with a shockingly disfiguring scar upon his chest.

Without warning, tears stung his eyes.

The following week, Brad was pronounced able to receive visitors. His first was Mrs. Elizabeth Custer.

"We've missed you so at our table, Captain."

"Thank you, ma'am, that's nice to hear."

"The general plans to visit you himself today, if his schedule permits, of course."

"You are most kind to remember me."

Libbie Custer's pretty face tilted coquettishly. "We have a surprise for you, Captain, but you'll have to wait four more days to receive it. Do you think you can wait four days? I promise you, it will be worth the wait and you will be so terribly happy." She laughed girlishly, delighted with herself.

Brad nodded and smiled and wondered what the woman was blathering on about. All he could concentrate on at the moment was the crushing pain in his chest; where was that surgeon with another shot of morphine, anyway?

General Custer arrived without ceremony just after two. A groveling orderly, the one who always smelled as if he had been into the hospital rations of whiskey, scurried about and found a chair to place at Brad's bedside.

The general, not attired in buckskin for a change, stretched his long legs out from the chair and folded his arms across his chest with a broad smile.

"Some men will do anything to get a furlough," he said with a teasing smirk.

Brad tried to smile at the joke but found himself too ill at ease. He had been rehearsing what he would say to his commanding officer ever since he learned of his impending visit from Mrs. Custer.

"Treating you well, I presume?"

"Yes, sir, just fine."

"The surgeon said you had a very close call."

"Yes, sir, I'm happy to still be here."

"As are we all."

Brad drew a deep, still painful breath and plunged into the remarks he had prepared. "General, I must inform you that . . . that I will be resigning my commission as soon as I am released from the hospital."

The cordial smile fell from Custer's face. "Randall, you don't mean that. You've had a rough go and some bad luck, but that's no reason to throw it all away, man."

"I'm sorry, sir, my mind is made up."

"You'll grow into this job. I know that putting up with me is no holiday at times, but that's no reason to forgo the opportunities—"

"I'm done with the military." Brad left unspoken, *I'm done with you.*

Custer sat forward in his chair and braced his elbows on his knees to lean in close. He now spoke in a low voice so as not to be overheard by the surgeons and other patients. His words came in short bursts. "Now look, you ungrateful, incompetent—" He struggled to curb himself as his anger spiked. "I brought you out here as a favor to General Markham. I will not have you embarrassing me with an untimely resignation."

The color rose in Custer's face just as it had that dreadful day of Benteen's letter. Brad swallowed hard and kept his voice low and even. "General Markham was instrumental in getting your suspension lifted early. I think everyone's back was well scratched in the matter, *sir.*"

"Listen carefully to me. I know enough about what happened that day at the stockade to place you in arrest. You could be court-martialed and executed for treason for your role in that little farce."

"And you have proof to support these allegations?"

"Do you think I'm stupid? There was no coincidence in *which* Cheyenne prisoner managed to escape that day. Especially after that Murdoch woman came to my office begging for her lover's release. How that woman disgusts me."

Brad struggled to keep his temper. The angrier he became, the more his chest hurt.

Custer tilted back his head and looked down his long nose at Brad. "She got to you, didn't she? Oh, yes, women like that can wrap men around their pretty fingers. The pair of you were seen openly embracing right in front of the stockade. You've been in league with her all along. Don't think I don't know whose hand I saw behind those letters she wrote. I'm surrounded by traitors. First Benteen, now you."

"Mrs. Murdoch and I are quite close, as you suggest, but not in the *manner* you suggest. And I believe it was you who got to *her,* if you'll allow me to say so, sir. But don't worry. I said nothing to your wife when she came to visit me this morning. Although she did ask some questions that went far beyond the state of my health."

"Questions? On what subject?"

Brad smiled inwardly. He knew an Achilles' heel when he saw one. Ignobly playing this trump card felt much more satisfying than it ought to have. "A variety of questions about the winter campaign. About the

Cheyenne women who accompanied us to Cobb and to the Sweetwater. About the rumors that are circulating."

"What rumors?" Custer almost barked the words.

"About your reported fondness for one of them."

"And what was your reply?"

"I had no opinion to share on the matter, sir. None whatsoever."

Custer relaxed. He once again sat back in his chair as though this were a mere social call, but he could not resist taunting Brad with a trump card of his own.

"She recanted, you know. Your *dear* Mrs. Murdoch. Sat in my office and wrote out a statement admitting she had lied about the Washita. Took back everything. She even *thanked me* for rescuing her. I have it all down in her own hand. Would you care to read it?"

"No, I would not," Brad growled with a clenched jaw. He gritted his teeth against both the outrage and the pain in his chest, which had reached such an intolerable level, he had trouble concealing it. So now he knew the secret Eden refused to share with him. He felt certain that what she gave up to try and free Hanging Road had hurt and humiliated her far more than any sexual indignity could have.

"I hope you're proud of your actions, sir."

"I'm always proud of my actions, Randall. Come on, now. You're just in low spirits from your injury. That's what the surgeon tells me. You'll perk up in a day or two. In *four* days to be precise. In the meantime, I'll have my cook fix something special for you and have it sent over tonight."

Brad grudgingly nodded his thanks as his guest rose to leave.

"General Custer?"

"Yes?"

"I will never forget my winter on the frontier."

Custer nodded curtly and withdrew.

Four days later, Libbie Custer's promised surprise arrived on the 12:07 P.M. train. Brad had just finished eating his midday meal when the door of the infirmary flew open and the bright May sunshine flooded in around the tall, elegant silhouette that could only belong to Amanda Markham.

She surveyed the hospital ward with a disapproving squint, then her eyes found her target and she broke into the most wondrous smile. She dashed to Brad's side, a vision in pink and gray tulle. He was so happy to see her, he could not hide the tears. She, too, wept at the reunion, though her first words to him were, "Oh, my darling Bradley, you look just awful!"

He listened to Amanda rattle on about the hardships and adventures of her travels west, but her words blurred into the sheer delight of hearing her voice again, of seeing her beautiful, animated face bursting with its vibrant energy which always astounded him.

If he had known she was coming he would have shaved. She tolerated his mustache for the sake of fashion, but she abhorred the slightest stubble on his cheeks. And a haircut. He hadn't cut his hair all winter. It hung in a shaggy, golden-brown mass well past his collar.

And yet how would she react to his news, his plans? Her excited talk gave no hint that the general or his wife had let on about his intended resignation. Probably they did not think it genuine. Their reaction was no doubt that he was simply low and melancholy during his recuperation and not thinking rationally.

"I can't believe you traveled halfway across the country all by yourself," Brad marveled.

"Well, Libbie—that is, Mrs. Custer—went to Leavenworth to meet me and accompany me the final, Kansas, part of the journey. But yes, the entire rest of the trip, Bradley, I was completely on my own. Aren't you proud of me, darling?"

"Utterly astonished, but in a good way."

"Mrs. Custer and I had the most wonderful talk. She has assured me that I will *love* living in a tent all summer. I told her I could not imagine such privation and hardship and she told me I was being silly and that I was in for the grandest adventure of my life. She said that every evening after dinner, she and the general go riding and that we may accompany them if we wish, and that there is a party or a hop every Friday night and—"

"Amanda—"

"I'm looking forward to spending the summer living in a tent. Truly, Bradley, I am. But is it always so humid

here?" She vigorously fanned herself with the little ivory fan that had belonged to her mother.

Brad decided there was no use holding off telling her the truth. "Amanda, you won't be living in a tent this summer."

Her fair eyebrows shot up in surprise.

"We will be returning to Washington as soon as the surgeon pronounces me fit enough to travel."

"You're being reassigned?"

"No, I'm leaving the army."

Her expression did not change and he assumed she did not take his meaning. "Amanda, I've decided to resign my commission. I have other plans for my future . . . our future."

Amanda stopped fanning herself. "This is a shock."

"I'm sorry if this disappoints you, darling. I know your dream was always to be a general's wife, but I'm afraid that will never be. My only hope is that you will find it more expedient to find a new dream . . . than a new husband."

She rose to her feet and placed her hands firmly on her hips, or the nearest thing to her hips given the yards of bunched tulle and the fortress of structured undergarments. He braced himself for a scene.

"Bradley James Randall, don't you know that I would be happy anywhere, doing anything, so long as we are together?"

A smile of relief and utter astonishment broke over his haggard features. "But didn't you have your heart set on my becoming a general?"

She sat again with a swish of her pink and gray tulle and resumed her fanning. "That was my *father*'s dream for you, not mine, you silly goose. I thought it was yours, too. That's why I always pretended such enthusiasm." She suddenly sobered and stilled her fan to peek over it. "Do you want to know something just awful? I always feared you wanted to marry me . . . because of my father and the help he could offer to advance your career."

"To advance my career? Oh, my darling girl, how could you think that of me?" He shook his head with a wry smile. "Kiss me quickly. We've done each other a terrible disservice."

She leaned down and gave him a peck on his cheek, but he caught her gently by the neck and pulled her to his lips for a more passionate kiss.

"Bradley," she scolded with an embarrassed smile as she eyed the other patients and orderlies who now watched their display of affection with undisguised interest.

Brad did not care who watched and pulled her close for a second kiss and a third.

The enlisted men with the measles, whose number had now doubled since Brad first entered the infirmary, broke into an impudent round of applause.

Amanda finally drew away, sat back down on her little bedside chair, and smoothed her skirts. "I have one request for our future, darling."

"Anything." Brad shifted back into his semireclining position, holding his bandages so as not to irritate his healing wound. The slightest flex of the musculature of his chest still caused him exquisite pain.

"You'll be very surprised to hear me say this."

He waited.

"I think we should be married right here at Fort Hays. It's a rather crude place, but Mrs. Custer has promised to help me make all the arrangements and she says that she and all the other officers' wives would have a jolly time with the preparations."

"I think it's a splendid idea."

"You haven't even heard the best part." She leaned close and covered her face and his with her fan. "Papa says if we get married out here he will give us as a wedding present all the money he was planning to spend on our wedding. And believe me, it's nice sum."

"If that's what he wishes, it's certainly fine with me."

She sat up straight with a glowing smile. "Oh, Bradley, you must get well soon. I can't wait to be married. And I can't wait to start our family. I mean, you did write and tell me that you looked forward to the prospect of fatherhood that day you held the little Indian babe in your arms."

In a sudden, playful mood, he beckoned her to lean in close again. "If there were not so many people in this blasted ward, I'd pull you into this bed and start our family *right now.*"

"Shame on you!" She giggled with delight and thumped him on the shoulder with her little ivory fan.

She drew herself up to her full height and arched one eyebrow provocatively. "You are a naughty boy and

you need to save your strength for our wedding night."
She delivered this command with the lewdest wink Brad
had ever seen on a decent woman's face.

Brad laughed out loud and Amanda sighed, "I'm so
relieved I won't have to spend the summer living in a
tent!"

Twenty-four

The Great Spirit Spring . . . is situated in Mitchell County, Kansas, 3.5 miles below the junc-
tion of the North and South forks of the
Solomon River. Before its tragic submergence
beneath the waters of the Glen Elder Reservoir, it was a natural artesian spring supplied
with highly mineralized waters from the Da-
kota sandstone, which rose through a fissure
to the surface under hydrostatic pressure.
—WALDO R. WEDEL, CENTRAL PLAINS PREHISTORY, 1933

In the confusion and outright bedlam of the stockade
insurrection, Eden and Hanging Road found it surprisingly easy to make their exit.

A fire bell sounded with an ominous *clang-clang-
clang* some fifty yards distant the moment the two of
them let the heavy stockade doors swing shut behind
them. The bell brought soldiers running from all directions. Many poured from the mess hall with napkins still
hanging from their collars.

Eden resourcefully shouted at the oncoming throng
of infantrymen, "Hurry! Hurry! The savages are trying
to make a break for it!"

She gestured wildly toward the stockade doors and
all the men followed her direction, running straight past

Hanging Road, who shielded his face with the brim of the hat Eden had given to him.

Eden untethered Brad's horse and tossed the reins in Hanging Road's direction. She mounted Hugh Christie's bay mare and they rode out of the fort at a cautious trot to avoid suspicion. Once they had covered a safe distance, they urged their horses into a full gallop and did not look back.

They headed north simply because the Seventh Cavalry was camped to the south of the garrison, but beyond that, Eden had made no further plans for their escape.

After fifteen minutes of hard riding, Hanging Road shouted to Eden, "Where are we going?"

"I don't really know," she said. "I never expected to get this far."

He took the lead and they rode for an hour more as fast as the horses could tolerate before they stopped and rested. Hanging Road walked the exhausted animals down to the banks of the Saline River beneath the flickering shade of a stand of cottonwood trees.

"We're close here," he said as she followed behind him. "I recognize this river. We could not be more than half a day's ride from the spring."

"The Sacred Spring? Are you certain?"

He nodded confidently.

"I suppose it's dangerous staying here so close to the fort. As soon as they realize you're missing, they'll send out search parties. They'll try to hunt you down. Hunt us both down."

"Let them come," he spat out with an arrogant contempt.

"Are you suggesting we might actually go there? Today? Really?" Eden was so delighted by the prospect of finally seeing the fabled Sacred Spring, she momentarily put aside her fears.

"We're this close. I think we ought to go."

When the horses had been watered and rested, Hanging Road and Eden rode on in silence for several hours. At last, a strange object came into sight on the vast horizon. From the prairie floor rose an enormous limestone dome, astounding in size, looking man-made in its perfect symmetry, yet touched by no human hand.

They tethered their horses at a brushy growth on the bank of the Solomon River well below the amazing dome. Hanging Road's countenance took on an expression of reverence as they began the long walk up the side of the swelling yellow limestone. Eden followed, her amber-green eyes glittering with excitement.

When they reached the highest point the dome flattened to reveal a large, perfectly round pool of clear water. To birds winging overhead, it must have seemed like an enormous eye staring up to the heavens.

"This is the strangest sight I've ever seen. It's wondrous, just as you described it," Eden said with a look of rapture on her face. She slowly walked the perimeter of the huge circle.

"I thought so many times of bringing you here. I'm glad it's finally come to pass."

He walked to the edge of the ancient pool and beckoned Eden to join him. They knelt, and he scooped up a palmful of the hallowed water and splashed it over Eden's face and throat.

"It's cold!" she yelped with surprise. "I thought it must be a hot spring, the way it was bubbling."

"What is it like to feel the water of your namesake?" he said, smiling.

"I'm new baptized!" she proclaimed, but Hanging Road did not take her meaning. She dipped her own hand in the water and brought it to her lips to take a cautious sip. She recoiled at the unexpectedly tart, mineral flavor.

Hanging Road then grew serious again and returned to his task. He stood at the edge of the watery circle and pulled out the medicine bundle she had returned to him at the camp outside Reliance. He withdrew the necklace of severed fingers and placed it around his neck, then he closed his eyes and began to sing in a high and mournful voice.

Eden sat by his side on the edge of the spring and contemplated its eerie bubbling waters. So much had transpired in the last few hours. She felt the oddest sense of peace and calm as she lost herself in Hanging Road's mesmerizing song.

The sun barely held its grasp on the western horizon when Hanging Road finished his prayers and seated himself next to her again. "Are you coming with me, Seota, or will you rejoin your own people?"

"I want to come with you, of course."

"Epehva." It is good. "I was hoping I hadn't lost you completely."

"I want to help you now. I once thought I could change things by merely speaking the truth, but I found out that speaking the truth means nothing if no one will listen. Blood will matter when words don't."

"I'm a little surprised you want to come with me. I often wondered whether you would be happier back with your own kind."

"I wondered that myself, on occasion. But I've gotten my answer well enough." She chuckled bitterly.

They chatted for some minutes about the severity of Brad's wound and his chances for survival, before Eden realized they were not behaving like two fugitives who might be set upon by the United States Army at any moment. The Sacred Spring really did provide a sense of serenity, a mystical protection from all the violence and hate in the world, just as Hanging Road had promised her. All her fears had vanished. What a miracle that in itself was. She wished she could remain in this blessed state of tranquility indefinitely.

Yet she knew the time had come to broach a delicate subject. "Before we leave, I need to tell you something, and if it changes how you feel toward me, then I'll understand." She did not dare look at him as she spoke. "I'm with child."

He turned to her, both concerned and curious. "Do you want to be rid of it?"

"No, not at all. I'm thrilled about it."

"Whose is it? That soldier's?"

She nodded.

"What does *he* say about this?"

"He doesn't know. I had no reason to tell him."

"Why not? A man would want to know."

"It would have served no purpose. He's promised marriage to another."

"What manner of man would behave so?" Hanging Road made a face of raw contempt.

"Don't blame him. It was all my own selfish doing." She couldn't bear for Hanging Road to think Brad some kind of libertine. "One night I was so miserably unhappy I just decided to take what was never mine to begin with, to pretend for one night . . . oh, well, it doesn't matter now."

She felt guilty about that promiscuous night, though she treasured memories of every moment of it. How passionate Brad had been. And how potent, consummating their union three times in as many hours. And how tender. So much so she was put in mind of the marriage vow, ". . . and with my body, I thee worship." The most literal sense of those words found voice in her heart, for Brad's caresses had seemed to bear an almost worshipful intensity. And afterward, while he slept, she had lain still as a lake at sunset, praying that his seed would find purchase.

For the longest time, she had been afraid to hope. She feared her symptoms were caused by her long illness rather than a pregnancy, but just within the last few weeks, she had noticed that her small breasts had swelled and her flat abdomen had begun to assume an unmistakable curve. Even at that very moment she could feel the faint fluttering signs inside her of a new life making its presence known. She placed her hands on her belly and caressed its rounded shape. She already ached with love for the child that grew there. My second chance, she thought, she prayed.

"I know you only too well," Hanging Road smirked. "That *ve'ho* soldier was no match for you when it comes to getting what you want."

"You're cruel."

"I'm truthful."

"Well, you've had three wives. I suppose I'm entitled to at least three husbands. Aren't I?"

He chuckled, then surveyed her up and down. "You look like a *ve'ho'o* in those ridiculous clothes."

"I *am* a white woman!" Eden laughed at his joke. It was an old favorite between them. For one particle of a second, it was as if their old days together had sprung to life. As if the long and terrible winter were over at last. But Eden knew it would never really be over. Not until justice was called out.

"You're sure you don't hate me after what I just told you?"

"I don't know. I'm not sure I have any normal emotions left."

"I know what you mean."

"It's getting dark," Hanging Road said. "I'm going down to saddle the horses for our journey. We'll have a full moon to travel by tonight."

Before following him, she paused to lean over the edge of the Sacred Spring to see her reflection in the bottomless depths of its crystalline waters. She beheld the thin face of a young woman she seemed only vaguely to recognize.

She wished she could somehow see the future in

the sacred waters. She wanted to know if Brad would survive. She wanted to know if Hanging Road would find justice . . . and peace. Most of all, she wanted assurance that her child would live and grow, happy and strong. But the only thing she saw was her own undulating reflection in the churning waters.

Still she believed in the future. After all that had happened, the unknown promise of the future was the only god she knew how to worship.

Epilogue

Benteen—Come on. Big village. Be quick.
Bring packs. P.S.—Bring Packs.
> —G. A. Custer's last order, Little Bighorn,
> Montana Territory, June 25, 1876

Seven Years Later

Office of the Hon. Bradley J. Randall
Commissioner of Indian Affairs,
Department of the Interior,
Washington, D.C.
October 7, 1876

My dear Hugh,

Your recent letter gave me no end of cheer. Forgive me for taking so long to respond. The duties of my office overwhelm me at times. I seem to fall behind on all my personal correspondence. My days are more challenging than I would wish.

May I offer my congratulations on your new business venture. I hope the cattle trade will prove immensely profitable. I can remember sitting in

your saloon the day we met and your telling me of
your plans!

My wife, Amanda, and I have also had reason
to celebrate of late. On August 14, we welcomed
our daughter, Sarah Louise, into the world to join
her brother, Bradley James, Jr. Poor B. J. doesn't
know quite what to make of this sister business yet.

I thank you for your kind remarks on the job I
am doing, though I often feel profoundly unequal to
the task. My early successes in administering to the
welfare of the native tribes now seem eclipsed by
the recent unrest on the northern plains—a conflict
occasioned entirely by the wholesale disregard by
American citizens for the Indians' treaty rights. I am
afraid those same railroads that brought you your
longed-for prosperity now shall complete the extermination of the tribes of the Plains. I find myself
in almost daily conflict with the War Department,
my former employer. How the army must rue the
day they supported my nomination to this post,
thinking they were promoting one of their own.

But enough of my tedious complaints. I am
afraid I let the stressing events of my profession
creep into every avenue of my life, including a letter to a dear and trusted friend. Forgive me. I am
anxious to share news about a woman who once
meant a great deal to us both: Eden Murdoch.

Last week I dined with a gentleman whom you
may remember, Hugh. He attended that birthday
dinner we celebrated for General Custer in Reliance in December of 1868.

His name is Thomas Weir. He was seated opposite Mrs. Lowell on that memorable night. He recently came through town on his way to New York.

Tom was on active duty last summer during the debacle in the Montana Territory. In fact, he believes himself to be one of the last officers to see General Custer alive on that fateful Sunday afternoon in June.

So many details of that terrible day put me in mind of my own experience at the Washita. How the general divided his forces into several parts in order to attack from multiple vantage points. All so reminiscent of nearly eight years ago.

Many, including Tom Weir, now criticize the failure of Major Benteen to come to the aid of General Custer's surrounded companies as ordered. Tom says it was almost as though he deliberately took his time in following the general's order to provide backup and bring the needed pack train with its critical supply of ammunition. And yet, was this a conscious decision on his part not to waste the lives of men to try and save those already hopelessly lost? General Custer once made such a bitter decision at the Washita and Major Benteen never forgot it.

Do you recall my story of how critical Major Benteen had been of Custer's conduct at the Washita in that controversial decision, tactically supportable or not, to retire the field without determining the fate of Major Elliott? Benteen wrote a vicious letter ridiculing the matter which was published in several newspapers. Over the years, the regard of the two men never warmed, according to Tom Weir.

Tom said when Major Benteen was told of Custer's death he refused to believe it. He reportedly opined that the general had gone off and left part of his command at the Battle of the Washita and would very likely do so again. When Tom and the other surviving officers returned to the scene of Custer's demise two days later, Benteen's usually combative attitude had changed quite noticeably. He pulled off his hat and stared for some minutes at the naked, death-stilled body of his slain commander. "There he is, God damn him," said the major, now looking quite pale and disturbed. "He will never fight anymore."

Tom made a desperate attempt with his own company to reach Custer, but he unfortunately did not know where to find him. He reached a high promontory and looked off to the north where the smoke and noise of battle had been evident so recently, but all was quiet. Tom would soon learn that this unnatural calm was the stillness of death and that all the five companies lay dead on that hill to the north. This wholly forgivable failure has broken Tom's spirit as well as his health, I fear.

Why, you must be asking, have I labored to tell you this tale? Other than the remarkable similarities I see between the destruction of Custer's five companies at the Little Bighorn and the annihilation of

Major Joel Elliott's lost detail at the Washita, one fact Tom Weir confided and one fact alone brought the woman Eden Murdoch to my memory with the most vivid clarity. I am now certain I have evidence she is yet alive.

Tom stated that when they found the bodies of the slaughtered men, they were gratified to see that Armstrong Custer's person was not as mutilated as the rest. He was not scalped, and save for a gouge in the thigh and an arrow thrust into his private parts, the only noticeable mutilation was that one of his fingers had been severed.

The moment Tom spoke these words, I must have turned as white as a sheet, for he immediately asked me if I had seen a ghost. I absentmindedly mumbled something like, "Not a ghost, but a Ghost Woman." He did not take my meaning—why should he?—so I assured him I was simply moved by his tragic story. I dared not share with him the true import I gave his revelation.

Eden Murdoch explained to me on the day we arrived in Reliance, Kansas, that the Cheyennes often sever the finger of an enemy as a trophy of war.

Indeed, her Cheyenne husband, the medicine man she called Hanging Road, possessed a necklace composed of severed human fingers. Eden apparently salvaged this horrific necklace from the fires of the Washita and carried it upon her person concealed beneath her clothing the entire time she resided in Reliance. I witnessed her return it to its owner when I reunited the pair outside Reliance on our return to Kansas in April of that year.

I had actually seen the grisly necklace before that day, however. I saw it in dreams, nay, in nightmares. I know this sounds impossible, but I swear it upon my life. Throughout that bitter winter, vicious nightmares tormented me in which I lay helpless on a stark prairie, being menaced by a Cheyenne warrior wearing an identical necklace to the one I saw Eden give to Hanging Road. How could I have known what it looked like, down to its smallest, most gruesome detail? How could I have known such a thing even existed in the world? I ask myself these questions over and over again.

I thought in the dream that I was envisioning my own death, yet I now wonder if I foresaw an end that awaited . . . someone else?

Did Eden Murdoch sever the finger of my dead commander? I shudder to imagine it, though perhaps I tend to idealize the female sex too much. I hate to think they could possess the taste for such vengeance, such blood lust, and yet my mind's eye can see her clearly enough on that killing field, toiling away with the other women, robbing and desecrating the dead. At such a moment, I remind myself that the Cheyennes have no word for "forgiveness." Maybe to understand that fact is to understand Eden Murdoch a little better.

And how am I to grapple with the possibility that I played a role in Custer's death? Hugh, you are the only one who knows the full extent of my actions the day Hanging Road escaped from Fort Hays. For the sake of discretion, I shall not dwell on it here, but I cannot avoid the possibility that I freed the man who came to kill General Custer, a man I once considered a friend, and that Eden Murdoch made it her business to sever his finger and add it to her husband's necklace.

If all this ghastly supposition is proof that she still lives, then I am glad of it. I have longed to know what became of her. I have waited all these years for some word, some hint, some chance encounter to come my way.

I thought I might have found her in the spring of 1873. A report came to my desk through a circuitous chain of events that enlivened my speculation. It seemed that a white woman appeared in Fort Laramie at a sutler's store. She was dressed in Indian garb and had a small child with her, but both were unquestionably of the white race. She was accompanied by two Indian woman whom the sutler claimed were Cheyennes.

The sutler tried to speak with her, but she remained silent. He assumed she must have been stolen by the Indians at so young an age she had forgotten the English tongue.

He noticed—and this is what brought the story to my attention—that she appeared to read the price tags of the merchandise. Then she picked up a discarded newspaper and began to study it in such a manner that he could only conclude she was reading it, as well. This event caused the man to try afresh to engage her in conversation. She again refused to speak and quickly placed her purchases on his counter. She bought some fabric, a sewing kit of the type soldiers carry in the field, and some tinned peaches. Then she placed the exact sum of money due along with the items before the sutler had even asked for the amount.

That she was able to compute her bill confirmed in his mind that she could not only read, but count. Then there was the astonishing fact that she possessed cash money—something most Indians consider a meaningless item. (Tom Weir told me that the men of the Seventh Cavalry had just been paid their wages before the Little Bighorn engagement and that their cash lay untouched and blew about on the prairie winds after the battle.)

When the sutler tried to detain the woman and her child to make further inquiries, she and the other women dashed out, mounted their horses, and were gone.

When I heard this account, I wanted desperately to believe that woman was Eden Murdoch. I've longed for a reason to believe she was alive and well. I've longed to know that she somehow found happiness. But given what I now surmise, I have to wonder, does revenge bring happiness? It does not bring back the dead. It will not bring back the old days, the free prairie days the Cheyennes long for. That much is unfortunately certain.

I have devoted my entire career to bringing about a peaceful solution to the Indian Question

and, toward that end, I feel I have failed utterly. This fills me with grief.

Am I mad to hang on to this story of the severed finger of Armstrong Custer as more proof that she survives? Or am I creating a fantasy no more legitimate than finding shapes in clouds?

In the passing of all these years, in all that has happened to me, she has never left my thoughts. She has haunted me as thoroughly as a ghost woman could. I do not mean to disparage or diminish in any way the joy I have found in my marriage, my children, my career, and yet I sometimes fear I will never be free of her strange and enfolding sorcery.

If I could but see her once more—just to spend an hour in her company and know the details of her extraordinary life since we parted—I would be truly a happy man.

Let us continue this correspondence, Hugh. Our friendship keeps the winter of 1868–1869 alive for me and you cannot know how much that means. Let it always be so.

Your friend,
Brad Randall

Historical Note

Though Eden Murdoch, Brad Randall, Hanging Road, and all the residents of the fictional town of Reliance, Kansas, were products of the author's imagination, every attempt has been made to render an accurate account of the Washita incident and the contemporary controversy that surrounded it in its day.

Eden's character was inspired by a cryptic remark Custer made in his field notes the day after the battle. He claimed to have found the body of a white woman in Black Kettle's camp that morning. He failed to make any further identification of her and never mentioned her again though he wrote extensively of his Washita "victory" in later years. (This reference is not to be confused with the discovery, a week later, of the body of white captive, Clara Blinn.)

Modern historians have not been able to identify this mystery woman nor explain why Custer never mentioned her again, yet this sole and unsubstantiated remark was used by General Sheridan to entirely justify Custer's actions at the Washita when he testified before Congress on the matter. This historical enigma served as the author's fictional starting point.

As many actual historical details as possible—from

the bright star that was visible on the horizon on the morning of the battle to the Cheyenne prisoner insurrection at Fort Hays the following spring—have been incorporated into the narrative.

Public outcry in the Eastern press was intense after the Washita and a heated debate ensued over U.S. Indian policies. Indian Agent Edward Wynkoop resigned his position in protest over the Washita and publicly likened it to the Sand Creek Massacre, comparing Custer to Chivington. He sparred in print with General Sheridan on the editorial pages of *The New York Times*.

Though Sheridan eventually won his campaign for public opinion, the controversy caused the remainder of Custer's winter offensive of 1868–69 to remain peaceful.

The Sacred Spring at the fork of the Solomon was located in Mitchell County, Kansas, and was also called the Waconda Spring or the Great Spirit Spring by whites who moved into the area in the early 1870s. They eventually seized control of the land from the various local Indian tribes and the mineral waters from the unusual geological formation were bottled and sold as a cure-all elixir under the name "Waconda Flyer." In the 1880s, a health spa operated at the site, though Native American pilgrimages continued to the area well into the twentieth century. Sadly, the Spring no longer exists. It lies under the reservoir created by the Glen Elder Dam.

It is not known who killed Custer at the Little Big Horn, but one of his fingers was severed.